FIRST EDITION

Mirror's Hope © 2013 by Justine Alley Dowsett and Murandy Damodred
Cover Art © 2013 by Sara Biddle
All Rights Reserved.

*This book is a work of fiction. All of the characters, organizations and events portrayed in this novel are either products of the authors' imagination or are used fictitiously. Any resemblance to actual locales, events or persons is entirely coincidental.

Mirror World Publishing
Windsor, Ontario
www.mirrorworldpublishing.com
info@mirrorworldpublishing.com

Edited by: Robert Dowsett

ISBN: 978-0-9920490-1-0

To Robert who taught us that
It's only water until you add the leaves...

Mirror's Hope

Mirror's Hope

Justine Alley Dowsett

and

Murandy Damodred

M|W mirror world publishing

Mirror's Hope

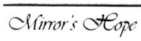

Prologue

"*E*xcuse me?"

"Look, I don't have all day so I need you to keep up with me here," the fair-skinned woman told a bewildered Tendro in a no-nonsense tone of voice, rounding on him and pushing her long white blonde hair out of the way. She looked him in the eye, making sure he was paying strict attention to what she had to say. "Do you know who the Creator is?"

"Uhh.." Tendro Seynor struggled to get his bearings, feeling confused by the lush grass all around him and the pleasant birdsong that filled the air. He got to his feet slowly, looking around at the non-descript rolling hills and the obscuring mists that limited his range of vision.

We could be anywhere... The thought came to him. *Only I know that moments ago we were indoors and not here... wherever this is.*

"Really?" The reedy woman demanded incredulously, staring him down, even though he was, in fact, the taller of the two of them. "Do I have to start at the beginning?" She took a deep and exasperated breath, widening her already large blue eyes at him in an expression that stated bluntly how uneducated she thought he was. "The Creator created the world and the Destroyer sought to unmake it..."

"I know who the Creator is..." Tendro told her, putting a stop to her history lesson at the same time as he took in the details of the robes she was wearing. White, with silver scrollwork on the hem and sleeves, the clothes marked the woman as a full Mage, maybe even a teacher of majik. Tendro amended his tone to show the proper amount of respect for this stranger. "At least, I know as much as any of us do. After creating the world, the Destroyer punished the Creator by sealing her away in a prison outside of time and only the 'Avatar of the Light' can free her and restore balance to the world."

The woman nodded like this was more along the lines of what she'd been expecting to hear and impatiently put her hands on her hips, accentuating through her robes how thin she really was.

"All right, what are you waiting for, then? Get to it."

"Get to what, exactly?" Tendro asked, wondering for what reason this Mage had shown up out of nowhere and chosen him specifically to bring here.

'The Creator was sealed away in a prison at the dawn of time...' The history lesson he'd learned in school came back to him unbidden. *It's from the history of the Avatar of the Light.*

I don't know how much stock I put in the tale of the Avatar, but could this woman be a Sympathizer of the Light? She's impatient and rude; she hardly seems the type to follow the selfless ways of the Creator's faith.

But what would I know of Sympathizers?

I may have been promoted to one of the Panarch's Generals, but I'm hardly qualified to be a Truthseeker. I haven't even been given my first assignment yet...

"Tendro Seynor and Mirena Calanais. Welcome, both of you."

The female voice that spoke was melodious and somehow everywhere at once, not seeming to come from any particular source in the dampening mists.

"Who's there?" Tendro questioned, calling out into the mists and wondering if his own voice would sound as ubiquitous to this new and mysterious arrival.

What's going on here...? Who is this and how do they know who I am?

"I brought him as you requested," Mirena informed the newcomer. "Is that all you need?"

"Yes, mostly," the melodious voice continued and a light began to build in the mists, causing Tendro to squint in its brightness until it threatened to blind him entirely. "That should be enough to allow me access to the world," she continued, the light encompassing everything now and searing with its intensity.

"Yes, he is the one... and now, finally, I am free..."

Mirror's Hope

I.

When Mirena received the letter, she knew it could only contain bad news. Some part of her had accepted long ago that something was always lurking in the shadows, just waiting for those times she allowed herself to hope, before reaching out of the dark to stifle the meager light of her dreams for the future.

Today, the unexpected had happened, causing that small flare of hope to surge within her once more.

He had finally spoken to her.

Well, not spoken, precisely, but he had taken notice of the rough time she was having and he'd gently pushed his slice of pie across the table to her to cheer her up. It was a small gesture; he'd left immediately after, before she got the chance to thank him, but it was the first sign that Odark Dalessandro had finally noticed her existence.

She had been staring at him for months.

The room was dark save for the small panel light set into the wall above the night table, put there and powered by the majik that coursed through the Capital to illuminate the hourglass suspended next to it, giving indication of the time. It was early in the morning, still over a full turn of the hourglass before dawn.

Mirena's bedroom was by no means a large space, containing only a double bed, a chair and a wardrobe. She was lucky enough to be housed in the Magi Dormitories, but she wasn't a Mage yet herself, not even one in training. There had simply been no other rooms left to rent to her in the sprawling and populated Collegium complex, so she paid double for this room that was too small for any of the Magi to want.

The little bedside light was enough for her to see by and to read the letter that she had found waiting for her when she returned to her room after her overnight shift in the Collegium's cafeteria, where she worked to afford her room and hopefully save up enough to start paying for classes.

The letter was from her parents. This was the first they had communicated since she'd left home for the Capital and she was pleased to hear from them, even if the tone of the letter wasn't exactly heart-warming.

Mirena,

It looks like your sister wanted to follow in your footsteps because she's run off to the Capital. She's not staying with you, is she? If she is, tell her that she is needed here on the farm. We need her to come home. I don't trust her in the big city by herself and I can only imagine the trouble the two of you could get into together. If you can't convince her to come of her own free will, then I swear I will come there and get the both of you myself.

It occurs to me that it's possible that she's not with you. If that's the case, Mirena, you'd better find her, because I fear that she's gotten herself into trouble and if you don't send her home, I'll be holding you responsible. We both know Elizabeth well enough to know that she'd take it upon herself to do something foolish just to spite me.

Don't you dare keep me worrying longer than I have to.

Your Mother.

Mirena folded the letter back up and placed it on her side table. Rubbing her face, she laid back on her bed, feeling defeated. *What does she think that I can do to get Elizabeth home? When has my sister ever listened to me? I don't even know where to start looking...*

With a frustrated sigh, she covered her eyes with her hands and so she was startled when the light from her bedside seemed to grow in intensity, the soft golden glow brightening to a fierce white.

Sitting up and removing her hands cautiously, Mirena turned towards the lamp, squinting as she reached over and shut it off. This action didn't seem to dim the light in any perceptible way.

What is going on here?

Inexplicably, the brightness was not coming from any normal source. As her eyes adjusted, Mirena realized that the light came from a point in the center of the room a few feet off the ground. Before her eyes the abnormality widened; then, with a flash, it was gone, and in its place was a man.

He hovered impossibly in the air for a moment before he crumpled with a thud, causing Mirena to jolt to her feet in shock. She stared, fixated on the sudden stranger in her midst. He was tall and fit looking, in a black jacket and pants with the tell-tale embroidered gold trim along the cuffs and hemline.

He's a Collegium-trained Mage, Mirena realized, taking note of his clothes and the meaning behind them before she realized that he was unconscious. From what she could see his expression was peaceful, but his brown hair flopped into his eyes and obscured a part of his face. *What happened to him to bring him here like this?*

Unnervingly, the air around the stranger continued to glow in the aftermath of the bright light that had so suddenly and inexplicably invaded her bedroom. Mirena swallowed uncomfortably, having trouble accepting the reality of the situation in which she found herself.

Snapping into action as the glow faded, Mirena found herself suddenly concerned for the stranger's well being.

Is he alive? She questioned, looking down at him and finding herself inexplicably drawn to his peaceful features and feeling a sense of familiarity she couldn't explain. She hesitated before reaching forward and gently moving his hair aside to get a better look at his face and felt a jolt of *something* like a spark pass through her fingertips on his brow. *Do I know you from somewhere?*

He was handsome and would no doubt appear regal and confident when awake, but as it was he just looked vulnerable. Mirena's heart fluttered in her chest with an unexplained feeling as she examined him, placing her hand close to his mouth to confirm that he was still breathing.

He was, but as she studied him something else caught her eye. The glowing she had mistaken for the aftermath of his strange arrival was not actually coming from the man himself, but from a silver ring hanging from a chain around his neck.

She couldn't tell if he was likely to wake up soon, but figuring she was safe enough, Mirena reached for the ring.

I wonder what this is for?

Her hand closed around the ring and with a start she dropped it again; with her touch the light went out entirely, causing the ring to appear no more unusual than a simple unadorned silver band inscribed with a single word.

Hope.

A sharp intake of breath startled her even further as the man before her proved that he was still very much alive.

Mirena quickly and sharply pushed away from the stranger, feeling suddenly embarrassed that she had gotten so close to him. She was very much aware that they were in her bedroom and it was very late at night. They were in nearly total darkness, now that the light coming from his ring had disappeared so completely.

"What's going on?" The stranger sat up quickly and looked around himself in confusion. "Where are we now?"

"Excuse me?" Mirena questioned, wondering at how he seemed to be speaking as if continuing a conversation he'd been involved in only a moment ago.

His eyes locked onto hers; they were an intense and startling grey and Mirena found herself unable to look away from the depth of them. "Mirena...? That is you, right? Where have you taken us? Why is it so dark?"

Mirena felt her face heat with his familiar tone and the directness of his gaze. *How does he know who I am? Does he have me confused with Elizabeth? No, he said my name... but...* She turned away, overwhelmed by a confusing flood of emotions and got to her feet so she could reach the panel light control on the bedside table.

"I'm sorry..." She began, not really knowing what to say or having any answers to his questions.

Slowly getting to his feet as well, the stranger started to look around himself now that there was light enough to see by.

"The Collegium?" He asked, guessing where they were. "This looks like a girl's dormitory room. Is it yours?"

"Yes." Mirena covered herself up with her blanket, aware that she was only in her nightclothes as she had been ready for bed before his arrival. "And why are you here, if that is okay to ask?"

He cocked his head to the side, confused.

"Why am I...? But you brought me here...after..." He trailed off, looking a little sheepish, his mouth curling up in a self-deprecating smile that gave him a playful air. "Did all that really happen...or did I dream it all?"

The shock of everything overwhelming her, Mirena stood staring blankly at him, unable to process any of it. He seemed so bold toward her, so full of assumptions about what their relationship to one another was, but she'd never seen him before in her life, she was sure of it now, whatever vague sense of familiarity she'd felt upon his arrival.

What does he mean "after"? After what? I am going to kill Elizabeth! She did this on purpose and is probably waiting somewhere nearby to see my reaction!

Taking a deep breath, Mirena clenched the sheet she held tighter around herself.

"I think you may have me confused with someone else," she stated as confidently as she could. "Perhaps my twin sister?"

His jaw visibly dropped. It was a common reaction when someone learned that Elizabeth had such a shy and unassuming twin.

"I'm so sorry...I didn't mean to presume." If his expression was anything to go by, the pieces seemed to fall together for him. "If Mirena is your twin, then that would make you....?" He fished for a name.

This is too far, Elizabeth. Too far! You may have soiled your own name but you will not do the same to mine!

"I'm Mirena," she insisted. "I think my sister gave you my name instead of hers, which is Elizabeth, by the way. She does that to some men when she wants them to not find her... after she's done with them."

His eyes widened perceptively and Mirena couldn't help but notice that the grey of them was like the colour of steel and unlike anything she'd ever seen before.

"Let me get this straight...you're Mirena and she's Elizabeth? And you think I...? No. I only just met your sister, I swear."

Like it makes any difference how long you've known her... Mirena thought callously, her mouth thinning into a line of distaste. *A man as handsome as you wouldn't stand a chance against Elizabeth if she was determined to have you.*

He hesitated a moment, as if unsure whether or not to trust her with what he was about to say next. "Tell me something," he continued, "do you have any idea why your sister might drop me off here with you?"

Mirena sighed, feeling pity for this stranger for being another victim of her sister's games. He was obviously naïve, even if he was a Mage. "She always plays pranks like this on me...wait, where did you come from, anyway?"

He smiled somewhat ruefully, shaking his head in a kind of awed disbelief. "I was kind of hoping you might be able to tell me that..."

"Well you showed up in a ball of light on the floor here, unconscious."

"I what?!" He exclaimed, his eyes opening wide once more. "So it did happen, then..."

Stumbling backwards a little, he felt behind him for the chair against the wall and fell into it. In contemplation, he reached for the ring around his neck, looking like the world had just shifted beneath his feet and he wasn't sure where he stood anymore.

*I am so confused...*Mirena admitted silently. *What is he talking about? What happened? If he didn't bring himself here with his majik, there is no way Elizabeth could have...*

"Look, I won't tell anyone what happened to you if you do decide to tell me," she told him, not wanting to pry despite her mounting curiosity, "but I'm looking for Elizabeth. So if you know where she is I would appreciate if you could share the information."

He looked up from his contemplation of the ring, as if remembering that she was still there. Watching him closely, Mirena could see a deep sadness behind his eyes that she couldn't begin to fathom the reason for, though a part of her inexplicably wished that he would confide in her so that she could comfort him.

"What? Oh, I'm sorry. I wish I could tell you where Mirena...I mean, Elizabeth is, but I don't know where she went. I thought she was responsible for sending me here, but maybe it wasn't her after all..."

How many women does he associate with? And who has the power to send him here like this? Even if she has run off to the Collegium, Elizabeth is the furthest thing from a Mage...

This is getting out of hand. I can't involve myself with a Mage's problems... I need to get him out of here.

But what if someone sees him leave my room at this hour? People would talk...it would be a scandal.

"Well, I'm sorry I can't help you further, but I don't know what to do for you..." Mirena realized that her words were true. She couldn't explain why she felt drawn to this stranger, but something about the memory of his vulnerability a moment before and the pain in his eyes made her want to help him in any way she could. "I really wish I could help you, but I can't do the things that your friends can do..."

"What are you talking about?"

"I'm not a Mage..." Mirena clarified, "and I'm not sure what is going on right now. The only thing I know is that you appeared out of nowhere and I am currently not in a decent state to receive a man in my room, especially at this hour."

He blinked a few times as if trying to process her words, before standing abruptly. "Oh...I'm so sorry...I didn't realize. Forgive me," he added with a slight bow in her direction. "I'm a little out of sorts right now. I'll stop imposing on you." Awkwardly, he took a few steps toward the bathroom door, not really knowing which of the two closed doors led out of the room.

"Hope, wait!"

He stopped, turning towards her. *That must be his name I saw written on the ring then*, Mirena realized belatedly.

"That's the bathroom..."

"Oh, sorry," he turned and gestured questioningly to the only other door in the room, which was also closed. Mirena nodded and he continued, stopping with his hand on the doorknob. "Wait...what did you call me?"

"Your name...it's Hope, right? It was on the ring, so I assumed."

Hope picked up the ring dangling from his neck and inspected it a moment.

"Huh, so it does," he noted, shrugging. "Well, anyway, I'll be going now. Sorry to have bothered you."

"Stop! You can't go out there..." Mirena panicked, scurrying to put herself between Hope and the door and leaning on it to force it shut again. "I can't be seen with you...I mean, if someone sees you leaving my room at this time of night…"

He covered his mouth with his hand to hide a smile. "What would you have me do, then? Stay here with you until the sun comes up?"

What is it about him? He's not like anyone I've ever met. There is no hint of seduction in his voice, and though he's amused, he's not making fun of me.

"There's always the window?"

Hope smirked, his mouth quirking to one side, almost laughing at himself. "The window leads out to the courtyard. If you want to avoid a scandal, that's the last thing you should have me do. Mirena, is it?" He asked, confirming one last time which sister it was that he was dealing with. "Do you have somewhere to be in the morning that you need to be resting for, or would it be alright if I just stayed here for a little while? Personally, I'd rather avoid a scandal myself."

Stay here? In my room... Mirena couldn't explain why even just the thought of it made her heart thump nervously.

"I only have to find my sister in the morning," she told him, speaking a little too quickly. "You can sit on the chair over there. I am going to go get more appropriately dressed in the bathroom, if you would excuse me a moment."

Mirena selected a dress at random from the wardrobe and didn't give him the chance to stop her from slipping into the bathroom to change.

He might be fine with spending time with a half-clothed woman he's just met, but I'm not that kind of girl...

Looking over her appearance in the mirror, Mirena adjusted her white-blonde hair; truthfully, it wasn't even mussed as she hadn't yet been to sleep. It was long, framing her thin oval face and trailing partway down her back. The dress she had pulled out of her wardrobe was thankfully one of her favourites. Form fitting on top and loose in the skirt, the simple white sundress was comfortable but flattering to her thin form, while still being conservative.

I don't know why I care so much; he doesn't seem to have noticed me that way. A handsome Mage like that wouldn't bother with a girl like me...and why would he anyway after he's been with my sister?

Feeling inexplicably peevish, Mirena washed her face and pinched her cheeks to get some colour into them; trying to make herself look more like she hadn't been up all night.

Hope, if that was even his name, smiled in an attempt to be friendly as she exited the bathroom to rejoin him. His polite demeanor continued to catch her off guard and she found herself watching him, unsure of what to think.

Is he for real?

"So, Mirena," he began, leaning back in the plush chair and making himself comfortable, "since we're stuck in here together for the time being, why don't you tell me a bit about yourself?"

Okay... She thought, taking in his relaxed posture and wondering at his easy confidence. *I suppose talking to him can't hurt anything. It might help me to find out more about him and why he's bothering to be nice to me...*

"I am working at the Collegium's Cafeteria to save up for the entrance fee to study majik here," she began. "It's nothing too exciting, really. You're the one who seems to have a more interesting story."

Hope's expression got serious for a moment, his grey eyes dark.

"I think it's probably safer if we don't talk too much about me right now," he commented with a frown. "I'm sorry if that sounds strange, but I'm not quite sure what is going to happen to me now. After what I've just done, I may need to sneak out of more than just your room…"

What did he do? Mirena found herself questioning. *What type of man is in my room?*

Stay calm and just pretend like nothing is wrong, she instructed herself. But despite her rational thoughts, panic was written all over her face as she brought her hands up to cover her mouth, her eyes wide.

"It's not what you think!" Hope protested at once upon seeing her expression and he sat up straight in the chair; his hands out to calm her. "I mean, I don't know what it is that you're thinking, but I'm not a criminal, I promise...I just…

"Now, this is going to sound crazy, but I figure that you don't know who I am and you'll probably never have to see me again after this, so I owe you an explanation for showing up in your room like this..." He paused, looking into her eyes searchingly, like it was he who was wondering if he really could trust her, instead of the other way around.

"I..." He started then stopped. "Look, I may have done something that a lot of others would see as a mistake...

"I think I freed the Creator...I'm the Avatar of the Light."

Overwhelmed by the sheer impossibility of his claim, Mirena felt her eyes roll back into her head as she slumped backward into unconsciousness and only had enough presence of mind to be grateful that her pillows were positioned sufficiently to catch her.

Mirror's Hope

II.

Mirena woke up alone sometime in the late afternoon. Sitting up, she looked down at herself and realized that she was still dressed from earlier that morning.

So it wasn't a dream...or was it?

Shaking off feelings of disorientation, she got up and walked purposefully to the bathroom. *I guess there is only one way to find out...and besides, he was the last person who presumably saw Elizabeth.* The man called Hope was her only clue to begin looking for her sister, even if that wasn't his real name.

Now, where would I find him?

Oh no, she realized, bits of last night's strange encounter coming back to her as she brushed her hair and got ready for the day. *He mentioned that he might have to leave the Collegium...will I even be able to find him if I try?*

Realizing that the best place to look for anyone around midday would be the busy Cafeteria, Mirena opened the door with purpose to set out on her way. She froze, startled, as the doorway revealed exactly the person she'd decided to look for, his hand frozen in the air in the action of knocking.

Tall and broad shouldered, Hope filled out his Mage jacket nicely and it was something again to see him in the light of day, very much real and standing in front of her.

The Avatar of the Light...

Mirena felt unsteady on her feet, taking him in with the light from the hallway windows streaming around him like a halo. Confident and with a regal bearing, handsome and with a kind expression, he really did look the part, even if it was impossible that it was true.

"Mirena..." Hope spoke hesitantly, and Mirena felt a moment of elation that he'd remembered her name. "I wasn't sure if I should come back or not after...I mean, I didn't want to leave it like that. Are you okay? You seemed pretty peaceful when I left, so I figured you were just sleeping."

They were in the girl's dormitories of the sprawling Collegium complex and she could see light traffic in the hallway as other residents of the center of Magi learning went about their business.

Feeling her heart beat rapidly in her chest, Mirena took in the few passersby in the silent hallway and realized what this must look like. Almost in a panic, she stepped forward quickly and shut the door behind her, moving a few steps to the side so it wouldn't appear as if the two of them had just exited her bedroom together.

"What is it?" Hope asked. "Is there something wrong? I'm sorry if I shouldn't have come, but I wanted to make sure that you were alright."

"We need to watch what we say," she reminded him, looking side to side, but it didn't seem that there was anyone paying attention to them. "Scandals, remember?"

He looked side to side himself, checking the behaviour of the people around him. "I don't think anyone else cares, but if you're that concerned about it...would you come with me to the gardens? I know a spot where we won't be overheard."

He's strange, Mirena found herself contemplating him. *He doesn't seem to have an ulterior motive... Most men would only offer to take a girl my age to a private spot for a secret rendez-vous.*

Does he not see me that way? Maybe he's not attracted to me because he has feelings for my sister.

"That should be fine." Mirena lowered her eyes, feeling slightly disappointed by his perception of her, but then she smiled to cover her momentary slip. "Thank you for understanding."

Why should I care? Anyways, at least he doesn't seem to want to take advantage of me.

Hope gestured for Mirena to precede him and waited for her to lead the way at least as far as the gardens. He was the perfect gentleman, conceding to her wishes that they not appear 'together' and walking far enough behind her that others wouldn't mistake them for a couple under any circumstances. As they exited through one of the Collegium's open archways into the courtyard and the late afternoon sun, Hope took the lead and hurried Mirena down a tree-covered pathway.

The Collegium gardens were beautiful, even this late into the season. The inner courtyard was full of walkways and foliage well-tended by those who were in the pay of the Panarch to do just that. Many people lived and worked in the Collegium complex, which was the heart of the Capital city, and not all of them were Magi.

There were a fair number of those, however, and it was far more likely for a Mage or apprentice Mage to have leisure time than it was for anyone else. The majority of people Mirena passed were dressed in tell-tale black robes or suits or occasionally the rarer white ones. The level of detail of the gold trim or silver trim respectively marked whether the person was a full Mage or one still in training. Watching them chat idly amongst themselves, Mirena found that she felt somewhat out of place.

Soon enough, they came to a beautiful, gurgling stone fountain that she had never seen before, even though Mirena had walked through these gardens more than a few times since coming to the Capital over a month ago.

This place is beautiful, Mirena thought appreciatively, taking in the flowers in full bloom, trailing lazily in the fountains gentle current.

"Have you taken many girls here before?" She asked, idly curious.

Strangely, Hope blushed as she might have done if asked a similar question.

"No, just one, but it's not what you might think. This fountain is a good place to talk. No one can hear you over the noise of the water as long as you speak softly and because of the Panarch's decree, it's not often that anyone comes this far into the gardens."

"What if the Panarch comes by now, won't we get in trouble?"

Hope smirked again in his usual way and she found herself watching for the way the side of his mouth lifted familiarly in amusement.

"The Panarch doesn't use these paths."

How does he know that? Mirena wondered. "Do you come here often?" She asked instead.

"As a matter of fact I do," he answered, taking a seat on the fountain's edge and gesturing for her to do the same. Then he frowned, that sadness she'd noted in him the night before back again. "Or at least I used to. I probably won't be doing so anymore..."

Did he make the Panarch angry with him? Is it because of what he said… that he's the Avatar…?

Thinking to herself, she suddenly came to her own conclusion and gasped, covering her mouth with her hands. "The Panarch kills followers of the Light. He hunts them down…"

Hope's eyes sank downward to look at the grass at his feet.

"I know," he stated after a moment, too calmly in light of his own circumstance. "I suppose I really am a criminal now…" He added, with a defeated shrug. "I didn't mean to mislead you. You could likely be found guilty just for meeting with me. Should I go?" He asked at last, looking up and meeting her eyes, imploring her silently to help him.

The vulnerable look on his face reminded her forcefully of the way she'd found him unconscious and needing her help. Despite herself, she reached a hesitant hand in his direction, shuffling a little closer along the carved stonework of the fountain's edge.

He actually trusts me enough to tell me this?

"How did you guess that I support the Light?" She whispered tentatively, knowing that her words were just as treasonous as his, especially here where the Panarch ruled absolutely. "Is it that obvious?"

Hope seemed to be holding his breath, like he wanted to let it out in relief, but didn't dare trust himself or her enough to do so.

"…You're serious?"

"I'm not a liar," she told him in a serious voice. "Do I make you think that I am?"

"Most people," he explained, "even the honest ones, would lie to protect themselves at this point. I mean, what we're talking about is dangerous to us both. I wouldn't hold it against you."

"I'm not most people."

"I'm starting to believe that."

Mirena felt sudden panic grip her as an awful realization dawned. "Are you here to find me out and report me to the Panarch?"

Thoughts of the Panarch's Truthseekers sent to infiltrate everyday places and search out Sympathizers of the Light, or simply treasonous talk, filled Mirena's mind. They were said to be everywhere and trained in the art of getting people to trust them and tell them what they needed to hear to find the guilt in their targets. It was possible that Mirena had just walked into the biggest trap of her life, one that she'd never be able to walk out of.

I'm so stupid and naïve... She cursed herself silently, wondering if it was too late to try and flee. *A Mage as good-looking and powerful as he is wouldn't be kind to me without an ulterior motive... he was playing me for a fool.*

This is his chance to drop the ruse and turn me in...

"Unfortunately for us both, I wasn't lying when I told you that I'm the Avatar of the Light. I freed the Creator. It happened; I remember it clearly." Hope took a deep breath.

His expression said it all. No matter what she might want to think about him, it seemed that Hope really was being sincere and putting it all on the line. He wasn't lying and he wasn't making things up; he was in a desperate situation and he knew it.

"So either I'm crazy and will soon be put out of my misery, or we both are and you'll agree to help me figure out what to do, now that I've done something that will turn the whole world against me."

Mirena studied Hope's features for a moment and then closed her eyes. *This is it. This is what I have been praying for my whole life. If I stay and help him, I will be giving up everything I've worked for, but if I walk away now I will always regret not taking this chance to follow what I believe in.*

Opening her eyes, she looked into his and lost herself once more in the deep pools of wintry grey. "If I don't help you now, I would be a hypocrite," she stated, sure of herself. "I will help you, but first I need to find my sister and get her out of here so she doesn't get blamed for our crimes. She's not supposed to be here anyway. Elizabeth may be callous and mean, but she doesn't deserve to pay for my mistakes."

"Okay," Hope agreed. "I'll help you find Elizabeth. Truthfully, I'd like to get some answers out of her and you're right that she shouldn't be punished for what we're about to do. Whatever that is," he amended.

"Though, you should probably know," he added, "that your sister was the one to bring me to the Creator's prison. If it wasn't for her, this wouldn't have happened."

Feeling a little lost by the impossibility of his words, Mirena tilted her head questioningly. "And how did she do that exactly?"

"You know her better than I do," Hope responded, seeming just as confused by her reaction. "Is your sister not a Sympathizer like you?"

"Umm, not exactly," Mirena said, knowing her words were an understatement. "She knows about my beliefs and doesn't say anything, but she is more of a person who does things to benefit herself. Elizabeth would be more likely to use you than to help you willingly."

"I see," he commented, considering. "Well, that fits what I saw of her. Either way, I'm telling you the truth. For some reason, your sister took me to a place unlike anywhere else I've ever seen and that was where I met the Creator."

He looked somewhat bewildered, remembering such an otherworldly occurrence. "She thanked me and left. I swear it was the Creator; she was far too powerful and had too much of a presence to be a Mage, even a strong one.

"Then the next thing I remember," he continued, meeting her eyes once more; his own gaze intense, "is you."

Feeling somewhat overwhelmed by being the sudden focus of his attention, Mirena pulled her eyes away and looked down at her hands uselessly picking at the folds of her dress.

I thought I was naive. The thought came to her unbidden. *She played him like a fiddle. Elizabeth must have gotten a Mage friend to play along and then had that person drop him off in my room with their majik.*

Mirena felt tears sting her eyes. "I really thought you were real."

"I suppose I should have expected that reaction," Hope said, his tone suddenly bitter and his lips pursed. "It's the only thing that's made sense about you since we've met. Though I suppose you're right, it's foolish to think that what I saw was really real, but I guess a part of me deep down just wanted to hope that there could be some truth to the prophecies that one day the Light would return."

"No, that's not what I meant by it," she amended, still looking down. "I do believe that you could have met the Creator. I have to believe that it can happen, that the prophecies can be true, but I just can't believe that my sister would do the things you said she did.

"If it was Elizabeth, it was probably a cruel prank of some sort. I am sorry you were dragged into this. She probably meant to hurt me and you just got caught in the middle. Do you understand now?"

Hope nodded. "I do understand where you're coming from. But think," he added, his eyes lighting up, "if it wasn't a trick. What if by some miracle what I'm telling you is the truth? Whether your sister was involved in it or not, don't you have to take a chance on that?

"I know that for me, no matter what you decide, I can't go back to my old life after this. I believe in what I saw and I will find the Creator and prove it to you and everyone else if I have to."

Mirena wanted to believe him, she really did, but he was asking so much of her and they had only just met. *Can I trust him? He seems to believe in what he said that he saw. If he's right, then for the first time in my life, I might actually be in the right place at the right time…*

Her thoughts were interrupted by a crashing noise that almost caused her to jump to her feet. Hope had promised her that this part of the garden was rarely frequented, but what if he was wrong?

Or worse, if he was lying to her?

She'd heard somewhere that Truthseekers sometimes like to play with their victims before turning them in to the Panarch, like it was a game for them. And that sometimes they would take that game much further than necessary just for the sheer pleasure that it brought them to have power over another human being.

She was beginning to trust Hope, no matter her reservations. *Is it possible that I could be so completely wrong about him?*

Raucous laughter filled the air and she heard a further smash of a glass bottle hitting the wall with force, followed by a playful shriek that fell just shy of sincerity. Turning her head sharply in the direction of the sounds, Mirena was startled to find that the newcomers weren't just approaching, they were already here.

"Dipaul," Hope identified the man who was a stranger to Mirena.

Tall and very broad of shoulder, his black Magi jacket looked strained to the limit where his muscles bulged and rumpled around the waist where the jacket hung more loosely. The coat was open, showing a stained white shirt beneath and a hint of curly blond chest hairs.

The man's dirty blond hair fell into his eyes. When he moved the locks out of his way and focused somewhat blearily on Hope's face, Mirena could see that his eyes were a dull brown and somewhat lifeless, showing a decided lack of intelligence.

He's drunk, Mirena realized. *Maybe he didn't hear us after all. He looks like he just stumbled in here, not like he's looking to catch two conspirators talking.*

"Tendro?" Dipaul questioned; his deep voice slow and deliberate as he wrapped his arm tighter around the girl he'd brought with him. Leaning on her to support his unsteady legs, he peered closer as if to confirm who he was looking at through lidded eyes. "Is that you there?"

Tendro? Mirena questioned in silence. *So, that's Hope's real name. I will have to ask him about that later, but either way this man seems to know him well enough. But what kind of person gets drunk so early in the afternoon? He can't even stand up!*

"Yeah, it's me," Hope answered, but seemed unwilling to say more.

"Oh, well you should come back inside," Dipaul told him, wagging a cautionary finger at him. "You know we're not supposed to take them out of the garden."

Dipaul followed this pronouncement with a somewhat sly wink and a pinch to the bottom of the girl he was draped all over. She was a dark-haired and curvy thing and she let out a gasp of real pain when he squeezed her with his large and powerfully muscled hands. Then she simply plastered that playful expression back on her face before forcing a laugh and batting him on the shoulder affectionately.

Mirena looked away from Dipaul and blushed in embarrassment for the girl before lifting her eyes to regard Hope from the side.

"Maybe we should get going and give them their privacy," she suggested quietly.

Dipaul laughed then, an overly loud and obnoxious sound that made Mirena feel uncomfortable, despite his jolliness. The sound of his mirth made her question just what this man was capable of and she decided right then and there that she never wanted to find herself alone with him.

"Well, whatever you want to do with them, I can't really object," Dipaul noted, studying Hope with a malicious expression that belied his drunken state, "but I wouldn't let the Panarch catch me, if I were you."

"Duly noted," Hope responded with a serious expression. "Either way, don't let us interrupt you; I can see that you're busy."

Dipaul smiled again, the hint of malice disappearing and leaving Mirena to wonder if she had imagined the whole thing.

"I sure am," he agreed amiably. "It looks like you've found something to your liking as well," he commented. "Terrence was looking for you. Watch yourself, Tendro."

Why is he threatening Hope and why does he refer to me as a thing? That is just completely uncalled for. He might be used to the kind of women who enjoy being called 'things', but I am certainly not one of them!

"Excuse me, sir..." Mirena began, but then trailed off as Dipaul turned his attention onto her and she remembered her earlier feelings of warning in regards to him.

"You too, blondie," Dipaul said in her direction, his brown eyes dark, "you know what'll happen to you if you get caught..."

"Have a pleasurable evening, sir," Mirena replied, feeling shaken and unsure of how else to respond.

Dipaul smiled, nodding as if what she had said was exactly what he expected, before tipping a non-existent hat to Hope and turning toward the garden wall, leading his companion before him.

There's no exit there...

Unless Mirena was mistaken, or the drunken man intended to turn about at the last possible second, Dipaul was walking straight into a wall and taking the girl he was fondling with him. Despite this, he continued forward until Mirena was certain that she'd hear a smacking sound, but then the two of them simply disappeared before her eyes, phasing right through the solid carved stonework.

What the?! Mirena blinked a few times in astonishment. *Where did they go?*

"Who was that?" She asked aloud, looking to Hope for the answer.

"No one," Hope answered just a little too quickly. "Come on, let's get out of here."

He got to his feet and held out a hand to help her up. Mirena gave him a worried look, hesitating before cautiously accepting his offer. But when she put her hand in his, she felt her heart beat faster with the simple contact.

"I thought you said not many people come by here unless they have the Panarch's permission?"

"That's true," Hope admitted, "but he does, so let's go."

"What about you, then?" She asked, fighting the urge to leave this place as quickly as possible, planting her feet and showing her intention not to go anywhere with him until she got some answers to her questions. "He seemed to know you...Tendro."

Hope paused and regarded her, his eyes searching. Then he frowned. "Okay," he admitted, "so you know who I am now. Does that change anything? Dipaul is a dangerous man and he would be the first one to hand my head to Terrence Lee on a silver platter for even the slightest hint of what we've been discussing."

"Know you?" Mirena questioned "I've learnt your name, but who you are is still a complete mystery to me."

Hope sighed. "I know and I'm sorry for that, but believe me when I say we have to go. It's not safe for either of us in the Capital."

"I agree with you, but you are forgetting the fact that you agreed to help me find my sister." Mirena paused for a moment to shudder before continuing. "I hate to say it, but the man you call Dipaul is exactly the type of man that she would be hanging around."

A look of sharp recognition passed across Hope's face before he managed to cover it up.

"What is it?" She inquired. "Do you know where she is?"

"Don't take it the wrong way, please," he urged, "but I know where I've seen your sister before and you're not going to like it."

Mirena couldn't help the expression of disgust that crossed her face, thinking of Dipaul or someone just like him fondling her sister the way that he'd been fondling that brunette.

"Where would that be?"

Hope took a deep breath. "Are you really sure that you want to get her back?"

"How could you ask such a question? Of course I do! She is my sister!"

"I was afraid you would say that. But I did offer to help you and unfortunately, I'm a man of my word." He sighed. "You're not going to like what we're going to have to do, but I need you to trust me if we're going to get out of the Panarch's private garden alive…"

Mirror's Hope

III.

Taking a deep breath to steady herself, Mirena still didn't feel any more comfortable with what she was about to do. The short black dress she had changed into and altered according to Hope's instructions felt more than a little immodest, but she had promised him that she would do whatever it took to see her sister free of where the Panarch was holding her.

His own private garden…

Why hadn't she even known a place like that existed within the Collegium? It certainly fit with what she had heard of Terrence Lee's personality, but the thought of such a place right under everyone's nose was sickening to her. Willingly or unwillingly, her twin sister, physically her mirror, was a part of it.

"We don't ever speak of this again," she told Hope, feeling herself on the verge of tears. "This never happened, okay?"

Mirena stood tall and stiff, her face flushed with embarrassment and she was conscious of Hope's presence and how little of her own form she was leaving to the imagination.

If my mother learns of this, I will never hear the end of it.

"You're going to have to act more confident and relaxed," Hope told her, leaning over her shoulder to speak directly into her ear, his breath on her neck sending shivers down her spine, "at least a little, all right? Some of the girls in here are scared, but they learn pretty quickly not to show it if they want to survive. Just remember what I told you and you'll be fine."

Mirena was very much aware of Hope's nearness, punctuated by the warmth of his breath and the whispered quality of his words. She whimpered quietly, her nerves threatening to cause her legs to give out beneath her, but she took strength from his reassuring grip on her shoulder.

With Hope guiding her, Mirena was able to take the single step forward and the false stone wall enveloped her, sending her into a lush garden paradise.

Lined wall to wall with vibrant exotic flowers and foliage, she hadn't expected the hidden garden to be so beautiful. Still, the fear remained and she had to force herself to remember Hope's advice.

Walk tall, Mirena repeated to herself, *act like you belong here and if all else fails just pretend to be Elizabeth.*

She pretends to be me all the time; I'm sure it can't be that difficult.

They had worked out a quick story beforehand. Hope insisted that it was unlike him to be seen with the girls in the Panarch's garden, but not completely unbelievable. He would simply act as if what Dipaul had assumed of the two of them was the truth; that he was spending time with one of the girls that Terrence Lee kept in his garden to entertain himself and his personal guests.

Mirena had been shocked to learn of Hope's familiarity with the Panarch, his secret garden, and what went on behind the high walls, but she had been too concerned with her part in the mission to rescue her sister to ask too many questions.

When Elizabeth is safe and this is all over, 'Hope' is going to have some explaining to do…

Despite her misgivings, his arm around her waist was comforting as they moved deeper into the false paradise, even if she would have considered the gesture to be overly familiar under any other circumstances. The garden's walls were high and the foliage thick and concealing, giving a sense of privacy and a feel of things better kept hidden.

If someone were to scream in here, Mirena wondered, *would anyone hear them, or would the plants muffle the sound?*

"This way," Hope whispered for her ears alone as he led her through a vine-covered archway and into a veritable maze of thick hedges covered in all types of flowers.

They were alone in the shade of the greenery for which she was grateful, but it wasn't long before they began to hear voices and Mirena realized that they weren't the only ones in this forbidden place.

The voices were male and getting closer as they talked loudly without fear of being overheard; unlike Mirena, they belonged here.

She considered warning Hope, but by his sudden change in posture, he had heard the voices too and reacted instinctively, giving her a quick push into a nearby hedge.

"Shh," Hope whispered sharply in warning. "Stay hidden, I know that voice."

Mirena nodded and moved herself deeper into the foliage where she hoped no one would be able to see her, as Hope stepped away from the hedge and the two men came around the corner and into view.

"Tendro." It was Dipaul again, though he didn't look drunk anymore, despite it having been less than an hour since their previous encounter with him. "We were just talking about you."

"Nothing bad, I hope," Hope replied casually, greeting the second man with a respectful nod. "Panarch."

Mirena felt her heart leap to her throat as she peered through the bushes at the man standing next to Dipaul. Blond and aloof, the Panarch, Terrence Lee, was a good-looking man, so much so that he could have the pick of any girl he wanted, even without the power attached to his position. He stood proudly, his lean body relaxed, yet confident in his own domain. His blue eyes were cold and calculating and there was meanness to the set of his perfect jaw as he oversaw the beauty of the garden he had created.

How can Hope be so casual around the Panarch? Mirena found herself wondering. *Who is he, really? Tendro, Dipaul called him... I don't know that name, but I've never paid much attention to the people close to the Panarch. And Dipaul also has the Panarch's ear...what is that about?*

"No need to be so formal, Tendro," the Panarch commented familiarly, "we're all friends here."

"Yes, sir," Hope agreed, seeming somewhat uncomfortable in the Panarch's presence.

Terrence Lee smiled expansively. "This garden was a wonderful idea, wasn't it? A place where we can all be ourselves and enjoy the *fruits* of our labour…"

Fruit? Mirena felt her jaw drop at the implication in the Panarch's tone, thinking of how Hope had told her that Elizabeth was in here somewhere. *My sister is not a fruit!*

"You're too kind to us," Hope told him, his words deliberate and careful.

"I just like to share with my friends," Terrence Lee replied with the open tone of a host at a very exclusive party, "and we are friends, aren't we Tendro?"

"Of course," Hope agreed cautiously.

"Good," the Panarch answered, walking forward and putting his arm around Hope in a familiar fashion, "because now that I've gotten you and Dipaul here together I have a proposition for the both of you. You know how I hate to talk business in the garden, but it seems like that's all I've been doing lately…"

Mirena felt her panic escalate as the Panarch led Hope away from the spot where she was hidden, Dipaul keeping pace with them.

Oh no, Mirena realized as their voices faded out of her hearing. She didn't dare move from her hiding spot, even though every bit of her wanted to hear more of what they were talking about. Half of her was morbidly curious, the other half wanted to see if Hope was going to sell her out.

They are both Truthseekers, her instincts screamed at her, *and I have just been trapped. I don't know where I am or how to get out of here. Any moment now they are going to come back for me and I'll be lucky if they throw me in with Elizabeth and let me live. I am so stupid to have trusted him!*

Despite her own immediate danger, her sister's well-being was still foremost in Mirena's mind. It was foolish, but if these were going to be her last few moments of freedom, she wanted desperately to see her sister with her own eyes and confirm whether or not Elizabeth was okay.

Her heart pounding with fear, Mirena pushed herself out of the bushes and took off at a run in the opposite direction than the Panarch had taken Hope. If they wanted to take her in for treason, they'd have to catch her first; which meant that she had some time.

Running hard, Mirena rounded a corner and tripped on the carved stone walkway, landing badly and scraping her knee. Wincing as she climbed to her feet, she realized her own foolishness. Not only did she have no idea where she was now, she also had no clue as to where Elizabeth might be held.

That's if she's even in here, Mirena thought bitterly. *'Hope' could have been lying about that too...*

Not knowing where else to go, but wanting to be further from where she had been, she started walking down the path in front of her. Mirena kept her head down, not bothering to look for Elizabeth. She knew without a doubt that if her sister was here and saw her in this place, she wouldn't hesitate to stop her.

Lost in her own thoughts, Mirena barely noticed the sounds that began to fill the air around her until the birdsong was all she could hear. Lulled by the soothing natural birdsong, she almost forgot where she was and looked up to see that she had wandered into a sort of aviary.

Fanciful gilded cages hung from wrought-iron hangers covered in the vines that decorated the whole garden. Inside the cages were birds of all kinds; they were chirping happily to one another, as if they didn't know that they were held prisoners for the pleasure of the Panarch who had trapped them.

Forgetting herself momentarily, Mirena slowly drifted over to a cage that held a multitude of vibrantly-coloured little birds. Reaching slowly, she brought her fingers up to a small blue bird perched delicately near the bars and ran her fingers down the side of its feathers. Her breath caught in her throat as it tilted its head to regard her curiously.

"Beautiful, aren't they?"

Startled, she pulled her hand away from the cage with a sharp intake of breath and froze. The voice that had spoken was undeniably male, and there was no doubt in Mirena's mind that she had heard the deceptively friendly tones before and very recently at that.

"Don't worry," the Panarch, Terrence Lee, continued, "they're meant to be admired…"

Not turning around, Mirena nodded quickly and lowered her head. Feeling apprehensive, but too scared to react, Mirena felt more than heard the Panarch approach. Sooner than she would like, he was no more than a few inches from her, close enough that she could feel his breath on the back of her neck.

She held herself as still as possible, not sure how to act, but knowing that she didn't want to do the wrong thing; whatever that was. Mirena felt Terrence Lee's hand reach up and caress the side of her neck, his fingers running along her skin, just as hers had run along the small bird's feathers.

"…Just like you."

The simple motion sending a spike of fear through Mirena, she was too afraid to move. She closed her eyes and prayed to the Creator that it would be over soon and the Panarch would somehow lose interest in her, leaving her alone and free.

Does he know about me? Her panicked mind questioned. *That I'm not Elizabeth? Or does he think I'm my sister and this is how he treats her?*

Changing abruptly from soft and caressing to a firm grip, the Panarch's hand tightened on the back of her neck without warning and Mirena flinched despite herself.

This is it, she couldn't help but think, *it's over. The Panarch has found me out...and he's come now personally take me away.*

Moving his hand from neck to shoulder and massaging with a firm grip, Terrence Lee whispered in her ear, "You're so tense, Elizabeth...that's not like you."

Mirena felt her eyes begin to fill with tears and she never even considered letting out a breath in relief at the news that he thought she was her sister; even though it meant she wasn't going to be executed as a Sympathizer of the Light.

What have you gotten yourself into, Elizabeth? Mirena questioned, filled with horror at the thought of her sister acting the whore with this man.

"My apologies..." Mirena began in a whisper, not trusting herself to speak any louder.

The Panarch's grip tightened once more, drawing her in to his body until she was pressed up against him, unable to escape. "You know that kind of formal crap doesn't work with me, dear," he growled dangerously.

Be Elizabeth! Think like Elizabeth, Mirena reprimanded herself. *That is what Hope told me to do...*

"Let me make it up to you..." she said in as sultry a voice as she could manage. Reaching up to her shoulder, she placed her hand on top of his as seductively as she knew how, which was not at all, but she hoped that her meaning was clear.

The Panarch turned her around so quickly that Mirena felt her head spin and before she could react, he took hold of her chin forcefully and lifted her eyes to his.

His blue eyes were ice cold.

"Who are you?" He demanded, his gaze boring into hers.

Elizabeth's eyes are green and mine are blue; it's the only physical difference between us.

"No one," Mirena whispered, shaken.

"I don't take well to imposters," he continued, his tone dark but his eyes still too bright, too intense. Mirena didn't doubt for a moment that every word he spoke was true, and that every threat he made would be carried out. "If you're here as a spy, you'll regret this day."

She began to cry, unable to help herself as her fear caused the tears to roll down her face. There was nothing she could do to stop them, any more than she could save herself from whatever the Panarch chose to do to her.

"Pathetic," he said and letting her go, Terrence Lee took a step away from her in disgust.

She began to hope that maybe he would let her be; that this was going to be the worst her punishment would get. She thought that right up until the moment he backhanded her sharply across the face.

At first, Mirena felt nothing but shock as the back of the Panarch's hand made contact with her face, the heavy gold rings which adorned it scraping along her nose and cheek. Seconds later, searing heat engulfed the place where he had struck her like an explosion going off under her skin.

Feeling like everything she had ever eaten was about to resurface, Mirena recoiled from the man who hadn't hesitated in the least to strike her so violently. Hitting the ground, she scurried backwards away from the threat, not being able to see past the swelling forming around her nose.

With her eyes shut tight against the pain, Mirena didn't see the Panarch's boot coming. If anything, the blow to her stomach was worse than the first strike had been and the beating kept on coming. Over and over again, he drove his heavy foot into her midsection and back like a hammer driving in a nail; no matter how she writhed or cried out, he didn't stop.

"I've considered your proposal."

The sudden absence of the boot striking her middle shocked Mirena more than the distant words and it took her a moment to realize that the cold and calculating voice hadn't come from the Panarch.

"And?" Terrence Lee questioned, giving the newcomer his full attention and dismissing Mirena for the moment.

Mirena rolled over, her mangled body hunching inward from the pain and fearing another blow. Past the blurriness of her vision she could just make him out.

Hope stood there, in the vine-covered entranceway of the aviary. His pose was relaxed, despite the scene before him. His eyes were locked on the Panarch and the woman that he'd reduced to a mangled heap at his feet.

It's like he doesn't even see me here... Mirena's mind supplied distantly.

"It seems that I have no choice but to accept."

IV.

All was quiet in her little corner of the secret garden until finally the birds that had been silenced during her brutal beating began to chirp again, their little wings fluttering within their cages.

The Panarch had long since led Hope away, chatting amiably with him as if he hadn't just beaten Mirena nearly to death and left her bleeding on the tiled floor of the aviary to die.

She wasn't dead, however. For some reason, Terrence Lee had left Mirena alive and she didn't even have it in her to be grateful.

"Elizabeth," she tried to say her sister's name, but it came out as only a cough of blood. She didn't have it in her to scream for help and there was no way of knowing if anyone was near enough to hear her if she tried.

"Hey," a voice whispered sharply to her right.

Mirena fought to turn her head to the sound, but the pain it cost her wasn't worth the effort. A flurry of small steps coming towards her informed her that it was a woman and not the Panarch or Hope returning.

"It is you," the woman said, reaching her side and kneeling down to move some of the blood-matted hair out of her eyes.

It was a struggle for her sluggish mind to pull up a memory of the face before her, but after a moment she had it. Her unlikely rescuer was the woman she had seen earlier with Dipaul. Dark-haired and curvy, she was wearing a short black dress not unlike Mirena's own, only she filled it effortlessly and looked comfortable despite how revealing it was.

"Elizabeth," Mirena coughed again with much effort.

"Hey now, don't try to talk..." the brunette said gently. "You're not her, are you? Elizabeth's your twin or something, right?"

Mirena couldn't help herself, the tears started flowing again; she wasn't capable of much else.

"It's all right," the woman continued, "it probably wouldn't surprise you after what you've just been through, but this happens all the time. We'll take care of you, don't worry."

With the fear finally leaving her, there was nothing left but the pain. The world around her darkened and finally went black as consciousness finally and blissfully left her.

Mirena woke up in a surprisingly plush and comfortable bed, though her body still ached and she felt drained and weaker than ever before in her life. Pink fabric was draped up to her chin, fluffy and soft, and she was propped up on countless pillows. From her vantage point the rest of the room continued in much the same style, with gauzy pink curtains over a window on the far side of the room and dizzying floral patterns cluttering the walls.

As she became more aware of her surroundings she began to take notice of an argument going on outside the closed wooden door.

"There's no way in hell I'm letting you in there. I don't care who the fuck you are or who you work for!"

Mirena smiled to herself, taking comfort in recognizing her sister's voice and her characteristically caustic attitude. A male voice responded more quietly and she was unable to make out the words, but her sister's response told Mirena what had likely been said.

"The Panarch can go fuck himself!"

"I'll be sure to tell him that," Hope replied sarcastically as he opened the door and stepped past a fuming double of Mirena who was dressed in a floor-length pink gown more elaborate and decorated than Mirena would have thought possible.

"What are you doing here?" Mirena croaked feebly, looking at Hope and feeling numb at the sight of him. "Have you come to take me back to him?"

"Creator," he gasped, taking in her ragged appearance, "what has he done to you?"

"Same thing your precious Panarch does to all of us," Elizabeth noted with scorn, placing her hands on her hips and looking down her nose at Hope. "Have you seen enough yet?"

"I am so sorry," Hope said, coming forward to kneel at Mirena's bedside and take her hand lightly in his.

"You brought me here knowing this could happen," Mirena damned him with her words, pulling her hand out of his grasp. "Then you stood by and watched...I think you should leave."

"I..." Hope began.

"You heard the woman," Elizabeth interjected.

Hope started to get to his feet, when Mirena took note of the real pain in his stricken expression and the way that emotion caused his eyes to fill with tears.

He didn't mean for this to happen... Mirena realized suddenly, *He wouldn't be here if he had... not like this.*

"Wait," she said more gently, reaching after him despite the effort it cost her to move.

Startled as he was turning to leave, Hope turned his head back to look down at her and Mirena noticed that the tears had started falling now and he made no move to stop them or wipe them away. Unless he was a superb actor, Hope wasn't faking this emotion and it was easily identifiable as regret.

"I believe you," she whispered softly. "The Panarch hurt me, not you..."

"I wish I could fix this and make it so it never happened," he replied just as softly, his head lowered in shame, "it's my fault that this happened to you... I should have just gone in and brought Elizabeth out to you."

"You couldn't have known," Mirena protested, taking his hand and hating that she was too weak to lift herself enough to wipe the tears from his eyes, finding herself wanting to comfort him even though she was the one who had suffered.

"Of course he knows!" Elizabeth broke in suddenly. "He's one of them… he knows what it's like here, what happens to girls who aren't clever enough or lucky enough to keep the Panarch's interest."

Mirena's head snapped up at Elizabeth's words, the very action causing her pain, but what happened next distracted her from even her sister's shocking revelation.

"I will make this better somehow…" Hope stated determinedly and Mirena gasped as from beneath Hope's white shirt the ring he had worn there since he had appeared from nowhere in her room began to glow once more.

Her eyes locked onto the glow, unable to look away, but it seemed that Hope didn't even notice the odd phenomenon. His steel grey eyes were focused on her and as she watched, light began to shine from him. It gave him a white aura, bathing the room in an otherworldly light.

She let go of the hand she held in surprise, but Hope caught her wrist with a determined expression crossing his features and continued to hold her. The white glow strengthened until it was all she could see and it blotted out everything else in the room, everything except for him.

In no more than a moment the light was gone, leaving even the ring dull again, but with its departure went the pain in her body and the overwhelming weakness she'd been feeling; leaving her feeling blissfully light and unburdened.

"What the hell was that?!" Elizabeth exclaimed, breaking the silence that had fallen over the room.

"I am so sorry I doubted you," Mirena whispered to Hope, her mouth open in shock and amazement.

He really is the Avatar… no mere Mage could have healed me like that.

"I would have doubted me too," Hope told her, his steel grey eyes shining in the aftermath of the glow created by his strange and otherworldly power.

"Can someone please explain to me what the fuck just happened?" Elizabeth repeated herself, standing bewildered in the middle of the room. "Because last I checked, majik doesn't look like that…"

"Do you see what I mean?" Mirena asked with sudden good humour, pointing to her sister.

"She's got quite a mouth on her, doesn't she?" Hope smiled in agreement.

"I'm standing right here," Elizabeth tapped her foot imperiously, the motion causing the pink ruffle of her dress to bob and the full skirt to sway, trailing lengths of pink ribbons, "and this is my bedroom we're all standing in, so I think I deserve an explanation if nothing else."

Hope's expression grew abruptly serious. "Close the door."

Elizabeth did what he wanted despite herself and shut the door to the small room, leaving the three of them alone in a tense kind of silence.

"So are you going to answer me or not?" She demanded after a moment.

Meanwhile, Mirena had managed to sit up in the bed with a surprising lack of difficulty and she found herself looking into an ornate round mirror on the opposite wall. Her face was perfect; there wasn't even a single mark or blemish.

And I'm sure the rest of me is miraculously the same way… Mirena thought. *Hope did as he said he wanted to… he made it so that it was like it never happened. He took the pain away…*

She touched her face to make sure that what she was seeing was actually real. *How is this even possible? Elizabeth is right, majik doesn't work like that. It can heal, but slowly and with great effort…. This, is a miracle.*

"Sit down," Hope instructed.

"I prefer to stand, thank you," Elizabeth insisted peevishly, putting her hands on her hips once more.

"Suit yourself," he told her with a sigh, "but what I have to tell you may be a little bit hard to swallow and completely treasonous."

"You don't say," Elizabeth countered, pointing to Mirena who suddenly felt self-conscious at being so vain as to continue to check her appearance in the mirror.

Gesturing in an absentminded fashion, Hope used his power as a Mage to seal the room from anyone who might be listening to what he was about to say. Wanting to become a Mage herself, Mirena was familiar with the motion, even though it was considered bad form by Magi and scholars alike to rely upon gestures when using majik.

"Now what I have to say won't be overheard," he informed them, taking a deep breath before his next words. "As crazy as it might seem, I'm the Avatar of the Light and I'm responsible for freeing the Creator."

Elizabeth stared at Hope for just a beat too long and then she burst out laughing full force from her gut, not at all in a ladylike fashion.

"Yeah, right, and I'm Theia Prosai, the female Panarch," she managed after a moment, "nice to meet you."

"Elizabeth! That's uncalled for, don't you think?" Mirena squeaked, shocked at her sister's lack of respect for who and what Hope had just proven himself to be.

"I wish I was lying to you, but I'm not," Hope told her. "It's the truth."

Elizabeth sobered quickly. "You're serious, aren't you?"

He nodded.

"Well after what I just saw, I'd be a liar if I said I didn't believe you," she continued, "but I will say that you are one unlucky bastard."

"We came here to rescue you and bring you with us," Mirena told her.

"Rescue me?" Elizabeth snorted. "What in the world makes you think I need rescuing?"

"Well Mother said that she was going to come get the both of us if you didn't come home…"

"That old harpy?" Elizabeth questioned. "That's an empty threat; she'd never leave the farm to Dad's care."

"Mother isn't a harpy, she just cares about your well being and you have done irresponsible things in the past to make her angry."

"You're one to talk," Elizabeth countered with her typical attitude.

"So are you saying that you don't want to leave here?" Hope asked, raising a brow in question.

Elizabeth turned her ire onto Hope. "I don't see how it's any of your business," she told him, "but I've got a good thing here. I'm the Panarch's favorite and…"

"And how long is that going to last?" Hope spoke quietly, but his words caused Elizabeth to fall silent. "You know what'll happen once Terrence finds a new 'favorite.' You'll be passed around to the other Generals and who knows who else."

"Generals like *you*?" Elizabeth spat. "I know what my position means, do you?"

"Stop it, both of you!" Mirena said loudly, getting out of the bed, amazed at how easy it was to stand, and putting herself between the two of them. "Don't you see this isn't helping anyone?"

The wordplay stopped, but Elizabeth's glare shot daggers in Hope's direction.

"So what it comes down to," Hope said after a moment, "is do you want our help or not?"

"Hmm..." Elizabeth made an exaggerated sound while tapping her lips with her finger. "Do I want to lump myself in with two admitted traitors to the Panarch's rule and be hung with them when they are found out? No, but it doesn't seem like you've left me much choice in the matter!"

"He beat me almost to death and he'll do the same to you!" Mirena pointed out. "Especially now!"

"You think I don't know that, Mira?!" Elizabeth demanded, rounding on her sister. "You've ruined everything by coming in here when this is the last place you should be! Now my life is going to be just as crappy as yours, but that's what you've always wanted, isn't it?"

"How could you say that to me? I'm your sister!" Mirena countered. "And sleeping with the Panarch isn't something you should be proud of!"

"Now ladies, I think that's enough," Hope interjected in a pacifying tone. "I'd be more than happy to let you both continue this once we get ourselves safely out of here, but for now we don't have the time to get into it."

"And how do you propose we get out of here now?" Elizabeth questioned. "Are you going to use your special VIP pass?"

"We have more of a chance with Hope than we do on our own," Mirena informed her.

"Hope?" Elizabeth exclaimed startled, her eyes going wide before she pointed incredulously at Hope. "You let her call you 'Hope'?"

"Come on, let's go," Hope instructed instead of rising to her taunts, undoing the majikal protection he'd placed on the room with another gesture and heading for the door.

"Oh Tendro!" Elizabeth said in the most high-pitched and annoying voice that she could manage. "You can be my Hope and I'll be your Miracle! Get it?" She dropped the fake voice, laughing at her own joke. "Mira, Miracle?"

"That's not funny Bethwee!" Mirena snapped, using her sister's hated childhood nickname.

"Girls," Hope cautioned from out in the hall. "I'd like to get us out of here without anyone taking notice."

"It's a little late for that, don't you think?" Dipaul stepped shirtless out into the hallway from a room down the hall, a half-naked, red-haired girl leaning her head out of the door behind him. "I told you to watch yourself, Tendro."

Dipaul lifted his hand, the tell-tale gesture warning Mirena that things were about to get a whole lot more dangerous. She dove instinctively toward Elizabeth in an attempt to shield her sister with her own body as Dipaul's majik raced through the air to attack Hope.

Mirena didn't know what the intended effect was and looking over her shoulder back at Hope once the immediate danger had passed, she couldn't see that anything had changed, but that didn't necessarily mean that Dipaul's majik had failed.

"I think you'll find that binding me won't do any good," Hope told Dipaul through gritted teeth.

A binding would stop Hope from being able to use his majik, Mirena realized, *and without it, there's nothing to stop Dipaul from delivering us right to the Panarch.*

But she hadn't accounted for Hope's newfound gifts. Without warning, light split the air in between Hope and Dipaul, burning with a fiery intensity. The searing white caused Mirena to bury her head in Elizabeth's shoulder, but doing so didn't stop the piercing scream from reaching her ears as the light found its target.

It went on and on, the ear-splitting sound and the burning light, until Hope's words somehow broke through it all.

"Come on!" He yelled. "We have to go!"

Mirena turned at the sound of his voice, peering through the brilliance to make him out. The hall was filled by an intense white light and in the middle of it all was Hope, his hand held out towards her. Without hesitation she reached for him and followed his lead, pulling her sister up with her. She didn't know what else to do; Hope was their only way out now.

Ten steps.

It was ten steps from where she'd huddled on the floor to protect Elizabeth to where Hope's power had ripped a hole in the air, much like the one she remembered from her room the night he'd appeared. The light plagued her senses every step of the way, but even still she found she could not shut her eyes to block out what the intense light allowed her to see.

At three steps, she hesitated at crossing the threshold of the hole in the air to the unknown, but two steps from the hole in the air she saw Dipaul's severed hand on the floor. She distantly heard the panicked shrieking of the red-headed girl as she took in the sight of the bloody stump that was all the remained of Dipaul's arm and realized that after what Hope had done, they had no choice but to take the way out he had provided.

For his part, Dipaul just glowered, unable to reach past the searing edges of the hole made of light that had already taken his left hand. Mirena could see no hint of stupidity or dullness in Dipaul's brown eyes now; there was only hatred and a promise that one day he would see her dead and he would laugh over her beaten and mangled corpse.

Creator, help me! Mirena prayed. *May the day never come that I have to face this man again.*

One more step and Hope pulled Mirena and Elizabeth into the unknown and the escape he'd provided for them closed behind their passage, the light abruptly disappearing and leaving them in total darkness.

Mirror's Hope

V.

"Blinding light, then complete darkness," Elizabeth commented wryly. "Nice work, holy boy."

"Is everyone okay?" Mirena asked; her voice too loud in the otherwise silent darkness. "Where are we, anyway?"

"This place feels familiar..." Hope responded, his voice growing distant as he let go of Mirena's hand.

"Where are you going?"

"This place…" Hope continued from a little ways away. "It feels just like the hills where I met the Creator."

At his words a dim light began to glow from no discernable source, illuminating grass beneath Mirena's feet. As the light grew it allowed them to make out rolling hills continuing in the distance and to see one another, if only barely.

For once, Elizabeth was speechless.

Hope looked around himself, not as bewildered as they were, but more like he was remembering a different time and a place; somewhere more real in his imagination than the featureless landscape on which they found themselves.

"It was daytime then, of course," Hope said and as if he had summoned it, the sun began to crest over the hills with the early light of dawn, "and there was mist everywhere…"

Mirena looked to her sister for confirmation of what she was seeing as, true to Hope's words, mist began to gather around them; it swirled around their feet as it rose.

Elizabeth met her gaze and simply shrugged as if to say 'who are we to question?'

"But this isn't the place," Hope continued.

As he spoke the mists retreated and the sunlight began to fade, taking the view of the rolling hills with it. It was like the breath of life he'd given this place had suddenly wilted with his lack of belief in its reality.

"No! Wait," Elizabeth exclaimed, hurrying over to Hope. "Can't you see what you're doing?"

He looked around himself for the first time, confused. "I don't know where we are, Elizabeth."

"I don't care about that," she told him. "Look, you moron. Look at what your words do to this place. Everything you say happens."

Hope gave Elizabeth a look that said she was crazy. "I don't know where I've managed to take us, but I hardly think that I have the ability to shape reality. The Creator may have blessed me with some of her power, but I sure as hell don't know how to use it."

Mirena walked over to join Hope and Elizabeth. "Think of a place that you know very well," she told him. "Think of all the details and imagine that we are there. It can be anywhere in the world."

Hope shook his head. "I can't teleport us anywhere right now; Dipaul really messed with my majik. I don't know what use I'm going to be as a Mage for a while. We might be better off just laying low, once we figure out where my crazy power has taken us."

"You're not listening," Mirena pressed. "Think about a place you want to be right now. Close your eyes and describe it to me."

He gave her a flat look and then closed his eyes, humouring her.

"There's a cottage in Lasalle," Hope began describing a place as she had requested. "It's a quiet place where you can see the stars. There isn't much around it, just long grass and a dock where the water laps gently from the lake.

"I wouldn't want to be at that exact cottage right now, since it's known by too many of the wrong people, but a place just like it; somewhere private and safe, with access to only those who know how to find it through the trees."

Mirena smiled, watching the scene he was describing unfold in front of her eyes. Even Elizabeth looked overawed as a long row of trees created a canopied walkway to a small cottage at the end of a dirt path through the grass that lengthened under their feet. She could hear the gentle sounds of water from beyond the tree line and she could only presume that the lake would be there just as he'd described it.

When the scene was complete down to the last detail of the light dimming to reveal a multitude of stars in the sky, she lightly reached out and touched Hope's arm to bring him back to the present and let him see what he'd created.

He opened his eyes and Mirena watched his jaw drop.

"That's more like it," Elizabeth commented, "now you look like the rest of us. Come on," she added, taking off down the path before her, "let's go explore."

With Elizabeth taking the lead, they walked the short path to the cottage. Once there, she reached for the door with a flourish and swung it open wide, not thinking for a moment that it might not be as solid as it looked.

"Here we are: one super secret hideout in a place no one will ever find us and we'll probably never be able to get out of on our own! Ta da!"

"I think we should bring her home now..." Mirena suggested, only half-joking. "Objections, anyone?"

"I object," Elizabeth stated, taking a few steps into the cabin and looking around at the homey wooden table and functionally-designed kitchen. "If you take me home now, then there will be no one here to chaperone you two in your private cabin getaway. We can't have that now, can we?"

She just has to open her mouth and make things awkward for me...

"I wish I was an only child," Mirena muttered peevishly.

"So do I, dear sister," Elizabeth responded with a smile over her shoulder back at Mirena, "so do I."

"It's the same, but not a perfect replica of the real thing," Hope informed them, lost in his own world, his expression awed as he took in his handiwork. "Exactly as I imagined it. We didn't teleport here; I made all of this, somehow."

"I meant what I said about taking her home," Mirena repeated her earlier statement, remembering the whole point of all this now that they'd somehow managed to leave the Capital behind. "Mother is expecting us."

"Mother can wait," Elizabeth countered with her usual attitude. "I think the little matter of the price on our heads is more important than making it home in time for dinner."

"Then that's all the more reason we should go home and warn them. They may be targeted as well!"

"Mirena's right," Hope agreed, putting the miracle of the cottage out of his mind for the moment and turning to face them both across the wooden table in the center of the room. "We do want to make sure they're not in danger because of us, but more importantly we need to get there before the Panarch can think to send someone after us. Where are you two from, exactly?"

"Maredon, the same place the Panarch grew up. Just a few farms over from his adoptive parents, actually," Mirena supplied, knowing, as everyone did, the reason for which her hometown was famous.

"Convenient," Hope commented sarcastically. "Well at least I know the place you're speaking of. It's too bad that the distance won't keep Terrence Lee from checking there."

"But it'll take him a while to get there, won't it?" Mirena asked hopefully. "And with the Creator's majik we might be able to find a faster way?"

"I'm afraid that the Panarch is quite the accomplished Mage," Hope frowned. "Teleportation is his specialty; it's not possible to outrun him."

"Balls," Elizabeth muttered.

"Shouldn't we go now, then?" Mirena felt a hint of panic at the thought that Hope might not be able to free them from this strange realm he'd brought them to. "How do we get out of here and to Maredon?"

"I can get us out of here, I think," Hope told them. "I mean, I got us in, so it should be a simple matter to do the same in reverse. But as for getting to Maredon, I can't do it myself until Dipaul's binding fades and I don't know how long that's going to take. Elizabeth, can you take us there?"

"Me?!" Elizabeth exclaimed. "I don't have even the tiniest bit of majik. That's Mira's department. She's the one who wanted to train to be like you...well, not like you exactly, but like other Magi that don't glow."

"How can I help?" Mirena asked.

"But I thought..." Hope began. "Never mind...I'll have to stop getting the two of you confused. I suppose it'll help that your personalities are so far apart. Okay, we can try it. It's really quite easy as long as you have the ability to use majik; we shouldn't have any problems."

With their decision made, they trooped out of the cottage and back down the path, though if Hope could send them back at all, he could probably do so from anywhere.

"I want to walk a ways from here so that when I open a hole back to the outside we don't end up in the same place we left," he informed them, continuing on and furthering the path beneath his feet as he walked. "I'm not sure if that's how it works, but I'd like to be safe about it if possible."

Hope's words made sense and it was true that he was the only one of the three of them who might have some knowledge of how this place worked. After a time they stopped and Hope announced that this was likely far enough.

"Stand back," he instructed and Mirena did as she was told, the image of Dipaul's severed hand lying on the floor in a pool of its own blood fresh in her mind. Once the two of them were clear, Hope closed his eyes to concentrate and after a moment, the ring around his neck began to glow with a familiar white pulse.

The pulse widening, a spot of light appeared in the air, the edges of which were tearing into a hole much like the one they had used to get here, only less violent and eruptive than before. Within moments, more natural lights and sounds intruded upon their private sanctuary as the bustling Collegium marketplace was revealed.

Generally a busy place, it was even more so in the early evening after most people had eaten supper and this evening was no exception. Foot traffic filled the indoor marketplace, visiting the various merchant stalls who rented the space from the Collegium, and therefore ultimately the Panarch.

The people stopped and stared, pointing at the anomaly in the air before them, but having begun to tear a hole in the fabric of reality, Hope didn't dare stop until he'd completed it. The hole widened until it was large enough for them to step through and then with a wave of his hand, he directed them forward.

"Go first; I don't know if this place will still exist once I leave it."

Mirena did not hesitate; she knew what was at stake here. Running toward the only possible exit from the world of Hope's creation, she leapt through the hole in the air; one leap taking her from grass to solid ground.

Once firmly back in the real world, Mirena raised her head to get her bearings and her eyes locked onto the monorail station platform accessible by a large curving staircase along the outer wall of the marketplace.

That is our best shot of getting out of here fast and if we're lucky, the crowd will let us blend in so no one can stop us.

The marketplace was complete chaos around them, but their unorthodox arrival was still enough to draw attention. With luck the scene they were causing would be a good enough distraction to give them time to get out of the Capital, but the Panarch and his Generals would soon hear about this no matter what. They couldn't pretend that Terrence Lee wouldn't care enough to send someone after them; or worse, he might come himself.

Opportunistic as ever, the confusion and the chaos caused by their desperate flight only served to give people an excuse to give into lawlessness themselves. While shop owners stared after them as they exited from a bright and gaping hole in the air, passersby took the momentary opportunity to make off with whatever they could, stuffing food, jewels and everyday necessities into their bulging pockets or their shopping bags.

As they ran through the crowd and toward the stairs that would take them to the monorail platform, so too did the thieves and cutpurses that preyed on the unwary. They, however, went in whichever direction would hide their thievery, only increasing the general chaos in the market square.

Hope led the group of them up the stairs to the platform of the monorail and people made way for him as he passed, either because they recognized him and his relation to the Panarch, or because of the scene he'd just caused downstairs. Mirena found herself hoping that it was the former, and that the bright light he'd created would somehow just fade from their memories as another Mage's trick.

As Mirena reached the top of the curved stairway and used her momentum to swing around the banister, something about the scene below caught her eye and caused her to pause despite her panicked flight.

A petite woman, no older than herself, with long black hair, pale skin and light blue eyes that matched her dress stood in the midst of the throng as it surged around her, her pose completely still and calm, her gaze steady. Her expression could only be described as unimpressed as she followed Hope's every move until he was no longer in sight.

Then the woman's expression turned bitterness as she tore her gaze from the stairs and turned about to go back to her business. In that moment between watching Hope and looking away, her eyes caught hold of Mirena's and there was a spark of recognition there and a deep and unexplained hatred.

I've never seen this woman before…who is she?

With that, the dark-haired stranger turned and went about her business as if nothing had happened and Mirena distantly became aware of Elizabeth calling her name.

"Coming!" She shouted back, turning from the mystery of the dark-haired woman and scurrying past the crowd of people to rejoin Hope and Elizabeth as the three of them boarded a timely monorail car that had just pulled into the station powered by the majik of the Collegium.

It was less than a turn of the hourglass from one end of the monorail track to the other, but they passed the journey in silence, each of them saying their own silent goodbyes to the lives they were leaving behind in the Capital.

Mirena had ridden the monorail only once before, on her way to the Collegium from Maredon, but it still fascinated her how something so large could move so quickly powered only by majik.

The Generator is a miraculous device, Mirena found herself appreciating the finer points of the Capital city, even if she didn't appreciate the man who controlled it now.

The Generator was the largest majik item ever made and it had taken the power of many Magi working together to create it, but its sole function was to harness the excess majik wasted by Magi and recycle it to power all of the Collegium's and the Capital's conveniences, which were largely majik items themselves.

If it wasn't for Terrence Lee, the Capital would probably be the paradise it was built to be. As it is, most of us either work for him, try to curry his favour or live in fear of him. I'm obviously in the third category, but Elizabeth until recently was in the second and Hope, the first.

Speaking of Hope… Who was that woman and why did she hate me so much? She seemed to know Hope, but if she did, why didn't she try to stop us if she was so upset?

I'll ask Hope about her later. Right now is just not the right time to bring it up; he already has so much on his mind.

Mirena was lost in her own thoughts, but even still the journey from the Collegium to the city's southern border seemed to take forever. Perhaps it was simply that she didn't really want to leave.

She had to admit that she believed in Hope and wanted to see him succeed as the Avatar in returning the Light to this world, but she also missed the days when her simple dreams had been enough for her.

It had been such a whirlwind, discovering Hope and getting caught up in his destiny, and a part of her wished that she was still in the Capital, working hard to one day save up enough to pay for her education as a Mage. Now she didn't know if she'd ever get the chance to realize her own potential and the realization saddened her.

"It's not far," Hope informed them, leading them away from the monorail station and into the darkened tree line at the edge of the Capital's sprawling expanse.

True to Hope's words, they soon reached a clearing in the forested area they had been traveling through. There was no real path through the darkened trees, but Hope seemed to know his way and he led them without faltering. In the middle of the clearing stood a ring of standing stones with a smaller stone in the middle of the circle which looked too perfectly circular to be made by nature or man.

The stones were tall and smooth, towering over them like frozen giants of ancient times past, but it was the stone in the middle that was the most interesting. It was shorter than the others and looked less weathered than the outer stones. Along the surface there were hundreds of small and intricate symbols, difficult to make out in the fading light, but still undeniably there. The symbols were aligned perfectly and covered the rock from the top to the bottom, seeming to fade from light to dark as they descended toward the earth.

Hope stopped when they reached the circle as if this was the place he'd been trying to lead them to, never mind that this was as far as it was possible to get from Maredon. Mirena, however, couldn't help herself. Not feeling the least bit intimidated by the ancient stones, she approached the pillar in the center and ran her fingers along the symbols that decorated its length. They were slightly indented.

"I've seen stones like these before," Mirena stated. "There's a circle of them like this one just outside the farm in Maredon. I go there sometimes to think."

"Really?" Elizabeth asked, hiking up her pink skirt to get close enough to study the stones on the outer ring. "Why have I never seen them then?"

"You always went the direction of the town; you were never interested in anything to do with the farm or the area around it."

"Well, you're right about that," Elizabeth agreed. "Now, as fascinating as these rocks are, my dress is wrecked, my shoes aren't much better and I'm starting to wonder about the point of this little trek through the woods."

"If I can show Mirena what to do, these rocks we've trekked out here to see will take us directly to Maredon without us having to cross the space between here and there," Hope explained as patiently as possible. "The Sentinal Stones will save us weeks of travel. Now, Mirena, do you see that symbol there, the one that looks a little like an oak leaf falling?"

It was dark now, the sun almost completely set, but looking over the symbols she thought she found the one he was referring to. "Yes."

"Good," he said. "Now how much do you know about majik? Can you access it on your own yet, or are we starting from scratch here?"

"Sometimes, it depends on the situation…"

"I see, well, how about you give it a try and we'll see how it goes," he suggested. "All you have to do is direct your power to the central pillar and choose the symbol you want. It takes a fair bit of power, but it's nothing more complicated than that; the Sentinal Stones do the rest."

Feeling a little nervous about using her power untrained, Mirena tried to relax and feel the majik within her, closing her eyes and taking a deep breath to calm her nerves and give herself confidence. She drew on the power of the world around her, the air, the wind and the earth itself feeling the energy they gave her build inside of her until she had to find an outlet for it or risk losing control.

"Here goes nothing."

Mirena felt the majik leave her with a whoosh and she did the best she could to direct the power to the stone before her, but she didn't know what Hope had meant about choosing a symbol. In her mind she thought about the oak leaf she had seen right before she'd closed her eyes and held onto that image, hoping that it would be enough.

The world lurched around them and Mirena staggered, feeling the majik leave her faster than it had come. She opened her eyes to a different and darkened landscape with fewer trees to block the view and gentle, rolling hills instead of a forest.

Wherever they were now, it wasn't the Capital…

Mirena had done it.

VI.

It was full dark by the time Hope had recovered enough of his majik to create them a small light to see by as they reached the homey looking farmhouse.

Trained Magi were a rarity in the town of Maredon, being as it was so far from the Capital, but Mirena figured that there wasn't likely to be anyone out here to see them as far as they were from anything but her parent's farm. The usage of majik was therefore probably safe enough and the light gave off a comforting glow to help lead them where there was no path.

"Mirena? Is that you there?" A deep male voice called from open doorway where he was lit from behind, causing his sturdy, broad form to appear in silhouette.

Mirena smiled, taking in her father's reassuring presence. It had been months since she'd seen him last, but she hadn't realized just how much she'd missed him until now.

"That's my dad," she whispered to Hope, "You're going to love him; he's really nice."

Mirena surged forward to wrap her arms around her father's waist as she'd always done. "Daddy!"

"Elizabeth!" He exclaimed. "What on earth are you wearing?"

I guess that would be a natural reaction to Elizabeth wearing a fluffy pink dress, but I thought he would be a little more excited to see us both home safe.

Mirena pulled back and looked up to meet her father's gaze. She realized that he was staring down at her and that he'd just called her by her sister's name. He'd never made that mistake before and she found that she was a little hurt by it, even if the skimpy black dress she was still wearing was more Elizabeth's style than her own.

"It's me, Daddy, Mirena..."

Her father pushed her back at arm's length to examine her and for a moment Mirena thought that perhaps he was only teasing, but when he spoke again her hopes were dashed.

"Whatever game you're playing, you two better get inside. You're mother is beside herself with worry after the stunts you've both pulled.

"Especially you, Mirena," he added, looking down at her once more before releasing her and stepping out of the doorframe to let them pass. "Who's your Mage friend?"

I just received Mother's letter yesterday...maybe it got delayed and she expected me home weeks ago. Creator help us if Mother is beside herself already. After the day I have had I don't think I can take being yelled at by her.

Mirena lowered her head as she entered the small farmhouse, mentally bracing herself for the harsh words she was sure to hear.

"I'm sorry I disappointed you, Mother."

"Elizabeth?!" Mrs. Calanais was on her feet in an instant, the knitting she'd been working on falling from her lap to the floor in a heap. "Oh my god, you're alive! I was so worried you'd gotten yourself caught up in your sister's schemes. We've heard such awful..."

She trailed off, her eyes lighting onto the real Elizabeth and Hope as they came through the doorway to fill the small room and make it feel almost crowded.

"Mirena?" Her mother looked from one twin to the other, confused; she never could tell them apart, not like Father could. "What's going on here, girls? Is what I've heard from the Capital true?"

What is with her being so concerned? I expected a callous remark about my clothing and how I can never do anything right. Mirena looked from her mother to her father and back again, her mouth open in shock.

"Has the Panarch already been here?" She asked, unable to explain her parents' reaction otherwise.

"The Panarch?" Mrs. Calanais gasped, bringing a hand up to cover her mouth.

"Are we to expect a visit from the Panarch, then?" Mr. Calanais demanded at the same time in a tone Mirena could only describe as dangerous, implying that she or Elizabeth, perhaps even both of them, were on thin ice.

She'd never heard him speak like that. Mr. Calanais was usually the understanding one, with her mother being more quick to anger and judgment.

"It's not what you think," Mirena said quickly, alarmed by the unsteadiness of her voice, "things just got really out of hand and we had to leave the Capital in a hurry."

Elizabeth walked past Mirena, her walk a confident swagger until she flopped down on the worn two-person sofa, her pink dress billowing around her like a sea of pink ruffles.

"Relax," she instructed them in an offhand manner, leaning her head back on the sofa and making herself comfortable. "We're home now. That's what you wanted, right? Take a seat, Hopey, it looks like we've reached our hideout and can take a load off."

Their father put out a hand to move Mirena gently out of the way before rounding on Elizabeth. He took up a firm stance before her, hands on his hips as he regarded her authoritatively.

Mirena watched in a shocked kind of silence as her father took charge of the situation like he'd never done before and prepared to give Elizabeth a piece of his mind.

"Get up," he spoke coldly, his voice hard. "I'm only going to say this once, Mirena. Get out of my house. We don't need your kind here."

"Gabe!" Mrs. Calanais protested.

"No, Abigail," he responded, silencing her. "We've talked about this and this is how it's going to be."

What did I do to deserve this? Mirena wondered, feeling numb with shock. *He was always supportive of me being a Sympathizer. I thought he was one also, though he'd never admitted it out loud.*

Is it possible that the Panarch sent a man here to scare them and Mother is making him say these things?

Tears began to form as she desperately tried to search for an answer as to what would make her father act like this.

"At least look at me, Daddy, if you are going to tell me to leave!"

"Not now, Elizabeth," Mr. Calanais said, barely throwing a glance in Mirena's direction, "I'm dealing with your sister. We'll talk about your part in all this once Mirena leaves. Unless something you saw can clear your sister's name, I don't want to hear it."

This is getting out of hand.

"Have you been drinking or something, Daddy? I'm Mirena!"

Mrs. Calanais was the first to react to this statement, taking in the identical confused expressions on both of her daughter's faces.

"She's telling the truth, Gabe, look closely. Mirena's eyes are blue. They may have brought a Mage with them, but there'd be little point in changing their eye colour just to play a trick on us."

Her father leaned into Elizabeth, noting the green of her eyes before grunting, realizing the truth of his wife's words.

"It's possible. If Mirena's on the run, I wouldn't put it past her," he stated.

"I can assure you that I haven't altered their appearance at all," Hope spoke up from the door, where he'd been unobtrusively standing the whole time, "if my word is worth anything to you."

Turning to Mirena at last, her father's first real words to her were still completely out of character. "Explain yourself then, Mirena. What are you trying to pull?"

Mirena took a deep breath and tried to be as honest as possible, hoping against hope that she could somehow get this situation under control.

"We fled the Capital because we are suspected Sympathizers, but you knew that already, Daddy. The Panarch found out about me and is likely hunting us now. He's especially upset because we took Elizabeth away from where he was keeping her captive. She's special to him; she's become his favorite, you might say..."

She let it all out. *Maybe if Father knows the whole story he'll be calmer*, Mirena rationalized. *This isn't like him, though he had been concerned something like this might happen when I went off to the Capital in the first place...*

"We have to hide or we will be killed for treason. Can you help us?"

Mirena cautiously lifted her gaze to meet her father's, hoping to see concern in his eyes. What she saw instead was a boiling anger bubbling to the surface as his face turned a deep red, as if he simply couldn't contain the emotion anymore. Despite herself, Mirena found that she was leaning back, fearing that the worst was about to happen.

"Help you?!" He sputtered, his words forcing themselves out as his outrage became vocal and his voice rose with each word. "I should hang you for treason myself! Sympathizer of the Dark? My own daughter! I knew you were always the wild one, Mirena, but I thought for certain that we'd raised you better than this. Get out!

"You'd better believe I'm getting word to the Panarch about this as soon as I'm able and by the Creator, I'm not letting you and your Light-forsaken friend stay in my house after what happened in the Capital.

"You will not bring further shame to us, Mirena. You are not my daughter anymore."

Mrs. Calanais was crying now, but for some reason her usual spunk did not surface and she didn't speak out against her husband's harsh words. Elizabeth's face was as shocked as her own and for once Mirena's brash and outspoken twin stayed silent, having no words that could lighten the mood or take away what had been said in such anger.

"Daddy?" Mirena whispered, incredulous.

"I think maybe we should leave," Hope suggested quietly from the doorway. "We are clearly not welcome here."

"No, you're not," Mirena's father continued, his tone cold. "Thank you for bringing my only daughter home. Elizabeth," he turned to Elizabeth who was still on the sofa, having not yet made the decision to leave it, "go to your room. We'll talk later."

This, unlike the words before it, seemed to get through to Elizabeth.

She stood abruptly, her pink dress falling around her feet. "Like hell I will," she stated; her eyes fierce and her back straight with pride. "I'm a Sympathizer too, Dad! What do you have to say about that?!"

Their mother fainted, passing right out in her chair at the kitchen table, but Mr. Calanais paid Elizabeth's words little mind.

"I know you think I'm being unfair, Elizabeth, but acting like a child is not going to make this situation any better and nothing you say is going to make me change my mind. Your sister is leaving this house and that's the end of the discussion."

"Then so am I," Elizabeth declared, pushing past him for the door. "Come on you two," she instructed to Hope and Mirena. "The old man's off his rocker and there's nothing here for us."

"I'm sorry to have caused you so much trouble," Mirena choked out through her grief, turning to follow after Elizabeth.

She was concerned about her mother, who lay still with her head on the table, but there was nothing she could do for her now. Mirena didn't know what had come over her father, but he'd clearly made his decision and he didn't want to ever see her again. The pain of that knowledge was intense, but putting one foot in front of the other she made herself reach the door before saying her last words to the man she'd always loved the most.

"Goodbye, Father."

She got the door slammed behind her for her troubles.

"That was not our father, Mirena," Elizabeth stated once they were out of earshot of the little farmhouse and Hope had made his little glowing ball of light again for them to see each other. "I don't know who those people were, but they are not our parents."

"I will agree that they were acting very strange," Mirena allowed, having found voice enough to speak, "but don't you think you're being a little extreme in saying that they are not our parents?"

"Extreme or not, it's true," Elizabeth insisted. "Hope, back me up on this one," she told him. "It's possible, isn't it?"

"Sure, I guess anything is possible, Elizabeth," Hope agreed with a shrug, "but it's highly unlikely. I mean, a talented Mage could have made two similar people look exactly like your parents with small alterations and some makeup, but why would they have bothered? And it's not Terrence Lee's style, if that's what you're thinking."

"Maybe they are just stressed after learning about what happened to us and it will all blow over soon. People do crazy things when pushed to their limits, right?"

Mirena was searching for anyone to take her side in this discussion, because if she was wrong and Elizabeth was right, that would mean one of two things: either her parents had been taken prisoner by the Panarch or they were dead.

I just can't accept those as possibilities right now...

The silence that followed her question was uncomfortable, but it was clear that neither Hope nor Elizabeth had a good answer for her. Nor did the three of them really have anywhere to turn to, now that their one safe haven had turned out to be quite the opposite.

"We can't stay here, anyways," Hope noted, "not if the threats your father made are true. Do either of you have any suggestions as to where else we should try?"

"Well, we've always got your perfect little hideaway," Elizabeth suggested as if the answer were obvious. "Heck, if you barely know how we got there in the first place, it's highly unlikely that anyone could figure out how to get in there to follow us. It's the safest we could ever be, if you're that convinced that the Panarch is going to send someone to drag us back to the Capital."

"Whatever you two think is best," Mirena agreed, feeling tired and resigned.

Having made their decision, there was no more reason to stay out in the open fields around Maredon where they might raise suspicion by their presence.

Taking deep breaths and concentrating fiercely, Hope summoned the strange power that had been granted to him by the ring around his neck, the Creator, or both, and ripped a hole in the air, filling the empty farm field with a sudden burst of light.

It was only there long enough for the three of them to hop into the realm that lay beyond, but even still the light was a beacon to anyone in the area and the strangeness of it would not be easily forgotten. All they could rely on was that no one could possibly know who or what had caused it and therefore they couldn't report it to the Panarch or his Truthseekers if they came asking about the three of them.

The world of Hope's creation was the same as they had left it, the neat little cottage on the water and every other little detail of Hope's imagining waiting for them. It was as if time ceased to pass here in their absence.

"Home sweet home," Elizabeth commented, rolling her eyes at the both of them before taking the short path through the trees to the front door. Once into the tiny cottage she pointed to a door on the main floor. "That the bedroom?" At Hope's nod, Elizabeth went for it. "Well, I call this one. Good night, you two."

In less than a heartbeat, she was gone and the cottage was still and silent around them.

It took Mirena less than a moment to realize that Elizabeth's departure left her alone with Hope for the first time since he'd helped her to infiltrate the Panarch's secret garden. Before that, the only time had been the night when he had unexpectedly turned up in her bedroom unannounced.

What should I do now? Mirena felt the nervousness she'd felt both those other times resurface a little. She trusted Hope now, so it wasn't fear, but something else that made her very aware of his presence. He stood not far at all from her and his nearness was almost palpable, like a fireplace heating a chilled room, she felt drawn to him, but still she didn't act on her feelings.

He watched my father disown me and kick me out of my house...I am so ashamed. I don't know what to even say to him.

His eyes as they regarded her were gentle and kind, but for once he seemed to really be looking at her, taking in the curves of her form with his gaze. He too, looked as if he wanted to close the distance between them, but something held him back and Mirena was at a loss to know what it was.

"I..." Hope began, then paused, watching Mirena's expression shift through the variety of emotions she was feeling. "There's another room upstairs..."

She felt her face flush at the subtle implication in his tone, despite her best intentions. *Is he asking me to share his room?*

No, he can't be... I must be imagining his interest in me because of how he makes me feel. He's never given me any indication before this. How many bedrooms does this cottage have, anyways?

"You can have it," Mirena said quickly. "I can sleep in here or make my sister share her room. I mean it's your house...technically."

"I guess it is," he smiled a little lopsidedly, and Mirena found herself watching the corner of his mouth for where it lifted slightly, "and since that's the case I guess I can always make you another room."

Hope considered this for a moment, regarding Mirena with curiosity. "What do you want in it? I mean, what have you always wanted your room to look like?"

"You don't have to do that for me," she said softly, politeness dictating that she refuse his offer while secretly she felt joy bubble to the surface at the thought of having a room to herself made for her especially by the Avatar of the Light himself.

"Come on," Hope insisted, perhaps reading her true desires on her face. "I've got this power now and who knows how long it's going to last. This could all fade away on us the moment I fall asleep, so we might as well make use of it while we can."

"And besides," he continued, "I'm not an architect or an interior designer and I've got absolutely no idea what to picture for your room unless you describe it to me."

"I appreciate the offer," Mirena found herself smiling back at his simple joy in his newfound abilities, "but if it does fade, won't I just end up on the floor anyway?"

"Probably," Hope grinned, "but what've you got to lose, right?"

"Nothing, I guess," she agreed, tapping her lips in thought. "I don't need anything special though… just a bed and a pillow would be enough for me."

Hope shook his head, smiling ruefully. "I offer you anything you can imagine and all you want is a pillow? Well, that's not too much to go on, but I'll see what I can do."

He closed his eyes, standing still in the center of the room. Mirena held her breath watching him. It was so strange what he could do, but somehow so natural at the same time. This time, there were no flashing lights and no strange glow beyond the white light through his shirt that came from the ring around his neck.

Is this what it would be like to be a Mage? To have things happen just because I will them to, or is Hope something entirely different...something special?

In no more than a moment, he opened his eyes again. "It's done," he said, then added, "I think..."

Gesturing for her to precede him, Hope motioned to the stairs beyond where Elizabeth had already retired for the night. The short staircase led them to a nondescript second floor with a wood-paneled hallway and only two doors and a small closet beyond them.

"This one's yours," Hope indicated the door on the right. "I'm just across the hall."

Did he plan it that way? Mirena wondered. *That he would be nearby when Elizabeth is all the way downstairs, or am I reading too much into a coincidence?*

Eyeing him out of the corner of her eye to try and judge his intentions, Mirena opened the door, subconsciously holding her breath. Inside, the room was simple, just as she had asked, but every detail was just right. It was if Hope had known exactly what she wanted, even though she hadn't done a very good job of explaining it to him.

There was a bed large enough for two with a fabric canopy, blue like the sky and patterned with billowing clouds. The pillow she'd asked for was sitting on the bed, also blue, except instead of just one, there were half a dozen of them strewn about. The walls and the rest of the room were decorated simply with light colours and faded flowers, the walls a pale yellow and the round throw rug on the wooden floors a soft pink.

How did he know I wanted a canopy bed? And that blue was my favourite colour?

She smiled, unable to contain her excitement, running over to pick up one of the soft pillows and hug it to her chest gratefully.

"Do you like it, then?" He asked, watching her with a slight smile on his face.

"Of course! It's perfect! Thank you," she whirled around and beamed at him. "I couldn't have pictured it better myself."

Hope stood awkwardly framed in the doorway for a moment seemingly at a loss for words as the silence stretched on just a beat too long. Looking at him like this, from amidst the wonderful gifts he'd just created for her, Mirena suddenly felt as if she didn't want him to just leave like this.

I made him make me a separate room…but did he really mean for us to share, before?

She found herself staring at him, her heart thudding loudly in her chest. He was tall and regal with a confident bearing, just as she'd assumed he would be on that first night when she'd seen him so vulnerable on the floor of her room in the Collegium. Suddenly those two images of him seemed to combine for her and she understood that as powerful as he'd become, Hope was still afraid of what he could not do and he was uneasy within the role he'd been cast into.

He's the Avatar of the Light… but he's also just a man. A man who's forsaken everything he's ever known to be the savior I've been waiting for my entire life.

I want to thank him for this…for everything, she realized, *but the words just don't seem to be enough.*

"Well, good night, then..." Hope said a little awkwardly, breaking the silence. "I'll be just across the hall if you need anything."

Mirena hesitated, raising her hand as if she wanted to stop him and tell him to stay just a little bit longer, but her silence cost her and the moment passed.

The door closed softly behind him as he left.

Mirror's Hope

VII.

Mirena was the first one up in what she assumed to be the morning, though the view out the cottage windows was the same as when she'd fallen asleep. Coming down the stairs she found more furniture in the main room than she remembered from the night before. There was a sofa just as worn-looking as the one in her parents' own home with a comfortable blanket draped across it and a sturdy wooden chair that looked less than inviting with its stiff back and hard wooden seat.

She found Hope passed out in the wooden chair as if he'd stayed up late fighting sleep, sitting in the uncomfortable chair that he'd created to torment himself to wakefulness.

I guess that proves that if he sleeps the cottage won't disappear, Mirena thought, smiling as she approached the couch as silently as possible and reached for the quilted blanket. *That's good news.*

She continued over to Hope, laying the blanket across him gently. *This is the perfect time for talking with my sister. Hope's asleep and I want to ask her what she thinks of him. If she believes I might have a chance with him at all.*

I hate to admit it, but I just might need to use some of Elizabeth's expertise with men.

Leaving the main room, Mirena slipped through Elizabeth's door quietly and found her sister sound asleep, her limbs splayed out in all directions on a bed big enough to sleep three people. The blankets and decor in here were darker and richer in colour than the room upstairs, but they were not luxurious either. Rather they were comfortable and practical, just like the rest of the cottage.

This is why I hate sharing a bed with her, Mirena noted silently, taking in her sister's sprawled position, *she kicks and hogs the blankets.*

However, I'll never get another chance like this one to repay her for all the times she's tormented me...

Acting on impulse, Mirena ran for the bed and propelled herself into it, aiming for her sister.

A sharp gasp came from Elizabeth's throat as her eyes snapped open and Mirena caught a split second of genuine fear on her sister's face. Elizabeth scrambled to right herself and escape the tangled blankets holding her down as if she was fleeing for her life.

"Mirena?" Elizabeth choked out after a moment, forcing her breathing to return to normal and righting her expression in order to pretend as if the momentary slip had never happened. "What the hell are you doing in my room?" The sharp words lacked their usual playfulness. "Did you miss me or something?"

"Did someone really hurt you, Elizabeth?" Mirena asked, pausing and regarding Elizabeth closely, honestly concerned by the reaction she'd witnessed.

"What would make you say a thing like that?" Elizabeth asked with a dismissive wave of her hand, rolling out of the bed and getting to her feet.

Her sister regained her composure as she went looking about for something to throw over herself. Then she remembered where they were and that her only clothing was the dirty pink dress lying in a heap on the ground.

"Elizabeth, what happened in the Panarch's garden to make you so afraid?"

"Nothing, okay? Just drop it."

"Don't lie to me..." Mirena cautioned.

"Look Mirena," Elizabeth began, her tone serious, "whatever self-righteous bent you're on this time, I don't want to hear it. I chose to go to that garden and I chose to place myself where Terrence Lee would have no choice but to notice me. The garden had its faults, but I carved myself out a place there and no matter what you think about my choices, they were mine to make!"

"No one has the right to hurt you," Mirena stated forcefully. "No one! I can only imagine what the Panarch has done to you, even after my experience, but that isn't a choice that you should ever make."

"You don't get it at all, do you?" Elizabeth demanded heatedly. "You just refuse to see that the world isn't the happy scrappy place you pretend that it ought to be. We don't live in a nice world where bad people occasionally do bad things, we live in a rotten world where bad things are normal and you're the freak, Mirena!

"You're the one who doesn't fit in and one day someone's going to push you hard enough to make you realize that. Me?" Elizabeth pointed to herself, her face red with anger now. "I do what I have to do to get ahead and to protect myself. You should try having a sense of self-preservation for a change!"

"And you should have a sense of self respect."

"Self-respect doesn't keep you alive," Elizabeth noted bitterly, her anger fading somewhat, leaving only an emptiness in its place, "and it doesn't insure that you get anything more out of life than your parents' lousy old farm. I want more than that, Mira."

"There are other ways to get what you want. I am...I was working towards that before we met Hope. I was going to have a better life and I would have asked you to come live with me in the Capital once I made something of myself."

"Yeah, I guess I could just aim to find myself a great man like you did," Elizabeth said, a teasing smile coming to her lips as her voice rose to a mocking tone, "then together we could change the world and make it a better place for everyone!"

"It's not what you think!" Mirena protested. "Hope and I just have a common goal."

"Oh Hope," Elizabeth continued, "will you help me save the world?" She lowered her voice to imitate Hope's. "Of course I will, my Miracle...we'll change everything and then we can be together forever!"

"I'm not like you! Getting a man isn't the first thing I think about!"

"Ahem," there was a loud and exaggerated throat clearing from the other side of the door and Mirena blushed scarlet realizing what Hope had overheard, "are you two done in there? I was hoping we could venture out and maybe find something to eat. I'm starving."

"Do you think he heard everything?"

"Nah," Elizabeth waved her hand in dismissal before lowering her voice to a conspiratorial whisper, obviously making fun of her. "I think you're safe. Breakfast sounds lovely," she added only slightly louder for Hope's benefit, "just let me get some clothes on."

"Good," he answered, clearing his throat again, this time somewhat uncomfortably. "I'll just wait out there then… until you girls are ready."

When they had all gathered what meager belongings they'd brought in with them, they met in the main room of the cottage, the twins looking to Hope with identical expectant expressions.

"So I've been doing some thinking," Hope began.

"I'm sure you did, what with being up all night," Elizabeth commented with a sly wink. "It was either to do some soul searching or because thoughts of *someone* were preventing you from sleeping."

"Yes, well," he continued, giving a small smile in response to Elizabeth's caustic humour, "I was thinking about how this place works, actually. I was testing it out. I think I know what sort of place I've brought us to, even if I don't know exactly where it is…if that makes any sense."

"It doesn't," Elizabeth noted, uncharacteristically patient, "but go on."

"There's a form of majik used to travel across great distances quickly," Hope explained. "Most Magi don't know that the possibility of teleportation exists, but as I already told you both, Terrence Lee is an expert at it.

"I, too, have some limited experience with it, or I wouldn't know enough to tell you about it," he continued. "Anyways, what I think I've created here, or at least accessed somehow, is a place between one place and another. That's why it doesn't change unless I will it to and time doesn't really pass.

"Look," he continued, closing his eyes a moment and gesturing vaguely toward the window as he did so. Mirena and Elizabeth did as they were instructed and to their amazement they watched the sun rise in the sky outside the little cottage window…to the west.

And it wasn't a slow climbing sunrise in any way that would be natural, either. The sun shot up into the sky, filling the empty blue backdrop with its golden light and beaming in through the window to drench them in sudden and unexpected daylight.

"Wow Tendro, way to overdo it. You think you can turn it down a bit?" Elizabeth complained, shielding her eyes from the intense brightness.

"Elizabeth, don't say that! It's so beautiful," Mirena said in awe, before rounding on her sister. "You could never do something as amazing as making a sunrise from nothing! So don't scoff at the miracle that just occurred in front of your eyes."

"It's not like that..." Hope said, modestly underplaying his display of power. "I mean, the point is that I think I can take us anywhere from here. Well, maybe not anywhere, but any place that I know really well. Just like I can control this place, I think I can control where the door from it leads.

"Think about it," he continued. "We got here from the Capital last time and then last night when we came here from Maredon we arrived in the exact same spot. I don't think that's a coincidence and I don't think I carry this place around with me, so it has to be accessible from anywhere and that means it has access to everywhere."

I know what the words mean and the theory in itself seems correct; at least Hope seems pretty confident about it, but the concept is way beyond my comprehension as far as majik is concerned, Mirena reasoned, coming quickly to a decision. *I will just have to take his word on this particular instance, and hope he knows what he is doing.*

"Where are you thinking of taking us then?"

"I thought about that, too," he answered, "and none of us are going to like the answer. We have to go back to the Collegium."

"What?!" Elizabeth exclaimed. "That's where we're running from, you dolt!"

"I know that," Hope grimaced, "but we can't stay here without supplies and whatever we decide to do, we'll need more information before we can make any plans at all.

"The Collegium has it all and provided that we can get in and out of there safely, everything we need would be free for the taking. You ladies can get clothing from Mirena's room, we can stockpile some food from the Cafeteria and if we can get close enough to hear the gossip among the Magi that would at least give us more information than we've got now."

"I can get us food from the Cafeteria. I used to work there, so I know the back ways to get around there unnoticed," Mirena offered.

"Good," Hope agreed. "That's a big help, actually." He turned to Elizabeth to see what she could offer. "Elizabeth?"

"What?" She questioned, putting her hands up defensively. "Don't look at me for help; this is your crazy plan. Besides, the only places I know in the Capital are those that we need to stay far away from."

"Well, let's get going then," Mirena decided. "The sooner we get there, the sooner I can get back with the food and we can start making our plans."

Elizabeth put her hand up like she was asking a question in a classroom. "Plans to do what, exactly? Or is it too soon to ask that?"

Hope's face took on a difficult expression. "Too soon, maybe, but I'll get back to you on that one, I promise."

"Fine," Elizabeth sighed, "but I'm telling you right now that the only reasons I'm coming with you fools is because I don't know if this place will still exist without holy boy here and I really, *really* want to get out of this dress."

Mirena frowned in Elizabeth's direction as Hope closed his eyes to access his power over this place once more. They felt no change, but after a moment he opened them and said, "Okay, here goes nothing."

A pinprick of light appeared in the air in what was becoming a familiar fashion, before it expanded into a doorway to a room Mirena recognized better than anyone, as it was her own.

Her bedroom in the Capital was unchanged, though servants had come in to make the bed and straighten what few belongings she'd left strewn about. She was a fairly neat person by nature, but even the letter from her parents had been neatly tucked away on the night table for her.

"Ladies first," Hope gestured as Mirena and Elizabeth passed through the hole he had made for them.

*Nothing's changed...*Mirena realized. *Maybe that means that the Panarch hasn't yet realized that I'm a part of this...or that he doesn't know who I am.*

He left me for dead...maybe, he just doesn't care.

She went to the wardrobe and opened it to get what they had come here for. There was no use taking chances by dallying here, but as much as Elizabeth wanted to change, Mirena had also been dressed very inappropriately for some time now.

Perhaps we should have thought to switch, Mirena sighed, looking over her options.

She didn't have much, just a small assortment of nondescript simple gowns; some had flowers, but most of them were just plain, light colours. None of her clothes would suit Elizabeth, but maybe that would be better to help her sister hide.

What's this? Mirena questioned, her hands brushing up against a heavier silky material at the back of the darkened wardrobe.

It was richer fabric than she thought she owned. When she pulled it out to see it more clearly, she discovered that it was pure white with thick silver embroidery, the detail making it clear that it was something Mirena would never have been able to afford.

These are Magi robes, Mirena realized with a gasp, almost dropping them in her surprise. They were not even apprentice robes, they belonged to a full Mage...*what are they doing in here?*

Maybe the servants put this here by mistake...I'll just put it back.

Placing the robes back where she found them, Mirena reached for a plain white dress when Hope stopped her with a hand on her arm. "Wait, where did you get that?"

"They aren't mine," Mirena answered openly, but found herself staring down at his hand on her arm, unable to look away.

This is the first time he's touched me, other than to pull me to safety and save my life...

His hand was warm on her skin, the simple contact sending a jolt through her. *Is he becoming more comfortable around me, or am I simply wishing that he would?*

"Come on, Mira," Elizabeth interjected, "hand me that dress already."

Startled by the reminder of her sister's presence, Mirena looked up only to find that Elizabeth had already shimmied out of her fluffy pink dress and let it fall to the floor around her to lie in a heap. Elizabeth was completely careless of the fact that Hope was standing right there and had only to turn his head to see everything she had to offer.

Elizabeth! You're a twin! Was Mirena's first startled thought. *Looking at you is the same as looking at me!*

Reacting instinctively, she threw the dress in her hands at Hope's head, aiming to cover his eyes before he saw Elizabeth in all her naked glory and everything was ruined.

"What the...?" Hope floundered, startled as Elizabeth snickered, taking in Mirena's reaction to her lack of embarrassment.

"Put your clothes on! Now!" Mirena hissed angrily.

Elizabeth put her hands on her bare hips, just above her low-cut frilly pink panties. "I would, if you'd pass me some," she commented, with a frustrating lack of modesty.

Hope froze in the act of removing the offending garment upon hearing these words. He slowly turned himself about until he was facing away from both sisters and tossed the dress back behind him to land in front of Mirena.

Watching him to catch his reaction and to avoid having to look at her naked sister flaunting herself, Mirena noted that the back of Hope's neck had turned a deep red.

Unimpressed, Mirena reached into the wardrobe and pulled out the most unattractive dress she could find at a glance. It was older and faded, but was covered in tiny yellow flowers on a light green backdrop.

"Here!" Mirena snapped as she threw the dress at her sister with as much force as she dared. "I'll be changing in the bathroom, like a proper person would!"

"Suit yourself," Elizabeth called back to her and as she shut the bathroom door, Mirena could see her sister stepping out of the sea of pink fabric to select her own garment from the meager supply.

Once fully dressed, Mirena examined herself in the mirror. *Why does Elizabeth always have to embarrass me in front of other people? Especially men...*

...Especially this man.

Shaking her head to clear it, she washed her face with cold water and brushed out her hair before packing herself a small bag of toiletries.

Heading back out to join the other two, she avoided both Hope's and Elizabeth's gaze, feeling inexplicably self-conscious.

"I should get going to the cafeteria..."

"You shouldn't go alone," Hope noted. "It wouldn't be safe."

"Right, because she'd be a lot safer with you around for people to recognize, or with me there so people can stare at the sight of identical twins walking the halls together," Elizabeth retorted.

Does he like me, or doesn't he? Mirena found herself questioning as Elizabeth ranted and Hope seemed focused on what she had to say. *He seems protective of me, but that could simply be because he's put me in this situation. A Mage like him...no, he's more than that now; the Avatar of the Light...I'm nothing compared to him.*

"All right," Mirena heard Hope agree from behind her, "but just be careful, okay, and if anything goes wrong, just run and try to find someone you can trust."

She waved a hand over her shoulder to indicate that she'd heard him before letting herself into the hall and softly shutting the door behind her. Her thoughts and feelings were all jumbled in her head, but she had a mission now. She put one foot in front of the other and started down familiar hallways, keeping to herself as she'd always done.

As long as the Panarch wasn't looking for her or hadn't told people to apprehend her on sight, then she should be safe enough to head straight to the stockroom through the less populated corridors of the Collegium. It would be risky of course, there were so many people who lived and worked here, but before her daring escape from the Capital, she had been fairly anonymous.

"Mirena!" The deep voice stopped her in her tracks.

Creator, help me! It's Dipaul…and by the sound of his voice, he's drunk again.

He knows who I am…

I'm going to die.

She didn't dare move from her location, frozen in fear. *I'm so stupid! I should have been more careful and kept a closer eye on where I was going instead of thinking about Hope!*

Dipaul was standing before her in the hallway; he had a half-eaten pastry in his hand, as if he'd just come from the Cafeteria.

"You're back!" He exclaimed, a happy smile on his face on his open features. Mirena found herself looking for the malice in his expression, knowing it had to be in there somewhere even if she couldn't see it.

Wait… he has both his hands… Mirena realized, still not moving a muscle. *Were the Magi able to replace the one he lost?*

That shouldn't be possible…

"Come with me to the Cafeteria," Dipaul suggested excitedly, still in his guise of drunken happiness as he took hold of her hand with a vice-like grip. "We have to let everyone know that you're here!"

Mirror's Hope

VIII.

Terrence Lee wants to publicly execute me in the Cafeteria...

It was the only possible explanation. People turned and stared as Dipaul dragged Mirena down the hallway. His large hand had a firm grip on her smaller one, but that wasn't why she didn't try to break free and run away; she was terrified.

More importantly, Mirena didn't know what Dipaul was playing at. Running like an excited child through the rows of mostly occupied tables, Dipaul led her where he pleased and she was powerless to stop him.

He takes pleasure in this, torturing his victims before he has them killed, she realized. *Creator save me, he's taking me to his friends to show off his catch before bringing me to Terrence Lee or denouncing me in front of the whole Collegium as a Sympathizer of the Light.*

Mirena gasped when she recognized the people around the table he was leading her towards; or at least most of them.

I didn't know that Dipaul was friends with Odark...

He was short and stocky but also handsome, with short black hair and pale skin and serious-looking green eyes that only seemed brighter when contrasted with the black of his gold embroidered Mage's outfit.

Mirena remembered long nights spent working in the Collegium's Cafeteria and dreaming of Odark Dalessandro and wishing that he would take notice of her, but the last time she had seen him had been on the very same night that Hope had come so unexpectedly into her life…

She sat alone at the table the furthest from the doors, just trying to get a moment to herself. Customers could be so nasty to her sometimes; on nights like this one Mirena was glad that she worked the nightshift, so that there would be less people around to see her cry on her breaks.

Odark always came by late at night or sometimes into the early morning. Occasionally, he would come with friends like Venson or Powell, but most often he came alone and kept to himself.

She'd been infatuated with him since her first shift in the Cafeteria. Despite herself, Mirena had always kept an eye on the noble and handsome looking young man and wondered what his life was like. Sometimes she foolishly fantasized about what their life could be like together if Odark ever took notice of her feelings for him and miraculously reciprocated them.

She heard the chair across the table from her scrape back and she sat up straight in surprise, her eyes widening as she took in his sudden presence. Not a tall or imposing man, Odark was from the neighboring country of Mor Gann and his stocky build, raven black hair and pale skin showed it. His green eyes didn't meet her gaze, nor did he even act like he knew she was sitting there with tears streaking down her face, but instead he placed his plate of pie on the table, arranged his fork just so, and took his seat.

The shock of him taking a seat so confidently front of her stopped Mirena's tears; Has he finally taken notice of me after all this time?

Unable to think of what to say or do as she wasn't very experienced in talking to strangers, especially one that she'd spent so much time thinking about, she looked down at her dish-worn hands uselessly. Sniffling a little to clear her nose so she could finally say something to Odark for the first time, she looked up just as he was sliding his untouched pie towards her.

Too startled for words at this show of kindness, Mirena missed her opportunity to speak and before so much as a thank you could rise to her lips, Odark was walking away and leaving her with his unexpected gift.

…And now here she was, her shame being paraded before Odark and his friends. Both the good-looking Venson and the blond, angular-faced Powell were present, as was a dark-haired and fox-faced girl that Mirena remembered was named something presumptuous like Starr. Thanks to Dipaul, Odark would have no choice but to take notice of her now, but it would never be in the way she had wanted for so long.

"Mirena?" Venson noticed her first, getting to his feet in his surprise.

I didn't realize that Odark's friends even knew my name...has he mentioned me to them?

Powell scowled, but Mirena didn't spare him a glance, instead focusing all of her attention on Odark. He whipped his head around and then caught himself, no doubt figuring that Venson was probably playing a prank on him. But then Odark caught sight of Mirena out of the corner of his eye and did a double-take before he locked onto her, his green eyes intense.

Mirena felt unfounded hope surge within her but when Odark spoke, his words were unfeeling.

"What are you doing here?"

"Don't be mad, Odark," Dipaul urged, still in his thick voice; subtly mocking her intelligence with the use of it. "She's come back."

"You're awful," Mirena told him, trying to tug her hand free of Dipaul's grasp and figuring she was beyond reproach at this point. She felt tears sting her eyes as she realized that Odark would be forced to watch as she was executed for treason against the Panarch for her beliefs. "Is this a game to all of you?"

Powell snorted. "We should be asking that of you, Mirena. What are you playing at this time?"

"Does the Panarch know you're here?" Odark asked intently, surprising Mirena with this line of questioning and the serious nature of it.

"I see that you're good friends with him, then," Mirena lashed out at him, unable to describe the feelings of betrayal that welled within her as she regarded him, "to be so concerned about what he knows."

"Me?" Odark questioned, seeming confused. "I'm not the one who runs to him with every little problem and then turns around and tries to take the Capital from under his nose."

"I have never even talked to the Panarch before yesterday, when he tried to use me like one of his whores!" Mirena protested her voice growing louder despite her efforts even as she wondered what Odark was talking about. "He beat me and then left me for dead when he found out that I wasn't his favorite, Elizabeth!"

Odark's jaw dropped and Powell froze in the midst of taking a sip of his drink. After a moment in tense silence, Powell snorted suddenly, spraying the red liquid everywhere as he burst out laughing, unable to contain himself. He doubled over, lost in a fit of laughter, as Venson merely regarded her with a shocked sort of expression.

"Is she for real?" Venson asked, indicating Mirena with a thumb.

"Mirena, why would you say a thing like that?" Dipaul questioned still playing the fool.

"Because she's sick, that's why," Odark concluded disdainfully. "She needs to spend some serious time in the Sanitorium."

Strangely, even through her muddled feelings in regards to him, Mirena still felt the sting of his words. She knew that it was too much to hope for that Odark would continue to be kind to her after the pie incident, but it still hurt to face the reality of his scorn.

He belongs to the Panarch, just like everyone else. He'd never love a Sympathizer of the Light…

"I wasn't lying!" Mirena stated, realizing that above all else, she was angry.

If I'm going to hang for my beliefs anyway, then I might as well take this last chance to say what's on my mind.

"You probably use the Panarch's private garden as well," she accused Odark, her words a whip, "because you can't get a girl to like you, so you force them to accept your attentions!

"Thank the Creator," she continued, "that Elizabeth won't have to be bullied anymore by someone as insignificant as you!"

"What are you even saying?" Odark demanded, his tone heated as he got to his feet to face her at eye level. "Do you even think about the words that are coming out of your mouth before you speak them?"

"You know exactly what I am talking about!" Mirena yelled; ignoring the stares of those around her in the crowded cafeteria as she secretly hoped the whole room would hear her damn one of the Panarch's men. "You're a heartless monster!"

Belatedly noticing that Dipaul had released her arm at some point during her outburst, Mirena broke away from them at full speed, despite knowing the instant retribution her escape would bring. She didn't know what method Odark or Dipaul might use to stop her or how far she might get, so she didn't bother to look up or wipe the tears from her face, just in case the sight of the doors proved to be too much hope for her to bear when she was inevitably struck down.

"Whoa there," a familiar voice said softly, but the recognition and the words themselves weren't enough of a jolt to get her to slow down before she ran full force into the speaker.

Hope caught her, his hands on her arms, and she found herself looking up at him with bleary eyes. Her breath caught, taking in his change in attire and how striking he looked dressed in formal black Magi garb. His long black jacket was embroidered with gold thread and the high collar made him look taller and gave him a more confident bearing.

He really was one of Terrence Lee's Generals, Mirena realized. *I can see it now; he has a presence about him.*

"Mirena, is that you?" Hope asked, staring into her eyes intently. "Are you back so soon? Did Caralain come back with you?"

"What are you doing out here?" Mirena questioned with mounting confusion, her panicked flight halted for the moment. *Who's Caralain?* "Where's Elizabeth?"

"It is you," Hope replied, his tone strange and still somewhat intense. "I thought so. Where are the others?"

"What are you talking about? I came here with you."

The expression on his face was odd and Mirena found that she couldn't place it or read the reason for the intensity of his gaze.

"Something must have gone wrong," he concluded after a moment, sounding genuinely concerned. "Come with me," Hope held out his hand to her, "we'll get this straightened out."

Something isn't right about this... Mirena's panicked mind supplied. *Hope is supposed to be hiding from Dipaul and the others, but instead here he is in plain sight, standing in front of them as if he doesn't have a care in the world.*

"I'm going back to my room," Mirena stated, pulling out of Hope's grasp and watching carefully for his reaction as she backed away from him, unable to explain why his presence suddenly filled her with unease.

She could see the open archways that led from the Cafeteria just beyond Hope and she made for the exit, pushing past him in a sudden flurry of motion.

"Mirena, we haven't seen each other in two months," Hope noted casually, falling in step with her despite her hurried pace. "Don't be like that."

We haven't seen each other in two months?

She stopped again, turning to face him. "I just..." she struggled to explain herself to him. "You were..."

It's been no more than twenty minutes since I left him in my room with Elizabeth...what's going on here?

Hope took a deep breath as if trying to be patient with her. "I know this must be really confusing for you," he told her. "I don't know why you're here right now, or why Caralain left you alone like this, but that's why I want to go sort it out. Will you come with me or do I have to go on my own?"

"Did I miss something?" Mirena managed at last. "Who's Caralain?"

"Oh dear," Hope muttered, shaking his head, "this is worse than I thought. This likely means there is no sense in asking what happened to you. I suppose you're just lucky that I found you, because I'm probably one of the few people who could explain all of this to you."

"I just left you in my room!"

"Okay, good," he answered inexplicably, making Mirena feel more lost than ever, "at least you remember that much. That gives us a starting point, anyways."

"Where's Elizabeth?" She redirected.

"Upstairs, I think," Hope answered, though Mirena knew full well that Elizabeth should still be on the main floor in the dormitory she'd left not long ago. "I can take you to her if it'll help you to see another familiar face."

Mirena nodded, still feeling disoriented and let Hope lead her through the Collegium's halls. There was no attack from Dipaul or Odark and no condemning words ringing out through the Cafeteria as they exited. None of it made any sense at all, but what else could she do but trust in Hope and follow where he led?

I might be making the wrong choice, but I trust Hope...I'll no doubt be safer with him than without.

Hope took her through the Collegium's maze of corridors until she was in a wing that Mirena had never been to on her own before, though she knew where they were from other peoples' descriptions. The Political Wing was the section of the Collegium where Terrence Lee and his female counterpart, Theia Prosai, held council meetings and where the ambassadors of the various countries and districts were housed. It was nearly as large and comprehensive as the Mage's Wing, but it was a place of government and administration instead of a school.

Why would Elizabeth be here? Mirena questioned before Hope's destination became a little clearer. Instead of heading to the large, domed council chambers, he took a set of stairs to the left of the entrance and started upwards.

He had mentioned that she was upstairs. Maybe he sent her here to gather information from the ambassadors or something.

Mirena expected meeting rooms or offices, but instead the top of the stairs led only to a single hall that headed in two directions. Hope unfalteringly chose the path on the right and before long they found themselves in a small, semi-circle area that Mirena could only describe as a waiting room. There were chairs lining the curved walls, which were covered in floor-to-ceiling windows looking out over the bustling Capital.

The semi-circular room was by no means empty but Hope went straight to a woman with a short bob of red hair who was seated behind a large desk that took up two thirds of the straight edge of the wall. Behind her was only a simple wooden door.

"Helen, I know he's on lunch, but would you mind paging him for me?" Hope addressed the woman behind the desk familiarly, reaching back to take hold of Mirena's wrist and pull her in close. "I've got someone here that he'll want to see immediately."

"I thought you were taking me to Elizabeth?"

"I will," Hope answered as the woman behind the desk nodded and placed her hand on a panel inset into her desk, "just as soon as I get the okay."

Mirena felt panic welling within her but she didn't get a chance to question Hope further before the panel lit up under the woman's touch and her voice filled the air around them, drowning out all other sounds.

"Terrence Lee, your presence is requested in your office."

He's betrayed me... Mirena concluded as the sheer pain of it rushed through her and it felt as if the floor had given way under her feet. *He was playing me all along. I knew he was too good to be true.*

"How could you?" It was what he no doubt expected to hear, but Mirena felt she needed to say it anyway, even if she was playing right into his hand. "I trusted you. I thought you cared..."

Hope's expression was hurt, of all things.

"I do care, Mirena," he insisted, playing his game until the very end. "This isn't a punishment; I'm trying to help you."

How is turning me in supposed to help me? Mirena questioned numbly. *Does he really believe that what he does as a Truthseeker is right? That it's helping people to catch them and prove to them the 'error of their ways'?*

I saw this coming all along...why didn't I run away when I first suspected the truth?

"I wasn't far," the Panarch's voice came suddenly from the doorway. There wasn't even enough time to escape, even if she somehow managed to get away from her captor. "What can I do for you, Tendro?"

Terrence Lee took note of Mirena and his expression betrayed his surprise at seeing the woman he'd beaten to half an inch of her life in front of him, alive and well. Either that, or he was seeing his 'favourite', Elizabeth, returned to him by one of his trusted Generals and struggling feebly to escape his hold on her.

"Oh," was all the Panarch said, standing out amongst the other Magi in the lobby of his own office with his white Magi jacket with silver trim where others mostly wore black and gold. He gestured for them to precede him to the door beyond the desk. "Into my office, please."

"Please don't hurt me," Mirena whispered, cringing at the thought of entering a small space with the Panarch, the fight completely gone out of her as she came face to face with Terrence Lee again, despite or perhaps because of the relaxed nature of his expression. "I'll do whatever you want."

Terrence Lee raised an eyebrow but said nothing. Mirena did as she was expected to and entered the small office with two of the most powerful men in the country, maybe even the world.

There is no use fighting them...the Panarch owns this city and Tendro knows everything about me; I can't hide what I am anymore. 'Hope' played his game well... 'The Avatar of the Light'... I bet he'll laugh later when he tells his friends how easily I believed him.

Once in the little office, the Panarch gestured at the two chairs across from his desk before crossing the room to take his own seat on the other side of the heavy wooden desk. Mirena took each step with dread and she found that she couldn't help but take in the details of the room around her, wondering what sort of space the infamously cold-hearted Panarch would spend most of his time in.

The bookshelves that lined the walls and the cluttered desk with its miniature Sentinal Stone paperweight seemed almost homey. They were definitely not what she would have expected from the office of the Capital's cruel tyrant, but nor were they comforting.

Mirena took in a deep breath and felt something within her snap.

No matter what happens in here today, she resolved, *I am not going to take this beating in silence. Not like the last time. I will fight them. I will fight for Sympathizers of the Light everywhere. Even if I can only do it with words or by being brave, followers of the Light everywhere who hear of what happened to me will know that someone fought for their beliefs...*

"If you intend to finish what you started in the garden," Mirena stated boldly, as unlike her usual self as it was possible for her to be, "I would prefer to get it over with and skip the formalities. I know what I'm guilty of and I can't and won't change it now."

Terrence Lee considered her a moment, his hand covering the lower half of his perfect face to hide his expression. Tendro too was watching her, but for his reasons of his own he chose not to interfere.

This is the Panarch's show now. I have to remember that Tendro only calls the shots when his ruler commands it. I have to find a way to make sure my execution is public so I can show the world a woman who can stand up to the Panarch even if she is going to be killed for it.

"Well," the Panarch said after a moment of tense silence, "this was not what I was expecting. You've changed, Mirena. Either way," he took a deep breath as if reconciling himself to the way things were, "welcome back."

"Um, sir," Tendro interjected hesitantly and Mirena realized just how intimidating of a man the Panarch must be, even to his Generals, if Tendro was that apprehensive about addressing him directly. "There's a more of a problem with Mirena's return than you are aware of. She seems to be confused and missing pieces of her memory."

"What do you mean?"

"She doesn't remember Caralain, for one," Tendro answered cryptically.

"Can I ask that I see my sister one last time before the trial?" Mirena ventured, ignoring what she didn't understand and hoping against hope that they'd allow her one final request if she was going to be hanged anyways.

A look of surprised crossed the Panarch's face. "What makes you think that there is going to be a trial?"

I suppose I have already been found guilty by the Panarch, Mirena realized. *I guess there would be no need for a trial if he's just going to decide my punishment personally. Just please let him do it publically.*

"Oh..." She felt her voice break, but she needed to get the words out. "Can you tell her I love her, then?"

"Mirena, you're home," Tendro said to her, imploring her to listen to him. "No one is going to send you away this time."

"You may get some harsh judgments from people in the Capital because of the rumours of your involvement in the attack on the Collegium, but I'll issue a formal statement that you are cleared of all suspicion in the matter. That should help things settle down a little bit," Terrence Lee added in a gentle tone.

Why are they pretending to be nice to me? Do they not have enough evidence to hang me? This has gone on too long to simply be a part of their games. Even so, I am not going to ask for punishment if they are not going to give it…

"So am I free to take my leave then? It's all over?"

"I guess it is," the Panarch said against all expectations. "I can't legitimately hold you here and honestly, I don't have a reason to. You are free to go but I'd recommend staying close to Tendro for a bit, just until you get your bearings again."

"No, I'll be fine," Mirena insisted, thinking about how she never wanted to see Tendro again after this. "I'll just go back to my room. Thank you for your time."

She stood and reached for the door, her steps tense and cautious in case they were still playing her and the Panarch cruelly changed his mind or revealed his true intentions toward her. The punishment never came and the door handle twisted easily under her grasp.

Tendro followed her out.

"Mirena, wait," he said, catching up to her out in the waiting room, "I thought you wanted me to take you to Elizabeth?"

She took a few more steps to place herself in the hallway where she'd have a better chance of escaping before she answered him. "You can just tell me where she is. I don't think we should see each other anymore."

"I'm relieved to hear you say that, actually," Tendro said, surprising her with the genuineness of his response and the familiar smile that accompanied it. "I've been trying to let you down gently for some time."

"Oh, okay," Mirena felt surprisingly numb. She couldn't believe that it was all playing out this way. After all the lies and deceit this was the last conversation she expected to have. "I think I might leave the Capital as well. It's just too much to bear to be here anymore. I can't walk these halls without the memories of us coming back to me."

He frowned. "I'm sorry. I didn't mean for any of this to happen this way, but if it's any consolation, I like the new you a lot better."

The new me? Have I really changed that much? And since when?

"It good to finally meet the real you," she told him honestly. *At least now I know where I stand…*

It is better to know once and for all that 'Hope' was a lie.

Tendro smiled, the charm of it breaking the severity his expression had taken on since he'd decided to turn her in to the Panarch at last.

"Fair enough, I guess. Listen, I know you said that you're leaving and all, but let me at least take you to Elizabeth. I'd like to leave you with someone who knows you and the circumstance that you're in."

"I guess it can't do any harm," Mirena agreed with a tired shrug worn out from all the shocks she'd lived through in the last handful of minutes. "Sure, lead the way."

Tendro led her back the way they'd come and back into the Magi quarters near where the hall to her room was, but instead of bringing her back to her own rooms, he took her up flight after flight of stairs until they'd climbed much higher than Mirena thought the Collegium went.

At long last they reached the topmost floor and what could only be described as the penthouse apartments.

Where is he taking me now? Mirena wondered numbly.

The hallway had few doors and Tendro selected one to knock on. After a moment it opened, revealing a bemused looking Panarch. Tendro laughed upon seeing him and the sound sent a sharp spike of fear through Mirena.

"I should have known you'd beat me here," Tendro commented, still smiling.

No…no, this is not fair. What a cruel joke! They've lured me here, after making me believe I was free… Now they can execute me in private and no one will ever know how I suffered for the Light. I'll be just another silent victim of the Panarch's rule.

Feeling the ultimate sting of betrayal, Mirena couldn't control herself as she let her hand fly full force towards Tendro's face and even the resounding smack did not make her feel any better.

"What the hell was that for?!" Tendro demanded, his hand flying to cover his stinging, reddened cheek as Terrence Lee's mouth dropped open in shock. "I thought we were getting along!"

"You can't fool me anymore!" Mirena declared sharply.

"What's going on out there?" A voice called curiously from within the room and Mirena was surprised to recognize it as Elizabeth's.

"You are not putting Elizabeth and I back in your garden for your pleasure!" Mirena was now beyond caring what they thought of her words. "I won't allow it!"

"What are you talking about?" Tendro questioned, his voice angry.

"You know what I am talking about. Don't you remember? The Panarch beat me senseless!"

Elizabeth's concerned face was finally visible in the frame of the doorway beside Terrence Lee when a look of recognition passed over the Panarch's face.

"Creator save us, I think I might know what's going on here..."

"Thank the Creator somebody does," Tendro noted sourly, "because I sure as hell don't. The last time I saw Mirena was when Caralain told us it would be three years before we saw her again."

"This isn't her," Terrence Lee stated, confusing them all, "this... is her Mirror."

IX.

"Let me explain," the Panarch began; his voice calm and patient as he sat across from them in the sitting room of his private quarters. "As most of you know, I was trained in a secret school for Magi where I learned a lot more than your average Mage has access to. Among what I was taught were the skills and knowledge necessary to travel from place to place using majik."

Mirena listened with rapt attention, but she couldn't help but stare at the girl who called herself Elizabeth and looked exactly like her twin sister but was not her sister. Wearing a light pink and blue floral dress, this 'Elizabeth' sat demurely and listened to the Panarch's explanation with polite attention, never once rolling her eyes or looking like she wanted to break in and speak her mind.

It's like watching myself from the outside...

"We were taught about the Sentinal Stones, what they are and how to use them," Terrence Lee continued. "Not everything is known about the ancient majik relics, even to the Sophists who were my mentors, but we have uncovered enough to know that the fourteen stone circles that are scattered about this continent are powerful enough to send even a moderately strong Mage to places far away.

"We've studied the symbols for this world and this time period extensively, but as some of us have experienced firsthand, time travel is also possible through the Stones. There were also rumours, though unproven until now, that realms other than our own could be reached as well.

"I was warned that something of this nature could be possible, but I didn't fully believe it," he finished, his tone kind, sincere and forthcoming. He was so different from Mirena's memory of the man who had found her trespassing in his private garden. "I know when to admit that I've been proven wrong."

"So this isn't our Mirena?" Tendro questioned when the Panarch was through, studying her intently. "Did you come through the Sentinal Stones on your own, or did anyone else come with you?"

Made slightly uncomfortable by their stares, Mirena unconsciously copied Elizabeth's demeanor, crossing her legs and folding her hands into her lap.

"We did use the Sentinal Stones…*He's* in my room," she told them, pointing at Tendro to show who she meant, "with my sister, Elizabeth."

"There's another one of us?" Elizabeth questioned, looking concerned. "That could get confusing pretty quickly."

Tendro shook his head. "That certainly explains your reaction to me," he noted, obviously thinking back to the words that had passed between them since he'd found her in the Cafeteria. "I'll admit that I wasn't able to follow half of what you were saying."

"I'm sorry about slapping you..." Mirena apologized. "I thought you were the other you, betraying me."

"So you trust me, then?" Tendro asked. "The other me, I mean."

"Sometimes," she answered honestly with the words she couldn't yet say to Hope. "A lot of the time I don't know if you are playing me or if you're sincerely being nice to me."

Tendro swallowed uncomfortably, but it was Terrence Lee that spoke. "What everyone needs to understand about this Mirena's realm is that, if I am correct, she is from the world that scholars theorize is a complete mirror to our own. They call it the 'Mirror World' for lack of a better name.

"It is believed that in the Mirror World, there are doubles of all of us, or Mirrors, if you will, and those people are the exact opposite of us in some crucial way. The theories also say that the whole basis for the world is flipped, meaning that our beliefs here would be turned on their heads over there. Basic things like morals and political views would likely be opposite.

"Mirena, can you confirm this with what you've seen here so far?" He asked, genuinely curious.

"From what I can tell, you're much kinder than the Panarch in our world," she ventured cautiously.

Mirena swallowed hard. *If this isn't real I am going to pay for my words, but they need to be said and I'm fairly sure that they can't all be in on this. Elizabeth is certainly proof enough of that.*

"In my world," she continued, "you have a private garden filled with women for your pleasure and that of your Generals, like Tendro. I sure hope that it is different here..."

The Panarch's mouth fell open and Tendro's expression wasn't much better. Elizabeth, however, gasped and placed her hands over her mouth, scandalized.

"I can assure you that that is not the case," Terrence Lee stated. "I can show you the private gardens if that would put your mind at ease."

"No, no," Mirena said quickly. "I have bad memories of that place...you, I mean he, almost killed me there..."

The Panarch looked extremely uncomfortable at this news.

"Maybe we should round up the other two," Tendro suggested. "If Mirena here is any indication, they are both probably pretty confused by now, if they haven't figured out yet that they aren't in their own realm anymore."

"Good idea," Terrence Lee agreed, recovering slightly. "Where did you say they were again?"

"My room on the first floor, first door on the right."

"And would it alarm them too much if I were to accompany you down there to speak to them?" He asked.

"If I go in first and explain it to them it should be fine," she answered, knowing Hope would believe her and Elizabeth would go along with what they decided whether she did or not.

Terrence Lee nodded his agreement and together they headed down flight after flight of stairs back down to the first floor, bringing this realm's Elizabeth and Tendro along for proof to show to Hope and Mirena's sister.

"Just give me a moment," Mirena instructed, opening her bedroom door slowly and slipping inside, leaving the rest of them to wait for her out in the hall.

Me, leaving the Panarch waiting for me in the hallway outside my bedroom...who would have ever thought?

"Should we be out looking for her, then?" Hope was saying as she entered.

"Mira!" Elizabeth exclaimed, taking notice of her as she entered. "What took you so long and where's the food you promised us? I'm starving here!"

Hope spun around to take notice of her also and his facial expression showed his relief before it turned to one of caution.

"Wait, Elizabeth, as I was telling you, something is not right about this place. That might not be your sister..."

"Oh, so you already know?" Mirena asked. "Then, can I bring in the others? They're waiting in the hall and are curious to meet you both."

"Others?" Hope questioned. "Who did you bring back with you?"

"Just a few people..." Mirena began hesitantly, almost mumbling as she was afraid of the reaction she'd get when they heard who was waiting outside the only exit to this room, "including the Panarch..."

"What?!" Elizabeth exclaimed, jumping to her feet with a look of outrage on her features. "Okay, Tendro, you're right, that's not Mira. It's an imposter!"

"Hey!" Mirena protested. "I'm me. I thought you'd be proud that I figured something out, instead of getting us into more trouble."

"Let him in," Hope instructed, calmly determined.

"Are you crazy?" Elizabeth demanded. "Tendro, wave your arms and take us to your majik bunker, okay? This isn't the time to face down the Panarch. We're not ready."

"It'll be fine," he assured her. "Mirena, let him in. I trust you."

He trusts me? Mirena questioned. *He trusts me and all I have been doing is doubting him at every turn. What kind of person am I?*

Shaking her head, Mirena opened the door to admit the Panarch and the two Mirrors from this realm. At least with their presence here to confirm they were in another realm, Mirena could prove to Hope and Elizabeth that she wasn't wrong about this Panarch; he really was as good as his Mirrored self was evil.

Terrence Lee nodded to Hope as he entered and Tendro behind him cautiously did the same, though he couldn't help the shocked expression on his face at seeing his own Mirror standing there before him. The two Elizabeths just stared at one another, neither one of them speaking or making any move to react to the other's presence.

Mirena's Elizabeth was the one to break the silence, however.

"There's three of us?!" She exclaimed somewhat peevishly. "How come mother never told us we were triplets?"

"Elizabeth, knock it off!"

"There's not three of you, but four, technically," Hope noted, taking in the three identical girls in the room all wearing similar dresses in different colours. "This is the Mirror World, isn't it?"

"You've heard of it?" Terrence Lee asked, sounding impressed.

Hope nodded. "From Caralain."

"Ah," the Panarch responded knowingly and didn't question Hope any further on the matter.

Caralain, again…

"Okay, so we know where we are now," Mirena acknowledged, pressing forward. "How do we get back?"

"Am I the only one who has no idea what the hell is going on here?!" Elizabeth demanded.

"This world is a mirror to yours," this realm's Elizabeth explained in a sweet voice. "Certain things are exact opposites and every person has a Mirror who differs from them in some crucial way."

"I can see that," Elizabeth noted sourly, referring to her own double. "Go on, then."

"Getting you home should be simple enough," Terrence Lee informed them. "The Sentinal Stones brought you here, so they can take you back. It's simply a matter of discovering the right set of symbols. If we examine them together, our combined knowledge should help us to choose the right ones."

"I don't know which one I used to get us here," Mirena explained. "I know which symbol I tried to use though."

"That's a start," Terrence Lee told her as he stood. "What I'll really need help with is recognizing which realm is yours; I should be able to handle the rest. I can take us down there if you've gotten everything you came for?"

"Actually, some supplies would be very welcome, if it's not too much trouble," Hope ventured.

"Certainly," he agreed, smiling expansively. "It's the least I can do for you after you've just answered the largest unsolved mystery of my order and confirmed the existence of the Mirror World."

Mirena couldn't help but smile back at him, even though this man shared the face of the one who'd treated her so badly. He was clearly the opposite of the Panarch she'd always feared, at least in all the ways that counted.

True to his word, it was not long before Mirena, Hope and Elizabeth found themselves in the familiar clearing south of the Capital, where the ancient stone circle stood waiting for them. They were laden with packs that the Panarch had had filled to bursting with food and basic necessities.

The stones here, like everything else, looked identical to the place they had come from, only now Mirena knew how truly different this place was and she found that she was somewhat hesitant to leave it. There was so much to see and learn here about how her realm could be different if people could just change their attitudes toward one another. The people here made kindness seem so simple.

Terrence Lee looked like he had so many questions to ask, too. As a scholar, he'd want to know everything he could about the nature of the world he'd just uncovered. However, as a competent and responsible ruler he knew that it was simply a curiosity that he would have to live with, as he couldn't leave his own realm without direction.

"This row," he said, approaching the stone in the center of the circle without the hesitation that Mirena would have shown now that she knew their power, "is the one we use to travel from place to place here, in this realm," he explained. "Do you know which symbols you use in yours?"

He's asking me, Mirena realized. *Why would he be looking to me and not Hope?*

"I'm not sure which row I was supposed to use," she replied hesitantly. "Maybe you should ask Hope. He has far more experience with these than I do."

"These here," Hope joined the Panarch at the stone pillar, "the row just below yours. So it's that simple, then? We just have to use the symbols we would have used anyway to get home again?"

Terrence Lee nodded. "It seems like it. It's a wonder that something like this hasn't happened sooner. Then again, even fully trained Sophists leave the other rows alone, knowing the danger they can represent."

At Mirena's expression of confusion, he continued, "There are a number of realms and not all of them are inhabitable. Some, I've heard, are filled with a fire that never stops burning, or a black void that swallows men whole. These could be myths of course, but many who've attempted to disprove them have never returned from their travels."

"And with those possible outcomes fresh in our minds, let's experiment, shall we?" Elizabeth suggested, looking somewhat impatient.

The Panarch smiled. "Well, as much as I'd like to see your realm, my place is here," he noted, taking the handful of steps needed to put him outside of the circle of stones. "But I wish you the best of luck and please know that you are always welcome here if you need a safe haven. It might be a little awkward to explain that there are two Tendros and two sets of identical twins, but we'd manage it somehow, if it came to that."

"Thank you for everything," Mirena told him, sincerely, "and for your understanding as well. Also, if you could give Tendro my sincerest apologies again for slapping him in the face it would be much appreciated."

"I will," he agreed. "And Mirena, take care of yourself, okay?"

Mirena nodded solemnly to the kind Panarch and without warning Terrence Lee disappeared, leaving only an empty and silent clearing. Mirena looked about herself in confusion for only a moment before her mind supplied her with what had happened. Not being the one to operate the Sentinal Stone herself this time, she hadn't felt any sort of shift or change; they simply were elsewhere without seeming to have moved at all.

"Are you sure you got it right this time?" Elizabeth questioned.

"Hardly," Hope answered her with his customary half-smile, "but there's a good way to check that. I've taken us to Maredon; it's time that I meet your parents for real."

We're in Maredon, Mirena took in the trees and the familiar lay of the land, seeing it through new eyes after all the distance they had travelled since leaving the Collegium. *So that's why it looks so familiar...*

Abruptly, Mirena's thoughts shifted to another topic. *Why does Hope want to meet my parents? I mean, didn't he have enough of the drama last time we were here, even though they weren't my real parents? The drama will be the same, but maybe he doesn't realize that…*

"Should I just go ahead and check for myself, to avoid any complications?" She asked.

"I don't think separating is the wisest idea right now," Hope frowned. "If we did somehow get yet another wrong realm, there is no telling what we might find. If you girls want to go in first though, I don't mind waiting for you outside the house."

"Sounds good," Elizabeth agreed before Mirena had a chance to react, grabbing her hand and pulling her out of the stone circle and running down the slope of the gentle hill that would take them to their childhood home. "See you later, Hopey."

"Elizabeth," Mirena said breathlessly, "do you always have to do things the complicated way?"

Elizabeth slowed her pace upon reaching the bottom of the hill, but she still pulled Mirena along with her at a good speed.

"Complicated? What do you mean, complicated?"

"Well, you know, being difficult," Mirena answered vaguely, not really wanting to start an argument, "and calling him Hopey? What's that all about?"

"You started it," Elizabeth stated flatly. "I'm only following your example. And besides, we can't go around calling him Tendro and alerting the Panarch's spies to his whereabouts, now can we?"

"Well, that's true," Mirena agreed, "but in that case, his name is Hope, not Hopey!"

"Semantics."

It seemed like that was the best she was going to get out of her sister and for now it would have to be enough. As they neared the old farm house, Mirena knew immediately they were home.

"Girls!" Their father exclaimed, happy to see them and despite whatever he might have heard about them in their absence he ran forward to catch Mirena up in his arms, wrapping her in the familiar comfort of his scent.

"Daddy!" Mirena squealed. "I've missed you more than you know."

"Me too, honey," her father assured her, before addressing Elizabeth. "You too Elizabeth; come here, before your mother gets out here."

Elizabeth humoured him and reluctantly joined the family hug, but the warm reunion didn't last long.

"Gabe! Gabe, is that Mirena or Elizabeth?" A sharp voice called from the open kitchen window as their mother tried to peer past worn curtains to get a look at what was going on outside. "Both of them?" She questioned, getting a better look. "Mirena actually did as I told her to?! Don't you go anywhere," she admonished them. "I'm coming out!"

Clearly working herself up to one of her legendary furies, Abigail Calanais stalked out of the front door of the small farm house ready to take a piece out of Elizabeth's hide. Mirena felt sorry for the wrath her sister was about to face, she really did, but this moment had been building in their mother since Elizabeth had run away to the Capital without permission.

Mirena felt more than heard Hope arrive behind them, having walked quickly in order to catch up. Some instinct warned her of the disaster about to befall her, but not in time to stop it from happening.

"Mom," Elizabeth began in a jubilant tone, "meet Mirena's fiancée, Hope."

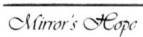

X.

How could you do this to me, Elizabeth?!

Mirena was outraged and she gave her sister the dirtiest look she could muster. *How could you throw me to the wolves after everything I have done for you?*

But her anger quickly shifted to panic as she felt her mother's gaze land on her and her mother's fury shift to her...exactly as Elizabeth had intended it to.

Creator, help me! Mirena silently screamed. *Why would Elizabeth even assume that Hope and I are romantically involved? When has Hope ever shown the slightest interest in me?*

Directing her gaze to Hope, she searched his face for a reaction. Even more important than the misunderstanding this would create with her parents was that this could ruin any chances of him ever wanting to be with her. Anything her mother could say right now would only pale in comparison to what Hope might think of her later.

More than anything, Mirena was embarrassed. Her panicked mind supplied her with no answers, no words she could say to dispel the announcement that Elizabeth had already made, even if it wasn't true. If she had to be honest with herself, some part of her wished that it could be.

Mrs. Calanais opened her mouth to begin the tirade that was sure to follow but Mirena didn't hear a word of it. She was already fleeing, her instincts taking her away from the source of her embarrassment and the tears on her cheeks whipped by the wind of her passage.

Mirena didn't hear anyone behind her and she didn't want to check; perhaps they were too stunned to follow her. She ran until she was stumbling and out of breath, not paying attention to where she was going, so she was startled when the first bolt of lightning arced through a rapidly darkening sky. The flash was followed by a loud peal of thunder that stopped her in her tracks.

I thought it was getting dark because of the time of day, but it's not that late, Mirena realized belatedly, coming to her senses. *I don't remember there being clouds earlier.*

There were clouds now, however; the sky was filled with them. Wiping the tearstains from her cheeks, Mirena tried to get her bearings in the failing light, but then quickly gave it up.

Even here, so close to her home, the copses of trees and rolling hills all looked the same. Turning back the way she thought she had come from, she slowly began the walk back. Even as upset as she was, it wasn't worth her safety to stay out in weather like this.

Another flash of lightning illuminated the way before her and Mirena thought she might have heard someone call out her name in the wind before thunder split the air again, but the storm was gathering strength and it was likely just wishful thinking that someone would have actually come looking for her.

Yet another flash revealed where she was as she crested the hill and saw the familiar shadowed form of the Sentinal Stones, standing impervious to the mounting wind. The stones didn't indicate shelter, but Mirena found her steps quickening, regardless. If she could just reach the stones, then she would be able to get her bearings by the next flash of light and know which way meant home.

Mirena reached the stones before the next bolt of lightning lit the sky and her hand brushed up against a stone in the outer ring. The first large drops of rain began to fall, splashing her hand and cooling the warm stone rapidly.

"Fascinating, aren't they?"

The voice came from her left, no further than the next stone. Whirling about, Mirena fought the darkness to see who was there, only to be almost blinded by the next flash.

"Who's there?" She asked, feeling suddenly apprehensive.

Blinking to adjust her vision, the figure before her took shape as it took a step nearer. He, or she, Mirena allowed, was cloaked and had their hood drawn up to protect against the increasing rain and it was hard to tell more than that it was a person slim of build, with a worn floor-length cloak and bulging pack strapped to his or her back.

"A weary traveller," the stranger answered and Mirena decided that by the voice it was likely male, though it was hard to tell for certain. "Tell me, do you know much about these ruins?"

It's the start of a bad storm and they're asking calmly about the Sentinal Stones?

"Shouldn't you be asking where the nearest shelter is? Besides, I hear that these stones are dangerous to stand by," she warned, "especially in a storm like this."

"Oh really?" The stranger questioned, his tone sounding intrigued of all things. He ignored the urgency of the wind and rain whipping his cloak about. "And why is that?"

"They are said to have majikal properties," she explained, wondering how much was safe to share, "and in a storm like this, with energy flying about, there is no telling what might happen."

Mirena hadn't noticed until now just how close the stranger had gotten during their conversation. It made sense for him to do so, so he could hear her voice over the wind and rain and be heard himself, but still she found herself feeling ill at ease with his nearness.

"You know, I've heard that somewhere before..." he commented at a normal volume, close enough now that he didn't need to bother raising his voice.

"Then we should both get going..." Mirena suggested, backing away from him, which coincidentally put her closer to the central pillar.

If I can just see the symbols, I'll know which way will take me home...

"Mirena!"

She heard her name this time over the wind, followed by another peal of thunder.

Hope?

The stranger spared one glance over his shoulder, before returning his attention to Mirena.

"You're right," the traveller agreed and a particularly bright flash of lightning allowed Mirena to see into the cowl of his hood for the first time. His blue eyes were not kind on his overly handsome face. "And it's time to get going, now that the heroes have arrived on the scene."

"Mira!" Elizabeth's voice screamed and Mirena caught sight of both her sister and Hope approaching the base of the hilltop where the stone circles stood.

She turned to run to them before the man could stop her, though curiously he didn't bother to try. The stranger with the cold blue eyes let her flee past him and out of the stone circle, but it wasn't until she was one step out of the shadow of the looming stones that she understood the reason why.

The rain stopped dead between one step and the next, causing Mirena to stumble to a halt, completely startled by the sudden lack of downpour. Even though they'd been standing in front of her only a moment before, Hope and Elizabeth were now nowhere to be seen.

And why should they be, for Mirena wasn't in Maredon any longer.

Here the trees here were solely coniferous and thick around the clearing. There was no longer anywhere for her to run and she didn't know where she was anymore, regardless.

"Just in time," the voice of the stranger came to her ears, but it only took her a moment to realize that he wasn't speaking to her.

A single coin flipped through the air over her head as Mirena focused on the newcomer to the scene. His hair was a vibrant orange and his long limbs were lanky. He looked young, but his expression showed a maturity and a strong sense of confidence in his own abilities.

"Good work, Nevodian," the orange-haired stranger praised the cloaked man, "there's more back at camp if you want to help me take her the rest of the way."

"I'll do better than that," Nevodian answered, focusing on Mirena again for the first time since bringing her here. "Go to sleep my little Sympathizer. You don't need to be awake any longer; we'll take care of you from here on out."

Mirena felt the world darken around her and this time it wasn't like the gathering rage of the storm; it was a sinking sensation that took her into involuntary unconsciousness.

Only one thought floated to the surface as everything else faded. *This only proves it…every time I start to hope that my life has changed for the better, something goes horribly wrong…*

"She's pregnant, isn't she?!" Abigail Calanais demanded, referencing the daughter who'd just run away embarrassed by her sister's blatant lie. "That's why this is happening. Didn't I tell you this would happen, Gabe?" She asked, but didn't wait for an answer before she rounded on Elizabeth, "I knew one of you girls would get pregnant by running off to the Capital, but I always thought it would be you."

"Hey, that's not fair," Elizabeth protested.

"Like hell it isn't," Mrs. Calanais continued, heedless of Hope's presence.

I suppose I'm family now, at least in her mind, Hope rationalized. *She doesn't care what dirty laundry she airs in front of me...*

"Little hussy," Mrs. Calanais noted disrespectfully. "I suppose this proves that your sister is no better. Though, at least in her case, she had the decency to drag her man home to own up to his responsibilities. So," she added, turning her wrathful gaze onto Hope at last, "what do you have to say for yourself?"

"Yeah, Hope, what do you have to say for yourself?" Elizabeth repeated; a nasty twinkle in her green eyes.

You're a piece of work, Elizabeth, Hope thought, pursing his lips before he answered the question, as ridiculous as it was.

"Ma'am, with all due respect," he began as diplomatically as possible, "I did not sleep with your daughter and I assure you that if she is with child, then it is no fault of mine."

Mrs. Calanais tsked in displeasure. "No fault of yours, is it?" She questioned; her tone severe. "Well, I suppose we'll see about that. A few months will tell us either way. So, Hope, is it? If you're not the father of my impending grandchild, then why in the name of the Destroyer are you here? You seem a handsome enough man; you could have any woman's daughter...why Mirena? Was Elizabeth too bold for you?"

Hope found that he was beginning to get annoyed with this woman.

Her husband stands there saying nothing, while his wife criticizes their children in front of a total stranger. I can see that Mirena doesn't take much after her mother and I can also see where Elizabeth gets her attitude from...

"If either were true," he replied in a controlled fashion, "it would certainly be none of your business. More importantly, there's a storm coming in and as much as I'd like to stay here and become better acquainted, Mirena is out there alone and upset. If you'll excuse me."

He turned, ignoring Mrs. Calanais' open-mouthed expression as she fished for some other line of attack.

Elizabeth broke the tense silence following his words by clapping suddenly and loudly. "Nicely done, Ten...I mean, Hope! Nicely done."

Hope ignored her; it was surprisingly easy as he was getting used to her antics. Besides, Elizabeth didn't mean any harm by her callous words and pointed comments. She said them to deflect attention, or to keep herself entertained and there was no harm in most of what she did and said.

This occasion though... Hope thought, *this could get serious quickly if the coming storm is going to be as bad as I think it is.*

Elizabeth caught up to him shortly and he realized that what he was doing could only be described as 'stalking off'. Smoothing his gait, he tried to calm his anger; there was no use wasting the energy he might need to locate Mirena in the inclement weather.

"That was unkind of you," he noted calmly to Elizabeth, partly to test his control over his emotions.

"Mother deserves a good shock every once and awhile," she responded without remorse. "Mira will get over it."

"If you say so," Hope allowed. "It's none of my business, of course, but I think Mira hurts more than you realize when you say things like that to her. She doesn't have your tough skin."

"I know," Elizabeth's voice sounded sincere for once, "but I just couldn't have all that disappointment on me, you know? So I told a white lie...it'll get cleared up and by then, after all the excitement, what I did will be old news."

It followed a perverse sort of logic and Hope found that he couldn't really argue with it. Besides, it was between sisters and his opinion certainly didn't belong, especially after only having known the both of them for so short a time.

"Besides," she added as the first flash of lightning arced through the darkened sky, "it was only an exaggeration and not a lie, right?"

Despite himself, Hope stopped dead in his tracks as thunder rumbled loudly, his mouth dropping open slightly.

Did she just imply...?

"Thought so," Elizabeth declared, not pausing her long stride as she left him behind and called back to him. "Better hurry if you want to catch your intended before the rain starts."

Covering up his momentary embarrassment, Hope hurried to keep pace with Elizabeth, saying nothing that she could turn back on him.

*She thinks she's so clever...*Hope thought, a smile playing about his lips despite his intentions. *The problem is, she's right.*

"Hope, look, up there on the hill near the Stones!" Elizabeth directed. The rain was coming down now and increasing in volume. It was getting difficult to see.

"Mirena?" Hope called out, loud enough that hopefully she'd be able to hear him over the wind. "I think that's her," he confirmed to Elizabeth, "but who's that with her?"

"Mira!" Elizabeth screamed, perhaps seeing something Hope hadn't, or realizing that a cloaked figure standing in the shadow of the Sentinal Stones could only mean trouble.

Mirena whirled to search for the source of her sister's voice and then made a dash for them before the rain swallowed her and the cloaked figure disappeared as well.

"No," Hope gasped, unable to mentally come to terms with what he'd just witnessed. Whoever that cloaked figure was had just used the Stones and taken Mirena with him...somewhere.

Elizabeth was already halfway up the hill now, but Hope knew that it was no use. There was no telling who it was who had taken her or where they'd gone to. The Sentinal Stones were the one form of travelling by majik that was nearly untraceable.

The rain beat down on his shoulders, drenching him in cold water that did nothing to ease his worries or the burden on his soul.

*This is my fault...*he realized, the weight of his guilt crashing down on him as suddenly as the heavy rainfall had. *She trusted me, followed me and I led them to her home, her family...I was so selfish and now she's been taken.*

She called me Hope, he thought despondently, *but her hope in me was unfounded.*

I'm nobody's hero.

Mirror's Hope

XI.

"Hark! At last she awakens; a merry twinkle in her eye!"

The voice that spoke expounded in a style familiar to a performer calling out lines in a play to amuse his audience. The tone was loud and jovial and brought Mirena fully out of the groggy sleep-state she'd been fighting silently for some time now.

Her left side hurt, her back ached uncomfortably and as she became aware of her surroundings, she realized that she was lying on her side on an uneven stone floor, her knees curled up to her chest.

"Sleep well, my dear?"

"Where am I?" Mirena questioned, feeling disoriented.

"Nowhere you need to concern yourself with," was the simple answer spoken by the young man with the orange hair who had been waiting for her at the Sentinal Stones. He sat in a relaxed posture by a small fire that he was prodding with a stick to keep it burning bright enough to see by, his long legs tucked beneath him and his shoulders hunched.

I'm in a cave, Mirena realized, slowly forcing herself into a sitting position and wincing, even in the dim firelight. *It's not very large, but I don't see any exits.*

"Then why am I here?" She asked, trying for mild curiosity, but falling just shy of the mark.

He turned his head to regard her a moment, his hazel eyes locking onto hers in the firelight. "I think you know."

He's a Truthseeker. The fact struck her like a blow to the midsection and Mirena's eyes widened in fear as she scrambled to a sitting position.

"I won't be of any use to you…"

"Oh, I beg to differ," he disagreed. "Actually, you and I have some important matters to discuss, but I'll let you take some time to get comfortable. I'm not in a hurry," he added, setting a black kettle carefully in the flames. "Tea?"

"What did you do to it?" She asked, rubbing her arms and feeling a chill despite the fire's heat.

"Nothing yet," the Truthseeker answered as he smiled disarmingly, unconcerned by this line of questioning. "It's only water until I add the leaves…"

"And if I refuse?"

"No matter," he said with a slight shrug as he urged the fire to burn hotter. "You'll answer my questions, tea or no tea."

He's going to torture me, the knowledge came to Mirena with the subtle implication in the Truthseeker's tone. *How can I even contemplate resisting something like that? I am not strong like Elizabeth.*

"Then why don't you tell me what you want me to say," she stated with false bravado, "so we can get this over with?"

"Are you in such a hurry to be executed?" He asked, regarding her once more. "Because if you want to plead guilty now, it would save me the trouble of digging for your sins."

He enjoys this…the Truthseeker game of hunter and prey…

"What did I ever do to you that would cause you to have such malice towards me?"

"You interpret this as malice?" The Truthseeker questioned. "Interesting idea, but you are incorrect. I hold no ill will towards you. This is a job; it is one that I am paid quite handsomely for and that suits my particular disposition. So, did you want to confess now, or shall we begin?"

Mirena's fear spiked, but huddled as she was in a cramped cave with her questioner so close and no exit in sight, she could only shake her head in refusal, wrapping her arms more tightly around herself.

"In case you were wondering, my name is Stiphen; Stiphy for short." Stiphy smiled, showing teeth and seeming to genuinely anticipate the challenge of the questioning that was about to begin. "I'm sure you're wondering about your captors too, but they didn't wish for their names to be disclosed to you. You understand why, of course?"

He thinks he so smart, Mirena felt a bitterness welling within her at his tone, *but I have had too many years of wordplay with Elizabeth to be made to feel worthless by a condescending tone.*

"As you probably already know, my name is Mirena Calanais," she supplied, knowing it was expected of her, "You may call me Ms. Calanais."

"Ms. Calanais," Stiphy considered the name a moment, rolling it around on his tongue. "Wise of you to co-operate. And since we are remaining civil, I'll begin with a simple question. Are you acquainted with a man by the name of Tendro Seynor?"

"Why are you asking a question you already know the answer to?"

"To see if you are willing to tell the truth," he responded easily, "it's no more complicated than that."

"I have no reason to lie to you."

"That in itself is a lie," he noted, "but no matter...let's continue, shall we? What does the name Tendro Seynor mean to you?"

"The name 'Tendro Seynor' is just a name," she told him, sticking to the letter of the truth. "It means nothing to me."

"I see," Stiphy answered, his tone ambiguous, "then I suppose the name 'Mirena Calanais' means nothing to him either?"

*It's probably true...*Mirena fought back the wave of emotion that accompanied the thought, unwilling to show weakness before this Truthseeker.

"You would assume correctly."

Stiphy nodded as if this was the answer he had been expecting.

"Very well. So if Tendro Seynor and Mirena Calanais mean nothing to one another, then is it Elizabeth who has the General's affections?"

He's lying...he has to be. Elizabeth wouldn't do something like that to me. Her sister's words abruptly came back to her. *She could have told mother that Hope and I were engaged to throw suspicion off of herself...she threw me to the wolves, then. What else is she capable of?*

"You'd have to ask them," Mirena told him, her voice shaking and betraying her uncertainty. "I don't meddle in my sister's personal affairs."

"Oh no? Then what of the daring escape from the Collegium?" Stiphy pressed. "Would you not consider that meddling?"

"I was simply following my mother's command to bring my sister home at any cost." The words came from her throat but they sounded distant to her ears, like someone else was speaking them.

"Then why, might I ask, would Tendro Seynor help you?"

Mirena said the first thing that came to her mind and hoped it sounded convincing. "I used him to get into the garden."

The kettle, sitting unnoticed in the campfire until now, suddenly split the air with a sharp whistle. Stiphy removed the red-hot kettle from the flames before giving her a look that said he knew she wasn't being completely truthful with him.

"Come now, we both know better than to think you were the mastermind behind the plan to undermine the Panarch's authority. You, a run-of-the-mill Sympathizer of the Light with no connections and no ambitions beyond working in the Collegium's Cafeteria so she can raise enough money to be like her betters? I think not."

Am I that obvious? I am smart enough to do something like that; I just wouldn't do it on my own, Mirena's cheeks reddened with embarrassment.

"What does it matter why he helped me?"

"Just call it idle curiosity," Stiphy said, turning his whole body to face her like he was sharing a secret with her and they were talking as two people around a campfire rather than a prisoner and her captor. "I want to know what makes a man like Tendro Seynor defect. From what I can tell, he had it all before he met you. The ear of the Panarch, the privileges of an esteemed General and a devoted and beautiful fiancée who'd given him the key to everything he could ever desire."

Fiancée? He can't be engaged! Mirena fought the doubt that creeped into her mind. *Hope would have mentioned someone that important to him...*

"You seem to know him better than I do, why don't you tell me, then?" She said aloud, turning her face to wipe the tears forming in her eyes before he could see them and know that his gambit had worked.

"Are you sure you want to hear it?" Stiphy asked, leaning forward until he was no more than a foot from her face. "Caralain is her name. Strange, don't you think? That he would take up with a farm girl like you when he's engaged to a prominent lady like Caralain Dashar. But maybe that's why he chose you; someone he could have on the side and no one would notice or question. What's your opinion, Ms. Calanais?"

Where's Caralain? Hope's Mirror had asked her upon meeting her. *Is she with you?* And later, Hope had told the Panarch of the other realm, *I learned about the Mirror World from Caralain…*

The pieces suddenly fell into place in Mirena's head and in her mind's eye she saw the petite woman with the long, dark hair that she'd caught watching their desperate flight up the stairs to the monorail platform. Her pale skin and light blue eyes stood out in the midst of the throng as it surged around her, the woman's pose completely still and calm and her gaze steady.

Caralain. She had followed Hope with her eyes until he was out of sight. Her unimpressed expression and the bitterness that had followed identified her as nothing else could have.

And Caralain had known who Mirena was; hated her, even.

Now Mirena knew why.

"I don't have an opinion…" She whispered. "I've never met Caralain Dashar."

Mirena was trying to be strong and confident, but her words were as unsteady as she felt. *I am such a fool to believe that Hope might have...* The tears started falling and once they had begun, she no longer had any chance of stopping them.

He's won. Stiphy's defeated me and he knows it.

"There now," the Truthseeker filled his tone with a false comfort as he lifted the now somewhat cooled kettle to pour tea into two mugs, "it's not so bad as you might think. At least now you know the truth now about who was using whom? Hm?"

Waiting out her silence, Stiphy slowly turned one of the mugs about before offering it to Mirena, handle out. She took the cup from him slowly, pulling it towards her to look down at the contents. Her eyes lingered on the steam slowly wafting from the water's surface before they snapped up to meet Stiphy's gaze, her expression filled with rage.

"Give my regards to Dipaul!" Mirena shouted, tossing the steaming liquid into Stiphy's eyes and crawling away as fast as she was able to get herself out of his reach.

"Stupid bitch!"

Mirena crawled, climbing to her feet as she went. She didn't care which way she was headed as she didn't know which way was out, but her lack of foresight soon cost her as she came up to the wall and realized that there was no exit on this side of the small cave.

Whirling about with her back to the jagged stone wall, she looked past Stiphy who was getting to his feet. She couldn't tell whether his face was red with rage or simply the burns from the boiled water.

The exit must be beyond him, Mirena thought, *just out of the light of the fire. He's too clever not to put himself between me and the exit.*

"You'll pay for that," Stiphy hissed dangerously, the red-hot tip of the wooden poker in his hand scraping slightly against the floor and sending sparks dancing as he approached her with a purposeful malice, "and we were getting along so nicely until now."

I have to get out of here, Mirena thought desperately, straining her eyes past the light of the fire in search of the exit.

Stiphy smiled; it was the first genuine expression he'd showed during their entire conversation and just for a moment Mirena caught a glimpse of the real Truthseeker. Standing no more than a few feet from her, he raised the poker and jabbed it forward with a deliberate motion.

Even in that last second with the burning tip of the stick poised in the air, Mirena found herself hoping that Stiphy only meant to scare her into answering his questions, but that hope was soundly dismissed as the white hot pain of the ashen tip seared through her shoulder.

A scream ripped its way through Mirena's throat, splitting the air and reverberating off the cavern walls so that the sound multiplied inside her mind like the pain did in her shoulder.

And through it all, Stiphy laughed.

When the scream had finally quieted to a desperate kind of panting, Stiphy began to slowly pull the wooden poker out of her flesh, like he was savoring the pain he had caused. Gasping with the shock of it, Mirena stood motionless, afraid that she would only make things worse if she moved.

"Please, stop...please," Mirena found that she was whispering the words over and over, her tone pleading, "please...please stop...I'm sorry...please."

The sharp crack of the wood across her cheek brought silence to the litany, the wooden stick snapping on her jaw with the intensity of the blow.

No, Mirena thought, blood filling her mouth, *I refuse to die here like this.*

Slowly turning her head back to regard Stiphy, her eyes were intense and filled with hatred. From no discernible source, a slight wind picked up in the cave, swirling around them and stirring the fire as it gathered speed.

"Ah, so there is a backbone in there somewhere," Stiphy commented with a smirk, his friendly demeanor back now that he felt he was in control once more. "I had begun to wonder with how docile you've been. Good," he noted, "that'll make this more interesting."

*So that's where the exit is...*Mirena silently thanked her majik for that piece of information, spitting the blood out of her mouth and onto the stone floor.

"Either way, I'm going to need you to stay put and as it seems you can't be trusted to behave..." Stiphy said ambiguously, reaching into a pouch at his waist and drawing something out. He fingered whatever it was in his hands before tossing it in Mirena's direction.

That was the only warning she got before vines shot out from the little seed that landed on the stone floor before her. Fanning outwards in the blink of an eye, the vines snapped around her, pinning her arms to her sides and wrapping so tightly that she wasn't sure how long she'd be able to keep breathing.

They were young vines, not very thick or strong under ordinary circumstances, but these were controlled by the will of a Mage and Mirena knew that she'd have little chance of breaking free of them without using majik of her own.

Using her anger as fuel, she pulled on the wind from outside that she had already begun to draw on. Mirena didn't know what good it would do her, but she had to try something and she already had a grip on the air currents that she'd instinctively brought into the cave.

They have to be enough to help me, Mirena willed. *Somehow it has to be enough or Stiphy will kill me and I can't let that happen.*

She pulled harder and the fire wavered under the growing strength of wind called forth by her majik. Some part of her wondered why Stiphy hadn't yet hit her again, or begun to ask the questions that she'd have no choice but to answer, but then she caught the look on his face.

It was fear; somehow the Truthseeker was afraid of her.

"You weren't supposed to have majik..." Stiphy began, taking a step back from her.

"I guess *someone* was misinformed," Mirena snapped in response, pulling sharply one last time on the wind.

A gust whooshed into the tiny cave, blowing over the fire and sending sparks flying at Stiphy. He swore, diving out of the way, but the moment of weakness cost him as Mirena saw her chance for escape.

A singular spark flew close enough that she could make out its every detail with her eyes. Switching tactics, she abruptly let the wind drop, reaching out to the fire with her mind and pulling on the strength of that spark, drawing its power into herself.

Stiphy got to his feet once more, thinking that the immediate danger had passed, when he was forced to shield his eyes as a sudden flare erupted around Mirena.

It hurt immensely, but with the fire she'd drawn from the spark, Mirena used her majik to ignite the vine that held her captive. It lit up immediately, burning hot and fast until only ash remained and burn marks across her skin where the vines had gripped too tightly.

It was over in a searing painful flash. Every bit of fire in the room was extinguished, but with that sudden burst of power Mirena was free and Stiphy was still struggling to regain his vision in the now darkened cave.

Mirena could see the starlight filtering gently into the cave, but more importantly she knew without a doubt where the exit was now. No longer hesitating, she ran for freedom.

Mirena veered sharply to the left past Stiphy in order to get around the remains of the fire pit and she felt her foot brush up against something which caused her to stop with sudden inspiration. Not pausing long enough to think her actions through, she reached down and took hold of the warm handle of the teapot, feeling the steam waft leisurely upwards from the freshly boiled water.

Gritting her teeth, she listened for the sounds of Stiphy regaining his footing in the dark cave. He was sure to come after her or try to grab her again.

In fact, Mirena was betting on it.

He probably thinks I've stopped because I don't know which way is out...he won't see this coming.

Sure enough, the Truthseeker made a grab for her shoulder. Stiphy was quiet and quick, but it wasn't enough to save him. Using every bit of strength she had and ignoring the wince of pain from her shoulder, Mirena swung the cast-iron pot with both hands, bringing it up high enough to strike her captor where it counted.

She heard the crack as the pot made contact with Stiphy's head. Then her captor's corpse hit the ground with a thud, blood leaking slowly from his skull as his face rested motionlessly in the still-hot remains of the campfire.

Mirena's breath came in ragged gasps; *I've killed him.*

Why did I stop? Her shocked mind questioned, immediately following the violent act. *If I would have kept running he would still be alive...*

What have I done?

The tears poured down her face. She wanted to take it all back somehow, but it wasn't possible to undo what she'd done.

"I'm sorry...I'm so sorry, Stiphy," Mirena whispered as she turned to flee and leave the evidence of her crime behind her.

I'm just as bad as them, now...

Mirror's Hope

XII.

"So?" Elizabeth pressed, impatient. "Are we going to follow after them or not?"

"This takes time and I'm not even sure I know what I'm doing," Hope told her, feeling his patience wearing thin at the delay also.

They huddled in the stone circle in the countryside of Maredon, heedless of the dangers that the Sentinal Stones presented. The ground was slick and muddy from the downpour, but the rain had largely subsided since Mirena had been taken from them; they had been working on how to follow her ever since she left.

"Well hurry it up," Elizabeth instructed waspishly.

"It would go a lot faster if you'd stop interrupting."

"Sorry," she muttered and then finally, blessedly, fell silent.

The stones looked like they always did; the same here as they had been in the Mirror world and not dissimilar from those near the Capital. The darkness made them hard to read, but not for him. His majik resonated with the inherent power in the stones and with an extreme amount of concentration he could see the faint glow of majik that had been used here recently. It wasn't a simple thing to do and hardly ever a power that needed to be called upon, but strong uses of majik left traces that could be followed by those who knew what to look for.

The problem was that the Sentinal Stones contained a majik of their own, so finding the trace the cloaked stranger had used to take Mirena away from here would be difficult at best.

At worst, it would be like trying to find a needle in a haystack.

Fortunately, these particular stones were used less often than most, being in such a remote location, so any traces of majik he found would most likely belong to the person who'd stolen Mirena.

"I think I've got it," Hope announced. "There are only three symbols with excess traces of majik. One is the one we used to get here from the Mirror World, the other is the symbol for the stones nearest the Capital, but the third would take us to just outside the keep of Nefall in the north."

"So which one is it?" Elizabeth asked.

He frowned. "Let's just hope it's not the Capital, because if it is we'll probably find a group of Magi and Truthseekers ready and waiting to take us in for questioning. As it is, we'd better be prepared that the same could happen in Nefall."

Elizabeth swallowed apprehensively, looking grim and without her usual nonchalance. "Okay, let's get going then."

Hope nodded. *I just have to hope that we're not too late...or worse, that the two of us coming after her isn't playing right into our enemy's hands...*

Standing, Hope set his feet in a defensive position and held his majik at the ready. It wouldn't be enough to save him if his former friends were waiting to catch or kill him, but he'd feel better going down fighting than being caught unaware.

At least he had the power to defend himself. Looking over at Elizabeth one last time before he sent them into possible danger, he was impressed with her bravery. She didn't have a weapon on her or any ability to do what he could, yet she was ready to fight alongside him to get her sister back.

Elizabeth nodded to tell him that she was ready, her expression set with determination. Taking this as his cue to stop wasting time, Hope took a deep breath and activated the Sentinal Stones to take them to the forests surrounding Nefall.

The scenery around them changed abruptly from a darkened hilltop to the middle of thick northern woodland. Coniferous trees surrounded them, limiting the distance they could see, but no circle of Magi stood waiting, at least not out in the open, and no attacks came at them out of the forest.

"Well that was anti-climatic," Elizabeth commented; her momentary show of vulnerability gone like it had never existed.

"Don't let your guard down yet," Hope warned. "We still don't know who took Mirena or why."

"I think the why of it is pretty obvious," Elizabeth noted wryly. "As for the who..."

He gave her a quelling look and Elizabeth wisely let the subject drop with a toothy grin in Hope's direction. Ignoring her for the moment, Hope looked around for any indication of a path or hint of which direction the kidnapper might have taken Mirena, but after a moment he gave it up as a bad job.

*I've never been in a forest in my life...*Hope admitted, albeit silently. *Who am I to think that I could track someone here and now?*

Elizabeth brushed past him on her way out of the stone circle, stepping carefully through the bramble as if she'd been born to this kind of terrain. Startled, Hope started after her, moving much less skillfully and making a lot more noise.

"I thought we were supposed to be keeping our guards up?" She questioned after a moment. "You look and sound like a drunken sailor trying to walk on land."

"Shut up."

With a dismissive shrug, Elizabeth turned back to what she was doing and before long she had led them through the trees and out the other side of the thicket.

It was there that they found her.

Looking down and muttering to herself, Mirena was headed in no particular direction, though it was perpendicular to where they stood on the forest's edge. At first Hope wasn't even sure it was her. She looked so defeated; her hair and clothes were singed in places and caked with blood. And the way she stumbled, as if in a daze, wasn't like Mirena's usual careful steps and the prideful tilt of her head.

Elizabeth's gasp of recognition confirmed it, though; this was Mirena and somehow she'd managed to escape her captor.

But at what price? Hope wondered; feeling horrified as he took in the sight of her.

"Mir-" Elizabeth began to call out but Hope silenced her with a cautionary gesture, some part of him still alert for a trap. He was too late though, Mirena had heard her sister's voice and her head snapped up at the sound.

"Elizabeth?" Mirena cried, her voice choking in a sob as she stumbled forward, intent on them both. "Help! Help me!"

The pain it cost her to run was obvious but she did it anyway and despite the dangers, Hope found himself running alongside Elizabeth to reach Mirena, his instincts screaming at him the whole time.

We're too out in the open here... They won't let her get away from them this easily.

"I'm so sorry..." Mirena cried. "I didn't mean to...I didn't mean to do it, but he's dead. I killed him."

She was scarred from head to toe. Burn marks in the pattern of fallen leaves - no, a trailing vine - covered her visible flesh and left it blackened in a most unnatural way. Her shoulder leaked blood slowly from a wound half-cauterized and her face was turning a blackish-purple from a massive bruise that seemed to emanate from a long and deep red welt.

Hope took Mirena in his arms gently, keeping in mind her injuries but wanting nothing more than to keep her safe now that he'd found her again.

"I'm so sorry," he repeated her words, but with a different meaning.

I shouldn't have let this happen to you...

"Who'd you kill?" Elizabeth demanded, her eyes dark with rage. "Who was he?"

"The man that did this..." Mirena said, looking down at her arms with a helpless motion. "Stiphy."

An unnaturally loud scream split the air, strong enough to knock them back. The sudden overwhelming sound deafened their ears to anything other than the anguish that poured from the man's lungs, strengthened by his majik. Elizabeth was quick enough to cover her ears, but Hope had his arms full and it was all he could do to hunch over Mirena and try to shield her with his body.

"I'll kill you!" The cloaked stranger screamed, still impossibly loud with his majik-enhanced voice. "By the Destroyer, I will see your soul devoured by the Void!"

Hope felt Mirena clench tightly to his shirt in fear, but Elizabeth's reaction was another matter. Turning to identify the man that was coming for them, Hope noticed Elizabeth waving her arms and screaming at their attacker, though due to the hearing loss caused by the man's majik, Hope couldn't make out her words.

He wanted to warn her, to tell her to be quiet and to stop drawing this man's attention to her. Hope knew this man, not well, but he'd met him before. His name was Nevodian and he was a travelling musician with a natural born talent for both music and torture.

Nevodian, like so many others, was in the Panarch's employ. He was a Truthseeker and a very successful one.

Today it seemed that Nevodian didn't have his usual patience or his love of a good chase. He wanted revenge and death and he didn't care who he had to cut through to get it.

The only question is why…

Lightning arced from a clear night sky, the stars not obscured by any clouds, as the Truthseeker Mage called down a more advanced form of majik. Elizabeth dove out of the way, expecting an attack of some sort even if she hadn't been prepared for the nature of it, as the ground where she had been standing erupted in a shower of debris.

Hope winced in sympathy but Elizabeth had managed to roll out of harm's way and now Nevodian was coming for his real target, Mirena.

Hope knew he couldn't let Mirena be captured again.

She wouldn't survive it…

"Get out of my way, Tendro," Nevodian commanded, his voice enhanced enough to be heard clearly, but not to hurt. "She's not worth it."

"What do you know about how much she's worth?" Hope retorted, hardly thinking about his response, just knowing that he had to keep the Truthseeker talking instead of killing.

"I know that we were only told to grab her in order to get you, friend," Nevodian responded, each deliberate step bringing him closer to where Hope safeguarded Mirena.

"Worth enough as bait then," Hope responded, his tone bitter. "So how does killing me to get to her make any sense?"

"Shut up!"

Hope tried not to show by his expression that anything was amiss, but he could see beyond Nevodian to where Elizabeth was creeping up with a heavy stick held before her like a sword that she wasn't strong enough to wield.

"Stiphy's dead, Nevodian, and killing me or her won't bring him back," Hope continued, mercilessly guessing at the reason behind Nevodian's intense desire for revenge.

He and this Stiphy were lovers…

Hope tried to keep Nevodian's attention focused on his pain so he wouldn't realize that Elizabeth was coming for him. "It won't make you feel any better."

"Maybe it will," the Truthseeker stated coldly. "Maybe crushing her skull in is just the therapy I need."

"Maybe crushing *your* skull in is just the therapy *I* need!" Elizabeth cried, swinging her stick wildly towards Nevodian's head.

Unfortunately, Elizabeth's need for a snappy comeback cost her the moment of surprise that she'd needed to catch the Truthseeker off guard. Whirling around, Nevodian took only a glancing blow to the shoulder instead of his head.

This left Hope with no choice. Prying himself out of Mirena's grasp, he ran forward as Nevodian advanced menacingly on Elizabeth, who was now powerless to defend herself from him. Without the element of surprise, a slip of a girl wielding a stick would be no match for a fully trained Mage, no matter how much moxie she had.

He was running full tilt now; it was only short distance to where they faced one another. But majik was faster than he was and before Hope could reach them Nevodian had Elizabeth suspended in ropes of air, strangling the life out his victim by the simple expedient of lifting her into the air by the neck.

Calling fire with his majik, Hope summoned a fiery blade to his hand and in the same moment he ran Nevodian through with it, causing Elizabeth to drop to the ground, coughing as the Truthseeker's majik was dispelled.

"Missed me?"

The deep, slow voice that rumbled in Mirena's ear and sent shivers of disgust running through her as she felt the warm heaviness of his hand settle on the back of her neck in a possessive way.

Why? She felt her whole body shake with fear. *Why Dipaul?*

"That's a girl," Dipaul encouraged, his hot breath wafting against the side of her face as he breathed in the scent of her.

Mirena felt Dipaul's other arm reach around her, rubbing inconsiderately against her many burns as it ran down her body. She was powerless to stop him as she shook like a leaf, held in his grasp. She felt his breathing come a little quicker in excitement as he reached down to paw at her skirt with the hand that ended in a misshapen stump.

Fear driving her to boldness, Mirena ineffectively tried to push his arm away.

"Please, no..."

Though he couldn't possible have heard her across the distance, especially after Nevodian's deafening attack, Hope's head whipped around, his eyes locking onto hers. Panic filled Hope's expression as he took in that she was at Dipaul's mercy.

Moving his hand from the back of her neck to reach across her chest, Dipaul pinned Mirena to him, pressing himself up against her as he forced her to submit. His grin and the sounds of his panting told her exactly how much he was enjoying her struggle.

The pawing of his stump resumed, more forcefully now, as he fought to reach past Mirena's attempt to resist so he could both enjoy himself and put on a show for Hope.

*He's going to rape me...*Mirena concluded. *Right here and now. I wish I had died in that cave if it would have prevented this...*

"Please, I'll do what you want just let me go."

"Hear that, Tendro?" Dipaul asked, still grinning and leaning into Mirena's neck, running his tongue up the length of it. "She'll do whatever I want. Maybe when I'm done with her, you can have a turn, eh? For old time's sake?"

"Run, Hope...please," Mirena cried out. "I'm not worth it."

"Aww...how precious," Dipaul said sweetly in his thick voice, ignoring both Hope and Elizabeth in favor of tormenting her further, "too bad it's you that I want."

He ripped free the buttons on the collar of her dress before reaching down inside of it to get at her flesh.

"Let her go," Hope commanded. "Stop lying to her. This isn't about her; it's about you and me. You've had your fun."

Dipaul laughed, the sound sending shivers down Mirena's spine, but with that comment he suddenly stood straight, all his attention on Hope and his voice surprisingly losing all trace of its former slowness. "I haven't nearly 'had my fun' but you're right about one thing... 'Hope'...my fun can wait, this time."

With a suddenness that sent Mirena reeling, Dipaul tossed her aside, discarding her like a broken doll. She hit the ground hard, feeling something crack beneath her and a scream rip her throat as pain took hold of her.

Barely conscious and fighting hard to keep her eyes focused, Mirena watched Dipaul summon fire and send it hurtling after Hope, bright lines of flame burning in her blurry vision. Desperately wishing she could help Hope in some way, Mirena tried to reach for her majik, but she just didn't have it in her and the effort was enough to send her hurtling into unconsciousness, Hope's fate hanging in the balance.

XIII.

Mirena's eyes opened slowly to soft sunlight filtering in through curtained windows. Her skin felt tender and her body sore, especially her wrist and shoulder, as well as the right side of her face. She remembered the pain of the red-hot poker stabbing through her flesh and cutting deeply into her cheek, but it took her a moment to remember when and how she'd broken her wrist.

Dipaul, she recalled, *threw me to the ground so he could go after Hope…*

Hope!

Mirena sat up quickly and looked around herself in some confusion. It was just like the last time she'd been beaten and bloody. She was sore and weak, but her wounds were mended enough that she could move around if she wished. Hope, she noticed immediately, was asleep in a light blue wing-backed chair next to her bed, his head slumped forward.

He must have healed me, again…with his power.

Mirena pulled back the covers and swung her legs over the side of the bed quietly, so as not to disturb him. She set her feet on the ground, trying to steady herself. Standing, she took careful steps towards Hope, stopping right before his chair.

He saved me.

He is the kindest man I know, besides my father. I feel safe around him; at home, even... Would he mind if I kissed him right now?

He wouldn't even have to know if I was gentle enough because he's sleeping and even if he were awake, I don't think that words would be enough to express my gratitude to him. Every time I look at him my heart starts to beat faster and he's the first thing I think about when I have a thought to myself.

I'm going to do it, she decided, *this might be my only chance.*

Taking in a deep but quiet breath, Mirena leaned in intending to kiss Hope lightly on the forehead, but she paused.

No, that doesn't seem right...

This close to him, the nearness was intoxicating and Mirena knew that a simple kiss on the forehead wasn't going to be enough. If this was to be the only chance she got, then she wanted more.

She moved in closer, lowering her head and gently kissed him lightly on the lips, noticing only a beat too late that his eyes were fluttering open slowly.

Mirena pulled away quickly, her cheeks flushing with embarrassment, but Hope put his hand on hers where it rested on the arm of the chair he'd made for her room.

"I'm sorry," she whispered, mortified.

"Don't be," he said over top of her apology.

Mirena didn't know what to do; nothing like this had ever happened to her before, not that she hadn't always thought about it.

He's touching my hand, her mind supplied numbly.

Hope opened his mouth like he was going to say something but didn't and the two of them stared at one another for just a moment too long, the feelings in the air between them remaining unresolved.

Feeling pulled towards him, Mirena found that she couldn't stop thinking of the feeling of his lips on hers. She wanted to feel them again, even though she knew it was too much to hope for. Despite her better judgment, she leaned forward until their faces were breaths apart.

The door swung open with a slight whoosh, breaking the moment.

"Is she awake?" Elizabeth froze in the doorway, speechless for nearly a full second. "My, my," she said at last, a wide grin breaking out, "so the good guy really does get the girl."

Instinctively Mirena raised her arm and with sudden motion the air in the room rose to do her bidding, forcing the door shut on Elizabeth as Mirena's face flushed an even deeper scarlet.

"Okay, okay, I get the message!" Elizabeth called brazenly through the door. "Don't need to paint me a picture! Just don't get too wild in there, I wouldn't want Hopey to lose his concentration and kick us out of here in a particularly vulnerable moment!"

"That's enough, Elizabeth," Hope admonished calmly, but loud enough to be heard through the door.

Mirena covered her face in embarrassment and then it hit her. *What is wrong with me? I kissed a man who is engaged to someone else.*

Caralain...

"I shouldn't have done that, please forgive me," Mirena said softly, "I don't know what's wrong with me..."

Hope met her eyes searchingly for a moment. "Nothing is wrong with you, Mira. You may lack a little bit of finesse, but you had the right idea using wind on the door like that."

He smiled, meaning his expression to be encouraging.

Hope doesn't know that I know...about his fiancée, Mirena recalled.

"Don't worry though, I can teach you. Some, at least," he continued. "I think it's better that you are prepared if something like this happens again. What we're doing...it isn't safe."

Should I really be someone to trust with majik? Mirena questioned, feeling somewhat distracted caught between what they should be talking about and what they were. *What if I hurt someone again?*

"I know what you're thinking," Hope said quickly, not letting her get too far down her current line of thought, "but trust me, you'll be a far bigger danger to yourself and others if you remain untrained. Majik is instinctual in some people, as it is in you. When you are hurt, angry or scared it can act with a will of its own. Surely, you've noticed that?"

Mirena nodded as she considered his words, pulling away from him to think more clearly. *I want to kiss him again…but all I keep thinking about is Caralain staring at me through the crowd in the market square and Stiphy's face in the ashes…over and over again.*

"Hey," Hope said gently, leaning forward in his chair, "are you all right? I'm not pushing you too quickly, am I? To learn majik, I mean."

"We should just figure out the next move we are going to make," she said, changing the subject away from majik and her feelings for Hope entirely. "I just don't want to think about what happened. I might say or do something that will make things…never mind."

"Okay," he agreed cautiously. "I understand and I won't pressure you. If you decide you want to talk to me, I'll be here. And listen; before we go down and talk things over with Elizabeth, I just want you to know that I'm very sorry about what happened to you." His voice caught, as if the emotions were difficult for him to face. "I wasn't prepared…I mean, it shouldn't have happened the way it did and I will do my best to make sure that it doesn't happen again. You deserve better."

I can't do this right now… Her mind recoiled from thinking about the trauma she'd lived through so recently.

"I believe in what we're doing, but even without this cause of ours, the Panarch would have eventually found out that Elizabeth had a twin," Mirena spoke in an emotionless voice, her words the simple, ugly truth that she was just beginning to realize. "I would have had this happen to me anyway or something like it. It would probably have been worse, because at least this way you were there to save me…"

She turned from him then and headed to the door, her hand gripping the cold metal handle, "I should be the least of your concerns, truly."

She left him there like that, letting herself out the door and down the stairs to where Elizabeth waited near the bottom, pretending not to snoop. Mirena had only just brushed past her sister without a word being spoken when Hope joined them on the stairs, no sign on his face of what he'd thought of Mirena's words or her lips on his earlier.

"Mirena's raised a good point," Hope mentioned, addressing the both of them with a businesslike air, "we should probably consider our next course of action. Where we should go and what steps we can take that won't get us killed, but might help our cause."

"That's a tall order," Elizabeth snorted.

Mirena ignored them both in favour of making her way to the couch. They might not know where to go or what needed doing, but she did. She'd thought about rebellion since she was a child and first learned of the way people like her were treated by everyone else.

And, she'd heard the legends.

"The Temple of the Light."

There was a place that still held the belief that the Creator was the rightful god of this world and the Destroyer was something to be reviled, not worshipped. It was a place Mirena had only heard of in stories, mostly from her father, but she knew that it existed, if not exactly where it was.

It was said that followers of the Light would make pilgrimages to the Temple to prove their faith. A pilgrimage such as that would have to be done in secret for most, but it could be done if one was brave enough to make the journey.

"What?" Elizabeth questioned as she and Hope convened around the couch and Hope took up a seat on the chair nearby.

"I've always wanted to go," Mirena confided in them with a shrug of her shoulders, "ever since father told me about it."

"Tell us," Hope instructed. "I've heard of the Avatar and the prophecy that says he will come and free the Creator from her prison, everyone has, but I didn't know that any holy places still existed. I would have assumed that the Panarch would have wiped them out to solidify his rule."

He believes in me and takes what I say seriously. He wants the same things as I do, Mirena realized. *I just can't be around him right now, because every time he talks to me I fall more and more in love with him...*

I can't do that to her...to Caralain, even if I don't know her. I can't be that girl.

Her thoughts flared with anger, more at herself than Hope, but the emotions all tangled so she didn't know who to blame. Inside her head, she raged silently, but her inner turmoil showed. No matter how she might want to she was no longer able to keep the confused bundle of emotions from her face. She had been through too much and it had all been because of Hope.

"Mirena?" Hope questioned, leaning forward to check on her.

"Just go away!" She told him, throwing up her hands and forcing him to back off with the force of her rejection. "Go away! I can't...it's too much. I just can't, okay?"

Hope and Elizabeth shared a meaningful look and then Hope stood up and put his hands up in defeat, nodding to Elizabeth as he exited from the room. Elizabeth, taking this as her cue, stepped forward and took a seat on the couch next to Mirena.

"Hey, Mira," she said softly, putting an arm around her sister's shoulders with a sympathetic motion, "why are you being such a bitch?"

"Go fuck yourself," Mirena responded uncharacteristically caustic, taking a page from her sister's book.

"Hey, let's not be nasty," Elizabeth admonished, "that's my job. You suck at it, anyways."

"Who's Caralain?" Mirena demanded without warning.

"What? How the hell should I know," Elizabeth began and then paused, some sort of recognition dawning in her eyes. "Wait, no, I do know that name...why do you ask?"

"He's engaged," Mirena stated bluntly, but the simple admittance of the fact brought everything crashing down on her and the tears began to fall.

"Oh, honey," Elizabeth murmured, wrapping both her arms around Mirena and holding her tightly, rocking her gently back and forth. "You poor naive little thing..."

"He couldn't even tell me himself...they used it against me, the Truthseekers."

"Shh," Elizabeth hushed her, "it's over now...we got you back and they can't hurt you anymore."

"Are you not listening?" Mirena accused, her voice rising despite herself. "I don't care what they did to hurt me, I care what Hope did to hurt me!"

"Mirena!" Elizabeth snapped to get Mirena's attention and then held her sister's gaze with intense eyes. "Have you even considered that maybe he chose this? Chose you? She's not here, is she? This Caralain person? She's not here hiding out with him when he's running from everything he's ever known; you are. You're the one he saved. You're the one he was frantic to find."

"Maybe he hasn't mentioned Caralain because he left her in his past, just like everything else he's given up to make your dreams come true," Elizabeth fell silent, her sincerity spent.

It happened like this sometimes, her sister showing her heart seemed to exhaust her, like letting her feelings out was harder on her then keeping them safely hidden.

"I can't be that girl..." Mirena answered quietly, defeated. "I kissed him...he's engaged and you only become engaged when you're serious about being with that person. It's a commitment and a significant one. Especially with what I know of Hope, he wouldn't make a decision like that lightly." She shook her head. "I... love him, Elizabeth. I love him and I'm afraid I've fallen too deep."

"Then tell him," Elizabeth responded just as quietly. "If he's as good a person as you seem to think he is, then he'll understand and he'll fix it." She stopped and considered, her old personality returning to her expression as her mouth lifted at the corners. "Or he'll toss you aside like a used rag, but then at least you'll know, right?"

Mirena couldn't help but smile; she knew her sister too well. "Thanks for the advice, Bethwee."

"No problem, Miracle," Elizabeth returned with an exaggeratedly sweet and innocent smile. "Now go find your Hope and tell him you think he's the sexiest man alive."

"I'll be sure to do that," she replied sarcastically with a roll of her eyes; a hint of Mirena's personality returning as well.

"I'm serious!" Elizabeth called to her back as Mirena headed for the stairs to confront Hope. "It works every time!"

Mirena made her way up the stairs, her heart thudding in her chest and her steps unsteady with nervousness she hadn't expected to feel so strongly.

It's just Hope's room. She told herself. *I've been in this hallway more than a few times...I mean, my room is just across the hall.*

Still, she couldn't help the butterflies that danced in her stomach or the nervous flutter of her thoughts. All too soon she was at his door, knocking on the solid wood and not having thought of a single thing to say.

Hope opened the door immediately, not giving her any further chances to reconsider her boldness in confronting him.

"I... umm..." Mirena's words dissolved into useless sounds as she tried to force herself to spit out something, anything. "I think you're the sexiest man alive..." She spluttered and then realized what had just escaped her lips. "Damn you, Elizabeth..."

"Excuse me?" Hope questioned, shocked and confused by her words, his eyes widening.

"Elizabeth made...said...it was her idea," Mirena dissembled. "I just..."

Hope smiled then, his whole face suddenly filling with mirth. "I don't care if Elizabeth put you up to it," he said, grinning, "it's the best news I've heard all day."

"What?"

The grin stayed on Hope's face and Mirena couldn't tell if he was simply making fun of her for what Elizabeth had gotten her to say, or if he meant every word. "If you truly think that...then I'm pleased to hear it, even if it came out in such a strange way."

"What are we talking about?" Mirena asked, feeling lost and overwhelmed.

Hope smiled; his expression softening as he took a step toward her in the open doorway.

"This," he answered, putting an arm gently around her waist and pulling her close as he leaned down to reach her mouth with a warm and deliberate kiss.

Mirena melted into his arms as her nervousness evaporated in the warmth of his acceptance.

XIV.

"Oh look, another pile of rocks..." Elizabeth commented dryly, kicking an offending pebble with her foot. "This pilgrimage sure is fascinating; where will we go next? To a field with a tree in it where monks used to sit and talk to themselves about how great the Creator is?"

"Shh, Elizabeth," Mirena cautioned, "it's not safe to talk like that. The Pilgrimage is a well-kept secret."

"Yeah," Elizabeth agreed wryly, "so secret that there doesn't seem to be a trail to follow anymore. It's been three days of non-stop hopping from desiccated ruins to boring little towns. Are either of you even sure that this place actually exists anymore? Maybe the Panarch really did wipe it out like he did the rest of these old temples."

Mirena gave her sister a quelling look, but Hope wasn't certain that Elizabeth was wrong. He wanted to believe that somewhere there might be people who would be on their side if they knew what he'd become. Unfortunately, every place they had visited and every lead they had followed had only led them to sites of ruined stone temples and old villages that had been burned to the ground sometime within the last couple of centuries.

"I know Magi live a long time but I didn't think that Terrence Lee had been around that long. I thought he was born in Maredon, like Elizabeth and I. That can't have been too long before we were born," Mirena noted, half to herself, "but most of these places have lain in ruins for a hundred years or more."

"He hasn't," Hope confirmed from where he knelt near a pile of still-standing stones that had once formed an ornately-carved temple wall. "Most of this destruction was put into motion long before Terrence Lee came into power. The Panarch then was just as bad as Terrence is now and the one before him was even worse, or so I hear. We've had a long line of terrible rulers.

"Depending on your perspective of course," he added, considering the issue from all sides. "I mean, to some, Terrence Lee and others like him have brought a lot of stability to our government and there's been a lot of progress too."

"Oh great, now we get a history lesson," Elizabeth sighed, her hands on her hips and her foot tapping impatiently. "Can we go now?"

"Wait, I think I've found something," Hope informed them, staring intently at the faded writing he could barely make out on the stone wall before him. "I know that symbol..."

"What is it?" Mirena asked, joining him.

"See here," he traced the carving that had once been part of a much larger inscription, "there are symbols and writing here, though it is much too faded to read and parts of it are missing. What bits I can make out, I recognize from the Prophecy of the Light; the one that tells us about the Avatar."

"Is there a point to this discovery?" Elizabeth demanded pointedly from where she stood, having no desire to join them in the rubble.

Hope grinned, standing and dusting himself off. "Why yes, as a matter of fact there is. I know where the Temple of the Light is...if it still stands, then we can be there in no time at all."

Helping Mirena to her feet and safely over the piles of loose rocks around them to join Elizabeth, Hope led the girls back to the Sentinal Stones. This stone circle, otherwise identical to the others they had visited, stood atop a platform of naturally formed stone, instead of upon a hill or in a forest clearing.

He had been using the Sentinal Stones to get them from place to place; relying on the strange power the Creator had gifted him with would only mark him for what he was and he wasn't quite sure he was ready for the world to find out about him yet. Not only that, but travel was difficult and uncertain when you didn't know where you were going and Hope had never heard of some of the places they had journeyed to, let alone knew them well enough to bring the three of them there using any form of majik.

Within the stone circle Elizabeth and Mirena regarded him as if waiting for an explanation of their next destination, but Hope merely held up a finger to forestall them, visually searching the central pillar for the symbol he wanted.

There it is, he located the carved symbol of a mostly eclipsed sun, halfway up from the base of the pillar. *I knew I'd seen that symbol somewhere before. It's to somewhere in this realm, though it's not a place I've ever been to.*

I guess it's time I went.

Drawing on his majik, he activated the Sentinal Stones and the scenery changed around them with no sense of transition between one place and the next. Hope smiled, taking in the sparse vegetation and the rocky outcroppings that now surrounded them. He remembered his first few times travelling by way of the stones and how long it had taken him to wrap his head around crossing that kind of distance instantaneously.

His reminiscing lasted only a moment before he really registered what he was looking at and realized that the broken and uneven terrain around them was really just the remains of yet another temple. Only this time, it wasn't just some site on the route of the pilgrimage of the Light. This was *the* Temple, the one they'd hoped to find still standing and waiting to welcome them; it really had been reduced to rubble like the others.

"Impressive," Elizabeth noted, looking around herself, her tone at odds with her words. "It looks so...exactly the same as every other ruin we've come across."

"You know Elizabeth, your attitude is not helping us at all. In fact you're starting to upset me now," Mirena told her sister.

Hope felt as if the weight of all of his decisions was trying to crush him. He'd been a fool to allow himself to think that there was some last bastion of the Light still standing defiant to the Panarch and ways of the Destroyer. There wasn't, of course; it had all been a foolish man's dream, a way to justify his own rebellion against the man he used to serve…

…with Caralain.

In a way, this all comes back to her…

Am I so afraid of commitment that I'm willing to go to such lengths to avoid admitting that I made a mistake? No, Hope told himself firmly, *no matter what excuses I made, she'd never accept me as I am now. She'd likely kill me on sight, or worse bring me straight to Terrence and denounce me as the traitor I am. Even more foolish than this hopeless cause of mine would be to trust Caralain with my life again.*

"...I know we will find something if we just keep looking," Mirena was saying, deep in an argument with Elizabeth's pessimism. "It's not supposed to be easy, so don't just give up when it gets hard."

"Something?" Elizabeth questioned scornfully. "What exactly are you looking for, Mira? Because if it's more rocks, then congratulations! You've found them!"

"I don't know, Elizabeth," Mirena replied, throwing up her hands in a frustrated fashion, "a temple, a sign from the Creator, anything!"

Hope considered interrupting them, but as it turned out he didn't have to. Not more than twenty feet ahead of them a robed and hooded figure darted between two pillars of stone a little too quickly and slipped in the rubble, making enough noise to startle the girls out of their heated discussion.

He dashed forward, partly out of concern for whoever it was that had fallen, but also because he wanted to confirm what this place was before it had fallen into such a sorry state. Hope managed to keep his footing on the loose, debris-covered cobblestones, having gotten a lot of experience navigating old ruins in the past couple of days. Mirena was right behind him as he reached the place where the figure had fallen.

The person, a frazzled-looking young brunette, was still there and she was ignoring a purple bruise rapidly developing on the ankle she had twisted in her fall. She was frantically tried to scoop up loose sheets of paper covered on both sides in cursive writing in a dark black ink, muttering under her breath as she did so.

"No, no, no..."

"Are you all right?" Hope asked, holding out a hand to the woman to help her up.

She looked up sharply, her expression betraying surprise and inexplicably, fear. Her mouth dropped open and it took her a moment to collect her thoughts.

"Um, no...I mean, yes. I'm fine, thank you for asking," she answered, not reaching for Hope's hand or acknowledging the gesture.

"Here, let me help you," Mirena offered politely, reaching down for one of the pages littering the floor.

"No! Don't touch that–" the woman began, but it was too late, Mirena's hand had already made contact with the thick parchment and a strange thing began to happen.

"What the hell?" Elizabeth asked no one in particular as she arrived and Hope found that for once he shared her sentiment. As he watched open-mouthed, the words seemed to crawl off the page and up Mirena's arm.

Looking horrified, Mirena dropped the paper abruptly and drew her hand back but it didn't seem to stop whatever process she had inadvertently begun. The words gained speed now and flew off the page. And not just the one, either, the ink from the other pages was running now, too. The whole mess of cursive script flowed through the air intent on the one who had awakened the majik within them.

"What's happening?!" Mirena demanded, her voice panicked, as she unsuccessfully tried to recoil from the phenomenon.

This is no majik I've ever seen, Hope thought, awed and more than a little concerned.

He looked to the woman who'd been carrying the documents for an answer, but by her expression this wasn't something she had been expecting either.

"What's going on?" He asked her, putting himself in the woman's line of sight and forcing her to acknowledge him. "Can you stop this?"

She shook her head mutely. "It's the prophecy..." she whispered, her tone filled with wonder.

"What prophecy?" Hope demanded, but before she could answer his eye caught the last line of the writing as it, too, flew through the air towards Mirena and the words told him everything he wanted to know.

"...And he shall be the key to the Creator's prison, the chosen one; the Avatar of the Light."

"No..." Hope gasped, but the moment was broken as usual by Elizabeth who erupted into a fit of giggles, clutching her sides as she doubled over laughing.

"At least now the Panarch will be able to tell us apart!"

"Stop laughing and help me!" Mirena shouted, alarmed.

She was waving her arms about and doing whatever she could to try to wipe the words from her skin, crying in frustration when nothing seemed to have any effect.

"Shhh, Mira, it's okay," Hope tried to sound comforting, wrapping his arms around her and trying to still her frantic motions. "We'll get this fixed. I'm sure that even if she doesn't know how to do it herself, she'll be able to take us to someone who does."

The woman in question looked extremely uncomfortable as she hesitantly rose to her feet, careful not to put too much weight on her injured ankle. "This is rather an...unusual situation," she said in a mild understatement. "I'm not sure..."

"Well, then start thinking, because this writing being seen by the wrong eyes could easily get her killed," Hope snapped, not sparing anyone's feelings. "Her life is already in danger as it is."

The woman nodded. "Yes, you're right," she agreed, "I suppose there's nothing for it then; you'll have to come with me. I know...a safe place."

Hope nodded his agreement and Elizabeth immediately sobered.

"You mean to tell me what after all that, you two fools have actually done it? You really managed to trick someone into revealing the location of the Temple of the Light? Damn..." Elizabeth smiled and the giggles threatened to resume. "I guess you got your sign, Mira."

"That's not funny, Elizabeth," Hope warned.

"My name is Jesabel," the woman identified herself with a resigned grimace. "Since you already know where we're going, I suppose there is no real point in being discreet. I'll be reprimanded for this, anyways."

"Not today, Jesabel," Elizabeth informed her with enthusiasm. "Hopey here is your golden ticket!"

"What is she talking about?" Jesabel asked.

"You'll find out soon enough," Hope told her, his expression wry. "Come on, I'll help you walk. Mira, can you get the papers? I think they've already done all they can to you..."

Mirena frowned, staring at the blank papers at her feet with disapproval. "I think that Elizabeth should get them," she muttered peevishly through clenched teeth. "You never know, she might just get a *sign* as well."

"It's too bad for you that I have a natural born aversion to manual labour," Elizabeth countered in an offhand manner, increasing her pace to catch up to Hope and Jesabel and leaving Mirena to the task that had been assigned to her.

Jesabel led them in a roundabout route between free-standing pillars, piles of rubble and around half-destroyed walls and caved-in sections of cobblestone streets. She never seemed to follow what anyone would dare call a path, but even still she seemed to know her way. Before long she stopped and gestured ahead of her.

"I should probably go in first, so I do not raise alarm," Jesabel told them with a concerned frown. "The entrance is only wide enough for one at a time, but I thank you for your assistance in getting me this far."

Hope nodded, letting her go and wincing in sympathy as she tested putting weight on her twisted ankle. Keeping close behind her in case she should fall again or need his support, he followed her to a particularly high vine-covered wall where she abruptly disappeared, slipping through a crack he would never had noticed if she hadn't led him directly to it.

"Do we even know if she is coming back for us, or could she be setting up a trap?" Mirena questioned as she and Elizabeth caught up to where Hope had stopped to wait for them.

"Are you that suspicious, Mira?" Hope countered with a smile, trying to put her at ease. "We found her, remember? It would be a pretty poorly-planned ambush if it involved someone like Jesabel genuinely injuring themselves like that."

"So are you saying that this would be beyond something that Dipaul would set up? I mean, he does like to play with his victims..." she retorted, defensively.

"She's got you there, Hopey."

He forced himself to smile reassuringly, but on the inside Hope knew that Mirena had good reason to be worried. She had suffered too much already at Dipaul's hands or because of his wishes or the Panarch's.

"I think we're a little outside of Dipaul's jurisdiction right now," he said aloud. "Trying to fool us is exactly what he would do, but creating a fake Temple to the Light all the way out here seems somewhat far-fetched. We can also probably safely assume that none of the Generals know what our plans are or that we'd be trying to search out this place. Until you mentioned it, Mira, it's honestly not something I would have even considered."

"Whatever you say," Mirena agreed, sounding unconvinced but dropping the issue for now, even though it was obvious that she wasn't going to forget about it.

Hope sighed but was saved from having to respond by Jesabel's hand waving out at them from the crack in the wall.

"Hopey?"

He groaned, but Elizabeth's renewed laughter showed what she thought of her oh-so-clever nickname for him spreading past the three of them.

Hope shook his head. *I suppose it's better that I have a pseudonym than use my real name here, anyway,* he thought.

"Coming…" he answered, "and it's Hope, not 'Hopey'."

"Sorry," Jesabel apologized as he reached her side and she made room for him to slip between where two parts of the wall almost met at a right angle, "I suppose I should have asked."

"That's perfectly all right," Hope allowed, giving her a friendly smile. "I can see how this might be an unusual circumstance."

Jesabel nodded. "We don't get many travelers anymore, no. I trust the three of you will be discreet?" She added, taking in Elizabeth and Mirena as they squeezed through the entrance to join them.

"Like we have a choice," Elizabeth commented. "Knowing this place exists is practically a death sentence."

"Yes, well..." Jesabel agreed uncomfortably. "Come, I'll take you to the Mother. Considering this," she gestured to Mirena and the prophecy that now covered her skin from the neck down, "she'll want to discuss some things with you immediately."

"Are you sure you can lead us there?" Hope asked. "With your ankle like that?"

"I'll manage," she grimaced.

"Here, let me help," he offered and taking a moment to concentrate he activated the power that he had been gifted by the Creator.

I'm not showing off; I really can help her, Hope rationalized. *And besides, I'm sure these people are going to want proof that I'm the Avatar and there is no better way to give them that.*

The ring on the chain around his neck, the one engraved with the word that had given him his new name, flared to life with an intense white light and from his hands shone a power that was nothing like the majik that people were used to seeing. Healing with majik was possible, but difficult, and it was nothing like this; he could make a wound seem like it had never existed.

"Oh," Jesabel gasped, moving her ankle about tentatively, her expression awed. "Oh my...I didn't truly think..." she met his eyes. "You really are the Avatar, aren't you?"

"I'm afraid so," Hope agreed with a slight grimace.

And whether I want to be or not, I suppose this makes me the person that you've all been waiting for...

Mirror's Hope

XV.

"You really are the Avatar, aren't you?" Mirena repeated in a mocking whisper, having fallen behind with Elizabeth as Jesabel led Hope further into the Temple of the Light and conversing softly with him in a manner that was clearly meant to imply that Mirena wasn't included.

"Jealousy is unbecoming, Mira," Elizabeth reminded her pointedly.

Mirena glowered, knowing she was being childish, but her pride was too hurt to do anything to change the way she was acting. Ahead of them Jesabel laughed at something Hope said to her, throwing her perfect oval face back so that the sun glinted upon her fair skin as she placed a hand lightly on Hope's arm.

Desperate to look anywhere but at the way Jesabel was throwing herself at Hope, Mirena found herself studying the courtyard and the people within it instead.

There were a fair number of people in the courtyard but a large majority of them kept to themselves, or at best they gathered in small groups of one of two adults and their children. A few were dressed as Jesabel was in light coloured robes of grey or beige. These walked quickly, crossing the courtyard and largely ignoring the people they passed as they headed to or from the still-standing parts of the sprawling temple building.

Of those who weren't in robes, however, the clothing could only be described as shabby or at best, well-worn. They huddled in on themselves, what meager possessions they had arrayed about them and their expressions were as desperate as their clothing.

As Mirena watched, a flurry of white-robed individuals swarmed out of an opening in the temple, a basket or steaming pot carried between every two of them.

"Seems like dinner time," Elizabeth noted, watching the newcomers. "I wonder if being Sympathizers means they'll want to share, I'm starving."

Typically Mirena would have risen to the bait and been scandalized by her sister's casual way of insulting those around her while still in their hearing, but instead she found herself without words as she realized what exactly she was watching.

The desperate people with their worn clothing and hungry children were reaching out gratefully for the meager offerings they were granted by the temple acolytes. As each person was handed a small bowl of soup or bit of bread they showered thanks upon those who showed them kindness, and Mirena could make out a chorus of "Thank the Creator" and "May the Light bless you."

The truth hit her with the force of a blow to her midsection.

The Temple of Light wasn't a place of equality and freedom, nor was it a center of philosophy and learning. It was a shelter and these people were refugees from the ongoing yet silent war against the will of the Panarch.

Yes, the acolytes of the temple were being kind to those they sheltered within this secret haven, but these were refugees, not rebels. These people were hiding from the Panarch and his Generals, not preparing to stand against them or living their lives in defiance of his rule.

"Mira, you can gawk like a tourist later, we're going inside," Elizabeth called and Mirena realized that she'd stopped halfway along the courtyard while her sister, not to mention Hope and Jesabel, had gone on without her.

Inside the temple was a little more like what Mirena had been expecting to find, but the sight of the people outside had left her with a feeling of unease. Everyone in here wore robes like Jesabel's, either in grey like hers, beige or occasionally white. These people were going about their daily tasks and a number of them stopped to stare at the group of them as they passed.

To her displeasure, most of the stares were directed at Mirena herself. They weren't the gazes of people curious about newcomers; they were scandalized and staring open-mouthed at the way the prophecy swirled darkly on her exposed skin.

They are staring at me like I don't belong... Mira thought, bitterness welling within her at the familiar feeling. *This is the one place where they should accept me with no reservations, even marked as I am.*

Jesabel and Hope had already reached the small room they were headed to by the time Mirena caught up and Elizabeth waved her in, looking impatient.

"He is the Avatar of the Light, Mother," Jesabel was saying as Mirena entered. "It's not a trick, I promise you. He healed me with power granted to him by the Creator out in the courtyard and there were at least a dozen witnesses to the miracle."

The Mother of the Temple was a young-seeming woman with long, honey-blond hair loose about her shoulders who wore a floor-length sky blue robe. She stood upon hearing Jesabel's words and taking in the strangers in her midst, revealing a lengthy figure and a confident bearing.

"This is a serious claim, daughter," she stated cautiously. "I know you are not one prone to exaggeration, but regardless this matter will need to be investigated thoroughly."

"Yes, Mother," Jesabel agreed.

"How do I prove that I am the Avatar?" Hope asked.

His question was addressed to the Mother, but she was not paying attention to him. Instead her serene gaze slipped by him to where Mirena stood and her eyes went slightly wide in astonishment.

"I think we may have all the proof we need right here..." the Mother noted, the controlled tone she'd used until now wavering somewhat.

Taking a few steps past Hope, the Mother approached Mirena and without waiting for permission simply took hold of her right arm and brought it to her face where she could inspect it more closely. Shocked by the sudden attention, Mirena said nothing as she looked from the Mother's intent expression to the line of prophecy she was reading on her arm.

She, once marked, shall name him Avatar and in so doing shall name herself, Prophet.

Mirena opened her mouth to ask what the meaning of this was, when the Mother stopped her with a long finger across her lips.

"Now, don't talk," she told her, a warning note in her voice. "You wouldn't want to spoil the effect."

"Excus-" Mirena began, affronted.

"Shh," the Mother interrupted her. "It is imperative that you await the proper time. I will gather the People of the Light together so that as many as possible can hear your announcement and know for themselves the truth of your words."

"So you believe me then?" Hope asked. "That I'm the Avatar of the Light?"

"It's the Prophecy," Jesabel explained, "the Mother reads some wisdom in it that the rest of us would not understand."

Elizabeth leaned over so she could see past the Mother to the particular line that had drawn so much attention. "It says Mira's going to tell all those fools out there that Hopey's their Chosen One...seems pretty self-explanatory to me."

Cheers erupted in the crowded auditorium, filling Hope's ears and drowning out anything he might have wanted to say to these people. Some of them must have seen the power he could wield when he'd used it in the courtyard, but most of them could only have heard about it from others.

Yet still, they believed.

The smiles on the faces of the people he passed were filled with hope. Their arms reached out as he passed, trying to touch some piece of him; his clothes, his skin, anything to confirm that he was real and had come to them at last.

These people, hidden refugees and pilgrims more than a secret rebellious force, had waited long years for the Avatar of the Light to be revealed to them and fulfill his destiny.

Now, somehow, impossibly, he was here.

But am I what they've been waiting for? Hope questioned silently as he made his way through the crowd, not sure whether to acknowledge these people and their faith in him or not. *I may have seen the Creator...at least I think I did, but that in itself doesn't make me a hero, does it?*

Whether he agreed or not, to these people he represented their hopes and dreams for a better world, a place of freedom and tolerance where they could openly worship the Creator without persecution.

"As the Mother," the Mother of the Temple began speaking, addressing the crowd, and the clamoring audience stilled to a sudden and reverent silence, "it is my duty to watch and wait for the Avatar of the Light to come to us and be revealed.

"This day, Acolyte Jesabel has brought me news of your arrival," she continued, turning to Hope, but still speaking for the benefit of the onlookers. "Though her words were brief, her account gives me faith that you are indeed the Creator's Chosen, as you claim. Further proof is, of course, necessary, but I also heard that you travel with the Prophet of the Light. If she could validate your claim, then all our worries would be put to rest in that regard and you would have our full support behind you."

Hope found himself lost in the melodious nature of her words until she paused and he realized that there had been a request of some sort in her speech.

"Yes, of course," he answered. "Whatever test you deem necessary would be fine."

"And the Prophet?" The Mother questioned. "Would she be willing to stand witness for you?"

"The Prophet?" Hope repeated, struggling to keep up and feeling slightly overwhelmed by all the attention.

"Me," Mirena said forcefully, surprising him with her brazenness as she pointing at her chest and spoke up despite the Mother's insistence that she remain silent. "I'm the one who is supposed to announce that you're the Avatar of the Light."

There was a collective gasp from the crowd at Mirena's words and at the way light shot forth from her arm; the writing there glowing fiercely white for a moment. Mirena stared down at her own arm in shocked disbelief and as the glow faded so too did the words on her skin, becoming dull and grey as opposed to the dark black ink that marred the rest of her.

Hope couldn't read the faded text from where he stood, but it wasn't lost on him that something significant had just happened and every single soul in the room knew it.

*That explains why I was sent to her, then...*Hope realized. *She's the Prophet; she's just as much a part of this as I am. I'm not sure exactly what happened the night I freed the Creator, but Mirena was there; I'm sure of it, even if she doesn't remember.*

"*She, once marked, shall name him Avatar!*" The Mother raised her arms above her head as she exclaimed and those gathered erupted in a cheer that drowned everything out save for the overwhelming sense of elation that the Creator had at last sent the People of the Light the savior they had been waiting for.

"Hope?" Mirena called out, trying to be heard over the throng, "Hope!"

She strained to catch sight of Hope as the crowd surged forward and Mirena was lost in a current of people whose only concern was touching some part of the hero that had been promised to them and confirming his reality for themselves.

He was still where he had been standing before, on the dais between the Mother and Jesabel, who held onto his arm possessively, falsely claiming that she had discovered him first.

That should be me up there, with Hope, Mirena thought bitterly, as her view of Hope was lost once more. *She's trying to take my place and they're all just helping her to push me aside.*

As if her thoughts were as much prophecy as that on her skin, Mirena was physically pushed aside, the followers of the Light swarming around her and treating her with as little regard as Hope had shown her since he'd taken up with 'Acolyte Jesabel.'

"You're the Prophet, aren't you?" Someone asked to her left, grabbing hold of her hand to steady her before the jostling of bodies could knock her over. He was young and fit, with broad shoulders beneath his white robe that hinted at a well-muscled form. "That was you up there with the Avatar?"

"Yes," Mirena answered, feeling pleased that someone had finally taken notice of her.

"You travelled with him here, right," the man continued, fiery zeal in his youthful eyes as he looked past her to where Hope stood on the dais. "What is he like? Does he intend to free the Creator and bring Light to the world... wait, what am I saying? Of course he does; he's the Avatar."

"Don't you mean that he will lead the followers of the Light to rise up against the Panarch, bringing light back into the world by defeating him and freeing them from his tyranny?" Mirena questioned, caught off guard by the intensity of his demeanor.

"Lead us?" The man replied, facing her once more, his green eyes shining with fervor beneath dark brows. "Of course the Avatar will lead us, but he can only do so by showing us the will of the Creator and how to live in the Light. Surely you don't think that we will *fight* the Panarch?"

"You can't expect to be free when you have done nothing to save yourselves!" Mirena exclaimed, feeling incredulous. "You can't just leave it all to Hope while you all sit by and watch him fight on your behalf."

"But he is the Avatar, is he not?" The young man questioned with a look of absolute incomprehension on his features. His words were filled with the polite tones of reason, but the words themselves were as nonsensical as any Mirena had ever heard. "He has the might of the Creator on his side. Surely she will not allow him to fail and see her people destitute."

Mirena couldn't believe what she was hearing but there was no more chance to argue further as she and the nameless Sympathizer were separated once more by the human current. She scanned the crowd, trying to find him again with her eyes, but to her horror she found that each and every person in the large and crowded auditorium had the same vapid and zealous expression plastered on their face.

They had blind faith; it was not logic or even conviction driving them. These were not a people ready to fight for their freedom or even the concept of it. They were just waiting for their 'Chosen one' to fight and die for them and leave them with a world they didn't have to make for themselves because of a promise from the Creator.

A promise the Creator had embedded into her very skin, forcing her to accept her role as if it wasn't a choice, but a responsibility.

Before long, Mirena found herself inexplicably back out in the hallway that led in to the massive auditorium. She was alone, save for Elizabeth, who strode calmly out of the doors as they slammed shut behind her with the finality of a dismissal.

According to the Temple of the Light and its followers, her part in this was done.

Mirror's Hope

XVI.

"Are you fucking kidding me?!" Mirena demanded, unable to control the feelings that welled within her and needing an outlet for her sudden outrage.

How dare he do that to me?

The closed massive double-doors to the audience chamber left her and Elizabeth stuck out in the hall while the followers of the Light greeted their long-awaited Avatar.

It was my dream to come here, not Hope's!

I found him, I helped him, I brought him here and proved he is the Avatar of the Light to these people and I'm treated like I'm no more than his baggage! I am covered in the Prophecy of the Light and yet somehow that makes me invisible compared to him. How is that fair?

"Well..." Elizabeth began, uncharacteristically hesitant, "it looks like Hope's going to be a while...did you want to," she gestured around herself vaguely, "you know...take a look around? We could...I dunno, break stuff?" She finished somewhat lamely.

"What makes you think I would do something like that?"

"Okay, suit yourself," Elizabeth shrugged, "but you're going to have to let that anger out somehow and with all those Light-crazed fanatics going all gooey-eyed over Hope, I gather you're not going to be able give him a piece of your mind anytime soon."

"Anger?" Mirena repeated; her words filled with sarcasm. "What reason would I possibly have to be angry with him right now? It's not like he's decided to be with that woman to fulfill his destiny while we're left out here, discarded and forgotten about…"

"Well, don't let me stop you, then." Elizabeth put her hands up in a defensive position. "You've obviously got some issues. Go on and get it all out."

"This was my dream, Elizabeth, and he's taking it for himself!" Mirena exclaimed. "And he was flirting with her, that Jesabel. Did you see the way he looked at her and then healed her with his power from the Creator? That's what he did for me, before."

"Yeah, you're right," Elizabeth nodded. "So, what are you going to do about it?"

Mirena stopped, collecting herself as she considered her sister's question very seriously for a moment.

Hope can gather his forces together here on his own. I wish him luck doing so, but I really think that the best way to beat Terrence Lee at his game is by using his own tactics against him. These people are going to be of no use, we need real help.

"We should go and leave him here to his 'Destiny'."

Elizabeth's eyes widened. "Seriously? I have to admit that's not the response I expected."

"What did you expect, then?"

"Anything but that I guess," Elizabeth answered. "Most girls as besotted as you obviously are would want to fight for him, or get revenge or something. You've always been odd, though."

"Well, if he wants to be with me, then he can come find me when he is ready."

"If we leave, where would you want to go? Home doesn't seem the safest place anymore and we certainly can't go back to our lives in the Capital," Elizabeth pointed out. "This thing between you and Hope has certainly led us pretty far afield."

The Mirror World, Mirena realized. *The people there are as good as the ones here are evil. If I go there will the Terrence Lee help me defeat his Mirror? He would know how to do it... he might be the only one who can.*

"The Mirror World," Mirena informed Elizabeth decisively. "We can get our own help there while he works his majik here."

Her sister looked crestfallen. "So you haven't given up your foolish quest to try and save the world. I should have known better than to think that was all Hope's idea."

"You don't have to go with me if you don't want to."

"Like hell," Elizabeth muttered. "Even in that pansy-ass world you still need someone to watch your back and if it's not going to be Hope, then it has to be me. Besides, you think I want to stay here? In the honest-to-goodness *Temple of the Light?!*"

"Follow me, then. There's no use wasting any more time." Mirena turned to head back the way they had come to the Sentinal Stones and Elizabeth scurried to catch up.

They picked their way carefully through the rubble in silence. Mirena didn't feel like she had much else to say and though she knew that Hope would wonder where they had gone to eventually, he would be trapped within the Temple of the Light for some time because of who he was.

It's a good idea, going to the Mirror world; it really is, Mirena told herself, calming somewhat as she reached the outer ring of the Sentinal Stones, *and it's something that Hope doesn't have the time to do personally if he's going to try and convince these people to do something to save themselves.*

But I shouldn't leave here without leaving some indication of where we've gone. He will worry and I really don't want that; he's stressed enough as it is. She reached down to pick up a jagged rock from the rubble and taking a firm hold on it, Mirena drew a symbol of a star in a circle in the stone before her at eye level. *It's the symbol for the Capital in the Mirror World. Hope should be able to figure out what I mean by that.*

Dropping the stone, she stepped within the stone ring and approached the central pillar. Waiting for Elizabeth to join her, Mirena felt her majik and filled herself with the confidence she needed to use it.

This is a good idea. I know it is.

Taking a deep breath, she reached for the symbol that would take her where she wanted and poured her majik into the Stone. The world lurched around her in a familiar way and the scenery changed.

From tall cliffs and the debris of a ruined temple to a familiar forest clearing, the world around them was suddenly different; even more than was immediately apparent. In this world there was no struggle for Light to shine in the Dark and for the Creator to defeat the Destroyer. Maybe it was the other way around here, but as far as Mirena saw from her last visit, this realm seemed a whole lot more stable and peaceful than her own.

"We should probably go see the Panarch and let him know we are here," Mirena suggested to Elizabeth, before heading out of the circle in the direction of the Capital and the Collegium.

It was a bit of a trek from the Sentinal Stones to the south side of the massive city, but the walk was a pleasant one in the cool and sunny weather. From there the monorail ride was nearly another turn of the hourglass, but it afforded a wonderful view of the bustling Capital city. The city here in this realm was a lot cleaner and in better repair than the Capital she was used to.

I wonder how I didn't notice the differences the first time, Mirena noted. *It's so obvious now that I know what to look for. This realm really is a Mirror to ours.*

Even the Collegium's marketplace had a more welcoming atmosphere than the one in their own realm. There were no thieves waiting in corners to prey on the unwary, at least none that Mirena could see and the customers haggling with merchants had smiles on their faces instead of unfriendly scowls.

Elizabeth shook her head, watching it all. "This place gives me the creeps," she muttered. "Don't you think so?"

"No, I think it's wonderful," Mirena responded sincerely. "I wish where we come from could be more like this."

People did stare at Mirena's scars and the inky black writing on her skin, but the stares were curious or maybe wary, not suspicious or angry. Still, she felt self-conscious and she hurried her steps, feeling glad when she left the busy marketplace behind in favour of the quieter hallways of the Collegium.

"Mirena and Elizabeth?" Terrence Lee's secretary questioned as they approached her desk in the Panarch's round-walled office, high above the Political Wing of the Collegium.

"Mira and Beth," Mirena corrected her. "If you could give the Panarch those names, he should understand."

The secretary nodded slowly before putting her hand to the panel on her desk and communicating silently somehow through the majik device. A moment later, the door opened and an immaculately beautiful woman with pale blonde hair exited, followed by a large and imposing muscular man with a serious expression.

Elizabeth gasped in recognition upon seeing the man, but Mirena tried not to react. *This is the Mirror World. Even if Elizabeth thinks she knows someone, she doesn't really...they're opposites.*

"Mira...and Beth," the woman said; her voice as rich and inviting as her appearance as she looked from one of them to the other. "I'm Jehenna. It's nice to meet you. I would say that I've heard so much about you, but truthfully this is the first that Lee's mentioned you." She smiled to soften the words that were obviously meant to poke fun at the Panarch, who stood not far behind her in the open doorway.

I have to remember that people are on friendly terms with their ruler here, Mirena told herself.

"Nice to meet you as well. I'm Mira," she added to differentiate herself from Elizabeth and this world's Mirena.

Mirena half expected the big man standing behind Jehenna to introduce himself next, but instead he chose to remain silent and imposing his Mage jacket and the confident way he wore it buttoned all the way to the top only amplifying how formidable of an opponent he would be if crossed.

"Oh, don't mind D'wann," Jehenna spoke for him, noticing Mirena's expression, "he's always like that. You get used to him...or at least, I did."

The stylish woman smiled again disarmingly and Mirena noted that her tanned face dimpled, expression drawing attention to her deep blue eyes and making her even more attractive.

It's not fair that she's so pretty, Mirena thought, trying to keep the bitterness out of her expression. *Look at me, all covered in scars and treasonous words; I'm only making her more beautiful by comparison...*

"Beth, Mira, why don't you both join me in my office?" Lee asked; using the names they had provided to clear up any confusion caused by the fact that they were the Mirrors of the people he knew from this realm. "D'wann and Jehenna were just leaving."

"We have a problem," Mirena announced as soon as the door was shut firmly behind them, blocking the sound from reaching the ears of the people waiting in the lobby beyond.

"I gathered as much or you wouldn't be here," the Panarch responded. "Is it Hope? I notice he's not with you."

"Naw, Hopey's good," Elizabeth told him with a wave of her hand. "He's got a whole crowd of admirers, Mira got jealous and she sprouted these words all over her skin. Well, maybe not exactly in that order," she amended, taking in her sister's reproachful expression.

"Thanks, Elizabeth, for that wonderful explanation," Mirena snapped, annoyed. "I have the Prophecy of the Light all over my body not because I am jealous, but because I'm the Prophet and I touched pages infused with majik. I would be killed on the spot if the Terrence Lee from our world, or anyone who worked for him, saw me like this.

"Hope is with the followers of the Light now and Jesabel, whom he healed with his Creator-given power to prove he is the Avatar of the Light," Mirena continued, feeling her anger returning. "That's when the doors of the temple's main hall shut, leaving Elizabeth and I alone with no protection, and I really just don't want to get hurt again."

"It really wasn't like that," Elizabeth countered. "I mean, other than the obvious threat of the Panarch and his Generals swooping down on us to destroy the hidden temple you were so dead set on finding, we were pretty safe amongst all those believers in Light and goodness. It's just that…"

"When Mira left those walls and was spotted, her new markings would be reported and make her easy to track down," Lee finished. "I understand. Is it the same for you, Mira, as the Mirena here? Would you girls be easily recognized by the Capital's citizens?"

"Well, yes, you know, because Elizabeth was sleeping with the Panarch," Mirena commented callously, still feeling peevish.

Elizabeth's mouth dropped open in shock. "You're going to say something like that in front of *him*?! That's highly inappropriate, don't you think?"

"Maybe if you cared about how I felt and didn't brush it off, I would care more about what you felt," Mirena countered, unwilling to apologize in her present mood.

"Girls," Lee cleared his throat uncomfortably. "You came here for a reason. If I can help you, I would be glad to, but you would need to tell me what it is that I can do for you."

"I need to hide," Mirena told him honestly. "This face is dangerous, the words on my skin are dangerous; I want to be someone else."

"Done," Lee responded without hesitation. "I know just what you need and I can provide it. Is there anything else?"

"I feel a little embarrassed to ask," she said, hesitant to broach the subject on her mind, "but I have been thinking on something for a while. Can I talk to you privately about it?"

"You have something to say that you can't say in front of me?" Elizabeth asked; her tone affronted. "You're something else, Mira."

"It's something I want to ask Lee's opinion on and I just don't want you to know about it yet," Mirena hedged. "I don't want to offend you, but I need to keep it secret and the fewer people that know about it the better. If it got back to certain people in our realm it would be more dangerous than the words on my skin. Please understand, Elizabeth."

"So you can blurt out my sexual exploits just to make someone uncomfortable, but you want me to keep things about you quiet?" Elizabeth commented disdainfully. "Fine, I hear you. I'm leaving, but mark my words Mira, you're going to have a lot of explaining to do to make Hope and I trust you after this."

With those words her sister stalked from the room, forcefully shutting the door behind her.

"I'm sensing some tension between the two of you," Lee commented carefully.

"Sorry about that," Mirena apologized after a moment. "Elizabeth was right about my words being inappropriate before. It's just that I've had this plan for a while…My sister kind of inspired me, actually.

"Our world is a dark place and everyone uses everyone else; everything has a price. The important people in our world use any kind of power they can in order to rule, including fear, manipulation, violence and sex to control those whom they feel are beneath them.

"I've come to understand that using the Panarch's tactics against him might be the only way to make things change. I want to break the system, but to do that I'll have to learn how to think like he does and get close to him."

Mirena took a deep breath before revealing her intentions. "I want to learn how to seduce and control the Panarch of my realm. I know I'll need a lot of help to do this, so I am asking you because there is no one better than Terrence Lee's Mirror to tell me what I need to know to defeat him."

Lee listened carefully to her words before making any acknowledgement of her unorthodox request. When she had finished speaking, he took a deep breath of his own and faced her squarely.

"You have very valid points, Mira, and I can see that you've thought this through very carefully," he began, "but I'm not sure I know how it is I can help you with this. The information you want is very personal…and truthfully, I don't know how much like myself my Mirror would be, or in what ways.

"I'm sorry," he finished, "but I don't think I'll be able to be of any use to you in this."

"I understand your apprehension, but I really do need your help in particular," Mirena pressed. "There's no one else I can ask."

She really had thought long and hard about what it would take to overthrow the system of power in her world. As much as the thought of it disgusted her, it seemed that getting close to the Panarch was going to be the only way to defeat him at his own game.

Only his Generals and his whores get close enough to him to do what I intend. I can't be either of those, but maybe I can be something more…

I have to do this myself. Elizabeth might be better suited for the task, but if I do it then I don't have to worry about her getting hurt. Besides, I owe him this after what he did to me.

The Panarch will fall and I will be the one to destroy him.

"Nothing too intimate," Mirena continued, not about to the let Lee hold out on her just because he was conservative, "just your likes and quirks. Please; you're the only one that I can turn to. Look, I can't let any other women get hurt by him, not like he hurt me. If I can do this and manage to keep his attentions focused on me, then he won't hurt anyone else."

Leaning back in his chair, Lee let out the breath he was holding. He raised an eyebrow, looking a little overwhelmed by Mira's line of attack. "Well, I think you already know well enough how to get me to listen to you," he commented after a moment. "Your sincerity certainly gets my attention, though that's going to be a little hard to continue with if you intend to fabricate yourself a romance with my Mirror."

She felt her face heat at the implication in his words. "It's purely for political reasons. I'm not going to sleep with him or anything…"

"Be that as it may," the Panarch looked uncomfortable and cleared his throat, sitting up straighter in his chair. "Beyond that, I'm not sure what you want to know about me…"

"I don't know…your favourite colour, your favourite food, your habits or hobbies? What you like in a woman, what you dislike, what you find attractive…simple things."

"I can see that it is going to take a while to answer your questions. I'm sure your sister is getting anxious out in the hallway," he hedged. "Can I perhaps write you a list?"

"Yes, that would be fine," Mirena answered with a smile, inwardly amused by this Panarch's modesty when she knew, at least theoretically, of the lewdness of the other one, "but do you know anyone who can teach me how to do the things on your list?"

Lee swallowed uncomfortably, closing his eyes for a moment as if trying to pretend he was somewhere else. "I'll see what I can do. I'm almost afraid to ask this, but is there anything else you need?"

"I would also like to request help in the starting a revolution in my realm," she answered, not quitting while she was ahead. "We simply don't have good people or the support that we would need. The followers of the Light are beaten down and the people in the Capital are all too afraid of standing up against the Panarch. It would be suicide for us to try and convince them otherwise without help."

"I thought we had troubles, but it's a very dangerous world on your side, isn't it?" He asked. "I would love to help you, but I'm not sure I have the right to interfere in a realm I don't live in. Here I'm directly responsible for the people, so I can only assume that my Mirror has the same responsibilities over there. As awful of a person as I have no doubt he is; can I realistically help you bring his realm down around him?"

"I'm not asking for an army, but a handful of kind-hearted, intelligent people, like yourself, who would be willing to help us," Mirena explained. "And besides, I'm the one asking for aid, so that would mean that you are not interfering, but enabling me to succeed.

"I will be doing this anyway," she continued, "but it will go smoother with your assistance and believe me, this change is necessary and the right thing to do. Why else would travel be possible between the realms if not to allow us to help one another?"

Lee smiled. "You'd make a good diplomat, Mira; you have a way with words. You're right, of course, but unfortunately my place is here. And as the responsible ruler that your Panarch isn't, I have my plate full with taking care of my realm.

"As for helping you to find people that might be interested in assisting you, I think I can do that. On one condition," he added, "that you let each of them know who is asking and why they would be risking their lives to help you. If anyone goes to the Mirror World to help you, they will have my full support, but I want going there to be their own decision. Does that sound fair to you?"

"Perfectly," Mirena answered, smiling. "Is it okay to just go ask them or would you bring the people I want to ask to your office to talk? Because I have some people in mind that might be able to be a great help in our circumstances."

"So do I," Lee added, "and I wouldn't be surprised if some of our choices overlapped. Why don't we each invite our intended prospects to a dinner this evening, say in two turnings of the hourglass from now? I'll reserve us a room in the Political Wing, on the third floor. How many people did you have in mind to ask?"

"Two."

"So few?" Lee questioned with a smile. "Very well…a small meeting room. You'd better go get your sister then, before she bursts in here demanding to know what has taken us so long. I'll see you in two turnings, then."

"Yes and thank you," Mirena agreed. "You don't know what this means to me."

"Truthfully, I pity my Mirror for what you will do to him," Lee told her as he rose to shake Mirena's hand before she left, "but more importantly, I wish you luck."

XVII.

By the time Mirena rejoined her sister, Elizabeth was stalking angrily back and forth across the small waiting room and wearing a path into the wooden floorboards beneath her feet. She had also managed to draw annoyed stares from the other more patient petitioners who were waiting for their turn to speak with the Panarch. She stopped in her tracks when she noticed Mirena exit Terrence Lee's office.

"Ready to take me home, yet?" She questioned, her tone angry but her words not quite the verbal slap in the face that Mira had been expecting.

"The opposite, actually," Mirena answered in a chipper fashion despite the reaction she knew she'd get for making light of her sister's bad mood. "We have to go invite some people to dinner."

"Excuse me?!"

"I have made arrangements with the Panarch and I have to go ask people to come to a dinner to discuss the plans. We should be able to find them in the cafeteria," she paused, taking in Elizabeth's unimpressed expression. "Don't worry, you're invited this time."

Elizabeth fumed silently for a moment before speaking in a dangerously quiet voice. "And what if I don't want to go to your little party?"

"You're welcome to wait in the hall until we're finished," Mirena responded pertly.

"I see."

Without further comment, Elizabeth gestured for Mirena to precede her out of the lobby. With a shrug, Mirena headed out into the hall to make her way down to the Cafeteria. Uncharacteristically wordless, Elizabeth followed her.

What's happening to us? Mirena wondered. *It's not like me to be so unfeeling…*

I don't think I can blame my attitude solely on my reaction to Hope. It was a misunderstanding and I overreacted. I know that, but I still feel angry about it. I need to apologize to Elizabeth, but maybe I should wait since she's acting strange as well.

The Cafeteria wasn't as busy as it would be come dinnertime, but it was never empty and there were still a number of people filling the tables, either eating or sitting casually with friends. Mirena stood just inside the main entrance looking about until she saw the people she had come here to find.

Even in this realm, Odark and his friends always sit at that same table.

The similarities between the two realms were just as noticeable as the differences.

"Odark," Mirena spoke his name hesitantly, remembering the Odark from her realm and how she had never quite managed to get up the courage to approach him.

Odark's head snapped up at the sound of her voice, his eyes an intense green as he regarded her with suspicion.

"I would like to apologize for my actions and harsh words the last time we saw each other," she began, hoping he would at least hear her out. "They were inappropriate, no matter what my reasons were. If you could let me explain to you what I was yelling about last time, I would be grateful."

"More games, Mirena?" Powell asked from the head of the table where he sat with a handful of cards in his hand and Mirena suddenly felt bad for interrupting their game.

"Shut up, Powell," Odark snapped, standing as he continued to stare into Mirena's eyes. "I don't know what's going on here, but this isn't Mirena. Is she back there?" He asked, gesturing to the far wall where Elizabeth leaned near a doorway waiting for Mirena to finish what she'd come to do. "Did she send her twin sister to talk to me because she didn't want to do it herself? Or was this your idea, Elizabeth?"

"It's not what you think." Mirena tried to explain. "Elizabeth has green eyes and mine are blue; we can't hide that difference between us. But you're right, I'm not who you think I am. You were always very clever and that is why I wish to talk to you.

"If you could meet me for dinner in the Political Wing on the third floor, the Panarch has arranged it and I promise that I will explain everything."

Odark's eyes widened perceptively, presumably noting the differences between Mirena and her Mirror. After a moment he found the words to reply.

"Okay," he agreed. "I'll be there."

"Thank you for understanding," she told him sincerely, "and I'm sorry if I interrupted your game.

"Also, have any of you seen Tendro?"

Hope sat before the Mother in her private antechamber; having finally, gratefully, escaped the awe and adulation of the People of the Light.

"Myself and those who worship here are convinced of your legitimacy," the Mother began, addressing him with her serene and melodious tones from where she sat cross-legged on a large pale blue cushion in this small room with no furniture to speak of, "because of the Prophet. None can doubt what they have seen here today, but how did you discover your destiny? Did the Creator show you the way in a dream or vision?"

Hope tried to imitate her relaxed pose on his own white cushion, but found it difficult to do so, being used to more formal seating than a few throw pillows on a cold stone floor.

"Vision?" Hope questioned, hating the way this woman so easily made him feel confused and out of place with all her talk of things she no doubt expected him to know as the Creator's 'Chosen one.' "No, I don't think it was a vision. It was real. I... met her."

"You *met* the Creator?" Jesabel asked.

Due to having 'found him' as far as the Mother was concerned, Jesabel had been the only other person included in this private meeting. *Not even Mirena was invited, not that I saw where she went once the crowd went wild. Elizabeth is probably fuming at being made to wait, but even if I'm their 'Avatar' there's not much I can do about their customs here and the Mother wished to speak with me alone.*

"I don't remember everything clearly from that night," Hope admitted, "but perhaps you can make sense of what I do remember.

"It all began in a small cottage near Shorelle," he continued, reminiscing about how his life used to be before all of this had begun. "I was working for the Panarch then, and I was meeting with some of the other Generals under his command when we discovered that our meeting place had been compromised…

"I want those Sympathizers caught," Dipaul's voice thundered loudly in the small cottage's main room. "We can't have them skulking about, not here. They shouldn't even know this hideout exists."

Tendro loved the little cottage in Lasalle with its homey atmosphere and its low-key feel. He loved how far away it seemed from all the pressures of life in the Capital and the Collegium, but he hated it when Dipaul used it for his meetings. Especially when the Panarch's General stopped kidding around and showed them his true face, his deep voice commanding instead of slow and thick; times like this one.

"Maybe they were just in the wrong place at the wrong time," Tendro spoke up despite his better judgment, his heart sick at the sight of the prisoners they already caught gagged with bonds of air summoned by Nevodian's majik. They struggled futilely in the worn old chair in which they had been unceremoniously dumped.

One was a nondescript fellow with medium brown hair and eyes smoldering with distrust of his captors. In Tendro's opinion he looked the least like a Sympathizer of the Light as anyone he'd ever seen, between the anger in his expression and the twin daggers sheathed in his belt.

The other prisoner, dressed in a white and silver Mage's outfit, looked the part, however. Scared, but trying not to show it, the thin and lithe young man with silver-white hair and ice blue eyes. He struggled more feebly, showing that though the bonds of air held him in an uncomfortable position, he knew there was little he could do to escape them.

But according to Dipaul, these two weren't the only ones that had been seen sneaking about in the woods outside the little cottage; they were just the only ones that Odark and Nevodian had been able to catch. Apparently two more had been spotted and Dipaul wouldn't let any of the Generals rest until they too were trussed up and waiting to be questioned.

Dipaul's eyes were dark as he regarded Tendro and Tendro found himself swallowing uncomfortably under the burly General's steady gaze.

"Either way, we'll find out," Caralain commented in an offhand manner from where she stood overseeing the prisoners, flipping her long black hair in a dismissive gesture, "and either way, they'll pay for having trespassed..."

A high-pitched voice cut sharply into the conversation, speaking loudly just outside the cottage's front door and causing Caralain to fall silent in shock.

"Why do I have to be careful? We are more powerful than all of them, Caralain!"

Caralain?

Tendro wasn't the only one in the room to question the use of his fiancée's name and to wonder who was creating a disturbance outside those doors.

Dipaul gestured a silent command to Odark, who stood closest to the closed door. With a nod, Odark pulled the door open in a sharp gesture, stepping boldly outside to see what was going on. Tendro sat up straighter on the couch, unsure of what to do; the prisoners, however, looked hopeful.

Odark got no more than a few steps outside the door before a blast of heat and flames pushed him back and he careened back through the open door to skid to a stop at Dipaul's feet, his face and clothes blackened and charred.

"See?" The same sharp voice questioned. "I told you they're weak! There's nothing to worry about."

"Mirena!"

The voice that reprimanded the first was more than simply familiar to Tendro.

It was Caralain's voice.

He was to his feet before he realized that he'd made the conscious decision to move, looking from Caralain in the room with him to where the sound of her voice had come through the open doorway.

What is going on here?

"I'm going to make this simple," the one Tendro presumed was named Mirena said, fully entering the room like she belonged there and pointing at the prisoners, "those two belong to me and the Caralain you have with you is an imposter."

Tendro's mouth fell open in shock. Caralain had never been a twin that he'd known of. In fact, she was an only child, but this woman sounded exactly like her and when she stepped into the frame of the open doorway he discovered that she looked exactly like her as well. Long black hair, a perfect oval face, and blue eyes; the newcomer Caralain was even dressed similarly in a thigh-length sky blue dress over black leggings; it was impossible at a glance to tell them apart.

How is this possible? Tendro found himself wondering, staring between the two of them and searching for any discernible differences. Physically, there weren't any, though the clothes were of different cut, the newcomer's a lighter shade of blue with lace trimming the edges.

I should be able to tell them apart if anyone can; Caralain is my fiancée...

Dipaul's mouth quirked in a smile; seemingly amused by this strange turn of events.

"Is she now?" He questioned. "I assume you have some proof?"

"This is ridiculous!" Caralain protested in an angry hiss.

Of course she's mad; this is her identity at stake.

"We knew there were at least two more Sympathizers out in the woods," she continued, defending herself. "Why are you bothering to listen to their lies?"

"Look," the one named Mirena said, sounding bored and walking forward, putting herself completely in the small room with Caralain's double on her heels. "I don't have time for this; I'm a little busy. I didn't come here to sort out your trash, I came here to get the two on the chair and be on my way."

"It looks to me that you came to cause confusion and distrust in my ranks," Dipaul told her, his smile never wavering. "Were you just going to leave her here then, in exchange for these two Sympathizers?"

"Exchange?" Mirena questioned disdainfully, putting her hands on skinny hips and throwing her long blonde hair over her shoulder. "Who says you're getting anything out of this deal? I'm walking away with these two and Caralain can do as she pleases."

*She has no fear...*Tendro found himself thinking. *Who is this woman? Did the female Panarch send her? Is she Theia Prosai's agent?*

Dipaul said nothing and didn't move a muscle, but he didn't need to. Nevodian stepped forward in his General's stead, leaving the spot where he'd lounged against the wall until now.

"The prisoners are mine," he stated confidently. "I caught them and I will question them."

"How are you going to question them if you can't even keep your eyes open?" Mirena asked in a condescending tone, simultaneously raising her right hand and snapping her fingers.

Nevodian fell to the floor, dead asleep; his dark hair falling in front of his eyes.

Dipaul followed the Truthseeker's defeat with an emotionless gaze. "Interesting use of majik," he commented tonelessly, "but what do you think of this?"

The burly General reached out both hands to either side of him and as one the two Caralains arched in discomfort, as if invisible hands had wrapped around each of their throats. Their feet scraped against the floorboards as they were lifted up just enough to slide through the air towards where Dipaul's actual hands waited eagerly for their necks.

Tendro was horrified, but powerless to do anything to stop what was happening before his eyes. Mirena, on the other hand, looked on dispassionately, seemingly unconcerned for the safety of either Caralain; she almost looked bored by the violent display.

Both Caralains choked and gasped on the infinitesimal amount of air Dipaul allowed them before his hands clamped tightly around each of their necks, holding them aloft with brute strength now instead of majik.

"Wow, nice party trick," Mirena commented sarcastically, showing her complete disregard for the human lives in danger before her, "but what exactly are you trying to prove?"

"Dipaul, stop this!" Tendro called out, deciding that he simply couldn't stand by and watch this any longer. "One of them is innocent!"

Dipaul's emotionless gaze turned to him then, the General's lazy eyes locking onto Tendro's and holding his gaze.

"Which one is it, Tendro?" He asked, his voice back to the dull and stupid tones he used when playing people for fools.

Tendro opened his mouth to answer, but paused for a moment. He'd watched the whole thing and noted their subtle differences in clothing selection, so he knew which Caralain was which, but something unsettled him.

Is this a trick? He questioned, the thoughts running quickly through his mind. *Dipaul knows which one is which; of course he does. Why would he ask me, unless he was playing some sort of game? Testing me, maybe?*

Innocent, Tendro realized. *I said innocent. In Dipaul's mind only Sympathizers of the Light are deemed innocent and he would eradicate any of those he could find...but I can't be responsible for that woman's death, even if she is an imposter...can I?*

He'll kill both of them right now if I don't choose one.

"That one," Tendro said, pointing to the imposter, the Caralain who had entered the cottage with this Mirena person. The one she had tried to claim was the real Caralain, before she had started blasting people with less regard than even Dipaul showed for the lives of those around him.

Without even a moment of hesitation, Dipaul dropped the Caralain that Tendro's words had not condemned. His fiancée crumpled to the ground, her hands automatically reaching up to her neck to protect it from further abuse as Dipaul turned his attention to the Caralain he still held.

He brought his free hand around, clearly intending to snap the neck of his victim before she could run out of air and deprive him of the chance to rob her of her last breath at a time of his choosing.

"Wrong one," Mirena said coldly and a dark aura arose in the air around her; her eyes blackening with power. She raised her hand in the same gesture she'd used to take down Nevodian and with a snap of her fingers, the impossible happened.

The world lurched as the Caralain on the floor and the one in the air changed places; there was simply no other way to describe it. Majik, as Tendro had been taught it, was not capable of a feat like the one this Mirena had just performed, yet before his eyes she casually, disdainfully, broke the laws of the universe.

The neck of the woman who found herself in Dipaul's hands snapped, while the one who had been freed cried pitifully on the floor at her would-be assassin's feet.

The only problem was that it was so unbelievable that Tendro found he wasn't certain if he'd imagined it all. No majik he'd ever heard tell of was capable of the feat he wasn't sure he'd just witnessed.

What the hell just happened? Was that real, what I saw? Which Caralain died and who is this woman who still lives?

However, he didn't have a chance to react or even feel anything beyond the shock of it before Mirena decided his fate for him.

"Time to go!" She yelled, barreling into him as she raised an arm to lash out at Dipaul and fling him into the wall behind where he'd been standing with a powerful burst of air.

Unprepared for the directness of her attack, Dipaul was knocked completely off balance and he slammed solidly into the cottage's wood-paneled wall, cracking the wood beneath his weight. Not bothering to check on Caralain, Mirena grabbed hold of Tendro's hand as she pulled him along, not losing her momentum.

Very suddenly Tendro found himself somewhere else, the two newly-freed prisoners following quickly behind them through the hole in the air Mirena had created effortlessly with her majik.

"Alastor, Nevirean," Mirena addressed the two she had freed without missing a beat, "I've got something I need Tendro to do, so I'll be back soon. Don't get into anymore trouble."

"What?!" Tendro exclaimed, still reeling from the events he'd just witnessed. "What do you want me for? What about Caralain?"

"Caralain can take care of herself," Mirena told him in a no-nonsense tone as she opened another hole in the air before her to somewhere misty and nebulous.

"Congratulations, Tendro," she announced, regarding her handiwork and speaking in a tone far too chipper given the circumstances, "you're the Avatar of the Light and you're going to help me free the Creator."

Mirror's Hope

XVIII.

"I knew you wouldn't be far behind," Lee noted with a smile as Hope joined them in the meeting room in the Mirror World. "We have something to discuss that I think you will find very interesting. But first, I'd like to introduce you to your team of recruits. Ladies and gentlemen, this is the man you will be helping to stage a revolution; meet Hope."

Mirena covered a smile while watching Hope's reaction. The shock was evident on his face; he may have been expecting to find her and Elizabeth in the Mirror World, but he obviously hadn't been expecting anything like this.

For Terrence Lee to give us his best men and women, it's more than we could have hoped for... Around the room sat a group of people that Mirena honestly believed might give her the edge she needed to outsmart and outmaneuver the Panarch in her own realm. *Lee must think so too or he never would have suggested these people. He's helping me like I asked, though he's being more subtle than simply giving me the answers.*

She had Lee's list held tightly in her hands. The Panarch had made her promise that the information would be seen by no eyes but her own and the person he had suggested help her learn what she needed to know. Looking across the table at Jehenna looking confident in her sultry red dress that hugged her figure in all the right places, Mirena couldn't help but think that the poised and elegant woman was the perfect choice for a tutor in the art of seduction.

Next to Jehenna sat her husband-to-be, D'wann, the Panarch's right hand man in this realm and maybe in her own as well, she didn't know. Powerfully muscled and taciturn, D'wann was intimidating by presence alone, but the two large swords he wore strapped to his back even in a meeting like this one didn't hurt his image any either. As Lee had informed her, D'wann was his personal bodyguard and had also been his best friend for many years.

I don't want to take his bodyguard away from him, but Lee assures me that he'll be fine in his absence. Besides, D'wann was the first to volunteer.

In addition to D'wann and Jehenna, Odark had also agreed to come. The serious-faced Mor Gannian had hesitated and thought through the request fully before answering, but once Lee had suggested that it might be a good training exercise for those who wanted to gain the skills necessary to defend this realm should it be needed, Odark had agreed wholeheartedly.

"I may have been a little hasty in that announcement," Lee allowed, "but almost everyone has decided to accompany Mira back to the Mirror World to help with your cause. We're just waiting on one...Tendro?"

Tendro's expression continued to betray no hint of which direction he was leaning, Hope's Mirror was a hard man to read.

Everytime I look at Tendro, or Hope for that matter, I never seem to know what is going on in their heads, Mirena frowned, considering them both. *Their thoughts are a mystery to me. They're supposed to be opposites, but they have so much in common.*

"I'm a little confused about the Mirror World, to be honest," Tendro began, addressing his concerns to Terrence Lee and not to Mirena or Hope who might be considered experts on the specifics of their realm. "I thought that the Mirror World was a place with ideals that opposed our own and people that are in some ways opposite to us. In fact, everything that's been said so far reflects that truth and even confirms it."

Lee nodded and Tendro continued, "So why is it then that Hope and I would be on the same side?"

"I think that's something you'll have to decide for yourself," Lee replied, not seeming concerned in the least by the difficult philosophical question Tendro had posed. "I, for one, believe that this is an opportunity to really explore the nature of our two realms and discover just how much choice is involved in who we are. Must we conform to the expectations of us or can we choose to be what we would like to be?"

Elizabeth sighed exaggeratedly, sitting up straight in the chair she had been lounging in throughout dinner and keeping her comments to herself until now.

"This is getting us nowhere," she commented tiredly. "Are you in or are you out?"

"I'm in," Tendro decided, his expression dark. "That is, if you'll have me."

"No problem," Elizabeth told him. "What's one more fugitive from the Panarch's wrath?"

"Elizabeth!"

Elizabeth flashed Mirena an impish grin, a hint of her usual personality returning.

"And now that everything is settled," Lee continued, "I have a present for you, Mira. I can't come to your realm myself, but I thought I would send you what protection I can offer."

Why is he giving me a gift? Mirena questioned. *If anything, I should be giving him something in return for his help...*

Inexplicably, Lee reached up and grabbed the sides of his face as if peeling off a mask that wasn't there, but all of a sudden what he was reaching for became visible in his hands. The featureless wooden mask in his hands appeared and was revealed to be nearly an inch thick and very solid-looking.

Tendro sat up quickly in his chair, his eyes wide. "How did you do that?"

"It's a majik item," Lee explained. "Perhaps it's better if I demonstrate further." The Panarch put the mask back on his face and as soon as the wood touched his skin, it vanished once more, transforming Terrence Lee's handsome features and blond hair into that of yet another Tendro Seynor.

Mirena gasped and Lee took the mask off again, smiling as he did so. The expression turned from Tendro's, or Hope's, half-smile into Lee's full blown one with the removal of the majik item from his face.

"And this," Lee continued, putting the mask on one more time and suddenly Mirena found that she was not alone in her shocked expression; the entire room was caught off guard.

The tall, proud and very male Panarch now appeared to be a perfectly believable woman. He...she had medium brown hair that draped past her shoulders, deep blue eyes and a sensual mouth set in a perfect oval of a face. She was beautiful and very feminine even in form; not just her face. It was difficult to believe that Lee was beneath the perfect disguise, even though his white and silver Mage outfit had not changed with the rest of him.

"That's for me?" Mirena whispered, overwhelmed. "How could you give me something as valuable as that?"

"You asked for my help," the woman the Panarch had become answered, her voice as alluring as the face, thanks to the majik of the mask.

Reaching for his face, Lee seemed to shift the image the mask cast over him, changing the details slightly. A beauty mark appeared above the lip, a light spattering of freckles danced across the nose and hands. The hair bounced a little shorter as curls were added and the highlights of gold darkened to low-lights of an even darker brown.

"There," said Lee, his male voice and appearance returning as he took the mask off, crossing the room to Mirena's side in order to hold the lifeless wooden thing out to her. "It's yours," he told her. "It's everything you asked for and with it, no one will ever know you're not as you appear; it cannot be removed except by the wearer under any circumstances excepting death, I presume. Just do me one favour, okay? Never wear it in my presence."

Mirena nodded, taking the mask from Lee's hands with extreme caution and a hint of reverence, never letting go of his eyes. "And what's my name?"

"Lyana." Lee pronounced the name with finality and a vulnerability Mirena hadn't known he was capable of before he turned from her to walk past Hope and out of the room.

The Panarch's departure left an awkward silence in the room that everyone seemed loathe to fill. Eventually, Hope let himself entirely into the room, but it was Jehenna who was the first one to speak.

"So I'm assuming we'll need to be briefed and trained," she noted, addressing Hope. "Where do you suggest we do this?"

Hope took a deep breath. "We have a secret place," he answered. "We'll need to gather supplies like food, water and weapons before we leave here. There will be nowhere to obtain them in our realm without taking them from people who need them more.

"The good news is," he added, "we have an army. They're not exactly soldiers, but we'll have to work with that we have. Hopefully we can avoid the physical kind of war, because if we can't, we're sure to lose to the Panarch's superior force and numbers."

"I guess that means we have our instructions," Odark stated, getting to his feet. "Where and when do we meet?"

"The Sentinal Stones," Hope informed them, "after dark. We'll wait for everyone to arrive before we cross over to the other realm, so try not to leave us waiting."

"Okay, just one problem." Odark laughed. "What's a Sentinal Stone and where do I find one?"

"I got this one," Elizabeth offered. "Stick with me, little man, and I'll get you to where you're going."

Odark's eyes darkened at the slight to his height and Mirena gave her sister a warning glance, but Elizabeth ignored them both in favour of holding the door open for Odark with an impish grin on her face.

Soon Jehenna and D'wann had left as well, leaving Mirena alone with the two Tendros.

"I want to apologize for what I said earlier," Tendro began, speaking to Hope as if Mirena wasn't present. "I don't want it to sound like I doubt your cause, because I don't. It's just..."

"I understand," Hope told him, leaving Tendro's reasons for doubt a mystery to Mirena, "and don't worry about it."

It is sad that I am getting used to being ignored lately...by both of them, it seems, Mirena thought, with an inward sigh. *Now they have secrets together. I don't know what I have gotten myself into, but I am thinking that I should be careful around them. They're so similar...it's hard to tell what the differences are between them.*

Tendro nodded; his expression serious. "So you know then that I'll do as I've agreed to. I'll help you through this; you can count on me."

Hope nodded in reply, his expression a true Mirror of the man who shared more than his face.

"Glad to have you," Hope held out his hand and Tendro took it, clasping his forearm tightly as they shook once before Tendro let go and let himself out of the room.

"So you've come alone, then?" Mirena asked Hope after a moment of awkward silence had passed between them.

"Yes," he answered cautiously, obviously confused by the question, "should I have brought someone else?"

"Well, you and Jesabel were becoming so close..." Mirena said scathingly. "After it was announced that she discovered you and proclaimed you Avatar of the Light and I was shoved out into the Hall, forgotten about after I fulfilled my 'duty' as your Prophet."

Hope looked taken aback by the anger in her voice and his stance shifted suddenly from relaxed to wary. "Mira...are you feeling all right?"

"Not sure," she replied, her tone filled with accusation, "maybe these words on my skin are getting to me, or did you forget about them, too?"

"Forget about them?" Hope questioned, seeming concerned. "Mira, I went into the Temple of the Light to find a way to get rid of them. The Mother assures me that they never expected this to happen to you, but that it's proof enough to them that you are the Prophet of the Light that they've been waiting for."

"Well, you're a little late in trying to find a solution," Mirena told him, holding up the mask. "Looks like you're not the only one that can get things done."

"Putting on a mask won't solve your problems, Mirena."

But it will help me, Mirena assured herself. *This mask is the best tool that I have against the Panarch.*

Why am I being so nasty? She questioned after a moment. *I'm mad, but Hope doesn't deserve this.*

"What's wrong with me?"

Hope frowned. "That's what I'm wondering. Did I miss something? Did something happen to you while I was talking with the Mother?"

"I'm angry with you," Mirena confessed, "but not this angry..."

"Okay," Hope allowed, tilting his head to the side and waiting for her to elaborate. "Do you want to talk about it?"

"Yes," Mirena answered. "I am upset with you for several reasons, some I don't even know if I have the right to be angry at you for, but I am none the less."

The words poured out now that she had the chance to speak them. "I feel like you took my dream away. I've always wanted to see the Temple of the Light and talk to the Mother and you were the one that got to go. And the only reason you were admitted was because I got the Prophecy of the Light on my skin. Everyone ignored me, but the only one that hurt me by doing so was you."

"Fair enough…" he said after a moment, seemingly at a loss for words. "I'm sorry. It wasn't right for me to be so welcomed at the Temple of the Light without you. I didn't think of how their reaction to me would make you feel. I was just caught up in it all…I didn't mean to ignore you."

"I didn't care that they were happy to see you. I cared about how you showed them who you were by healing *her*," she said, wiping the tears from her face as she turned away from him, unable to meet his gaze. "That was how I fell in love with you and you were just flirting with Jesabel right in front of me…like I didn't exist."

Mirena felt more than heard Hope take a step closer to her, cutting the distance between them in half and startling her with his sudden nearness.

"You love me?" He repeated and she felt something flutter within her at his words.

"What?" Mirena's head snapped around to look at him, her eyes wide. "I…"

I did say that, didn't I?

"You said you loved me," Hope smiled, the corners of his mouth lifting up and causing Mirena's heart to soar seeing the joy in his expression. "Just now."

Mirena met his eyes and in that moment she realized that the anger she'd been feeling had all been born of jealousy. *I love him and I want him to love me…when I thought I was mistaken about his feelings for me, I got upset.*

"I do," she admitted after a moment, unable to do anything else but tell the truth when faced with his open expression. "I love you."

The usual half-smile that Hope wore split into a full grin and in a rush he caught Mirena in his arms.

"But, I'm still mad at you…" She protested half-heartedly. "You just can't…"

"You can be mad at me later," Hope interjected, "but for now…"

Despite the implication in his tone, Mirena wasn't really expecting Hope to lean down and kiss her, but that was exactly what he did. It wasn't the first time he had done so, but there was a passion in the way his lips pressed against hers and something deep within her responded to it with abandon. Jealousy and anger completely forgotten with the warmth of his lips, she found herself kissing him back with as much fervor as he showed her, perhaps even more.

Hope's hand was warm and gentle against the back of her neck and his tongue moist as it found its way into her mouth. She was very much aware of his body against hers and the way his other hand caressed the lower part of her back.

Despite herself, she heard a small moan escaped her lips.

Mirena had dreamed of this moment. She'd thought of it often, especially since she'd begun to believe that Hope actually did have feelings for her. Despite her daydreams, she'd never expected it would be like this. Kissing him stoked a fire within her and caused it to build until it threatened to consume her.

Hope kept on kissing her and she didn't stop herself from kissing him back.

Every kiss made her desire burn hotter, but left her wanting more of him. It took away her sense of control, leaving her with a newfound freedom and a belief that she could be bold enough to do anything or be anyone.

Distracted by his mouth on hers, she fumbled blindly at the laces that held his white shirt in place. She wanted to be nearer to him, to feel his skin against her hands and against her body.

Hope, it seemed, felt the same way. Taking her lead, he reached for the buttons on her dress, but he stopped after undoing only a handful of them.

"Mira," Hope said, pulling back from her, when all she wanted was for him to never let go. "Are you sure you want this? I mean...."

"Yes," she told him firmly, inches from his face, before she took hold of the collar of his shirt again and drew him closer.

The fervent kissing resumed as they sought to free themselves of the layers of cloth that separated them from one another.

"Not here," Hope interjected after a moment, pulling back from Mirena once more. "Not like this."

"Please?" She whispered, the word coming out unbidden.

I don't want to wake up now and learn that this was all a dream.

"I won't say no to you, Mira," Hope smiled gently down at her, "but Terrence Lee's boardroom is not the place for us to tear each other's clothes off."

Taking a moment to think, he closed his eyes and the ring around his neck began to glow with a fitful pulse.

"What are you trying to do?" Mirena asked, her breath still coming quickly as she watched the way his muscles moved beneath the fabric of his shirt, illuminated by the majik of the Creator's ring.

Hope didn't answer her; instead he turned away and caused a familiar glow to erupt in the room.

"It works," he breathed, looking back at her. "I didn't truly think it would..."

Ignoring his words, Mirena rushed into his arms.

Here or there, it doesn't matter...

He caught her and together they fell back into a world where the grass rose at Hope's command to make the plushest of beds for them to lay on.

His kisses resumed and it was like they had never paused. The flames within her rose higher and she rose with them, kissing him back with more confidence and desire than she ever would have believed herself capable of. Her dress and his shirt were minor impediments and they soon found one another, their clothing forgotten in the grass around them as their bodies met for the first time.

She gasped in shock as he entered her. Pain cut abruptly through the other emotions that rose and swelled within her.

Is it supposed to hurt? Mirena questioned silently, but the moment passed quickly.

It was strange and unlike anything she'd ever experienced, but as Hope rose above her and started moving within her, Mirena found that more than anything else she never wanted him to stop.

He moved gently within her and Mirena felt her body respond to his, moving in time slowly at first, but with a rising intensity as something powerful built between them.

And it felt good; better than anything she'd ever known. It was as if Hope belonged inside of her; the two of them moving this way together. Like this, they felt like they were one and the same and that they were never meant to be separated.

If they could stay like this forever, then and only then would the world be as it should be; perfect.

When the moment they were building to finally came, it was with an overwhelming rush, bringing with it a crescendo of all the feelings she'd been riding like a wave. Mirena lost herself in the sheer bliss of it and cried out, unable to contain her reaction.

After this, her life would never be the same.

Part Two

Mirror's Hope

XIX.

"You little slut," Elizabeth accused, her sister's sharp words causing Mirena to stop in her tracks.

"You seem to have the definition of the word 'slut' confused..." Mirena answered, her tone unimpressed as she turned about to face Elizabeth's scorn.

"No," Elizabeth countered, "what you're planning to do fits the definition of the word quite nicely. Is there a reason that you've been plotting this scheme behind our backs? Oh wait, it's because you don't want Hope to find out that you're deliberately intending to cheat on him."

They were just outside the Void now, the place of Hope's creation so named by the rebels that had been living and training there over the past month. They had named it so because it was a place that by the laws of nature and majik shouldn't exist. Elizabeth and Mirena were outside of it and in the real world, nearby the Sentinal Stones bordering the Capital, but they were still too close to where Hope or the others could overhear them for Mirena's liking.

"Back off, Elizabeth. It's none of your business, even less so to tell anyone of it. Besides, I am not going to sleep around, I'm only going to try and find out what they are planning."

"They? Or *him?*" Elizabeth questioned, looking her up and down.

Mirena blushed despite herself and the intense training she had received from Jehenna these past weeks. She knew the clothes she was wearing were a little excessive. She had chosen them for exactly that reason; to get attention.

Terrence Lee's attention, to be specific; she hadn't given up her plan of revenge and was now moving ahead full force with it.

Accentuating her figure to its fullest potential, Mirena's dress was mauve and barely long enough to reach her knees. It was decorated in light blue accents, Lee's favourite colour, and complete with a sweetheart top and a wide blue ribbon belt. She stood confidently in her light blue heels as she had trained extensively on how to walk and even run in them on all types of terrain.

I'm ready. Mira affirmed. *I can do this.*

I have trained in majik with Hope, strength and speed with D'wann, politics with Odark and most importantly the art of seduction with Jehenna. I'm not a whore; I'm a spy and I'll be a damned good one.

Elizabeth doesn't get it, but I'm doing this for her and for Hope. I know my limits, but I will do what I can to protect those girls in the garden and keep the Panarch's attention fixated on me so they can do their part and overthrow the government under his nose.

"If you'll excuse me, I have somewhere to be," she said, her words a dismissal as Mirena brought Lee's mask to her face and became Lyana, the woman who would defeat the Panarch at his own game.

Lyana turned from Elizabeth as if she didn't exist. To this new persona, Mirena's sister didn't mean a thing.

"He'll tear you apart, Mira," Elizabeth spat, her words as cutting as she could make them. "You think you can stay above it all, but his words, his charm, his presence...he'll get into your heart and your head and then he'll have you. You'll be powerless against him. There's a reason he's the most loved and the most despised man of this world and why he gets everything he wants..."

Elizabeth's words fell on deaf ears. Mirena Calanais was gone for the moment and Lyana Morelle was already walking away; she had somewhere she needed to be.

And Lyana knew exactly where to go and exactly where to wait...

"Terrence Lee is a creature of habit," Jehenna lectured. *"He always appears at the same places throughout his day. To most,"* she added, *"the pattern wouldn't be obvious, but to those that know of his affinity for travelling by majik, it is unmistakable."*

"Should I stage a meeting by happenstance?" Mirena asked; her attention captivated as always by Jehenna's words and the secrets they revealed. "Would it get his attention if I appeared lost and confused?"

"Lost and confused, no," Jehenna cautioned, meeting and holding Mirena's gaze from across the canopied bed in Mirena's room where they held their late night meetings by candlelight. "That would give him the upper hand. He might want to be in control and you might want him to feel like he is, but you must never let him get the best of you. This is your game and only you know the rules. Understand?"

"Perfectly," Mirena nodded.

The garden near the training grounds was a still and peaceful place in the early morning, as she had expected. Whether D'wann's Mirror ruled here like D'wann did in the other realm or not, classes in the Collegium didn't officially start until after breakfast was served in the Cafeteria.

Lyana strolled leisurely along the vine-covered stone walls her eyes wandering casually over the well-tailored landscape. Her fingers reached out to brush against the occasional flower, lingering particularly on a fragile white lily hanging at eye level.

"Beautiful, aren't they?"

His voice cut through the air softly, just as it had to Mirena long ago in the stillness of the Panarch's secret garden. Inside, Mirena felt her fear spike but Jehenna's words whispered calmly in her mind, reminding her to let Lyana be in control.

"Now remember, he doesn't know you and you don't know him. Make use of that. First impressions are very important, but not to be overdone."

"To some..." Lyana replied simply, turning her head ever so slightly to regard the man who had came upon her unawares, looking him up and down as if measuring him with her eyes. "These however," she commented, plucking the white lily between her fingers and letting it drop, discarded, to the grass at her feet, "are common enough."

"Above all else," Jehenna coached knowledgeably, "the Panarch is a man like any other. Catch his interest, intrigue him, but never satisfy him entirely and you'll have him lusting after what he can't have."

"If I can do that, I'll be the first woman he's ever had to work for."

"And that is what he will love about you."

Having made her point, Lyana turned from the Panarch, striding with purpose back to the path from which she had strayed. She felt a smile creep to her lips as she heard his footsteps quicken to catch up to her.

"Are you lost?" She questioned pertly, not slowing her stride. "I believe the rest of the garden is back that way."

She didn't look back to catch his reaction to her words, but she knew she had him confused, if nothing else.

Who would dare direct the Panarch in his own garden?

Me, that's who...

"Where are you headed?" He asked, curious instead of angry.

I've got him, Mirena exulted silently. *Like a fish on a hook. Now I've just got to keep him long enough to reel him in.*

"Getting his attention is the easy part," Jehenna reminded her. *"Many girls before you have ensnared him, but so far none have yet weathered the storms long enough to keep him. Ride the waves. Use him more skillfully than he tries to use you.*

"Do this and he'll believe you're the one who understands him best. This is the way to earn his trust and his secrets."

"I'm not in the habit of letting strangers know my business," Lyana stated matter-of-factly. "Besides, what business is it of yours?"

There was an audible pause then in which the Panarch was obviously considering whether to reveal his identity or whether to continue with the scenario she had provided him, that of two strangers meeting by chance on an empty garden path.

"Consider my interest to be born of a friendly curiosity," he told her, deciding on chance encounter. "If you'd rather I go on my way, I will, but it's a fine day for company, is it not?"

"The Panarch is a man assured of his own power," Jehenna warned. "Know how to protect yourself, but know also how to appear vulnerable enough that he'll want to protect you and use his considerable power to keep you safe from harm."

Lyana sighed suddenly, as if dropping the charade of a confident woman who knew exactly where she was going and how she was going to get there.

"To be honest," she admitted, turning and looking Terrence Lee in the eyes for the first time, "I don't know where I'm going. I've only just arrived here from Lasalle and the Collegium is like a maze to me. I apologized if I've reacted poorly, but I wanted to believe for a moment that you were as lost as I was."

"Think nothing of it," the Panarch replied, holding out his hand invitingly. "I'm Terrence," he introduced himself, deliberately leaving off the second part of his name.

So he believes me about not knowing who he is, Mirena decided, *and that a newly arrived stranger from faraway Lasalle wouldn't recognize the Panarch on sight.*

Good...that makes this easier.

"Lyana," she replied, placing her hand gently in his as if deciding to trust him at least that far. "Pleasure."

"The pleasure's mine," Terrence replied, bringing her hand to his lips.

Lyana raised a brow but didn't protest at his presumption and with a slight smile he let her hand drop.

"So, was there anything in particular you came all this way to see?"

"I'm a graduate of the college in Lasalle," she replied, referencing the college that had trained Jehenna in beauty, diplomacy and illusion. "I'm here to enroll at the Collegium and further my studies."

Terrence smiled knowingly.

The college in Lasalle in this realm is known for training young ladies with enough money or prestige in how to be desirable and powerful in their own right. So trained, Lyana would be a great prize by any man's standard.

"I wouldn't want to trouble you," Lyana continued, "but would you mind pointing me in the right direction?"

"I can do better than that," he answered with a charming smile, "I can take you there myself. It's no trouble; I'm headed that way, regardless."

"Wonderful," she said, smiling at last as she gestured for him to precede her.

"Do you think I'm ready?"

"Would Lyana have to ask?"

"No," Mirena responded, considering the question very carefully, "I don't think she would."

"Then be Lyana," Jehenna urged, *"and we'll just have to trust that with her instincts and all that I've taught her, Lyana will know what to do when the most powerful man in the world reacts in a way none of us would expect."*

Terrence led Lyana through the bustling Cafeteria. Breakfast was just being served in a buffet style, but the powerful man paid no attention to the appetizing smells. Instead he brought her through to the hall beyond, to the place where in a short while the Magi of the Collegium would begin hearing petitions from citizens of the Capital and beyond.

The men and women lined up in the hall wore their best finery, as it was wise to prove one had the ability to pay the Magi who would decide one way or the other if they would grant what you desired. The system was subjective and unfair, but in the end those with the money or power to trade got what they wanted and the Panarch who ran the institution got richer and more powerful.

"Petition Hall?" Lyana questioned.

"You've heard of it, I assume," Terrence replied.

"Yes, but..." she began.

"You'll see."

Citizens in line, likely none of them Magi themselves, or at least not fully-trained ones, were whispering amongst themselves now. They weren't quite pointing and staring, they had more sense of caution than that, but it appeared that as Panarch, Terrence Lee, no matter what part of his name he chose to use, could not go unnoticed for long in the heart of the city he ruled.

Terrence ignored it all, however, either because he was used to it or because he chose not to credit it; Mirena didn't know.

Why are we here? He could enroll me himself in his own school if he chose, unless he's really set on continuing this charade that he's just a man like any other and not one to be feared.

The Panarch didn't hesitate in striding directly to the front of the long line where two Magi, a man and a woman as was customary, were setting down chairs behind a table obviously set there for them to use. A thick velvet rope held back the waiting throng, the first of which was a rather robust man in a burgundy and gold-tasseled suit with a multitude of heavy gold chains around his neck.

Terrence cut between the table and the man, ignoring the velvet rope altogether and that should have been that, but either the man was a fool or he hadn't yet taken notice of the Panarch's recognizable face.

"What do you think you're trying to pull?" The petitioner questioned belligerently at the same time as the female Mage behind the table looked up from her post.

"Terrence –"

"Yes, Marge, it's me," the Panarch cut her off with a winning smile before she could speak the other half of his name and spoil his secret, "and I have a favour to ask of you, though I know I haven't waited my turn for it."

"That's...quite alright," the woman stammered as the man in the burgundy suit finally took notice of who he had inadvertently challenged and his eyes bugged out of his head. "You don't have to wait; I'm sure this gentleman won't mind in the slightest."

"No sir," the man said quickly, his face flushing, "I'm sorry, Pa –" he began and then curiously fell silent, his face turning redder as he obviously struggled for air.

"What can I do for you?" Marge swallowed carefully.

If that even is her name, Mirena thought, eyeing the exchange critically.

Terrence smiled handsomely, leaning forward as if whispering to 'Marge' conspiratorially. "My friend is looking to start studying here as soon as possible. She's newly come to the Capital and needs a place to stay. Please tell me that with all your considerable pull around here that you can get her in on the ground floor, so to speak."

Marge's eyes were fearful, but her tone was as steady as she could make it. "I'm sure that something can be arranged, P– presently...Terrence. Yes, I'll see that all is handled...presently."

"Thank you, Marge," Terrence smiled. "As usual, you're a dear."

The Panarch turned from the two Magi then, dismissing them from his mind. Mirena found herself watching the second Mage, the male who until now had not managed to shut his jaw since it had fallen open sometime near the beginning of the exchange.

"Lyana, I leave you in capable hands," he told her. "I hate to have to run, but I've got duties of my own that I must attend to. I trust that we'll see each other again?"

"Perhaps," Lyana responded noncommittally but with a slight smile.

Terrence nodded, taking this for a yes. "I'll hold you to it. If you'll both excuse me," he added, nodding to Marge and taking his leave before making his way beyond the line of petitioners, the crowd soon blocking sight of him.

"Miss Lyana…?" The female Mage questioned.

"Morelle," Lyana supplied.

"Yes, well, if I could get you to follow me, then we can do as the Pa–as...Terrence wanted."

"We both know your name isn't Marge," Lyana whispered, letting the woman know that she was in on the secret, "so what should I call you?"

"Stacey," she responded quietly, turning quickly to head in the direction the Panarch had gone. "Right this way, Ms. Morelle."

XX.

Hope sighed with pleasure, stretching languorously and causing the soft white sheets to pull where they had wrapped around his legs in the night. Blinking as he came awake, he realized that he was forgetting something.

Oh yeah, he realized, *it's no longer nighttime.*

Hope had to force his brain to work sluggishly as he'd never been a morning person. He concentrated and the sun began to rise outside his window, just as lazily as he was feeling, slowly illuminating the master bedroom of the cottage he'd created.

I could get used to this, he thought, looking about the room as the sunlight filtered in and revealed the finer details. Large bay windows with the curtains drawn showed simple, rolling hills as far as the eye could see. Perfect clouds dotted the light blue sky and the grass wavered in a slight breeze as Hope willed it to do.

The room was not lavish, nor was it particularly busy; it was simply enough. Homey, for him at least; the wooden walls and sturdy furnishings gave him a sense of familiarity, even though this hadn't actually been his room for long. He'd designed every inch of it and so it fit his tastes perfectly.

And then there was Mirena. Turning his head to one side, he felt a smile creep to his face as he took her in; she was beautiful and graceful, even while sleeping. She had managed to wrap herself entirely in the tangles of the bed sheet and her long white-blonde hair was strewn haphazardly across the pillow.

She had taken to wearing the mask that the Mirror World's Panarch had given her at all times since she'd gotten it, except when she was sleeping. It gave Hope some satisfaction that he was the only one who got to see the real her, prophecies and all, but he still sometimes wished that she would simply accept her own beauty and let the words show.

Perhaps one day she would, when those words would no longer be enough to get her killed.

Reaching over ever so carefully, Hope traced a particularly telling line that draped across her lower back. Mirena was so far gone in sleep that she didn't twitch away at his touch, so with gentle fingers, he traced the line downwards, moving the sheet aside as he did so.

"And with the Creator's blessing, the Prophet of the Light shall bear him a son and the boy will be called Grace."

Hope and Grace, Hope thought, *fitting, I suppose, but she sure does pick odd names. But this says that I will father a son...with Mira.*

I love her, I do, but am I ready for that? At least I know it hasn't happened yet. The prophecies that have taken place already fade or disappear entirely; this one is dark and therefore still in the future.

The prophecies said a great deal more than simply the fact that he would one day become a father, but there was too much to dwell on now and the meanings of most of the lines were cryptic at best. In fact, the one on her lower back was one of the more obvious ones.

Shaking his head at the strangeness of such foreknowledge, Hope leaned in and kissed Mirena lightly on the shoulder. She likely wouldn't feel it, but he was loathe to wake her; she'd been working long hours for over three months now.

She trained with Jehenna, D'wann, Odark and himself well into the night and then more recently also started attending classes at the Collegium during the day in the way the rest of them couldn't with such recognizable faces.

Mirena was often exhausted and today was no different. Since it was a rest day at the school, it was best that she get what sleep she could.

So he left her there and quickly got dressed, pulling on his Magi robes. They marked him for what he was, but at the same time they allowed him to blend in better in the Collegium and today was the day that he'd have to make another supply run. Not only that, but there were some things going on in the Collegium that Hope felt he had to see for himself.

"Okay wait, let me guess," Elizabeth began as Hope came down the stairs and found her sitting at the kitchen table, ignoring her breakfast of a single stale piece of bread. Supplies were lower than ever; his last run had not been as successful as he would have liked. "Hope, am I right?"

Hope nodded. "Right as usual, Elizabeth."

"Thought so," Elizabeth responded, sounding bored, "this game used to be fun, but you two are too easy to tell apart. He's all broody and you're all…well, Hopey."

Hope smiled. "Well, we are Mirrors. Speaking of Tendro, have you seen him?"

"Right behind you," Tendro said, coming down the stairs to join them from the set of extra rooms that Hope had added to the second floor.

Hope turned about to face his Mirror. It no longer unnerved him to look at himself; it really was like looking in a mirror, but no stranger than that unless he dwelled on it. Tendro was dressed identically in a black and gold Magi outfit, his usual colour. The other option was the white with silver trim that Hope favored but wasn't confident enough to wear openly, as it could be construed in this realm as showing support for the Light, or at the very least that one was defying the will of the Panarch.

"I'll need you to stay here today, Tendro, or at least stay out of the Collegium," Hope requested. "I have to do a supply run and I don't need anyone reporting the sight of two Tendro Seynors."

"A supply run sounds like just the thing," Elizabeth agreed, getting to her feet. "When do we leave?"

"I'm going alone, Elizabeth," he told her.

"Like hell you are," she countered. "Last time you came back with barely enough to last us a week and we've stretched it for nearly two. You don't know how to shop or steal and somebody has to show you how to do it."

"Not this time," he replied, his tone firm, "I've got other things I've need to do. While it would be fine to have the two of us in the marketplace, we're more likely to be spotted in some of the other places I need to go and I can't be seen with you; it would undermine what we've worked for."

Elizabeth pouted. "Well, what am I supposed to do, then? You almost never let me go to the Capital and I'm dying of boredom in here. I'm not meant for cottage life; I crave the city."

"Tendro's free for the day now, too," Hope noted. "Why don't you two see what trouble you can stir up elsewhere to further our cause?"

"If you need trouble stirred and supplies gathered, I may know just the place," Tendro offered. "We can get there through the Sentinal Stones."

"Fine," Elizabeth sighed, "you're more fun than Hopey anyways. I'm in."

Hope picked up the discarded bread from Elizabeth's plate and opened the front door of the little cottage. The opening revealed the clearing south of the Capital where the Sentinal Stones stood proudly; he had set the door to always open to this place so that his allies could come and go. So far it had worked nicely; it worked even better with the addition of a back door to reach the field they had all been using as training grounds for both Majik and fighting.

He took a bite of the bread as Tendro and Elizabeth filed past him and almost choked on it for his trouble.

"I told you that you suck at getting supplies," Elizabeth noted with a wink and a sharp pat on the back. "Take care of yourself out there, okay?"

"Tendro's been in and out of there a hundred times and so have I," he responded once he got enough air to speak. "I'll be fine."

Hope regretted his blasé words now. He felt naked here, exposed for what he was. He'd left the Collegium and the Capital under suspicion of being a traitor, if not worse. Showing his recognizable face here now felt foolish, even with all the work he and Tendro had done to repair his reputation.

The marketplace had been bustling but the library was a quiet place. It was so much more dangerous to linger here where he couldn't blend in with the crowds of people. Still, what he'd come for was important and finding the meager section of the library dedicated to religious history would not take long.

There it is, Hope saw the volume he was looking for, *'Understanding Prophecy' and there's 'Avatar: A History of the Seekers of the Light.'*

It was perhaps strange that such 'blasphemous' texts would be in the Panarch's library, but it did serve to remind the people of the Light's repeated failures and the victories of the faith of the Destroyer over that of the Creator.

The first volume he hoped would help him to help Mirena with the words she now wore. The second, far from light reading, would give him a better idea of what the men who had taken on his title of Avatar had lived through while seeking to find the Creator's prison so they could free her. They had all failed by trying where he'd succeeded by accident, but maybe there was something to be learned from the type of people they were, or how they had become infamous through their good deeds.

Putting a cloth sack around the books to hide their controversial titles, Hope turned to head through the aisles to the checkout desk. Almost there, he froze in place before instinctively putting his back up to a bookshelf to avoid being seen.

It's her…

Tendro has reported seeing Caralain back in the Capital, but I'm still not certain which one we're dealing with. There were two Caralains there the night I met the Creator. Now that I know about the Mirror World, it's likely that the extra one was from that realm. Only one of the two Caralains made it through that night alive, but which one was it?

And if this is my Caralain's Mirror like I think it is…what is she still doing here?

He leaned out slowly from his hiding place to get a better look at her. Caralain's back was to him, her dark hair silky and straight reaching all the way to her lower back, and she stood at the very desk Hope needed to stop at before leaving in order to register the books he was taking. She wore a vibrant red dress, so different from her usual choice of light blue or white.

It was a rest day, so her choice wasn't overly odd, but still she looked…provocative.

Hope glanced from side to side as if trying to determine who Caralain was trying to impress. *It's not a day that Tendro has scheduled to see her again, but that doesn't mean she doesn't expect to run into him…or me, I should say.*

That's when Caralain turned around, feeling his eyes on her back. Spinning abruptly, her gaze locked on to his as this motion revealed her very large and pregnant belly.

Hope frantically fought to control his facial features and not betray the shock he felt.

Tendro has been seeing her; been seeing her like this, he told himself. *She'd expect you to already know about her condition.*

Why didn't he tell me something this important?!

"Tendro?"

It has to be mine... Hope realized, feeling his panic rising as Caralain began to approach his compromised hiding spot. *If this Caralain isn't the imposter...by the Destroyer, it has to be mine. She's got to be at least six months along...and I've been gone for almost four.*

"Tendro, what are you doing back there?" Caralain asked.

Caught like he was, Hope had no choice, so he stepped out from behind the bookcase. He reached for a book at random as he did so, not even looking at the cover.

"Just picking out a book," he commented in what he hoped to be a casual fashion. "I was bored."

"Well you could have come to see me," Caralain said, flashing an alluring smile. "What have you got there? 'Dream Theory'," she read, "I didn't know you were into that sort of thing."

"I wasn't," Hope replied with a shrug, putting the book back on the shelf where he'd found it, "but after you've told me so much about it, I thought it might be worth looking into."

"I was just returning some books on the topic myself," she said lightly and he found himself able to breathe a little easier at the very generic topic. "I think I might have a volume that would really appeal to you back in my rooms, if you're interested."

"I don't know..." Hope began, but then realized that he'd better do anything in his power not to wreck the groundwork that Tendro had lain in re-establishing a sort of relationship with Caralain.

This may be an imposter, or at the very least we may not be one another's intended anymore, but the rebellion needs the information that only Caralain, with her proximity to the Panarch and his Generals, can provide us. I can't make her suspicious of me.

"I mean, it sure is exciting in here," he changed his tone to light-hearted sarcasm, "I wouldn't want to miss anything."

Caralain laughed softly at his joke. "Come on, I'm certain we can find other ways to amuse ourselves."

Does she mean...? Hope questioned, wondering at the implication in her tone. *It's impossible to know which one I'm dealing with...if this is the Mirror Caralain, she's got the role down pat.*

What is she up to?

Letting Caralain take the lead like she had so many times in the past, Hope followed her out of the quiet library, having no other choice now but to steal the books he had tucked away into his cloth sack.

It's better that I don't sign them out legitimately anyway, considering their titles.

Caralain led him to her quarters in the dorms of Magi Hall. It was the room they'd once shared together and it was surreal for him to return and by her invitation, no less.

They talked of this and that on the way there, nothing too risky for either of them, and Hope found himself inexplicably beginning to relax somewhat. Obviously by her treatment of him, Tendro had done good work repairing his image and with Caralain at his side he had no fear of walking confidently through the Collegium hallways; for better or worse, he belonged there once again.

Caralain opened the door to her room and didn't hesitate walking through it, turning back to face him with a questioning smile once she was inside.

"Feeling shy?"

Hope realized that he'd stopped on the threshold of the doorway, no longer feeling that this room was his or that he would have permission to enter it.

"No," he answered, stepping into the room as she obviously expected him to do, "not really," he added cautiously, "it's just that everything is different now..."

What has Tendro gotten me into? Hope questioned. *His reports never prepared me for this...*

Caralain stepped toward him and reached for his hand. Hope didn't protest, still working under the premise that he'd have to try and go along with whatever she presented because he didn't know what she expected from him due to all the time she'd spent with his Mirror.

Taking his hand by the wrist, Caralain pulled him to her and to his surprise she rested his hand on her distended belly.

"I'm going to name her Eryth," she proclaimed, smiling and holding his hand in place with her own. "The healers tell me it's going to be a girl. They can tell, with majik; some arcane use of water. What do you think?"

Maybe this is her Mirror. Either way, this isn't the Caralain I remember. She's different somehow...happier. She's going to be a mother; maybe the only difference is that having a child is something she's always wanted.

"Eryth sounds like a wonderful name," Hope replied truthfully, feeling tears sting his eyes.

I'm going to have a daughter…a little girl named Eryth.

He felt Caralain regarding him then and his eyes met hers. They were no more than a foot apart, standing in the room they used to share with the knowledge that their baby was on the way. Hope didn't notice himself leaning down to kiss her, but when their lips met, he didn't put a stop to it.

It was just like before.

It was like his abandonment of her had never happened. She was kissing him, running her hands through his hair and reaching authoritatively for the clasp of his belt buckle.

Caralain was a woman who knew what she wanted; if this was her Mirror, then she was remarkably similar to the woman to whom he had been engaged.

"Don't ever leave me again," she ordered, unlacing and reaching into the front of his pants, punctuating her words with a squeeze.

Hope gasped; he was shocked all at once with the boldness of it and the desire that her actions and even her words sent coursing through him.

"I…" He stammered, wanting at the same time to give into her demands but also to have the strength of character to walk away from her and never look back.

But Caralain wasn't looking for an answer, at least not the verbal kind. Pulling him to her, she reached up with her free hand and forcefully brought his mouth back down to hers.

Within moments, she had him panting and gasping for air; all thoughts of escape driven right out of his head by the desire she rekindled within him.

As he entered her, mindful of the child between them, Caralain moaned and arched her back in pleasure and it was a simple matter to shut the door to their room with a gentle push of air…

Tendro and Elizabeth were back to the cottage before he was. Hope spared no more than a moment to put down his sacks full of supplies before he rounded on Tendro, grabbing the front of his collar and shoving his Mirror up against the wall. It was clear by his expression that Tendro had never expected Hope to do something like that.

"Holy shit," Elizabeth exclaimed, surging to her feet. "Where's Hope and what have you done with him?"

"Why didn't you tell me she was pregnant?" Hope demanded heatedly. "And when the hell did we start sleeping with her?"

"I thought you knew," his Mirror answered calmly, Tendro's expression controlled once he got over the initial shock of the violence, "and *I* haven't."

Hope dropped Tendro and walked away, feeling disgusted with himself.

"She's going to name the baby Eryth," Hope said, "that's all I have to report."

Mirror's Hope

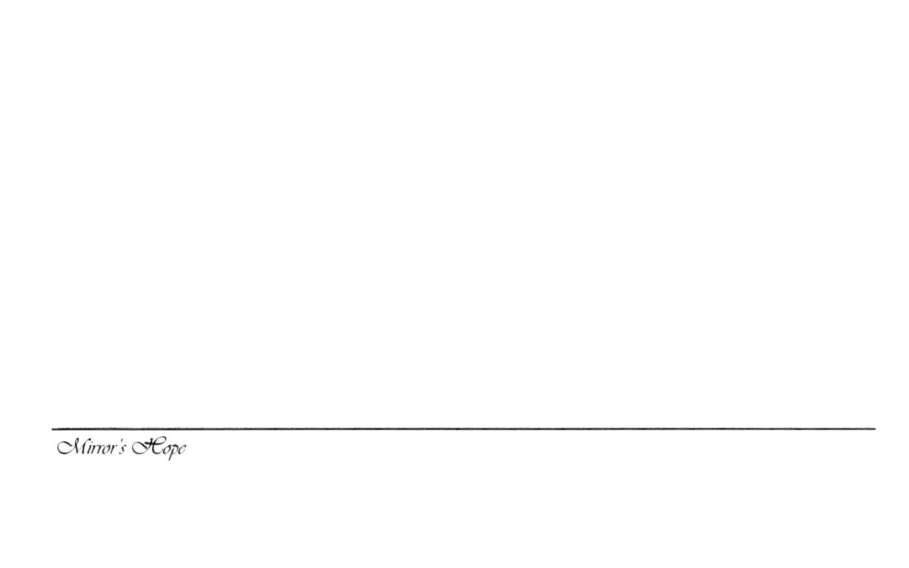

XXI.

Lyana found Terrence waiting for her at the end of her day of classes. He stood immobile in a gold-trimmed black Mage's outfit with his hands clasped behind his back, a sly smile playing about his lips, and a small bubble of space around him amidst a crowd of student Magi dispersing quickly from the classroom.

"You just don't know when to give up, do you?" She asked him with her lips quirking in a slight smile, inwardly pleased that he had sought her out.

It's working...

"I'm not known for it, no," he answered, pulling a bouquet of deep blood-red roses out from behind his back. "These are a little less common, don't you think?"

"They may not be common," Lyana noted, considering the flowers in his hands but not reaching for them, "but they're predictable."

"I'll do better next time," Terrence commented nonchalantly and the roses in his hands burst into sudden flames, the vibrant leaves and dark petals reduced to ash in mere moments.

"So you're a full Mage, I see."

"A talented one, I assure you," he replied simply.

"We'll see," she answered noncommittally. "Is there a reason you've arranged this chance meeting?"

"As a matter of fact, there is," he responded, his smile widening now. "We're late; come on."

"What?"

Without another word being spoken, Terrence took hold of her hand and tugged Lyana along the corridor. Soon he had led her down so many smaller hallways in the Magi section of the Collegium that Mirena, who knew the Capital even as Lyana pretended not to, was lost.

"Where are you taking me?" Lyana asked, once she'd caught her breath.

"You'll see," he responded cryptically, taking yet another turn, this one leading them conveniently out onto the monorail platform just as the train was calling out the last warning to board.

Without delay, Terrence leapt through the open monorail doors, tugging Lyana behind him as they whooshed closed.

"You think you're clever, don't you?" Lyana questioned, her tone amused and annoyed in equal measure.

"Don't you?" He repeated with a smile and then laughed with the knowledge that his ploy had worked. "I mean, I have you all to myself now and that was the point of all this."

"Some might consider this to be kidnapping."

"I suppose they might if you were a child, but you, my dear Lyana, are very much an independent woman who can make her own choices," Terrence replied, his smile knowing.

Mirena tried to ignore the stares of the other people aboard the crowded monorail car, but Lyana had little trouble dismissing their whispers; in fact, she silently reveled at the attention. These people were going to get to watch as she used Jehenna's teachings and her own instincts to masterfully manipulate the Panarch into fulfilling her every desire.

"Don't tell him what you want," Jehenna's words echoed in her mind.

"Reward him not with words, but with a smile or a gesture. A free laugh to show you are enjoying yourself and are relaxed in his company will let him know how to make you happy and in turn, allow you to direct him according to your whims."

Lyana smiled suddenly, turning her head to hide the blush she allowed herself to feel.

Let's see what he thinks of that, Mirena thought, her cunning mind carefully hidden behind the beautiful facade of a woman caught off guard by an ardent suitor.

The monorail's warning system chimed out the notes that indicated that they were stopping at a station. They weren't far from the Collegium at all, only a single stop down the monorail's full journey that lasted a turn and a half of the hourglass, but it seemed that this was the stop that Terrence had been waiting for, even though it was close enough to the Collegium that they might have walked instead of boarding the monorail.

"Let's go," he instructed, taking hold of her hand once more to lead her from the monorail car.

The platform here was small and not busy. It was late and the sun was just setting; Lyana's classes had not ended early. A light drizzle was beginning, but the oncoming soggy weather did not dampen Terrence's good spirits in the slightest.

"It's not far, but I wouldn't want you to continue to think I've kidnapped you," he noted, regarding her out of the corner of his eye. "Did you want me to call a hover cab or would you prefer to walk?"

I shouldn't be surprised that the Panarch would think nothing of calling a hover cab for such a frivolous purpose, Mirena thought, *but even still, having a magik-powered vehicle at your beck and call is exceptionally costly and it certainly isn't helping 'Terrence' keep his cover as just an average Mage.*

"We could both do with a little fresh air," Lyana responded, "Besides, I find the rain refreshing."

"Walking it is then," Terrence pronounced, holding out his arm to her.

Lyana put her arm in his, seeing little point in being difficult if he was going to act the part of the gentleman.

He was correct, their destination wasn't far. The small restaurant was tucked in an out of the way corner, with deep black velvet curtains hiding the interior from view and a lit bright red sign announcing the name of the establishment as 'Valentinos'.

"After you, my dear," Terrence directed, allowing Lyana to precede him into the small entranceway.

Passing by him in the small space, Lyana's eyes lit on the restaurant's host and she saw that she had an opportunity here. Working quickly, she walked a few steps forward to where the host stood and then tossed her head over her shoulder to regard Terrence.

Good, I have his attention, Mirena thought, reaching up and taking hold of the pen that held her hair in place, letting it fall loose as she simultaneously reached for the sack of coins she kept tucked in her Mage's robes.

Shaking her head gently so that the curls bounced into place, Lyana used the momentary distraction she knew she was causing to slip the host the bag of money, careful not to let the coins clink together as she did so. Locking eyes with the host, she took note of his imperceptible nod and knew that she had succeeded.

This man will do whatever I need of him tonight. There's enough gold in there for dinner and far more than that to cover any other expenses, no matter what Terrence Lee tries to impress me with.

Bowing with proper respect for his honored guests, the host led them to a small round table for two in an empty section of the restaurant, giving them the privacy she hadn't even needed to ask for. Either the Panarch had arranged that little detail in advance, or her money had bought the man's good sense as well and he was willing to do what favors might grant him more of her patronage.

Terrence pulled back Lyana's chair for her as the host offered to take her jacket. As Terrence looked up at her once more he was greeted with the sight of her Mage's robe being shrugged off into the hands of the waiting host, revealing what she had chosen to wear beneath them, just in case of an event like this one.

It certainly doesn't hurt to be prepared, Mirena thought, taking in the Panarch's rapt attention to her low-cut neckline and slim, form-fitting black dress. The material was plain, but hugged her like a second skin and it was just a tad shorter than the conservative Mage's robes he had been expecting her to continue wearing.

Pretending to ignore his stares, or take them as a matter of course, Lyana placed herself on the proffered seat, tucking her feet under the chair and allowing him a glimpse of her long, perfectly-shaped legs before they were hidden by the white table cloth.

Terrence leaned down over her, affording himself a lingering view for just a moment before he took hold of her hand and kissed it lightly.

"I'm so glad you've decided to join me tonight," he commented, then nodded to the host to dismiss him for the moment before returning to his seat across the table from her. "I didn't think you would after all the effort you've spent avoiding me."

The host retreated politely to a corner of the room where he would not be intruding, but would be near enough if his services were required.

"I don't want to have to say this, but with my status comes specific obligations," Lyana noted softly, her eyes downcast on the white napkin before her. "This can't be what you want it to be."

"A bottle of your best Claret, if you please," Terrence raised his voice and called out to the host, whom it seemed was going to serve them personally this evening.

It wasn't long before the wine was brought and poured. The round-bottomed wine goblets glistened with condensation and Terrence's eyes sparkled with amusement and something deeper as he regarded Lyana across the table, his hands steepled under his chin.

"May I?" Lyana asked; holding out her hand as the host tried to present the Panarch with a leather-bound menu.

Terrence gestured for her to help herself and with a mischievous smile Lyana took the menu, gracefully flipping it open and holding it in a way that way he couldn't see what it contained.

"Steak," Lyana said without hesitation, her eyes barely glancing at the menu. Instead, she looked over the top of it, locking her eyes Terrence's. "Rare. Firm, but tender; a fillet for a man who considers himself a cut above the rest and a desirable commodity.

"Potatoes, mashed with roasted garlic," she continued in the same fashion, "a dependable selection, but with a hint of added flavor. Well seasoned so as to be never boring and layered with sharp cheddar, so there is always something more to be discovered with every bite.

"Finally, garden fresh asparagus, lightly steamed just until they are tender, but still have a snap to them. A refreshing break from the richness of the rest and an aphrodisiac as well," she added with a sly look over the top of the menu, "since that seems to be what you're implying you want from this meal."

Terrence cracked a smile at this last comment, his eyes twinkling.

"Well done," he noted. "Very perceptive of you. And for yourself?" He questioned.

"Chicken Caesar salad," Lyana responded simply. "A hint of lemon, hold the bacon and light on the cheese. Thank you," she finished, closing the menu with a snap and handing it back to the host, smiling warmly in his direction. "Also, a glass of water, if you please."

The host nodded, accepting the menu with professional grace before leaving to prepare their meal to Lyana's specifications.

"You haven't touched your wine," Terrence noted, taking a sip of his own and placing his goblet back on the table.

A glass of water appeared on the table before her as the host casually walked by and placed it there. Lyana reached for it.

"I know."

"Beware the Panarch's pride. Play him like a fiddle. Push and pull him, taunt and tease him, but never bruise that fragile ego or you may risk losing all that you've worked so hard to gain."

Jehenna's words, a caution, entered her mind.

"You really must try it," Terrence insisted, taking his own goblet and spinning it so the place where his lips had touched its rim was facing her before reaching across the table and placing it before her.

Lyana reached out and placed her hand upon his, taking hold of the goblet with her other hand and pulling it to herself. With a knowing smile and a deliberate motion, she spun the goblet back around and took a slow sip of the fragrant wine.

"You're right," Lyana said. "It's divine. I commend your choice."

Their food arrived, artfully prepared and masterfully presented, brought by a team of servants on small plates, one at a time, with accompaniments that Mirena had never thought to ask for.

I'm starting to wonder if the gold I provided is going to be enough to pay for all this.

"Everything looks lovely," Terrence commented, ignoring the food in favour of letting his eyes take in their fill of her.

Mirena felt herself blush at his attention before she buried her personality back beneath Lyana's, sipping cautiously at her wine to hide her momentary lapse.

"You think too much of me," Lyana told him. "How many times must I remind you that you cannot have me?"

"Until it sticks, I suppose," Terrence laughed, "and that might never occur, so it's probably best if you just leave me to my delusions and cease mentioning their impossibilities, lest I be forced to face them."

"As you wish," Lyana pursed her lips in thought. "I suppose it would be cruel of me to take away your fantasies."

"I see we are agreed, then," he said with a smile. "Dessert?"

"By all means."

"Allow me, though I'm certain my skills at reading people aren't as adept as yours. But then, I wasn't trained in Lasalle."

Waving the host back over, Terrence didn't need to tell the man what he wanted; the servants simply followed his gesture and the plates before them were carried away without much fuss. Within a moment, a small, leather-bound placard was placed in the Panarch's outstretched hands.

"Steak is a simple choice for a man, even though your opinions were accurate enough, but a woman is not quite so simple a matter; especially a woman like yourself." He paused, considering her. "Bold, with a strong flavour, but not overwhelming, sweet and not bitter, though not sugary and without a false coating…

"I think that a tiramisu would do nicely. It stands up to all other flavors in a classic, yet unforgettable way and as it is carefully prepared in a mouthwatering liqueur in advance it is simply delicious when enjoyed at the proper time.

"How did I do?"

"Time will only tell if your presumptions are correct," Lyana smiled indulgently in his direction, "but you are correct that a woman is no simple matter."

"Like a full-bodied wine," Terrence agreed, swirling the last of the deep Claret in his goblet before downing the contents in one gulp. "I'd like to think I'm up to the task."

Lyana found herself smiling despite herself. "I am beginning to believe that you received a little training in Lasalle yourself."

"I didn't," he answered, grinning to show his appreciation of the compliment, "but since you're wondering, I was trained in Marroise as a Sophist, actually. Before coming to the Capital, that is."

"A graduate of the College of Communication and Geography," she nodded. "A good background in worldly things, but the real question is: what is the focus of your studies now at the Collegium?"

"What makes you think I'm still a student?" He asked, his expression teasing as the host returned with their dessert plates, placing them unobtrusively before them, complete with tall flute glasses of clear champagne decorated with tiny red berries.

"If this is the point where you tell me you are a teacher, then I must inform you that this is highly inappropriate," she told him, her tone abruptly serious.

"I'm not a teacher," Terrence stated, the smile never leaving his face, "though I do believe I did mention earlier that I'm a full Mage."

"I guess it slipped my mind, since you are so young that it didn't seem the case."

"Majik keeps us looking young," Terrence noted with a shrug, "the stronger of us even more so. I'm not as old as you might think, but I'm not as young as I look either. The truth is that I work at the Collegium.

"You might say that I'm in the business of granting petitions," he paused a moment, giving away the lie, in Mirena's opinion. "What about yourself, Lyana? What are your ambitions? What would you like to do once you've finished your studies?"

"You're a smart man. I am sure you will figure it out," Lyana redirected. "Besides, it is getting late and I have an early class in the morning."

"A subject for next time, then," he replied, gesturing for the host to bring the bill.

As summoned, the man arrived and slid the cheque to the exact center of the table between them, not an inch closer to either of them. Caught off guard, Terrence allowed his momentary surprise to show on his face before reaching for the bill.

Lyana made no move to stop him and instead waited with no show of impatience for the further shock she was about to cause him. Mirena knew she was bordering on the edge of Jehenna's advice with this move, but she felt that it was a calculated risk.

The cheque had no monetary amount listed on it, but Lyana caught just enough of a glimpse of it to see the words 'paid in full' written clearly in the host's fine hand on the bottom of the page.

Terrence's expression betrayed his confusion. He knew full well he hadn't paid for a thing and had intended to do so at the conclusion of the meal. He had to be wondering if his position as Panarch had bought him this expense without having to actually pay for it.

"There is no reason for you to go broke trying to impress me," Lyana commented after a moment, reaching across the table to pull the bill down so she could look Terrence in the eyes and show that she wasn't being condescending, but really meant her next words, "but I appreciate the gesture all the same. Goodnight, Terrence and thank you for the evening…

"It was a pleasant surprise."

Mirror's Hope

XXII.

"Hey, you..."

Odark, seated at the kitchen table, greeted Mirena with an odd expression on his face. The book he was reading was lowered for the moment and his eyebrow raised in question as she entered Hope's cottage in the void-world, pausing just inside the doorway.

"What?" Mirena questioned, feeling piqued. "Can't say my name? It's only one syllable."

He gave her a pointed look in response, raising his hand to mime removing a mask from his face.

Oh yeah, she realized, *I'm still Lyana.*

"One syllable, eh?" Odark commented as she hastily removed the mask that altered her features, picking his book back up and bringing it to eye level. "Mi...ra."

"Shut up," Mirena retorted, narrowing her eyes at him. "It's been a long day."

"I can see that," he replied, eyeing the hourglass suspended on the kitchen wall. "You're back much later than usual. Pretty much everyone else is in bed at this hour."

"I lost track of time," she mumbled, too tired to bother coming up with a better excuse for her actions.

"Ah," he replied, leaving it at that and going back to his reading, "well, don't let me keep you. I'm sure you've got another busy day planned for tomorrow."

"Can I ask you an honest question?" Mirena interrupted him.

"Do I have a choice?" He answered quickly, then seemed to catch himself, his tone softening. "I'm sorry, I didn't mean that. Go ahead."

"What do you know about Caralain?"

"This one or ours?"

"This realm's," Mirena clarified.

"Not too much," Odark answered cautiously. "Hope's had me hopping around to various places, moving people and supplies and gathering information, so I haven't spent any real amount of time in the Capital; that's where he and Tendro have been focusing their attentions.

"I do know that she is close with the Panarch," he continued, the book flat on the table once more as he used his hands to gesture as he spoke, "real close; maybe too close. People in the outlying areas think that maybe she's trying to manipulate him. Others think that she is more than just his General or his mistress, though most of them agree either way that the baby is his..."

"She's pregnant?!"

"Yeah..." Odark answered, seeming confused by her reaction, "I thought you knew; it's fairly common knowledge by this point. I think she must be about six months along by now." He mimed how large and round her stomach must be. "You haven't come across her in the Collegium?"

"No, I haven't," Mirena admitted, still reeling from the news. "Don't you think that's strange?"

"Maybe," he allowed, "but the Collegium is a big and busy place. It's possible that it's simply a coincidence, or that you don't move in the same circles."

"I can assure you that we do," she noted quietly. "Anyways, thank you for your time. I should be getting to bed...I have a lot to think about."

Odark nodded. "Good night, then. And Mira," he added, stopping her at the bottom of the stairs, "don't dwell too much on it. Pregnant or not, if she willingly panders to a man like your Panarch, she's not worth it."

Odark's well-meaning words stabbed her like a knife in the back and her guilt sent her up the stairs two at a time. All too soon, Mirena found herself at Hope's door and she threw herself at the handle.

Late or not, he was going to answer for this.

Let him deny his relationship to Caralain when I have proof of the contrary and witnesses to the condition Hope has put her in...

Mirena could do the math and it was all too easy to prove that the child in Caralain's womb belonged to Hope.

Six Months?! Mirena's anger threatened to overwhelm her. *Six months ago Hope and Caralain were engaged, probably publicly if Stiphy's knowledge was accurate. That means there was no way Caralain would had been seeing the Panarch at the same time. Stiphy had no reason to lie to me; the truth hurts too much.*

The handle didn't budge; the door was locked.

That bastard, she thought viciously. *He's known all along...or at least since we've been back. He's known his fiancée was pregnant with his unborn child and he's been sleeping with me!*

"So this is how it's going to be, then," Mirena stated, loud enough that if Hope was awake he would hear her and the anger in her voice.

Not waiting for a response, she turned from his door and crossed the hall to her own room, slamming the door behind her.

Alone in her room, sleep was a long time coming.

Morning came abruptly, sunlight illuminating Hope's void-world as if it rising at all was an afterthought. Despite this, Mirena had trouble discerning what time of day it actually was.

This place is so fake, she thought bitterly, still reeling from last night's discovery. *Just like the man who made it.*

Tossing her blankets to the floor disrespectfully, Mirena climbed from the canopied bed. With her arms strengthened by D'wann's physical training, she tore the cloth canopy from its support, throwing it haphazardly in a fit of pique and knocking the wooden posts to the ground in the process.

Not that it means much since he can so easily make another, Mirena sulked, *but this makes me feel a little better.*

Stomping on the fabric for extra measure, she disentangled herself from the mess. Perversely, Mirena folded her night things and placed them neatly in a pile as she dressed carefully, her rage smoldering until the violent flames were at last reduced into glowing embers.

At the bottom of the stairs, Mirena found an audience of unexpected stares waiting for her.

"Are you building a tree fort up there or something?" Elizabeth demanded with her usual flair. "Geez, Mira. I didn't know that waking up on the wrong side of the bed meant that you had to bring the house down around you and bury the rest of us in a pile of rubble."

Tendro, Hope, Odark and Jehenna all waited for Mirena's reply with varied expressions. Hope's was contrite, his eyes downcast and avoiding her gaze, Tendro's was simply curious; Odark and Jehenna looked concerned.

"A gallows, actually," Mirena answered in a flat tone, walking past them all. "If you'll all excuse me, I have somewhere to be."

"Mira," Hope said, catching up to her at the main door and grabbing hold of her arm, "wait."

"I think it would be wise if you didn't try and talk to me right now," she warned in a low voice.

"You've changed," he said, meeting her eyes at last.

"And you're not the person I thought you were," she retorted, meeting him stare for stare. "Was any of it real?"

"Mira..." Hope pleaded.

"Don't call me that," Mirena pulled her arm out of his grasp and reached for her mask, putting it to her face and becoming Lyana once more.

I need this right now, Mirena told herself. *I need to be someone else. It's too hard to be me and face him like this. I'm mad, but I love him too much and it hurts.*

What she didn't expect was how much it hurt to see his expression close off to her now that he was faced with Lyana and not Mirena.

"Fine, go," Hope said. "We can talk about this when you come back."

Without a backwards glance, Lyana left the cottage and its occupants behind; she had things to do.

The Collegium gardens were well populated as usual and even more so near the square patch of bare earth that marked the training yard. People had gathered there around the fenced-in yard to watch the physical contest of skill that was taking place.

Two swordsmen faced one another; the grace and intensity of their movements were clearly born of their great skill and not simply put on because of their rather large audience. No, these two fighters hardly knew or cared that the people watched them; they were far too focused on winning.

Both competitors were male and one was decidedly shorter than the other. Mirena knew them both, or at least their Mirrors, but Lyana could not claim to have ever met either of them.

D'wann faced Odark, the former with a blank expression on his face even while his sword arm was whirling to fend off the shorter man's attacks. Tall and broad of shoulder, D'wann was imposing even while cloaked and standing still. Here, shirt off and thick muscles rippling with the weight of his two broadswords, he was a terrifying predator and Odark was either brave or foolish to be facing him, especially with only the one slender blade in his hands.

The left side of this Odark's face was identical to the Odark Mirena had just left in the void-world not long ago, but the right side was another matter altogether.

Lyana was able to hold in Mirena's instinctively horrified reaction. *What happened to him?*

The Odark she'd once known, the man who had graciously slid her a piece of pie on the night she'd met Hope, was hardly recognizable now. The right side of his face was melted and scarred, as if someone had warped it with flames and then frozen it that way so that it would always look like it was still on fire.

I wonder if still hurts him and how long ago it happened... Mirena thought, studying Odark's deep look of concentration as he twisted and turned, bringing his sword down repeatedly to try and break through D'wann's whirling defense. *I haven't been gone that long, have I? I suppose it's been nearly six months; I would have noticed Caralain's pregnancy otherwise.*

Odark was breathing hard now, his motions slowing, but D'wann had still not broken a sweat and it was becoming clear who the better fighter was, even though Odark showed some real skill.

Driving forward suddenly, Odark made a risky maneuver that put him between D'wann's blades, forcing the bigger man to attack rather than defend and then Odark struck.

Swatting aside D'wann's swords one at a time, Odark made himself an opening and got in close enough to do some real damage. Unfortunately, having expended his efforts in keeping the broadswords from decapitating him, he didn't have enough time to make good on the opportunity he created for himself. In that extra moment it took for Odark to bring his sword around for a fatal strike, D'wann had him.

A sword blade to the front of his neck and another to the back of it, Odark was forced to freeze in place or risk losing his life in what had started out in a harmless training session.

"Why don't you pick on someone your own size?"

Lyana's level words cut through the sudden hush of the crowd following the realization of Odark's fate. Her unexpected taunt drew all eyes in her direction, including the two combatants.

With a release of the tension in muscles held taut, D'wann withdrew his blades and Odark stepped carefully free, very much aware of how close he'd come to real harm at the hand of his teacher.

D'wann looked around the crowd, his expression flat as he considered the onlookers. "I see no one my own size," he noted after a moment. "Either way, this is not a tournament or even an occasion for sport. I was teaching this man a lesson it would be better for him not to forget."

"The size of a man is not merely measured by his bulk but by his confidence and intelligence as well," Lyana stated with confidence, climbing over the short wooden fence with a smooth motion to walk out and meet D'wann in the middle of his playing field.

"What do you think you are doing?" The swords master demanded.

"Looking to get herself killed, apparently," Odark commented offhandedly, wiping the sweat from his brow with a cloth from his pocket.

"Proving I am worthy of your instruction," Lyana countered, prideful.

D'wann laughed without warning and there was no humour in it.

"If you value your beauty and wish to keep your head, I suggest you back down now," Odark suggested for her ears alone. "Your pride isn't worth this and he won't spare you pain or disfigurement."

"I value everything equally," Lyana responded quietly, her words sincere. "I am not afraid to die. As I see it, each scar marks a person's journey and what they've overcome, showing their strength for the entire world to see."

"Who are you?" Odark questioned, regarding her strangely.

"It doesn't matter who she is," D'wann stated coldly, sheathing his massive weapons on his back. "She's just a girl who's wasting my time. Get off the field."

"I thought you were a teacher and if I am correct, it's your job to judge everyone equally and fairly," Lyana retorted, just as cold. "If nothing else, since I am just a silly girl in your mind, take this opportunity to show your students a lesson in humility."

"Humility or humiliation?" Odark muttered, his eyes dark.

"Forget my students," D'wann stated. "It seems you are the one in need of a lesson in humility. Unfortunately, I don't teach girls. Fairness and equality aren't in it when you are weaker just for being what you are."

"Try me," she pressed.

"No."

Lyana looked around herself for a weapon. *A stick or something, anything will do.*

She was startled when a sword presented itself, held out by the one man who'd cared enough to try and dissuade her from this course of action.

"If you're going to do it anyways, you should at least do it armed," Odark noted, passing her his sword hilt first and taking a step back to clear the field.

Lyana nodded to Odark in appreciation for his timely gift before turning back to her quarry.

Remember your training with this man's Mirror, Mirena told herself. *He is going to hold nothing back. He will go for the kill if he has the opportunity. Hold your ground and show no fear or pain. Odark's right; this is foolish, but it's also necessary.*

This is what I trained for; I have to be ready.

Lyana took in a deep breath. She held nothing back, yelling wordlessly as she charged at the bigger man who stood there calmly, his swords still sheathed. At the last possible second, he moved faster than his size could account for and he drew one sword, not bothering to bring the blade around, but striking downward with the hilt instead.

The metal hilt sunk into her shoulder with a sickening crunch and Lyana took the sharp pain of it with as much dignity as she could muster.

He thinks I'm going to stop now, admit I was wrong and succumb to the pain he's inflicted, Mirena thought. *He's wrong.*

Her borrowed sword continued its forward motion, keeping a steady trajectory that was in no way altered by the mind-numbing pain in her left shoulder. D'wann was fast, but not quite fast enough to avoid a glancing blow to his left arm, the one that hadn't drawn the second sword he could have used to defend himself.

He's underestimated me, Mirena exulted. *I made good use of my first strike, but he won't make the same mistake twice.*

D'wann cocked his head to the side a moment, regarding her as if weighing his opponent at last.

"You know how to take a hit," he noted. "Do men strike you often?"

Lyana didn't even dignify that question with an answer. Launching herself forward, she did what D'wann would never expect and dropped her sword, diving into a handspring on her uninjured sword arm and flipping up over his head.

The swords master was tall, but she'd practiced this move a hundred times on a man the exact same size, shape and strength. Lyana didn't attack him physically, for she had no weapon, but she did reach down inside of herself for her majik to boost her high enough into the air to make it over the large man's shoulder. As she did, she took hold of the hilt of his second sword, knowing from training that she was just strong enough to wield it; at least for a short length of time.

The barest touch on D'wann's shoulder was enough to send her majik coursing through him. The sword easily slid free from his scabbard, as he had not sheathed it very firmly following his fight with Odark. In less than an instant, Lyana found herself on the other side of the man, his heavy broadsword in her right hand as she steadied herself to wait and see if her gambit had paid off.

He turned, just a fraction slower than he would have before her touch. Then, facing her, D'wann wobbled slightly and she knew she had him.

"What did you do?" He questioned while he leveled his remaining sword in her direction.

"What it took to win," Lyana answered; her voice level as she too raised her sword and then pulled hard on her majik to make a second blade. This one was birthed from fire and appeared in her left hand.

I'm not strong enough after what he did to my shoulder to hold anything more substantial than this, but a sword made of flames gets my point across quite nicely.

Taking one single step, she had both swords crossed before the General's neck, reminiscent of the way he'd trapped Odark. It wasn't a perfect hold and if it wasn't for her majik weakening his responses, he would be able to easily overcome her, but as it was she had him and everyone who was watching them knew it.

The crowd didn't know whether to cheer or remain silent. There were a few hesitant claps and a brave woman called out in support for Lyana's boldness, but mostly the atmosphere was tense and expectant. Odark, however, only looked pensive.

"All right," D'wann capitulated. "I'll train you on the condition that you stop relying on a woman's tricks. Your appearance aside, if I train you, you become a man."

Filled with sudden and exhausting relief, Lyana let the metal sword fall to the dusty ground and the fiery one in her hand dissipate.

"My name is Lyana, and I'll act whatever part you wish on the training field, but I'm very much a woman and you'd do best to remember it."

Mirror's Hope

XXIII.

I suppose I should go home and face Hope, Mirena reconciled herself to the thought. *I'd better get it over with it while I'm still feeling confident. While I'm there I should also have Jehenna look at my shoulder; it feels like something might be broken.*

Lyana took the short way back to the monorail station, which involved taking less well-known passages through the Political Wing of the Collegium. It was the route Terrence had shown her back on the night he had taken her to Valentino's. Even though the halls she travelled were less populated than most, Mirena wore Lyana's face here in the Capital as always; it was safer that way.

"Are you trying to say that it isn't mine?"

"I'm not trying to say anything...I'm telling you this child is Terrence Lee's."

Mirena couldn't help herself; she stopped dead in her tracks. She knew she was staring but she couldn't seem to tear her eyes away from the scene before her.

There in the hallway, between two minor embassies, Tendro stood next to a very pregnant Caralain. They were in the middle of a conversation that was certainly not meant to be overheard, but they had gotten louder as the discussion became somewhat heated.

Tendro, or Hope, depending on which one was actually standing before her, would no doubt have recognized her disguise and gone silent if he'd taken notice of her, but his back was to her. Also, to the best of Mirena's knowledge Caralain had no idea who Lyana was.

"Even if we weren't still sleeping together, I think we both know that isn't true," Tendro remarked, lowering his voice once more, "and the Panarch isn't a fool; he would know it too."

"The Panarch believes what I tell him and you'd be wise to do the same," Caralain commanded. "Whatever the two of us had is over. You made certain of that when you left, even if we have had some good times since you've come crawling back. Besides, in a few more months, maybe sooner, none of it will matter. Terrence and I are getting married and when I claim –"

Her words cut off abruptly upon hearing the gasp that Mirena hadn't realized had escaped her lips. With the sound, Caralain's gaze locked onto Lyana. She was the only person who had stopped in the hallway, clearly with the purpose of listening in on their conversation.

"Do I know you?" Caralain asked; her eyes piercing as she studied Lyana's face.

Mirena found herself breathing hard, even as she silently thanked Lee profusely for the precious gift he had given her.

"No..." Mirena stumbled, trying hard to regain Lyana's composure. "I just remembered that I have a test tomorrow...sorry to have bothered you."

"Lyana Morelle, isn't it?" Tendro asked; his demeanor friendly and his words casual.

Mirena found herself wondering which one she was dealing with and how he managed to seem so in control after the news he'd just received and with the knowledge that she might have just overheard it.

"You're new, right?" He continued, acting nonchalant. "I think we have that class together; History of the Ages, right? Test in the afternoon tomorrow?"

"Yes," Lyana agreed, even though they both knew full well there was no test in the one class they shared. "I thought you looked familiar. We're soon to have Physical Training together as well. I've just joined your class and I start tomorrow."

"D'wann doesn't train women," Caralain noted, her tone flat but her eyes still searching Lyana's face for some indication of how much she'd heard.

"He does now," Lyana replied with a self-satisfied smile even as she gave Caralain a once over, taking in her rather round and full figure. "Congratulations..." she added belatedly. "Perhaps once you've delivered and you manage to get back into shape, D'wann will consider letting you join us."

"Perhaps," Caralain responded, her lips pursed and her tone tightly controlled.

"I'm sorry, I didn't catch your name," Lyana said, turning subtly to face Tendro and dismissing Caralain from her view.

Tendro was trying to hide his amusement but Mirena knew Hope's face well enough to see it regardless, even if this was only his Mirror. "Tendro Seynor. It's nice to officially make your acquaintance, Miss Morelle."

By this point Caralain was practically fuming and looking impatient at the continued interruption; she didn't appear to be someone who could stand to be anything other than the center of attention.

"Yes, it is," Lyana agreed politely, drawing out her departure on purpose. "Perhaps we could get together some time to study? Tonight, if you're not otherwise occupied," she added, flirting only a little. "I mean, I know it seems forward, but the test is tomorrow, after all."

This is the deciding moment, Mirena thought inwardly sickened by the whole scene as she watched Tendro's expression carefully. *Hope would look to Caralain first to gauge her reaction because he wouldn't want to overstep his boundaries with her no matter how she treated him. But Tendro...I don't think he would hesitate in accepting this offer, as it would be a slight to the woman who just dumped him.*

Tendro smiled that familiar half-smile that both he and his Mirror were so fond of.

"Certainly. The gardens?" Tendro, Mirena was sure it was him now and not Hope, used their code word for returning to the Void-world. "Say, in about an hour?"

"Perfect. See you later, then."

"Perfect," Caralain repeated, mockingly. "Now, if you'll excuse us."

"Of course," Lyana agreed graciously, forcing a grin and showing teeth. "Good day."

Collected and centered; that's what I need to be.

The sword in Hope's hand flared, the flames licking his hand, but he didn't feel the heat of it. His own sword, controlled by his majik and made manifest by his will, couldn't hurt him.

If only it was so simple with everything else.

"Don't you think you're stretching yourself a little too thin?"

Her voice came out of nowhere, condemning him. "Did you honestly think you could play the game with me, toy with my emotions and assume I wouldn't figure it out?"

Hope's head snapped up, thinking for a moment that he was imagining her disdainful words, but Mirena, wearing the mask of the persona Lee had given her stood before him. She had just entered the void-world through the semi-permanent opening he had left between this world and the real one beyond it.

It's as if another soul lives inside that mask and it takes her over each and every time she wears it, he noted. *What sort of a gift changes a person so much?*

"Do you have nothing to say for yourself? I *know*, Tendro," Mirena stated forcefully, her words callous and so unlike her usual kind demeanor. "I know about *her*. I know everything that you tried to keep hidden from me. Caralain...your engagement...your baby!"

"The fact that you're still *sleeping with her!*"

She was yelling now, almost screaming, but her words were too controlled, the emotions not as raw as they would be without the mask. The voice wasn't quite right either and she'd called him Tendro; she'd never done that before.

"Take it off."

"What?" Mirena questioned, as if she didn't remember that she even still had it on. "This?"

She took the mask from her face and held it up. It was then he took notice of the massive purpling bruise developing on the left side of her neck, heading down toward her shoulder. There was blood seeping through her black Magi robes too, he could see it now; the wetness of it.

"Mira, what happened to you?"

Mirena's face got, if anything, more filled with rage. Her pale skin, tanned no longer by the illusion of the mask, reddened with the force of the emotions that threatened to overwhelm her completely, if they hadn't already.

"Are you kidding me?" She demanded, throwing her precious mask to the ground. "Did you hear anything I just said?!"

"I heard you, Mira, but your shoulder..." Hope gestured at the wound, concerned for her. It looked painful and it was a wonder she wasn't hampered by the pain she must be feeling. "What happened?"

"Fuck my shoulder!" Mirena yelled, beside herself. "This isn't about me, this is about the fact that you've been cheating on me with Caralain!"

"I..." Hope stumbled over a response to this, his mind and tongue going numb.

She really does know everything, he realized. *I should never have kept it from her in the first place.*

"It's not what you think..."

"Oh, so, you're cheating on Caralain with me, then?" Mirena demanded heatedly. "Which is it, Hope? Because it's one or the other."

The sword in his hands evaporated as he lost concentration. He was dumbstruck. *I did cheat...I only meant to keep my cover as Tendro, but I allowed Caralain to manipulate me...*

What am I saying? Hope admonished himself. *I am Tendro. I've done this and I have to take responsibility for it.*

"I'm so sorry, Mira," he whispered, knowing that his words could never be enough. "It was a mistake..."

"Me or her?" Mirena demanded coldly.

Hope looked up at her and met her eyes in shock. *How low her opinion of me has gotten. How did I not notice that she was beginning to feel this way?*

"Mira, I love you," He told her, meaning every word. "I've told you this before. Yes, I was engaged to Caralain, but that was before I met you."

"This is first time you have ever said that to me," she snapped. "How dare you tell me you love me now?"

"Haven't I?" Hope questioned, his mind whirling and trying to recall. Memories danced through his mind of the times they'd spent together. Happy times, sad times and the more intimate moments and he realized all at once that she was right...he'd never actually said the words.

"No."

"I've been such an ass to you, Mira...you deserve better," he hung his head, feeling shame overtake him.

"Choosing to play the victim again, are you?" She demanded.

"No, I'm not," he stated, raising his head to look her in the eyes. "I know full well that you're the one getting hurt in all this...for me. Leaving your family, your home and your studies; the words marking your skin and the games you've been forced to play. I know what it is that knowing me has done to you and I'm sorry for it.

"I had hoped that part of it was made up by the fact that you wanted to be here, with me; that I made you happy. But I've gone and screwed it up and that was never what I intended."

"It was worth it, before...but it was all lie, wasn't it? I was just a silly girl with delusions of happiness. I was a fool, but no more," Mirena stated decisively. "This is about me, now. Until you can figure out what you want, without the lies, then what we had is over."

Hope felt her words like a blow to the stomach. They came as such a shock to him, even though they were deserved a hundred times over for what he'd done.

"Even if you don't want me to…" he said quietly, hardly knowing what he was saying, the only feeling in his body the tearing of his heart. "I'll still love you, Mira. I can't help the way I feel, even if you want me to stop."

"Shut up," Mirena snapped at him suddenly, throwing her hands up as her face contorted in a sudden and fierce anger. "Just shut up! You don't have the right to talk to me like that anymore. In fact, you don't have the right to talk to me at all!"

She whirled and started away from him, toward the house, bending to scoop up the mask almost absently.

"Mira…" Hope pleaded, his voice sounding distant to his own ears.

But she didn't even hear him; she was putting the mask to her face, becoming Lyana once more…she was lost to him.

"I didn't mean to catch the last bit of that," Hope's Mirror interjected, Tendro's words coming from behind Hope and sounding genuine of all things, "though Lyana told me to meet her here in an hour and your conversation was too loud to ignore."

"It doesn't matter now," Hope sighed, too emotionally drained to feel anything but an immense sense of loss. "We've been playing this like it's a game, but these are lives we're toying with, Tendro, and people that we're hurting. This has to stop."

"By this, what exactly are you referring to?" Tendro asked.

"All of it."

"The revolution?" Tendro questioned searchingly. "Do you want to give up?"

"No," Hope sighed. "I don't. And whatever she says, I know Mira doesn't want to either. Just...this game with Caralain. We have to put an end to it. Publicly would be best."

"Then I have good news for you," Tendro smiled unexpectedly. "Caralain's decided to dump us anyway. She plans to marry the Panarch and claim that her child is his."

"Our child, you mean."

"Ours?" Tendro questioned, shaking his head. "It's yours, or maybe it's Terrence Lee's, but it's never been mine."

"Sorry, yes, you're right."

I have a child...and Caralain's going to give it to the Panarch to secure her own power... Hope hardly recognized the feelings that came over him with the realization.

That bitch!

"Leave me alone," Mirena headed off both Jehenna and Elizabeth by stomping up the stairs toward her room.

"Lyana, you're hurt," Jehenna reminded her. "It's not doing your body any good to push it like this."

"I don't care," Lyana yelled back, throwing the door to her room open and sending it flying into the wall with a crashing sound.

"Where's Mira and what have you done with her?" Elizabeth questioned pointedly as she stomped up the stairs behind her.

"She's gone; maybe for good. My name is Lyana."

"Like hell it is," Elizabeth protested with her hands on her hips in the open doorway. "You can change your face and your hair and act like a bitch, but that doesn't make you any less my sister."

"Watch it, Beth," Jehenna warned. "I've taught her to embrace a whole second life as Lyana. If that's who she says she is right now, then she means it."

"As of right now, you don't have a sister anymore," Lyana told her heartlessly, "not in this realm, anyway."

"I'm not listening to this," Elizabeth threw her hands up. "When you want to come to your senses and take that goddamn mask off your face then we can talk. But if this is how you're going to treat me, then I'm glad you're not claiming to be related to me, because that gives me the right to tell you to go fuck yourself."

"Are you quite finished?"

"Yes," Elizabeth answered, turning on her heels and stomping from the room.

Choosing to ignore Jehenna's continued presence; Lyana turned to the wardrobe and began efficiently packing her things into a bag.

Jehenna's touch was light on her injured shoulder and the majik she sent into the torn and mangled flesh was soothing. It wouldn't be enough to heal the damage completely, but it would hasten the process and help ease the pain.

"Has something changed?" Jehenna asked gently. "Must you move into your rooms in the Collegium now to accomplish what you've set out to do?"

"Yes, unfortunately," Lyana replied matter-of-factly. "I can't afford to be distracted by the drama of this place. Besides, if I am to get what I want, I need to be accessible to Terrence at all times. This has to be real."

"I understand, but what about your responsibilities here? What about Mirena's life?"

"She will check in once in awhile," Lyana responded, ensuring Mirena's personality was as far down as it could go; it wasn't only the drama of this place that was distracting. "But as for her life, it's no longer as important. She brings nothing to the table but useless emotions and I can't have that affecting my mission."

"It's your choice," Jehenna told her. "I can't stop you, but I can offer some advice. Let Mira out to breathe every once and a while; it won't do to lose yourself in the role you've created. Yes, Lyana feels real and is real, but Mirena is who you are and who you will have to be for the rest of your life. Don't forsake her, for she created you."

Lyana nodded. "I'll keep that in mind. Now if you'll excuse me, I must go."

Mirror's Hope

XXIV.

"Did you convince me?"

Lyana came to an abrupt stop, just about to exit through the permanent door Hope had made so they could all come and go from the Void-world as needed. D'wann was a man of few words, but those he did speak were usually very worth listening to.

He was leaning on the outside of the cottage, waiting, it seemed, for her. D'wann took full notice of her bags, packed to bursting with all of her belongings, but he didn't mention them. He spoke to her like he didn't care if she was Lyana or Mirena; his words to her would have been the same, regardless.

"Well, I did have the best person to train me," Lyana answered simply.

"So confident," he noted, regarding her with his customary level gaze. "Don't let one success let you become accustomed to it. I would use that as an opportunity to teach you a painful lesson, more painful than even your shoulder there."

"I don't feel confident," Mirena told him honestly, forgetting for the moment to be Lyana and to keep up the character she'd built to hide behind. "I feel like everything is falling apart and it's just as much my fault as it is anyone else's. This game is getting dangerous and I am afraid I am going to lose."

"Do you know whose face it is you wear?" D'wann asked suddenly, changing the subject in Mirena's opinion.

"Terrence Lee's ideal woman?" She ventured uncertainly.

"More so than you know," he answered in a low voice. "Lyana Morelle was Lee's first love. Not many people even remember that she ever existed, but he can't forget."

"What happened to her?" Mirena asked, sorrow welling up within her at the thought of how difficult it must have been for Lee to give her Lyana's face and see her wearing it in light of this new information. "Is that why he asked me never to wear the mask in his presence?"

"She is no more," D'wann answered simply. "The people who don't know her name and can't remember her are the ones who are right. She never existed because she was killed by a force of majik so strong that it was able to erase her from reality."

"Why are you telling me this?"

"Because you need to know," he replied. "By wearing her face, you honor her memory and because she doesn't exist without you, you are her. Lee loved her; he still does. And Lee believed in you enough to grant you the face of the woman he loved. Lyana could never let him down, so you will succeed because you are meant to."

"So I am Lyana's Mirror," Mirena realized in part what D'wann was trying to say to her.

He nodded. "Lee and Lyana were married for only a month before the incident which took her life, but from one of the only people who remember a time when she lived, believe me when I say that their love would have lasted a lifetime.

"You can do this," he added. "And trust me, it isn't a game."

Mirena felt the weight of his words crash down on her. *D'wann's right; this isn't a game. I am Lyana. Does this mean that by being given this face and wearing it so well, that I am destined to fall in love with Terrence and him with me?*

Maybe Lyana can handle that, but I can't...

"Thank you, D'wann," Lyana spoke. "As always, you are my mentor. I have a long day tomorrow, if you'll excuse me."

D'wann nodded, bidding her goodbye with a gesture. "Watch yourself, Lyana."

Lyana had to get an early start the next morning in order fit in a meeting with the Panarch before her first class. She still had to get the change in her schedule approved to be able to join D'wann's training class and for entering such an elite group, Lyana would need permission from the Panarch himself.

She was pretty sure she was ready to handle facing him in his own den, though she was fairly certain that 'just Terrence' would not be as ready to face her learning the truth of his identity.

"Name?" The secretary, a red-headed woman with a cool demeanor and dark, metal-framed glasses didn't bother looking up as she took the next petitioner in line to see the Panarch.

"Morelle," Lyana stated.

The secretary looked up then, meeting Lyana's eyes. "That's it? Just Morelle, no last name?"

"Morelle is my last name," she clarified, hoping she wouldn't have to say anything further.

"Fine," the woman sighed tiredly, placing her hand on a panel on the left side of her desk. "I have a Miss Morelle here to see you..." There was an audible pause before the woman removed her hand from the panel once more.

"Thank you," Lyana replied sweetly, pleased to have gotten her way as she headed for the closed wooden door beyond the woman's desk.

Opening the door, she entered swiftly, closing it behind her with as little noise as possible and keeping her back to the room's occupant throughout the process. She hoped that if Terrence looked up he would take notice of her before she had to acknowledge that she recognized him.

"Miss Morelle…to what do I owe the –"

Lyana smiled to herself as the Panarch's voice fell silent mid-sentence. *I've got him.*

"…pleasure," Terrence finished his greeting awkwardly, getting to his feet and trying to save face.

Lyana took this opportunity to turn around and face him, her expression carefully prepared.

"Terrence?!"

The Panarch smiled suddenly, the grin just a little forced as he threw his hands up in the air in an animated gesture. "Welcome to my office!"

"Saying that you worked in petitions was a bit of an understatement, don't you think?" Lyana questioned, her mouth open in feigned shock.

"Perhaps a little bit, yes," he agreed, clearing his throat, "but it's true, regardless. I do grant petitions on a daily basis. It's quite tedious, I assure you."

"Oh, I'm fairly sure running a country is a tedious business," she agreed, not needing to try too hard to sound unimpressed with the revelation of his status.

"So I take it you aren't here to see me?" Terrence asked. "I mean, you're here to see 'the Panarch' for business..." he smirked, "and not for pleasure?"

"Yes, actually," Lyana retorted, her mouth settling into a thin line. "I am here to speak to you about a man named Terrence who just doesn't know when to leave a girl alone."

Terrence laughed then, a real smile coming to his lips. "I thought that might be the case. Do you need me to pass him a message?"

"That his fantasy is a little far-fetched," she replied, then after a moment's hesitation she threw her hands up in defeat. "I can't do this. I won't be that girl; not even for you."

Her motions more frantic than he'd ever seen them; Lyana turned for the door, struggling to find the handle in her haste to be away from him.

"Lyana, wait." Terrence was around his desk in a flash, his hand thumping to the wooden door before her to hold it closed and his voice was in her ear. "I was only teasing. You don't need to leave, I'll grant your request like a proper Panarch."

"There is another Panarch," Lyana told him, feeling a little overwhelmed by his nearness and trying to regain her composure. "Theia Prosai would grant my request just as quickly."

"Theia would make you wait hours, if not days, to even hear your request," Terrence told her, his tone realistic without being overly arrogant. "Besides, we both know who wields the power in this city."

"You're getting married," Lyana stated, turning around and putting her back to the door to face him as she revealed what she knew as she met his ice blue eyes.

"A matter of political convenience, I assure you," Terrence responded quickly, "and Lyana," he added, their faces too close together now for anything other than an intimate conversation and his arm still holding the door shut over her shoulder, "one word from you could change all that. She's not important to me."

"She's carrying your child."

"I'll be honest with you, Lyana, because I want to tell you the truth and I want you to believe me to be a man of my word," Terrence told her, his tone as serious as a gathering storm and Lyana felt as if she was in the center of it. "The child is not mine. No one else knows it, but I don't believe I'm capable of being a father. I've agreed to marry Caralain because it was the one sure way to guarantee myself a successor."

"Things change. Majik can make the impossible, possible," Lyana told him in a whisper. "You can never say never when it comes to fate."

"That still doesn't make Caralain's child mine," he countered. "I think it's Tendro Seynor's."

"I caught them talking in hushed whispers in the hall yesterday," she confided. "She's dead set on saying it's yours."

"As she should be if she wants this marriage of ours to come to pass," he agreed in an offhand manner, "but that's not what's important here. I want to hear your opinion. Does what I am change what's between us?"

"Not what you are, but what you're implying me to be," Lyana protested. "I'm not a whore and I won't be one for any man."

Terrence frowned. "I do not consider you such and I hold too much respect for you to ever ask it of you. Do you think so low of me?"

"Do you not see that you put me at an impasse? You say you want us to be together, yet you are marrying someone else. What else should I be thinking?"

"The truth," he stated, not relenting. "That I want to be with you, not Caralain Dashar."

"Then prove it."

"I will," he answered, leaning down to place his lips on hers and kissing her lightly, not in a possessive way as Mirena might have expected.

"Starting with this," Terrence whispered, his lips still inches from her own.

He kissed her again and Lyana didn't stop him. It wasn't fear that kept her from moving or even passion, it was something else; something that she couldn't yet identify. She was curious and she felt something stirring deep within her and slowly rise to the surface to overtake her better judgment.

His lips lingered for a moment on hers, the warmth of him near enough to entice her into wanting more from him, but then he stopped, not giving in to the temptation as much as he, too, must have wanted to.

Terrence dropped his hand from the door, taking a half step back from her. "I'll grant your petition," he told her. "My secretary has my seal and I'll let her know to see to it that your desires are fulfilled."

"Are you not the least bit curious as to what you are agreeing to?" Lyana asked, feeling unexpectedly breathless.

Terrence smiled. "I trust you. Go; we'll talk later, over dinner?"

She nodded despite herself, looking into his eyes and searching for sincerity. *Is he playing me the way I'm supposed to be playing him?*

"If D'wann's training doesn't kill me first."

"Would you have me tell him to go easy on you...?" He began and then seemed to catch himself, looking startled. "Wait – you said D'wann's training you?"

"That is what you agreed to by granting my petition."

Terrence's gaze was intense. "You're sure that's what you want? Out of everything I could grant you, you choose to have that man pummel you for an hour every day?"

"I want to prove I'm the best and D'wann only trains the best."

"I have one condition for my approval, then," he added.

"You told me I could have anything I wanted and now you are imposing conditions?" Lyana asked, smiling in disbelief.

"I've already approved it," he dismissed her concerns with a wave of his hand, "and as I said, I'm a man of my word. This condition is for my General.

He's going to have to promise me that you'll live or I'll have his head."

Mirror's Hope

XXV.

I can't believe it's been nearly three months already...

Lyana sat patiently waiting for Terrence to join her in the Collegium gardens. It was brisk on a very early spring day, but they had planned to meet for a picnic lunch regardless and a checkered cloth was spread beside her on the fountain's edge with a large wicker basket balanced upon it.

Terrence really is completely different from what I originally thought, she reasoned. *It's as if this game we're playing just comes so naturally; I don't have to even think about it anymore. I wonder how he truly feels about me, if he is sincere when he tells me wants to be with me.*

And what about me?

Am I as sincere as I pretend to be? It's getting harder and harder to detach myself and know what's real and what isn't. That makes this game even more dangerous...but can I afford to stop now?

Do I even want to?

Lyana knew she was treading dangerous waters. She sat contemplating her predicament as her hand lightly skimmed the top of the fountain's clear pool, enjoying the feel of the icy chill on her fingertips.

A splash startled her before she felt the cold drops sprinkle her face.

Terrence? Lyana questioned and looked up, an expectant smile on her face and her heart feeling suddenly lighter in her chest. He was late, but she didn't mind; the Panarch was a busy man.

"I hear D'wann lets you play with the boys."

It wasn't Terrence; it was Dipaul.

Lyana had to mentally force Mirena's fear down; she could show no weakness in front of this man.

"It's called training, not playing," she informed him in a frosty tone. "Perhaps you don't know the difference, which is why I never see you in class."

"So you need to be trained to play with boys?" Dipaul turned her words on their head. "I can offer you a free lesson, if you'd like."

"Are you quite finished?" Lyana questioned, unimpressed. "I don't appreciate your tone with me. I can assure you that I am much higher class than the women you normally socialize with, so I will let your actions slide for today."

He smiled then and it was an expression that promised malice. Deep within Lyana, Mirena whimpered at the sight.

"That's generous of you," Dipaul told her, the smile only stretching wider as he spoke, "giving me a whole day to treat you as I please. A high class whore; I'll have to consider how best to take advantage of your offer."

"How dare you say that to me?" She demanded, standing abruptly to put herself in a more defensible position. "I would suggest that you leave now, before you regret it. I don't take kindly to men who call women whores."

"That's okay, I don't take kindly to women or whores," he said, advancing upon her and closing the already not-so-great distance between them. "I just take them," he finished, reaching for her with his solitary hand.

Lyana slapped his hand away from her. "Don't you dare touch me. I'll scream," she warned.

"I like it better when they scream," Dipaul told her honestly, leaning his face into hers until she could feel the rough stubble of his cheek and the heat of his breath on her neck.

"Your hand isn't the only thing that will be missing if you don't back off," she hissed, her words heated but her body frozen in terror.

"Oooh, feisty," he noted, grinning with anticipated pleasure now as he tightened his grip on her arm. "Do you fight this hard the whole time? Because that would be fun…"

Lyana spat into his face, not feeling that his line of questioning deserved a more respectful response and Dipaul's grin stretched from ear to ear as he licked the spittle from his lips slowly, savoring it.

This time when he used his greater weight and strength to push her down to the fountains' edge, there was no slapping his hand away, as he already had her in his grip and not much in this world could make him let her go.

A button on her dress popped off to splash in the fountain, sinking slowly and Mirena sunk further with it. This left only Lyana to taste Dipaul's tongue as it thrust its way into her mouth, only Lyana to feel Dipaul's hand groping her chest and the stump of his arm pressing her down so she didn't have enough leverage to escape between his heavy body and the rough stones at her back.

She jerked and made muffled screaming sounds, but they didn't do her any good. She scratched Dipaul's arms, his chest, his face; any part of him she could reach, trying to bite him when her screams sounded weak, even to her own ears. But all of her effort only seemed to fuel Dipaul's fervor and his pleasure, making him want even more to be inside of her where he could do the most damage.

Lyana was pushed down hard on the cold and uneven rocks of the fountain, her torso half exposed and Dipaul's knee separating her legs by the time anyone came to bear witness to her plight.

She saw him before Dipaul did, her face turned uncomfortably to one side and her screams silenced for the moment, as she had run out of breath and hadn't yet been able to draw in more air.

Shock was never a part of Terrence Lee's expression; he skipped that emotion and went straight to unbridled rage. His face didn't redden like another man's might have, but Lyana recognized the emotion coming off the Panarch in waves.

Logically her mind told her that she should feel relieved that rescue had arrived, but all Lyana felt were the tears that rolled uncontrollably down her face; she'd never thought it would come to this.

"Dipaul Valorence, you are a dead man."

The words were unexpectedly calm and steady, but as cold as ice.

To her surprise, Dipaul's rough and questing hand stopped prying at what remained of her dress. It seemed there was one force on this world that could bring the monstrous General to heel.

"Panarch," Dipaul acknowledged his master, releasing Lyana and getting rapidly to his feet. "Have I done something to displease you?"

"You are dead to me, Dipaul," the Panarch's cold words continued. "I gave you everything, every privilege you could want; the power to crush nations and make men cower in your wake, but no more. You take everything I have to offer and then still take more.

"Lyana is not a thing to be possessed or shared. She is *mine*!"

Terrence summoned a sword of fire and the flames licked his hand, the blade flaring wildly in response to his anger and offering a counter-balance to the chill in his voice.

"You will leave now, or I will kill you myself…or better yet, I will defeat you and have Lyana chop off your balls and then your head."

"Panarch..." Dipaul said again, backing up hesitantly in the face of his ruler's wrath, but it was a measure of his fear or his respect that Dipaul never thought to draw a flaming sword of his own, or unsheathe the real one he wore strapped to his back.

"Get out of my sight," Terrence Lee said, disgusted. "I never want to see your face again."

Unable to do much else unless he wanted to challenge his Panarch to a duel, Dipaul left by warping the air before him until he'd created a hole to another place far from the Collegium.

Lyana caught no more than a glance of tall reeds and a familiar dock over a pond before the hole in the air closed again, taking Dipaul with it and allowing her to surrender to the pain and the fear now that he wasn't around to keep hurting her.

Terrence didn't make any attempt to comfort her with words. He simply let his sword disappear and picked her up in powerfully-muscled arms, cradling her against his body. She whimpered softly; though she wasn't overly hurt, she was shaken and her pride was badly damaged.

It could have been so much worse...

Dipaul had taken advantage of her and forced himself upon her, but Terrence's arrival had come in the nick of time to save her from further violation.

The Panarch didn't take her to his secret garden. Deep down, Mirena silently feared he might have, since it was the closest and most secluded spot. Instead he, too, warped the air before them, opening a hole to a plush room bearing a décor of richly-themed black and silver.

Two steps took them to the edge of the lavish bed, where he placed her gently before retreating from the room. He was back less than a moment later with silky black cloth draped over one arm.

"Here," he said, "put this on."

Lyana made no move to accept the fabric in Terrence's hands or even to acknowledge his words. Tremors had begun and they made her rock back and forth somewhat with their intensity. She was unable to bring herself to even form thoughts, let alone words.

Taking a step forward, Terrence reached for her partially-opened dress. Lyana's instincts kicked in and she withdrew from him, getting ready to defend herself if necessary.

I won't let him finish what his General started!

"Lyana," Terrence snapped, forcing her to meet his eyes. "Lyana, listen to me. I'm not going to hurt you and I'm not interested in your body right now. You need to put this robe on," he shook the black silk robe at her. "It will help protect your modesty."

She nodded, giving him permission to help her and she scooted a little bit closer so he could do so.

The Panarch's hands were gentle as he undid the remainder of the buttons that still held her dress to her body. There weren't many of them left, perhaps only two. Despite this, Terrence remained a gentleman and he didn't look at her skin beyond what was necessary to help her from her clothes and wrap the robe around her.

"There," he said when finished, "that's better, isn't it? I'll be right back, I'm going to start running you a bath."

He left her for a moment, but it didn't seem overly long from her perspective. She heard his footsteps cross the tiled floor of the bathroom and then she heard the water start to fill a tub in the room beyond.

With Terrence gone, Lyana had a chance to look around at her surroundings. Tall posts, sleek and polished dark wood and gilded silver accents, the Panarch's private chamber was fit for a king, though it was simply elegant and not overdone. The bedding was sleek black silk like the robe he'd brought for her to wear and the floor had a thick black carpet that rose like grass to cushion one's feet in the morning.

It's so...comfortable, Lyana thought, feeling a little awed. *This isn't what I expected.*

Sliding her feet over the edge of the high bed, she felt the soft black carpet experimentally with her toe and was pleased to find that it felt as soft as it looked. She got so absorbed in the novelty of the feeling that she didn't notice Terrence's return until he was standing before her, a gentle smile playing about his lips.

Lyana blushed, seeing the way he regarded her.

"You're beautiful…" he noted softly. "Do you want me to help you to the bath?"

She nodded; wordlessly, Terrence stepped into her outstretched arms and lifted her once more. Lyana enfolded her arms around his neck, burying her face in his shoulder and felt the tension drain out of her as she was comforted by his strong embrace.

He knows exactly what I need…I think I'm falling for him. No, it's possible that I already have...

Terrence set her down on her feet on the first step of a massive black marble square bathtub inset into the black-tiled floor. The water was the perfect temperature as it lapped against her feet and she longed to lose herself in the dark depths of the deep pool, but there was something she felt she needed to do first.

Terrence had still not let go of her waist or moved from where he stood just outside the bath. Standing on the top step like this put her height just slightly above his and leaning her head down she placed her forehead gently on his, resting it there a moment.

"Thank you," Lyana whispered.

"You don't ever need to thank me for something like this," he replied.

She drew back ever so slightly, leaning her head down further and seeking his lips. His mouth rose to meet hers, wanting so much to have whatever she was willing to offer him.

A knock sounded on the outer door, shattering the moment between them.

"Shit."

Lyana's eyes snapped open; she hadn't even realized she'd closed them.

Who would knock on the Panarch's personal chambers? Is it D'wann?

"Stay here and make yourself at home," Terrence instructed. "I'll go see what this is about."

Lyana nodded, not knowing what else to do or say and Terrence left her, shutting the bathroom door behind him on the way out.

Alone again, for the moment at least, Lyana looked about herself once more. The room was tasteful and simple, with black marble, gold accents and a large mirror. Other than the obvious features of a bathroom, there wasn't really much to look at and she didn't want to study the image of herself in the mirror with the purpling bruises that were beginning to mar her skin.

I suppose there's nothing else for it... She lowered her gaze to the dark waters at her feet. *I might as well make use of this opportunity to try and relax.*

Moving slowly, Lyana removed the robe Terrence had lent her, placing it outside the tub. Luxuriously she entered the water, letting it cover her up to the neck and sighing with the pleasure of it.

"I'm not sure how much more of this I'm willing to take!"

The sudden sound of a familiar voice caused Lyana to snap out of her state of bliss and sit upright in surprise.

"Calm down, Caralain," Terrence responded, sounding unimpressed.

"I will not calm down!" Caralain protested. "First you use every kind of delay you can think of to postpone our marriage and now you're taking out your frustrations on Dipaul?"

"You will not speak to me in that tone," the Panarch warned; his voice low.

Lyana gasped sharply, hearing the dangerous quality in his voice. *Terrence nearly killed one of his Generals not more than a turn of the hourglass ago, will he rid himself of another now?*

"I'm sorry, Terrence," Caralain's tone softened, realizing she'd overstepped herself, "it's all this stress...it's not good for the baby. Our baby..."

"You mean Tendro's baby," Terrence stated flatly. "I hardly feel that we need to keep up the charade in private."

Lyana could imagine Caralain's outraged expression but also the guilty truth in her eyes.

"You knew." It wasn't a question.

"Of course I knew," Terrence assured her. "Did you think me a fool? Someone to be manipulated, perhaps? You cannot play games with me, Caralain Dashar. Not if you expect to keep the power I've given you."

"I understand, Panarch," Caralain replied in a more submissive tone than Lyana had been expecting.

"Leave me," he commanded.

Lyana heard the outer door of the private apartments open and shut and then she didn't hear anything for a long time. She tried to return to enjoying her bath, but she found that the moment was lost and the words she'd overheard were tumbling incessantly through her mind.

With a sigh, she reluctantly dragged herself from the water and after toweling herself dry, she pulled on the borrowed robe once more before heading cautiously back out into the bedchamber.

She found Terrence pacing the length of the large room.

"I don't want you to marry her," Lyana stated quietly, only partly surprised that her words were the truth and not simply a part of her game to seduce the Panarch into wanting no one but her. "You told me once that one word from me could change your mind...well, I'm saying it now; choose me."

Terrence stopped pacing abruptly, his head snapping up and his eyes as open and guileless as she'd ever seen them. She didn't know how it had happened or when she'd fallen so hard, but Lyana found that she trusted this powerful man; she trusted him so far as to put the fate of her heart into his hands.

"Of course I choose you, Lyana," he told her. "That's what I've been trying to tell you all along...so you'll marry me, then? And together we'll hope and wait to see if we can have children of our own..."

"I'm sick of the lies," he continued, startling her with his open honesty, "I want someone I can love and trust."

Lyana took one step and then, having overcome that hurdle, she ran the rest of the way into his waiting arms. The borrowed silk robe slipped from her shoulders and fell unnoticed to the floor around her as Terrence enfolded her into his embrace and brought his mouth down to hers, bringing all her desire for him rushing to the surface.

I love him, I can't help it.

She kissed him with abandon, throwing caution to the winds and not dwelling for a moment on what had almost been or who she really was inside. Here, with him, she was Lyana and she was safe in the arms of the man she loved.

And she wanted nothing more than to prove it to him here and now and give herself over to him completely, no matter what it might cost her in the end.

Mirror's Hope

XXVI.

"Choose your weapons and pair off," D'wann commanded. "Lyana, you're with me today; we have an uneven number."

The training class was often surrounded by spectators as long as the weather was fine. Today showed spring's promise and so the idle Magi had gathered in droves.

"I have a regular partner," Lyana reminded the swords master, indicating Odark with a wave of her hand. "Did I do something wrong?"

D'wann smirked, his expression showing just how much he'd come to treat Lyana as one of the boys in the past couple of months. "You've been too hard on the others lately. Practice with me and give Odark a break. It's good to challenge yourself every once and while."

"Thanks," Odark murmured sarcastically, rolling his eyes at the slight.

"Don't worry, he meant all of us, not just you," Tendro told him. "Lyana's got us all beat."

Tendro, Lyana identified which one she was looking at.

It had become a game to her, trying to figure out each day which of the two men had come to 'keep an eye on her'. She'd gotten pretty good at telling them apart; Hope wouldn't have said 'Lyana'.

He'd have referred to me by a pronoun to avoid saying my name, as if that made it any less who I am.

"Don't sugar coat it," Lyana teased D'wann in the way that only she or those in the training class could get away with, "you need a challenge yourself once in a while, huh?"

"I could use a challenge," a new voice entered the conversation as Terrence Lee bounded over the low fence and the crowd erupted into hushed whispers. Some of them were bold or foolish enough to point at the Panarch, caught off guard by his sudden presence in their midst.

"I thought you said you weren't a student?" Lyana questioned, startled by his sudden appearance despite herself.

"Well, the only thing I needed to join this class was the Panarch's permission," Terrence noted with a self-deprecating smirk, "and I had no trouble getting him to sign the paperwork. It must be my winning personality."

By the raise in murmurs, the crowd didn't know what to make of their Panarch's humour, but those in the training class were all his Generals or those men who were training to hold similar positions and they were used to Terrence Lee's overwhelming presence.

"Well, you may be the Panarch, but that doesn't mean I will go easy on you," Lyana teased, causing shock to ripple through the onlookers at her bold words and the familiarity they implied.

Terrence grinned. "I certainly hope not," he told her, "I'm expecting to get a workout today." He winked; his back to most of the spectators if not to his new classmates, letting her know he meant more than just on the field.

"Weapons!" D'wann cut in with a roar. "Now."

To the surprise of everyone present, excepting perhaps Lyana, Terrence took instruction as well as any member of the class. He was the first one within the weapon's locker in the training facility and he selected a thin-bladed practice sword.

Physical Training was a small class, only eight members in all. One was absent today, but the Panarch's presence made up for that and four groups of sparring partners danced across the field, metal practice blades ringing as they made contact with one another.

D'wann often had them use real swords when they fought one on one, but in large groups like this he made sure they used dull-edged practice swords. He didn't want any accidental deaths and he couldn't watch all of them at once for any underhanded moves.

There was often fierce competition between the class members and not all of it was for sport.

"I knew you were skilled, Lyana, but you're also a pleasure to watch," Terrence noted, as he parried a few close calls. "A little distracting, actually."

"You should remember that out here I am one of the boys," Lyana warned, feeling her face heat with the implication in his words.

"D'wann may be able to separate mind from body enough to think of you that way," he countered, "but I do not have that kind of self-control."

"You're going to get me in trouble," she whispered fiercely, having spun in close enough to speak the words so the others wouldn't overhear as she feinted with her blade.

"Then fend me off, if you can," Terrence retorted with a sly expression. "You wanted a challenge, did you not?"

"D'wann, will I get in trouble if I severely injure the Panarch?" Lyana called out, winking at Terrence to show that she too could play.

The swords master didn't dignify her question with an answer but the onlookers found it scandalous and Terrence laughed, clearly amused at the effect their banter was having on everyone else.

"Call me Terrence," he said in an offhand manner, loud enough for everyone to hear. "I'm a student now and I should be treated like everyone else."

Lyana struck while Terrence was distracted by pandering to his audience. Flipping her sword around with expert skill, she drove the hilt into the Panarch's gut, driving him backwards and forcing him to double over in pain. Pressing her advantage, she ignored the crowd's outrage at seeing their ruler so brutally assaulted and lowered her sword in favour of sweeping his feet out from under him with her foot.

The surprised Panarch fell to the hard-packed dirt of the training field, rolling onto his back with a grin across his face despite the pain she'd caused him. Swinging one foot over his torso, Lyana squatted on Terrence's chest, using her weight with a sudden motion to pin him to the ground. Lifting her sword once again, she brought the point of it to his neck and held it there with expert precision.

"Do you yield," Lyana questioned pointedly, "Terrence?"

"So this is the position you're going to take?" He countered with a smirk. "Can't say I'm too displeased, but yes, for now I yield, Miss Morelle."

Removing the sword and flashing a smile that showed teeth, Lyana got to her feet and offered the Panarch a hand up, feeling that she'd proven her point, though he still managed to twist everything she said or did.

They are certainly not going to forget this day, Lyana thought, considering the thick crowd of gathered Magi. *I'll be the talk of the Collegium for some time. I don't know if that's a good or a bad thing...*

"That's it for today," D'wann bellowed. "Hit the showers, boys."

The showers in the training center were off-limits to Lyana. Technically, she supposed she could have used the facilities either before or after the men were through. Typically she didn't bother, knowing that her rooms were not too far away on the main floor of the Magi quarters.

So as the men replaced their weapons and headed to wash up, Lyana waited until the weapons locker was clear and then went inside to hang her own weapon on the wall. Stretching on her toes, she gained the little bit of extra height needed to reach the last spot on the wall.

"Need a lift?" Terrence's voice came from behind her and she got no more warning than that before she felt an unfamiliar pressure around her waist and hips lifting her up into the air just enough to reach the pegs in the wall comfortably.

Lyana gasped, awed by the sensation of hands formed of air lifting her upwards. The grasp was firm but molded to her form in an almost intimate way. When she was lowered to the ground again, she had trouble understanding why she felt a blush creeping to her cheeks, but it was warranted regardless as Terrence was there to put his arms around her midsection as soon as he released the bonds of air that had held her.

"You were remarkable out there," he whispered seductively in her ear, the rest of his body cupping hers. "The sword hilt to the stomach was a little uncalled for, but you made your point; I was being an ass."

"Terrence, you shouldn't..." she protested weakly, her breath coming a little more quickly, despite herself.

She felt his teeth on the tip of her ear, followed by a series of slow, meandering kisses down the side of her neck. Lyana let a soft moan escape her and she bit her lip, trying to control her reaction.

This shouldn't be happening...someone could come in here at any moment and for all anyone else knows, he's still formally engaged to Caralain.

"It's alright," he told her, his voice low and throaty with anticipated pleasure, "they're all in the showers. No one's coming in here."

As if to prove how unconcerned he was about discovery, Terrence reached around to pull at the lacings of the loose-fitting blouse that she wore to give her some freedom of movement while training. The ties came undone with ease as they were meant to, exposing her bosom.

She couldn't fight him and truthfully she didn't want to.

So what if we're discovered, Lyana rationalized. *It's the Panarch and no one will dare speak out against him, not even D'wann who is the only person who is likely to come upon us.*

Lyana turned, all at once convinced and unable to fight against her body's desires. She wanted his mouth on hers; she wanted it all.

Her lips closed on the Panarch's and then her eyes fell on the man standing in the doorway, watching the two of them lost to their passions and with their hands all over one another.

It was Tendro.

Cutting the kiss off abruptly, Lyana pushed back from Terrence, startled completely out of the moment as her heart skipped a beat.

"What the...?" Terrence questioned, confused to no longer have Lyana in his arms as he looked up and took note of the panicked expression on her face.

Her face was pale and she looked like she had seen a ghost, but in reality she had seen the face of the man she had abandoned to lure the Panarch into this very position. It was a position Lyana had intended to use to destroy him and so far had only managed to fall for him herself.

"I brought you your towel," Tendro noted, seeming to ignore what he'd just interrupted.

*I completely forgot...*Lyana realized, frozen in panic, *Tendro or Hope, whichever one comes to class, always brings me a wet towel so I can clean myself off a little before making the trip back to my rooms to shower.*

He must have come looking for me...

"Just leave it over there," Terrence instructed; his voice calm and not at all the tone of a man who had just been caught in the throes of passion to a woman that was not his intended wife.

Tendro nodded and did as instructed, leaving the two of them alone once more.

"Now where were we?" Terrence asked, seeking to resume their clandestine activities.

"I can't do this..." Lyana whispered, feeling uncomfortable and ashamed and knowing that Tendro had likely not gone far. "Not now."

Terrence sighed, a frustrated sound.

"Fine," he said, "we'll pick this up later." He picked up the towel that Tendro had placed on D'wann's small work desk and thrust it at her. "Have a nice shower."

"Terrence..." Lyana protested, not wanting him to walk away angry.

The Panarch took a deep breath, turning around to face her instead of continuing towards the door. "No, really, it's fine. I understand and I'll just have to learn to be more patient...it's not one of my virtues."

Lyana forced herself to regain her composure and her control. She sauntered up to Terrence and reached up to kiss him lingeringly, biting his lower lip lightly in a promise for later.

"I promise to be worth the wait."

"You'd better," he growled, taking in her form hungrily with his eyes, including the flesh he'd exposed earlier. "You might want to...cover that," he added, gesturing down at her chest with a slight smile returning to his lips.

Terrence lingered long enough to watch her re-tie her blouse before creating a hole in the air back to his office and stepping through it.

"Until later, then."

Alone again, Lyana let out the breath she'd been holding. *I almost lost control there...I almost lost everything.*

Gathering herself, she took another breath and then strode purposefully outside the weapons locker to deal with Tendro.

As expected, he was outside waiting for her, his back to the wall of training facility. He was near the door and might not have been seen if someone didn't know to look back for him as they exited the building.

"Look," Lyana rounded on him, "it's really none of your business."

Tendro didn't answer, but waited patiently for her to continue.

"I have everything under control, don't worry about it."

"So you say..." Tendro replied casually, walking forward to join her, "but I see a very different picture. You don't look in control at all and this is a dangerous game you're playing. More dangerous, I think, than what Hope's planning."

"Well, as we both know," Lyana countered, she and Tendro walking together now as it meant less chance of being overheard or being seen speaking together as if they had something to hide, "men have been known to only see their illusions of control. Women are the ones who actually rule men's minds and hearts and I can assure you that I have his."

"I would think that gender would be a non-issue in a third party observer," Tendro noted calmly, "but I'll let you keep your illusions. Just answer me one question; do you love him?"

"Which 'him' are you referring to?"

"That's the problem, isn't it?" Tendro questioned innocently. "If you weren't in so deep, that would have been an easy question. I wish you luck, Mira," he gave her a slight nod of his head, "and I hope I'll see you in the gardens sometime soon; it has been months since your last visit and you've been missed."

"What do you know?" Lyana demanded to his back as he walked away. "You're no better; look to your own relationships!"

Lyana was fuming, but with the sudden absence of someone to blame she turned on herself. *I'm still in control. I still have him and he doesn't know anything. I haven't lost yet and as long as I'm careful, I won't. Terrence loves me.*

*But I love Hope...*Mirena's voice was small in the back of her mind. *I don't want to...he hurt me, but I can't help that I love him.*

What do you know about hurt? Or love? Or pain? Lyana retorted. *I protect you from it all. You hid there, watching, as Dipaul forced himself upon me. You're weak; you don't deserve a say.*

It's my life; this is what I wanted to do, Mirena insisted. *Seduce the Panarch, thwart him and eventually destroy him. This was my plan.*

*You gave it to me...*Lyana countered, taking full control and pushing Mirena down to where her silent voice could no longer be heard. *You gave me life and gave me everything. Now, I'm making use of what you weren't strong enough to manage on your own. I can do it and because you want me to succeed you're going to let me have what I want.*

And that's Terrence Lee...

XXVII.

Later that evening, Lyana found herself picking over her dinner in the Cafeteria, pushing the buttered vegetables around on her plate but not eating any of them. In her mind she still felt conflicted, a part of her wanting to go see Terrence as she'd promised and another part unsure, in her current state of mind, if that would be the best idea.

She'd chosen a table alone near the back of the Cafeteria. She could hear the whispers as people talked about her and the little show she'd put on with the Panarch this morning. She had known it would happen but the gossip still stung her ears and didn't bring her any satisfaction.

Even though they talked about her, they left her alone and didn't dare approach her; the Panarch's mistress was not someone to take lightly, no matter how popular she was or wasn't. So it was that Lyana was surprised when someone pulled out the seat across from her, setting down two small plates and pushing one across the table at her.

"Pie?" Odark offered. "You look like you could use a piece."

"Thanks," Lyana murmured, glancing upwards in surprise as her memory supplied her with the last time she had sat across from Odark like this. Only that time he hadn't had the disfiguring burn marks across the right side of his face and she had been Mirena, not Lyana.

Feeling suddenly thrust back to that time months ago and to the life she'd known back then, Mirena couldn't help but resurface in Odark's company. This was the man she'd always wished for the chance to talk to and now she had another chance.

"Chocolate cream pie is my favourite," she noted, meeting his eyes and having no trouble speaking to him now with the confidence she'd gained training to be Lyana. "How did you know?"

"Call it a lucky guess," Odark replied. "Actually it's tonight's feature, but it makes me look better if I don't admit it."

Mirena chuckled a little despite herself and then following a sudden instinct she reached gently across the table to touch the scarred side of Odark's face.

To her surprise, he didn't flinch away from her touch.

"What happened to you?" She asked. "Does it still hurt?"

She slowly took her hand away and was surprised to find something on her fingers. Bringing them to her face, she stared at her smudged makeup on her fingers in disbelief, rubbing them together and watching the complicated mass of colours combine to grey.

"What the...?"

"It still hurts," Odark answered, his tone falling just shy of complete sincerity, which he followed with a wink.

"You're a jerk," Mirena gasped, smacking him playfully as she realized which Odark she was really dealing with. "How long have *you*...been here?"

"Odark," the Panarch's cold voice suddenly cut into their conversation, his tone damning.

"Lyana," he added, almost as an afterthought. "Fancy seeing you both here... together. I see that our dinner date has been cancelled, then, Lyana? Seeing as you've already eaten...and enjoyed dessert."

"I was just leaving..." Odark spoke quickly. "I only just stopped by to drop this off," he said, indicating the pie.

"I see," Terrence noted coolly. "How kind of you to entertain the lady in my absence. You can go now."

Odark nodded and stood, bowing to the Panarch as he took his leave.

"Jealousy is very unbecoming in a man like you," Lyana stated in a frosty tone, standing in defiance of his accusations. "I am allowed to have friends."

"Oh, I see. You'd rather I didn't safeguard your reputation and let you create rumours of who you are sleeping with at any opportunity." Terrence gestured around at the crowded Cafeteria, which fell silent at his notice of them.

Until now, Lyana hadn't realized just how loud the whispers had gotten. She now saw the reproachful stares on every face and the condemnation as they looked her over.

"It's just a piece of pie!" Lyana stated forcefully, feeling anger overtake her and with a sudden motion she slammed her hand down on the table and caused the untouched pie plate to rattle. Having made her point for the listeners, she leaned into Terrence, getting close enough that no one else would hear her venomous whisper. "And I'm not the adulterer, you are."

Turning to stalk away, she was angry but not at all surprised when Terrence grabbed her arm to stop her.

"You forget yourself," he hissed dangerously, "and you forget who you are dealing with."

"I know perfectly well who I am," Lyana answered boldly, "and you're the man I love; why treat me this way?"

Her words were the painful blow she meant them to be, so Terrence let go of her arm, the strength going out of him. Taking the only chance at freedom she was going to get, Lyana strode from the Cafeteria trying to ignore the stares as she left the Panarch behind. She'd managed to grant herself a few moments of safety but there was no use lingering here where he could find another reason to be angry with her.

She went to her rooms first, but only to grab a change of clothes. She didn't feel safe within the Collegium because it was the Panarch's castle and he would be able to find her, no matter where she went. There was only one place to go, though she didn't look forward to it; the 'gardens' or Hope's void-world was the perfect escape plan.

Feeling the tears start rolling down her cheeks, Lyana left the Collegium behind and started the walk down to where Hope's void-world waited for her near the Sentinal Stones. Not long out of the city, she took off the mask and let herself truly cry for the first time in months.

I've lost everything.

The truth came crashing down on her. *I worked so hard for this and in one foolish moment I lost it all. I have become the whore and Terrence will no doubt marry Caralain now as she can give him everything he wants.*

I am so tired... The strain of being Lyana and keeping up the facade while manipulating such a powerful man was getting to her. *And it's going to be so hard to face them. Jehenna will be disappointed; they all will. Tendro has lost respect for me, Odark left me to fend off the Panarch myself and now I've done to Hope what I accused him of doing to me.*

I'm no better. I love him, yet I've slept with the Panarch to further my goals and even worse, I've fallen for him.

How can a person love two people at the same time?

I love Hope for his unique outlook and his kindness to me and others. He was my first love, but now I love Terrence, though it's different with him. He is strong and powerful, but somehow still gentle and usually kind to me.

Tendro was right, she realized. *If I wasn't in too deep I would have known how to the answer the question of who it is that I love. It should have been an easy question, but I've been a fool and now it's all so tangled.*

I love them both and my heart is breaking because of it. And the worst part is that I don't want to lose either of them, so I can't choose between them.

This isn't a game, Tendro, Mirena thought silently to him, as she entered into the void-world by walking through the familiar set of trees that Hope had used to mark the hidden entrance to their safe haven, *it's my heart and keeping it whole means a whole lot more to me than winning...*

~~~

Some instinct alerted Hope that someone had entered the void-world. He felt it like whoever had come in was standing right next to him, even though that wasn't the case, strictly speaking.

But everyone is accounted for, even Odark, who was supposed to stay in the Collegium tonight...

A little earlier, Odark had come back with unsettling news. He had been keeping an eye on Mirena as asked, when the Panarch had cornered her in front of everyone in the Cafeteria. It seemed that her secret was still somehow safe, but Terrence Lee been angry with Mirena for more...personal reasons.

Hope didn't know exactly what to make of that. He hadn't known before she left of her intentions regarding the Panarch but there was no doubt now what she was up to, even if her closest friends wouldn't confirm it and Elizabeth refused to 'get in the middle', as she termed it.

Hope had been to the Collegium himself on more than one occasion and he'd heard the whispers and even attended a Physical Training class or two to get to know 'Lyana' better.

Following his instincts, Hope moved the curtain aside to look out the window. He ignored the others as they debated amongst themselves what the best course of action would be for dealing with the information that had been gathered today. They were getting closer and closer to the time when they would actually have to act and set everything in motion, but they were all still having trouble agreeing on the particulars of the plan.

Mira?

She was there, within the two trees that marked the gateway between this fake world that he'd created and the real one outside, like a ghost of the woman who had been sent here to haunt him.

But she was real.

Hope wasn't delusional and even though he could have created an illusion of her here, he knew that he hadn't.

He ran to the door and threw it open to the quiet night where the stars were too perfect and the grass only moved when he told it to.

"Mira!" Hope exclaimed as he headed outside, his feet carrying him towards her without a conscious decision having been made to run.

She looked up, her eyes stricken and as she took him in everything seemed to fall apart and she fell to her knees, unable to stand any longer under the weight of her emotions. Hope reached her side in no time at all and lightened the sky a little so he could look her over.

"Are you alright?" He asked, checking her for bruises and seeing no sign of the mask she usually wore or kept in her hands if she wasn't wearing it. "Did he hurt you?"

"Not physically," she sniffed.

"Come inside," Hope urged, helping Mirena to her feet. "Your room hasn't changed a bit. If you...want to be alone, you can do so there. No one will bother you if you don't want them to."

"I'm sorry," she said instead. "I understand now, why you and Caralain...I shouldn't have judged..."

Hope swallowed with some difficulty, his mind returning to that time two months ago when they had fought in this very same spot. He felt all the guilt and the sadness of that argument and the weeks that followed it well up within him, stinging his eyes with the beginnings of tears.

"Don't..." he began, "it's not something so easily dismissed. I shouldn't have, and maybe you shouldn't have...but it happened." Hope struggled to put his thoughts and emotions into words. "We can't take it back, I know, but I meant it when I said I loved you, Mira."

"Did you love Caralain too when you...?"

"I..." Hope hesitated, wanting to be honest with her. She deserved nothing less. "I did, once. When that...happened, I suppose I just wanted to remember. It was so much easier then, when I didn't have to be strong for everyone else. But that wasn't really love, Mira; I know that now. I love you and I don't know if you still feel the same way about me, but I want to be with you, not Caralain. She used me...she always did, I just didn't see it clearly until after I met you."

"I still love you...but I love him too." Tears fell freely down Mirena's face as she struggled to speak. "I thought it was a game, but I lost myself in it and now it's too late..."

"Too late?" Hope questioned, wondering what she meant. For him, if she loved him, then that was enough. They could deal with everything thing else later, including the Panarch.

"I think I'm pregnant..." Mirena whispered. "I haven't told anyone, but I can't be that far along...I know it's not yours."

*The prophecy...*Hope realized, the words he'd read on Mirena's lower back coming back to him. *'With the Creator's blessing, the Prophet of the Light shall bear him a son and the boy will be called Grace.'*

The prophecy doesn't mean me...it's not mine.

"Grace," he said aloud.

"Excuse me?"

"Your son," he clarified, "it's a boy and you'll call him Grace. I read it on your back some time ago, only I thought then that...well, it doesn't matter what I thought. Congratulations."

Hope didn't know what he was saying. He felt numb with shock. *Not only did she sleep with him, she's in love with him and she's having his baby…*

"I wish it was yours," Mirena told him honestly, her words changing quickly from sad to angry. "I hate her for deciding my fate. Is this not hard enough as it is without the Creator choosing our paths for us? I hate myself so much for what I've become."

Hope recognized her words for what they were; she was lashing out in any way she could because she felt powerless. Under ordinary circumstances Mirena would never say these things. *She's the strongest believer in the Creator that I've ever met.*

"It's not over yet, Mira," he told her, feeling some of his personality returning, "you can still decide who you want to be and I'll support you no matter what you choose."

"You don't understand; it was never my choice…"

"Then make it yours now," he insisted. "I'm not saying you have to choose this instant; I'll be patient and I'll wait for you. I have to believe that you will choose me when you are ready…and Mira, I'll love Grace as if he were my own flesh and blood; I promise you that."

And what about your child, his conscience questioned, *the one Caralain is carrying? Will you love it just the same? Or will it be Terrence Lee's, the way that his child will be your own?*

That will be Caralain's choice…it's always been what she wants, Hope thought bitterly, *and what I want be damned…*

XXVIII.

"I still say that we need D'wann in there," Jehenna insisted. "With Dipaul gone, D'wann is Terrence Lee's right hand man, or close enough to it, and he'd be able to get in close enough to do what we need him to. The Panarch trusts him and why shouldn't he?"

Mirena came down the stairs to a breakfast meeting in full swing. She'd slept later than she intended to, having been exhausted from the revelations of the night before, but the noise of the discussion had lured her downstairs.

Everyone was present; Hope, Tendro, Jehenna, D'wann, Odark without his face makeup today and Elizabeth. Only Mirena had been missing, like she had been for months now.

They're used to meeting without me by now. I wonder if they even would have noticed if I hadn't come down to join them.

"What you're saying makes sense," Hope agreed, "D'wann do you feel that you can get the Panarch to entrust you to that position?"

D'wann nodded; there was nothing else to be said.

"D'wann won't have any trouble replacing his Mirror," Jehenna informed them. "There's little noticeable difference between them, not as much as some others," she added, glancing toward Odark and referring to his lack of facial scarring more than his personality.

"I agree," Mirena added, taking the remaining seat between Elizabeth and Jehenna, "he's practically the same man."

"Not in the ways that count," Jehenna countered, smiling in a knowing fashion, "but in all the visible ways, yes."

Odark got up as Mirena sat and went over to the kitchen cupboards to grab a plate for her. Bringing it back over, he reached for the bowls of food in the center of the table.

"Did you want eggs?" He asked. "We have toast and sausage as well..."

At his words, the smell of food hit her and Mirena felt her stomach turn. *Oh no...* She had no choice; she ran to the bathroom, losing what little was in her stomach.

When she returned with a somewhat sheepish look on her face she had everyone's attention. She looked to Jehenna first as she would be the one to know best what this meant and Mirena saw only a small nod of acceptance and a knowing stare. She searched her friend's face further, looking for some sign that Jehenna was disappointed in her, but Elizabeth interrupted her view by standing abruptly.

Her sister's hands smacked down suddenly on the table's surface.

"It's his, isn't it?!"

"Yes," Lyana calm and confident tones answered, though it was still Mirena's face that she wore.

"How could you?!" Elizabeth demanded, sounding scandalized. "I know I've called you a whore before, but I never meant it until now."

"Elizabeth!" Hope admonished her.

"What?" She demanded. "You disagree with that assessment? She's whoring around with the Panarch; I know better than anyone what that's like."

Mirena slapped her sister, hard. She hadn't even realized that she had crossed the room in her anger, but Elizabeth deserved the physical rebuke and more.

"You will keep your opinions to yourself," Mirena told her sister dangerously. "I am no one's whore."

Elizabeth fell silent, her expression stunned and her face red where Mirena had struck her. After a tense moment Elizabeth opened her mouth once more but this time the words came in a quiet and small voice, the voice of someone who had been frightened into submission.

"I never thought that you would treat me like he did...you're right, *Lyana*, we're not sisters anymore."

Mirena buried her face in her hands, feeling remorse wash over her in a wave. By the time she looked up again Elizabeth was gone. Mirena hadn't even heard the door slam because Elizabeth had shut it quietly; her intent hadn't been to create a scene, her sister actually felt the way she'd said. She'd let the whole room see her real self and then had taken herself away from Mirena forever.

Who am I? Mirena questioned. *I never would have treated Elizabeth like that before...no matter how angry or upset I got. I can't just blame Lyana; this is my fault and whatever else I decide, I've got to stop hurting the people I love.*

"Isn't the Panarch still marrying Caralain?" Odark questioned the room at large, trying to follow the events as they unfolded.

"I can change that," Mirena stated, letting Lyana's boldness take over as she met the eyes of everyone who was sitting around the table, "and I know how we can win this."

"What are you saying, Mira?" Hope questioned.

"I can marry the Panarch; he's already asked me to," she explained in a way they could understand, "and that will be his weakest moment. D'wann can get close, but no one can get closer than I can."

"But that would mean you'd be married to him," Jehenna pointed out. "Is that what you want?"

Mirena took a breath to steady herself; *this is what I want...what we both want.*

"I'll do it before the ceremony is complete. Hope can place the entrance to the void-world right where I need it and when the moment is right, I'll push him in."

"Cutting it a little close, aren't you?" Tendro asked.

"It has to be real," she countered. "It will be the moment he least expects and it'll come from the person he trusts the most."

"She can do it," Hope agreed, throwing his support behind Mirena like he'd promised to do.

It would hurt him to do it, but he was a man of his word.

"Well, we all knew that we would have to make sacrifices and take risks when we agreed to this," Odark pointed out, referring to the mission as a whole. "If Mira wants to do this, we should let her."

"Then we are agreed," Lyana stated, "and this is how it's going to go…"

⁂

"Terrence, it's me," Lyana announced, knocking on the closed door of the Panarch's apartments.

She'd gone early in the morning, before he generally left for his office, but there was still no guarantee that he would be in his rooms; he hardly ever used them other than to sleep. She had spent a whole day in the void-world planning with the others and now it was the next morning; all she could do now was hope that she wasn't too late.

The door opened, seemingly of its own accord, sliding open on silent hinges and revealing nothing but a still and impeccably decorated empty room.

Lyana let herself in, closing the door behind her just as softly as it had opened. She took a quick look around the sitting room, noting the unused furniture and the spotless cleanliness of it all. The servants either did a wonderful job, or Terrence never bothered to use this room except for show and to cross it to get to his own bedroom beyond.

"Terrence?" Lyana questioned, allowing the worry she felt to show in her voice.

Let him think me concerned, she counseled herself, holding tightly to every lesson Jehenna had ever taught her. *I have to play this right; everything hinges on this conversation.*

"In here." The reply, when it came a beat later than she would have expected it to, was cold; controlled.

This is going to be harder that I thought. I should have known he'd be waiting for me; expecting this.

The door was open just a crack but Lyana pushed it wider, trying to give herself a moment to take in the state of things before she stepped further in.

The room was nothing like it usually was. The sheets were ripped and covered in shards of glass, broken pottery and discarded luxuries. Their remains were tangled on the floor and mixed with spots of blood from where glass had cut his skin, as he paced the length of the room or walked about in search of more things to destroy. The pillows, too, had been torn open and feathers littered the bed and the free space on the lush black carpet surrounding it.

Terrence was in the room also, but he was not on the bed and the bottom layer of sheets appeared unused. He sat in a black leather chair, fully dressed for the day in a pristine black and gold Mage's outfit. His posture was relaxed and his face covered by his hand as he regarded her, ignoring the chaos around him.

Lyana let the sight of it all wash over her as she took it in and reconciled herself to it. *This is the man I've chosen to love. This is him; all of it. If I love him as I say, then I have to accept the bad with the good.*

But, dear Creator, do I ever want to be afraid of him right now...

"If you're looking for an apology, I don't have one," Lyana told him, forcing her voice to be firm and not waver or betray her nervousness, "because to apologize would mean that I have something to feel guilty about and I don't."

"I'm not looking for an apology," he stated tonelessly, leaning forward and watching her every shift in expression with intensity. "I want the truth and I want to be able to have no cause to doubt your integrity."

"I have given you no cause to doubt," she told him flatly. "This is not a game to me and I would not play with your emotions.

"I love you," Lyana stated it simply, straight out and with no frills. "I know I haven't said it before, but it's the truth."

A little hint of personality showed at the corner of his mouth around the visual impediment of his hand. "Actually, you have said it before, though I doubt you remember it. It was the last thing you said to me before you stormed off; 'you're the man I love.'"

"You're right," Lyana nodded, remembering the words she'd thrown in his face that night. "I meant it then and I mean it now.

"I love *you*, Terrence, not 'Terrence Lee the Panarch.' I love *you*."

"And what of 'the Panarch?'" Terrence asked, letting a certain amount of vulnerability show in his voice. "Can you love him too?"

"I love all of you," she insisted, telling the truth, though she would have never thought that this far into her plans that the truth would be the best tool at her disposal. "Your position is who you are, but it's not all that you are."

"Do you really mean that?"

He asked the question again and Lyana could see it now, the innocence, the vulnerability and the fear. The emotions she would have never believed possible from such a powerful man were there and the sight of them only made her love him more; she wanted to protect him from the harshness of the world.

She crossed the distance to his chair, heedless of the shattered glass and remains of his rage at her feet. At some point during their conversation, he had leaned forward so it was a simple matter for her to kneel before him, take his hands in her own and put her forehead to his.

"Of course I do," she told him, needing now to show him the truth, beyond words and beyond simple gestures.

"I love you," Lyana repeated one last time, emphasizing it with a kiss.

"I love you, too," he replied, letting her coerce him into kissing her back, healing the rift that had sprung up between them. "I'm so sorry, Lyana. I just needed to know; I needed to know how you felt about me. It's not that I don't trust you, it's that I don't trust myself...or anyone else with you."

"Shh, it's okay," she told him, kissing his mouth, his face and trailing kisses down the proud line of his jaw, "I know."

He cupped the side of her face in his hand, redirecting her lips back to his and kissing her passionately. She didn't hold back; she gave into his desire with no reservations, letting the fire he stoked within her build until it threatened to consume them both with its heat.

Surging forward, Terrence stood abruptly, startling her with the sudden absence of his mouth on hers. She looked up at him, confused for a moment but she saw the light in his eyes and the tightness in his pants; he was still aroused and she hadn't lost his attention.

With a determined expression he bent down and helped her to her feet. She tried to wrap herself around him and give him what he obviously wanted but he kept her at arm's length, as if trying to draw out his anticipation.

What he wasn't taking into consideration was just how much she wanted him. Lyana didn't want to wait; she wanted Terrence to take hold of her now and remove the layers of cloth that separated their bodies.

"Terrence," she whispered pleadingly, her breath coming quickly.

He shook his head and looked her form up and down, admiring her curves and the way her clothes hugged her body. "You made me wait," he noted with a slight smirk, "now it's your turn to be patient."

"Patience is a virtue," Lyana noted seductively, taking this moment to study him as well.

His Mage jacket was undone at the top and he wore no shirt beneath, having presumably dressed in a hurry upon hearing her enter the room. His black pants fit him snugly, even more so now, given his preoccupation with her.

"However, now is not the time for it," she added, reaching down to the hem of her dress to pull it up over her head.

"I would say you've ruined the view," Terrence replied, eyeing her now mostly bare form, "but I would be lying and you would know it instantly."

"So what are you waiting for?" She asked, taking a step forward and reaching to unbutton his jacket the rest of the way.

"I'm not waiting," he countered, scooping her up into his arms as the jacket fell to the ground, revealing his perfect chest, "I'm savoring."

He carried her to the bed, slowly and deliberately. His arms did not strain in the least from the effort and he was heedless of the crunching glass beneath his thick-soled shoes. Once there, Terrence laid Lyana gently on the bed in the center of the white feathers that littered its surface. That was when he let his pants fall to the ground, baring everything to her and letting her take in the full sight of him.

Leaning over her, he took hold of her waist and drew her to him, hooking his thumbs under the black lace of her panties and tugging them toward him.

Lyana watched his every move, feeling at once a mixture of desire and awe. She wanted him badly, but at the same time she found herself wondering how she had gotten to this moment of intimacy with the Panarch she used to fear.

He got her undergarments off with little trouble and then pulled her in closer, spreading her legs apart and bringing his lips to the soft skin of her inner thigh. She moaned with the pleasure of it, her back arching as he worked his way up her leg, his tongue roaming freely and driving any thoughts of doubt right out of her head.

He loves me and I love him; right here and now, that's enough.

It doesn't matter that he's the Panarch and I'm a rebel; together like this we don't have to be either of those things.

Terrence surfaced for air a moment later and Lyana reached for him, pulling him to her and wanting more from him than even what he'd given her so far. She took hold of his hair and pulled him down to her lips, driving her tongue into his mouth.

"I don't want to be patient," she told him after a moment. "I don't want gentle and I don't want to wait. Give yourself to me; make me feel like you are mine and no one else's."

"I will," he answered, his voice deep and throaty, "but not the way you're asking. I want you all to myself and I'm going to take my time to prove it to you, because Lyana....we're going to have all the time in the world."

He kissed her then, long and deep, and then he entered her; the strength and power of his body carefully controlled to bring her as much pleasure as she could handle and draw it out for as long as possible.

Terrence Lee's every motion was sweet and unexpectedly tender, so Lyana was surprised when she felt a single tear fall down her cheek to land in the feathered chaos around her.

She couldn't account for it but the very act of their lovemaking felt bittersweet to her. It was almost a goodbye, even though she didn't want this moment to ever end.

XXIX.

Mirena stretched luxuriously, feeling feathers against her skin before she remembered where she was, who she was, and who she was with.

She heard the Panarch's feet pad across the floor, careful this time not to step on any shards of broken glass and then she heard the bathroom door quietly open and shut, so as not to disturb her.

Lyana smiled to herself, her eyes still closed as she snuggled into sheets that smelled of him. *He'll be back momentarily and I'm going to tell him about Grace. I know now that he will believe me.*

He will be so pleased. This is the perfect day and my news can only make it better.

She heard the door open once more and footsteps make their way back across the room, this time to her side of the bed. Lyana smiled again to let him know that she was awake, even if she didn't want to open her eyes just yet and begin the day; the longer she could stay here with him, the better.

She felt his hand softly stroke her cheek.

"Rise and shine, my little whore."

The deep and familiar voice caused her to freeze with immediate terror, her limbs paralyzed and her lungs unwilling to take in enough air to scream.

"I've come to settle our debt."

Lyana's eyes snapped open and she tried to spur herself to action to push away from Dipaul. He was ready for her reaction and pain blossomed in her cheek as he backhanded her with the stump of his left arm.

She rolled with the impact, heedless of anything but her need to get away from him, but before she had even rolled over Dipaul was on top of her, pummeling every inch of her that he could reach. Lyana hunched in on herself instinctively, desperate to protect her unborn child; she had to survive this for that reason above any other.

Terrence, she thought desperately. *Where is he? What have they done to him?*

"Terrence!"

The scream escaped her, her voice sounding desperate to her own ears. Naked and pinned by her worst enemy, gone was the woman who confidently took down male adversaries with ease and in its place was a woman who was prey before a man like Dipaul; a man with no compunctions whatsoever.

"Go ahead," Dipaul told her, his tone filled with a sadistic mirth, "scream as loud as you want. No one is coming to rescue you and I want the Panarch to hear how much fun I'm having with his whore. Besides," he whispered, leaning in close to her ear so she could feel his warm breath on her neck, "I like it better when you struggle, but you knew that already, didn't you?"

Lyana started sobbing, her breaths coming raggedly.

"Please..." She begged. "Please...I'll do whatever you want."

"You're doing just fine as you are," he told her, licking the side of her face, "and it was so nice of 'Terrence' to get you ready for me and leave you lying here like bait. It makes for a pleasant distraction from the tediousness of overthrowing a ruler."

"Fuck you," Lyana spat.

"No, you," he countered, ripping his pants open with one hand and driving himself into her.

Lyana screamed as Dipaul entered her, the shock and pain of it suddenly making all of this more real and terrifying.

Last time, Terrence came in time to save me; now I don't even know if he still lives.

Pulling his cock out of her with as much suddenness as he had driven it in, Dipaul arched his back and turned his head over one shoulder to look over in the direction of the closed bathroom door.

"He needs to see this," the burly General called out. "Bring in the Panarch."

No...not Terrence...not like this!

She heard the bathroom door slam open and several sets of boots troop out of the small room and then she heard a body being dragged in, displacing some of the debris that littered the floor.

"Lyana..." Terrence croaked weakly, though she couldn't see the state of him as she was held down.

"Run!" Lyana screamed, twisting in an attempt to break free. "Save yourself..."

"I'm sure he would if he could," Dipaul told her, turning his considerable attention back to her naked form. "You're attractive and all, but you're not enough to risk his life for. Though, I'm afraid he's all tied up at the moment and my boys are going to make sure he watches every second of this...aren't you, boys?"

Male laughter chorused from the two or more men who held Terrence. Lyana didn't know whether they held him physically or with majik, but they must have caught the Panarch off guard because Terrence was the best swords master she knew besides D'wann.

Terrence was distracted because of me, Lyana realized. *He was happy and comfortable and felt safe within his rooms with me and they used that against him.*

A yelp escaped her as all of a sudden Dipaul's fist was in her hair and he was hauling her from the bed to the floor, where Terrence could get a better view of the proceedings. Lyana hit the ground hard; the black carpet that surrounded the bed did little to cushion her tailbone from the fall and the waiting debris cut into her flesh with the impact.

Dipaul was on his feet standing over her as he lowered his pants and further released his manhood. His back was to Terrence, but now Lyana could see clearly the look on her lover's face just beyond her assailant.

The Panarch's expression was a mask of horror.

It was a look Lyana had never expected to see on Terrence's face, a look that even now she had trouble comprehending. Then it hit her; Terrence feared for her because there was nothing he could do to stop what was about to happen.

Knowing the truth of this the instant she took in the sight of him, something within Lyana snapped.

If I want to live through this, to protect myself and my unborn child, then I am going to have to fight back with everything I have.

Kicking determinedly, Lyana attacked Dipaul's legs and tried to knock him off balance. She got one with a solid blow, causing the big man to stumble but as she went for the second leg, his heavy boot crashed down on her outstretched arm with deliberate suddenness, mercilessly crushing her wrist under his considerable weight.

She screamed with the sound of her bones snapping, but Dipaul didn't stop there.

He moved his foot and then bent down to take hold of her arm just above the mangled wrist, using it to drag her across the floor until he had spun her about entirely.

Lyana knew she was still screaming. She felt the rawness of her throat and she heard the almost inhuman sounds she was making but she was beyond the pain of it, feeling somewhat separated from her body.

She felt as if she was floating just above herself, taking in the whole scene. Terrence was just above her head, his view forced downwards by one of his captors; the one on the left was holding him down.

I know him, Lyana realized, *that's Nevodian. He brought me to Stiphy...*

Other than the hand on Terrence's head forcing him to watch her torment, there were no other bonds or restraints that she could see. *Nevodian and his companion must have used majik to detain Terrence.* There was no other method that could make the Panarch sit so immobile under the circumstances.

Dipaul executed this perfectly, Lyana realized.

Dropping her to the floor allowed Terrence the perfect vantage point. This also caused the broken shards of glass and pottery to dig into her skin, smearing her blood on the floor and creating a dramatic backdrop for the horror that was taking place. Then by swinging her around, Dipaul had made it so that Terrence had no choice but to look into his lover's eyes and he could watch his victim's face as he took his pleasure from Lyana's limp form.

Unable to truly escape her body, Lyana's undamaged hand reached unconsciously for Terrence, her bloody fingers just managing to touch his ankle and feel him start with surprise at her touch.

"Help me..." She mouthed silently and then, forcing air into her lungs, she drew on every bit of strength she could muster and tried to say the words again, this time with force.

"Help me!"

It came out not as a scream or even a plea. The words ripped through her vocal cords and were propelled by majik out into the air, louder than she'd ever yelled before.

Dipaul's back arched at the sound, his eyes rolling back into his head at the pleasure he felt in having broken her so completely. His lumbering form shuddered as he reached his climax and then he slumped, pinning her to the ground more thoroughly than before and driving the shards of glass and pottery deeper into her flesh.

He never saw the sword hilt coming for him or the sword that sliced off one of his henchmen's heads as D'wann swept into the room, a raging whirlwind of blades and death.

Dipaul fell to the side, knocked senseless, but even the sword hilt driven by D'wann's immense strength wasn't enough to take the big man down; it only disoriented him for a time.

"Let him go," D'wann commanded, leveling his sword at Nevodian's throat. He spoke the words so coldly that Lyana found herself confused for a moment which D'wann she was actually faced with. Was this man from this realm or the Mirror that should have replaced him by now?

Terrence slumped to his knees, the strength draining out of him as Nevodian obviously released the bonds of majik that had held him.

"Get out of here," D'wann continued, his voice and sword arm steady, "before I change my mind and kill you."

Nevodian backed up, his arms held before him in a pacifying gesture. Reaching Dipaul's side, he opened a hole in the air to a nondescript field and then urged his General to his feet.

Stumbling a little from the force of D'wann's blow, Dipaul allowed Nevodian to pull him through to safety, their plans for conquest shattered by one moment of vulnerability.

With strong arms, D'wann knelt to pick Lyana up off the floor and cradle her to his body. Leaving Terrence behind with no thought to the Panarch's well-being, D'wann turned from the bloody scene of chaos and made his way solidly to the chamber's main doors.

It was only there, a few steps from safety that Lyana felt the big man's arms begin to shake with the reality of the horror he had just witnessed and she at last became aware of which D'wann had come to rescue her.

"I'm taking you back to Jehenna," D'wann told her, his usually strong voice wavering around the edges as he paused to wrap his cloak one-handedly around her nudity. "Hold on."

"How did they get in?" Jehenna demanded. "You were standing guard over the Panarch's rooms, weren't you?"

"No," D'wann admitted. "I had only just made the switch; I wasn't there in time."

"You may not have gotten there in time," Hope told him, trying to keep the frustration and anger from his voice, "but at least you were there...at the end."

He wasn't angry with D'wann, but at himself. He had let Mirena get too deep, let her risk herself and he hadn't been there to save her when things took a turn for the worst. Hope would never be able to forgive himself for what had happened to her because of his inadequacies.

"Is Elizabeth back yet?" Jehenna asked, directing the subject away from more delicate matters.

"No," Hope replied, inwardly worried about the intensity of Elizabeth's reaction when she found out about what had happened to Mirena.

"That's perhaps for the best," Jehenna noted. "It would be better to let things settle down a little before bringing her into this."

Hope nodded, his attention distracted upwards by what only he could feel thanks to his connection with this place. Someone had just entered Mirena's room.

"If you'll excuse me," he told D'wann and Jehenna, taking the stairs two at a time.

On the second floor landing, Hope took a deep breath to prepare himself for what lay beyond the simple wooden door to Mirena's room before turning the handle and going inside.

Odark had dragged his chair closer to the bed and his hand rested lightly on Mirena's as she slept. The mask was still on her face, making her physically still look like Lyana. Sleeping like this, Hope could imagine the softness of Mirena's expression and he fancied he could see past the illusion she wore.

Startled by Hope's sudden entrance, Odark removed his hand quickly, no doubt thinking that Hope hadn't even taken notice of it. Hope found himself studying the man's face, noticing that it was still scarred down the right side; Jehenna's masterpiece of theatrical makeup was very convincing.

It almost looked like it still pained him.

"I'm sorry, I just thought that maybe she could use a...friend right now."

Maybe it's seeing Mira like this that pains him, Hope thought as he nodded noncommittally in Odark's direction.

"You're probably right," he said aloud, though inwardly he thought the opposite.

The last thing she needs right now is another admirer.

As if sensing their presence, Mirena's eyes opened wide and she took in the room around her with a fearful expression, which didn't seem to immediately quiet once she realized her surroundings.

"Terrence?" Mirena questioned, her eyes darting from side to side.

"He's not here, Mira," Hope assured her. "He can't hurt you now."

"I should leave the two of you alone," Odark said quickly, getting to his feet. "I'll just be downstairs..."

Hope let Odark go past him as he took his spot in the chair beside Mirena, who was struggling to get to a seated position.

"Don't strain yourself," Hope cautioned as the door closed softly behind Odark. "You're still healing. I did what I could, but it took a lot of your strength and you're going to have to take it easy for a little while longer."

"Is he alright?" Mirena asked in a small voice. "He was so badly hurt..."

Hope didn't know what to make of her words. "D'wann is fine, no one hurt him..."

Then it hit him like a blow to the stomach. *She's talking about the Panarch...*

"I'm sure he's fine," Hope said stiffly, getting to his feet. "The reports say he'll live, at any rate."

"I need to go back," Mirena insisted, seeming to ignore his words and the warning in his tone. "I have to finish what I started."

She struggled further, trying to swing her legs off the edge of the bed now.

"No Mira," Hope pleaded, "it's not worth it...he's not worth it."

Lyana met his eyes with a flash of anger. For the first time he saw and acknowledged the switch from the woman he loved to the one that lived within her and was trying so hard to take her from him.

"I'll be the judge of that," she said sharply, as if daring him to defy her. "I love him and not you or anyone else will keep me from him."

Hope stumbled back in shock, her words tearing a hole in his heart the way nothing else could have.

No, she can't mean that...this is Lyana talking, not Mirena. Mirena could never love a monster like the Panarch.

Mirena loves me.

"Mira..." Hope began.

"Get out of my way," Lyana cut him off, forcing Mirena's body to stand despite the beatings it had taken.

Hope had no other choice. He couldn't convince her like this and he would never use force to control her like the men who had put her in this state.

He let her go, though it tore the hole in his heart wider to do it.

Lyana walked out the door past him and didn't look back.

XXX.

Why are you doing this? Mirena demanded silently of her alter ego.

Internally she knew that Lyana wasn't really another person; she was just a mask she wore and a character she had developed with Jehenna's help, but right now it was easier to blame Lyana's boldness for her current troubles.

*Hope doesn't deserve this...*Mirena continued. *I love him and you're pushing him away; I can see his heart breaking. It's like you are trying to ruin my chance at having a happy ending.*

I've given you everything, the part of her that was Lyana countered. *You think that I'm not as real as you are? That I don't love as deeply? I love Terrence. You say you love Hope, but he doesn't seem to want me around. Every time he sees my face he grows angry; he hates me.*

*But I can't love Terrence...*Mirena protested, even though she knew it was too late now. *We were supposed to use our power over the Panarch to bring him down, to help Hope succeed. It wasn't supposed to be this way. I know you love Terrence, but you're not me...I created you; I can get rid of you.*

I don't believe that you can anymore, Lyana countered. *You use me to hide. You're too much of a coward to face the world on your own, so you turn to me. Do you think that's fair? I'm not just a mask to be used at your leisure...I'm a person too. I'm just as real as you are now, maybe more so.*

So how do we fix this? Mirena wondered. *I need you and you don't exist without me…can we keep on like this, loving two men equally?*

A sudden, firm grasp on her broken and bandaged wrist brought her up short with a painful gasp.

"Who the hell do you think you are?" A cold voice demanded and Mirena whirled to face her assailant, only to find herself face to face with a very angry and still very pregnant Caralain.

"Please, let go of me," Mirena whimpered, wanting to pull her wrist away but fearing how much it would hurt to do so.

"'Please, let go of me,'" Caralain mocked. "You're so pathetic; I don't know why he bothers with you."

"I said, let go of me," Lyana rose to the surface, repeating Mirena's words with force and pulling her arm from Caralain's grasp, pushing through the pain it caused her.

"Gladly," Caralain said, her tone disgusted. "I just want you to know your place. You're not his wife and you're not his intended. At best, you're a distraction to while away the hours until he's married to me and his son is born. At worst, you're just another of his whores."

"Excuse me?" Lyana questioned, raising her voice as she didn't care who heard them but she knew that Caralain did. "You're calling *me* a whore? Really? Do you even know who the father of your baby is?"

"Terrence Lee," Caralain said stiffly, lifting her chin with a determined pride as people in the hall of the Political Wing began to slow around them, intent on the possibly scandalous information that might be revealed by the confrontation between Panarch's bride to be and his favored mistress. "My fiancee. Ask *him* if you want to know the details."

"I know perfectly well that he knows the truth," Lyana said coolly. "I was there the day that you confessed to him that you're bearing Tendro Seynor's child. I remember you being all scared and submissive. I was in his private quarters. You know; the room *you're* not allowed to enter?"

"You bitch," Caralain gasped, but the truth was only strengthened by her reaction. "Making up lies only discredits you further. It won't matter, anyways; in two days I'll be his wife and you'll be yesterday's trash."

The wedding is so soon? Lyana questioned, not letting her emotions show on her face. *I thought he would have called it off by now…what else has he been keeping from me?*

"Unlike you, I have nothing to hide," Lyana stated confidently. "If you are so assured, then why are you on the defensive? If it is as you say, you should have nothing to worry about. So why don't you relax, Caralain?"

"You'll regret this, Lyana," Caralain said her name with disgust. "You'll regret that you ever tried to take what doesn't belong to you."

"In order for me to take something from you, you would actually have to possess it first," she noted calmly. "Last time I checked, the Panarch belonged to no one but himself."

Lyana expected the fire that inflamed her cheek as Caralain's hand struck the side of her face. She took the hit without much outward reaction for it didn't shock her, or even really hurt that much compared to what she'd been through recently.

She turned her head, deliberately showing the welt to the crowd of gathered onlookers. They couldn't help but gasp at the injustice but they would do nothing to interfere. *That's not how it works, here.*

Lyana lifted her head once more, meeting Caralain stare for stare and she felt something within her come to life. It was rage and she let it build until it burned hotly in her eyes.

The anger didn't just come from Lyana but from Mirena, too. Mirena hated this woman with all of her being and in this single moment she knew that Caralain could see it.

Soon, Caralain would know just how much danger she was truly in.

A look of fear danced across Caralain's face and just like a predator, Mirena knew she had her prey cornered.

"Caralain, don't do this to yourself," Tendro's voice, so much like Hope's, snapped her out of it and the fire within her died down to embers for the moment. "She's not worth your health."

Tendro had worked his way through the crowd after seeing what had caused the cluster in the hallway and now he stepped between the two of them, trying to guide Caralain away from where Lyana would strike her down.

The scene was tense for a moment but eventually Caralain realized that Tendro had given her the opportunity she needed to back down graciously.

"You're right, of course, Tendro. Thank you for being concerned for me. I should perhaps go lie down; the baby is restless."

"You're too hard on yourself, Caralain," Tendro continued, his tone gentle as he turned her about to lead her away but in Caralain's moment of inattention, he turned his head back over his shoulder to wink at Lyana.

Definitely not Hope, was all Lyana could think, watching the back of Tendro's gold-trimmed black Magi jacket as he faded into the crowd, trailing after Caralain.

Lyana was about to depart herself, disgusted with the spectacle that Caralain had forced her into when a low moan split the air, causing her to turn back instinctively. The crowd parted, revealing Tendro as he supported Caralain who was gripping her rather large abdomen with both hands.

Shit, Lyana felt the world around her shift and suddenly become a very uncertain place. *If she has that child before Terrence knows about mine...*

Lyana felt the wind of her own passage before she realized that she'd made the conscious decision to run. *I could lose everything. He could marry her instead just to claim her son as his own and to have the legacy he's always wanted.*

She ran and the Collegium passed by in a blur around her. Lyana ignored her fatigue and the pain that running caused her as she took the stairs up to the Panarch's office, moving as quickly as her legs would carry her.

She didn't stop at the secretary's desk in the waiting room; she just charged right through the office door, relieved to find that Terrence was within and that he was alone.

Lyana didn't bother shutting the door behind her; she was through caring who knew her business. If she wanted to be with the Panarch, then her life would be a public matter, regardless.

"I have to tell you something," Lyana stated, trying in vain to catch her breath.

Terrence's gaze was distant, as if he was listening to something beyond the round office walls. Then she noticed that his hand was on the panel inset into the desk before him and his attention was on whatever his secretary was telling him through the majik device.

"Terrence, it's important," Lyana tried to get the Panarch's attention, walking towards him.

He stood abruptly, his eyes lighting on her for the first time but they didn't seem to see her. His expression was distracted as he looked beyond her.

"I have to go," he stated, pushing past her for the door.

"Terrence, listen to me," Lyana reached for him but he was already well past her and still walking away.

It was as if he didn't even hear her words; she was like a ghost and he was so far away as to be in another world. To Lyana it felt like a nightmare where she could scream and scream but he would only continue to get further away from her. Her feet felt glued to the floor and no matter how badly she wanted to chase after him, she couldn't even put one foot in front of the other.

Terrence was out the door and into the lobby when she snapped and traitorous words ripped from her throat of their own volition, condemning him in a way she could never take back.

"I was raped because of you!"

Terrence froze, turning around slowly and ignoring the wide eyes and shocked expressions of those waiting in the room for their turn to petition him.

"My son is being born," the Panarch stated coldly. "We will talk about this later."

He walked away from her and Lyana only realized that she had fallen when her knees slammed painfully into the wooden floorboards.

I truly have lost everything...

It wasn't too difficult to get out of the birthing chamber while his own child was being born. Caralain wanted to claim that it was the Panarch's, anyway, so it wouldn't look right if the suspected father was there and Terrence Lee was not.

Hope tried to ignore his nagging conscience. *I'm not stepping out on my daughter; I'm giving her mother what she wants by leaving.*

Eryth really is a pretty name. I wonder what she'll look like and if Caralain will ever let me see her.

Hope shook his head to clear it; thoughts like that weren't going to accomplish anything. The only saving grace was that the child would be a girl. There was a strong possibility that the Panarch wouldn't want to claim her; Terrence Lee wanted a son.

And he has one...Grace, Hope realized. *Why the hell did Mira have to sleep with him?*

I can't judge her, though; I'm no better.

Someone bumped into him, startling Hope out of his thoughts.

"Panarch?" Hope said, startled to find himself suddenly faced with the man he'd just been thinking of.

Terrence Lee ignored him like he was no more than another of the faceless throng that had gathered outside of Healer's Hall to await the announcement of the Panarch's offspring. And, Hope supposed, perhaps he was just another face in the crowd to Terrence Lee, no matter that he'd once been one of the man's trusted Generals.

I've fallen so far, Hope thought with a slight smile, *which is exactly where I want to be so that he will be shocked when I take everything from him.*

A nobody like me; the Avatar of the Light.

He watched the Panarch scurry through the crowd that parted before him for a moment. *The end of your reign is coming, Terrence*, Hope thought in his enemy's direction, *and you may have stolen my daughter for now, but I won't let you keep her...or Mirena.*

Mira! He remembered where he'd last seen her. Hope had gotten caught up in all the commotion surrounding Caralain when she'd gone into labor, but Mirena had run in the opposite direction...towards the Panarch's office.

Hurrying his pace, Hope headed against the current of the people flocking to Healer's Hall after the Panarch. There would be few people still upstairs while all this was going on, but Hope knew he would find Mirena waiting for him.

Terrence,

I know that I cannot live without you. She doesn't deserve you. I thought I did, but you turned me into the whore I swore I'd never become. I'll always love you, but I don't want your son to be born in a world like this. As much as I don't want to leave, I have to say goodbye.

Lyana.

A teardrop hit the page before her as she signed the name she had adopted with a flourish.

Once, she might have written a letter like this as an exit strategy, a way to fake Lyana's death so Mirena could give up on the mission and go back to being herself. Now, in her desperation and with how far she'd fallen, she meant every word.

Not bothering to wipe away the tears that fell, Lyana reached for the letter opener on Terrence's desk and tested its blade. It was sharp enough and it would have to do; she didn't want to face the world outside of this office.

But what about Hope? Mirena hesitated, the blade of the letter opener held poised above her wrist. *I can't leave without saying goodbye to him too; it wouldn't be fair.*

"Is she still in there?"

"Who does she think she is? Just because she's the Panarch's kept woman..."

"I hear she's pregnant too," yet another whispered voice carried through the open door. "That's the reason for all the delays surrounding the wedding; the Panarch can't make up his mind which baby to keep."

"If it's a boy he'll have his answer and he'll marry Caralain within the hour; that's all Terrence Lee's ever wanted…"

Lyana simply couldn't bear it anymore. She brought the blade to her wrist and dragged it across her skin with as much force as she could muster. Then she quickly did the same to the other arm only higher up because of the bandage on her right wrist.

She couldn't help but feel satisfied by the clang of the letter opener as it struck the ground, having fallen out of her hand as she lost the strength to hold it.

It won't be long now and then it'll all be over. It won't be what they were looking for, but just maybe Terrence's grief over my death will give Hope and the others the opening they need to defeat him. It's all I can hope for now.

My part in this is done.

※

"Mira!"

Hope surged forward, pushing past the people that were trying to block his way to the Panarch's office. The secretary was deep in concentration, her hand poised on the panel on her desk but Hope didn't wait for her acknowledgement or her permission to enter; there wasn't time for that.

Abruptly, he pushed his way past the crowd and into the small room. There was blood everywhere and Mirena was lying in a pool of it.

Her body lay draped over the Panarch's chair, her outstretched hand dangling over a bloodied dagger the size of a letter opener. Her open wrist dripped at an alarming rate, the blood that fell from it pooling on the floor below.

"Hope?"

Mirena struggled weakly, lifting her head and her glazed eyes searching for him.

"I'm here," Hope told her, ignoring the audience as best he could and hurrying to her. He clamped his hand down over one of her wrists and then thought better of it when his eyes lit on her bandaged arm.

Thinking fast, Hope undid the bandage he had wrapped around her right wrist this morning, picking up the cursed letter opener and using it to cut the fabric in two. Then he re-tied the cloth, one strip to each arm, hopefully tight enough to stop the bleeding.

In the midst of this, Hope's eyes caught on a blood-spattered page lying open on the desk, the ink drying in time with the blood. *Terrence*, the letter began. His eyes scanned the page; *I'll always love you, but I don't want your son...*

Hope instinctively grabbed the letter and the page beneath it for good measure, crumpling them both in his fist. There would be time for reading the rest of the short message later, but he'd seen enough to know that it couldn't fall into the wrong hands.

"I love you," Mirena whispered, drawing his attention back to her and he leaned in to hear her. "I'm sorry...I wanted to say goodbye."

"No you don't..." Hope told her, his words low and fierce but his tone vulnerable as he took Mirena into his arms. "You don't get to do that, Mira. Not for him; not like this."

She was light in his arms, too light. She had lost weight recently as well as blood and she was weak from everything she'd been through. Hope stood, turning to face the crowd, his expression serious.

I can't heal her here in front of them and I can't open a hole to the void-world either, but I won't let them stop me from taking her out of here.

Perhaps it was the horror of the scene or Hope's intimidating expression, but no one said anything or tried to stop him as he carried Mirena toward the door. In fact, they parted to let him pass and some even wore sympathetic expressions.

Hope thought he'd made it when he reached the outer door to the waiting room but there he found the only man who had enough power to actually stop him.

He'd been running hard and his expression was haggard; this was not the controlled visage the Panarch usually displayed.

"Lyana," Terrence Lee breathed, taking in the sight of her in Hope's arms before he seemed to realize what was going on. "Where are you taking her?"

"She needs a healer," Hope responded, telling the truth, but not exactly the whole truth.

Mirena does need a healer, but I don't exactly have time to play this game right now.

"Give her to me," the Panarch commanded, holding out his arms. His tone implied that 'Tendro' ought to know that he could get her downstairs faster with the majik at his disposal.

There was no real objection Hope could make against giving 'Lyana' over to the Panarch, except that Mirena was the love of his life and he didn't want to give her up to this tyrant just to save appearances.

With Mirena's life in the balance, Hope found that he didn't care overmuch whether they won or lost this war they were fighting against the Panarch's rule in the end. He just wanted Mirena to get through this and come back to him.

"Tendro, I know she is your friend and you care for her," Terrence said in the most reasonable tone that Hope had ever heard him speak, "but I have the best healers in the land and I can get her to them as quickly as needed. You can trust her life in my hands."

"Can I?" Hope questioned, meeting the Panarch stare for stare. "Because if that were the case she wouldn't be dying right now...your games have done this to her, Terrence. She gave up because she wasn't enough for you. You chose the possibility of more power over her and made her feel worthless."

"I know," Terrence said softly, his head dropping forward in shame, despite the room full of people watching his every move. "I was wrong and I will pay for my mistakes...but not with her life. Please, you have to let me save her.

"She means the world to me," he added in a stronger voice, his head snapping up and his eyes bright with tears as he met Hope's gaze, "and she's running out of time!"

Mirena gasped in Hope's arms and then coughed weakly, her skin pale and her eyes rolling back into her head.

He's right...damn him, he's right!

Despite his better judgment, Hope found himself letting the Panarch take Mirena's limp form from his arms with bonds of air. She drifted gently over to Terrence's waiting arms and Hope could do nothing but watch impotently as the Panarch fled the room, leaving Hope to face the judgment of the crowd in the tyrant's place.

"He loves her, then," they whispered.

"He wouldn't have left Caralain during the birth for her if he didn't. She tried to kill herself for him...almost succeeded, too."

She told me she loves me, Hope silently denied the whispers around him. *Terrence Lee may save her life today, but in the end she'll choose me. She'll see what kind of person he really is and she'll choose me.*

I just hope she does it in time...

XXXI.

"Hope?"

"Lyana, I'm here."

It was Terrence's voice. Mirena recognized it immediately.

I must be in the Panarch's room...not in the void-world then, but why?

"Where am I and how did I get here?" Mirena asked, trying to raise her head to look around but finding that she was terribly weak.

The Panarch took hold of her hand and gently placed his other hand on her forehead, pushing her hair back. "Shh, rest now," he said, speaking softly as he ran his fingers through her hair. "You're going to be alright, but you'll need time to get stronger. You gave me quite a scare, Lyana. Please don't ever do anything like that again. I don't want to lose you."

Lyana? Mirena found herself searching for the familiar presence that was the persona she had adopted, but she couldn't seem to bring her bolder, more confident personality to the surface. *Where are you? This is your life, not mine. I don't belong here.*

"I can't promise you anything right now," Mirena said aloud, feeling hesitant and uncertain of her place.

"Don't say that, Lyana," Terrence pleaded. "I love you. I don't want to be the cause of your unhappiness. I'll do whatever it takes to keep you here with me."

"You wanted Caralain..." Mirena began, wondering at his mercurial nature. "What about the family you wanted? Your new son?"

"It was a girl and she's not mine," he answered with no hint of regret in his voice; his words were matter-of-fact. "She's Tendro's. They're calling her Eryth."

"How can you be so cruel?" Mirena demanded, crying out at the injustice of his words and actions. "You claimed that child publicly and now you deny it because it's a girl? What kind of man are you?!"

"Lyana, I don't know how your opinion of me has fallen so far, but I never publicly claimed that the child was mine," he told her, sounding concerned in the face of her anger. "I may not have been as quick to denounce the assumptions that I was the father, assumptions that Caralain fostered, but I never made anything official. I thought you knew that?"

"How dare you?" Mirena snapped, anger overtaking her better judgment. "You said 'My son is being born' in front of everyone in the office and to me. You can't just change your mind about it now because it's a girl and it is more convenient to do so."

"It's not about convenience, Lyana," Terrence stated firmly, denying the truth she'd placed in front of him. "You've given me no indication that you've considered my proposal of marriage, even though you've known that without it I would have no choice but to follow my given word to marry Caralain.

"If I had married her, Lyana, then her child, whether physically Tendro's offspring or not, would have legitimately been my own. As far as the rest of the world knows, Caralain Dashar is my intended wife."

"Stop saying my name!" Mirena protested suddenly, her anger rising to the surface and giving her the adrenaline she needed to pull her hand out of his grasp and get herself into a sitting position. "I know who I am, but are you so used to saying such things to Caralain that you need to remind yourself who you are speaking to?!

"I already asked you not to marry Caralain. I told you I loved you. I gave everything to you. I was fucking raped because of you and I still came back. And do you know what I got for my trouble? You claimed her baby as your own and left me so you could go and check on her. I wanted to die because of you!

"You made me into the whore I swore to you that I would never become. I am so angry at you and I don't even care anymore if you beat me like one of your whores, because it would be easier to deal with than you ever breaking my heart again."

"Damn it, Lyana," Terrence swore, standing and striking the bedside table with his fist. Mirena flinched with the sound of the impact, feeling fear overtake her and believing that the next blow that came would be meant for her. "You're not a whore; you're the love of my life! Why don't you believe me?

"Say you'll marry me and I swear to the Creator and the Destroyer both that you'll never want for anything and never have to fear monsters like Dipaul again. I'll hang anyone who thinks of touching you without your permission, or even imprison anyone who thinks to name you a whore, if that's what you want. Anything and it's yours. Just promise you'll never leave me!"

"You shouldn't have that kind of power over people!" Mirena protested. "You're a heartless tyrant."

As soon as the words were out of her mouth, she regretted them. The Panarch's face settled into a stony mask and Mirena knew that she'd gone too far and betrayed too much of her own opinions in a violent outburst of emotion.

No rational person would say such things to the Panarch's face and not fear retribution. She'd been a fool and now he would not hesitate in seeing her life forfeit.

"Is that what you truly think of me?" Terrence asked, betraying nothing by his facial expression. "I bare my heart and soul to you and you call me a tyrant?"

"No," Lyana rose slowly to the surface as if awaking from a deep sleep to reclaim what was hers and to look the man she'd pledged her heart to in the eyes. "I was so hurt by your words before in your office that I admit I wanted you to feel the way I felt. It was selfish and wrong and I'm sorry," she added in a whisper, letting the strength born of Mirena's anger drain from her. "I just didn't want you to lure me back with your words, so I would risk feeling my heart break again...I do love you, Terrence."

The Panarch let out a sigh of relief, gently wrapping his arms around her. "I know you do," he said softly. "We're made from the same mold you and I...quick to anger and even quicker to react to it and go too far. I hope we can remember to always give one another the chance to apologize."

"I love you and I want to marry you," Lyana assured him, confining Mirena's protests to the back of her mind. "Get rid of her..."

"As my fiancée commands," Terrence replied, a smile lighting his face as his grin spread from ear to ear before he leaned in to kiss her on the forehead. "Rest now, my love. I'll see to everything, but if we're to be married soon you'll need your strength."

Hope, I'm sorry, Mirena called out silently to the man she loved, *but really, Lyana is doing this for you.*

I hope...

⁂

"Are you sure about this?"

Jehenna's voice was calm and collected as always but Lyana could hear the note of concern, regardless.

"Aren't you supposed to tell me I look beautiful?" Lyana asked, smirking in mild amusement.

"There's little sense in saying it since you are already so aware of the fact," Jehenna chided, placing a lock of hair just so and settling a thin, white gold tiara atop a pile of curls, "besides, it is vain to complement one's own handiwork.

"But, being perfectly serious, I'm concerned that this may not go as you plan it to, or even as you want it to. Have you thought this through as far as you are able?"

"It will be fine," Lyana insisted. "I can do what I set out to."

Jehenna snorted in an unladylike fashion, pausing over a curl that didn't want to lay the way she wanted it to. "The words of a woman who is not quite as sure of herself as she'd like others to believe..."

Lyana turned abruptly in her seat, causing Jehenna to pull back her hands so she didn't risk ruining her masterpiece. "I may be in too deep," she admitted, allowing her fear to show for just a moment. "I fell in love with him; I couldn't help it."

"Hush," Jehenna said, wrapping her arms around Lyana and holding her close, even as she was mindful of mussing her makeup or hair. "Of course you did, hun. You didn't think that you could stay immune to his charms when you planned to have him fall so completely to yours, did you? We're all vulnerable to love and we love being loved in return. It's just human nature."

"What if I can't do it?" Lyana asked. "What if I can't push him in?"

"Then you can't," Jehenna stated simply, letting her arms around Lyana drop.

"It's just that simple?"

"Nothing is ever simple," Jehenna told her, "but we all must make our own choices and, I'm afraid, live with the consequences of our actions. I trust, no matter how conflicted you are feeling now, that in the moment you will do the right thing."

"I hope you're right."

There was a knock at the door, causing them both to look toward the curtained entranceway as a familiar face poked through the red velvet drapery.

"I hope I'm not interrupting anything," Hope said.

"You're lucky," Jehenna noted. "Not five minutes earlier and you might have disrupted my concentration in a very important task. As it is, though my work is a living art, I think for the moment I am done."

"In that case," Hope commented, stepping fully into the room and letting the curtain fall back into place again behind him, "would you mind if I stole a moment of the bride's time?"

"Well," she noted thoughtfully, tapping her full and red lower lip with a perfectly manicured fingernail, "I'm not supposed to leave her alone. Nor am I supposed to allow a man to see her unsupervised before the ceremony, but in your case, I suppose I can make an exception.

"If you'll excuse me, I'll just take my time on a trip to the ladies room…on the far end of the Collegium building. Don't have too much fun in my absence."

With a flourish of red velvet, Jehenna left Hope and Mirena alone together and an awkward silence fell over the lavish preparation room in the wake of her departure.

Hope cleared his throat. "You look lovely," he stated awkwardly.

"Thank you, Tendro," Lyana said carefully, trying to at least verbally keep up the charade of their relationship to one another, just in case anyone should be listening through the flimsy excuse for a door. Internally, she keenly felt the truth of their intimacy.

Hope was dressed in a Mage's jacket, as he was most days, but today it was of the formal kind with broad shoulders and more elaborate gold scroll-work decorating the breast of it. His whole outfit was dark and glossy with trim lines and it gave him an unconscious regal bearing. Mirena within her rose to the surface at the sight and she found that she couldn't take her eyes off of him.

I wanted the first time he saw me in a wedding dress to be at our wedding, Mirena's thoughts were as unruly as her emotions.

If I cry now with my face done up like this, Jehenna will kill me...

"I..." Hope began, then hesitated, changing whatever it was that he'd been about to say. "You'll be the focus of everyone's attention today."

"I did this all for you..." Mirena told him suddenly in a hushed whisper.

"I can't wait to see Mira in a dress like this," he said at the same time, his words tumbling overtop of hers.

"Me either," she confided, "this all feels so surreal..."

"Because it isn't real," he stated, straightening his back as he spoke. "I mean it is, but it isn't. This isn't who you are."

"I need you to look past this mask right now."

"I always do..." He told her, his voice thick with suppressed emotion. "I hardly even see it."

Mirena stood carefully, letting the bulky white gown settle around her feet so she could face him; her with a mask of a stranger's face and him wearing the mask of his former life.

"Is there any chance that we could just walk away from this now and forget any of it ever happened?" Mirena asked for the impossible, fearing even as she said it that he might try to give it to her. "I never wanted to hurt you..."

"Mira..." Hope said quietly, stepping forward and reaching for her face as if he wanted to pull off the mask she wore but stopping inches from her skin, knowing it was futile and unwilling to destroy all of Jehenna's hard work. "The only part of all this that hurt was how far you were willing to go to make it happen. I have to believe that if we make it through this next hour that you'll be mine and we'll no longer have anything to worry about."

"I need to succeed in the plan to give you everything you ever wanted."

Hope shook his head, denying her words. "The only thing I really want is you. The rest of it doesn't matter without you. What good is a perfect world if you're not in it?"

"Why did you wait until now to say this to me?"

"I've been saying it all along, you just haven't been listening," he insisted. "It's alright though, Mira, because I haven't been listening very well to you, either. I should have recognized how much you wanted to help and trusted in your capabilities from the start."

"I love you."

"Thank the Creator," Hope said, smiling suddenly in relief, "because I was beginning to doubt. I love you too, Mira, and I always will."

Mirena found herself leaning toward him, hoping for the kiss that would heal all the hurt that had come between them. He also leaned into her until their lips were inches apart.

"Tendro, Lyana?" Jehenna interrupted, sticking her head through the red velvet entranceway, reminding them of where they stood and what awaited them. "It's time. I'm needed up at the front.

"Lyana, are you ready?"

Hope met Mirena's eyes, as if asking her silently if she was still going through with this.

Mirena felt every possible emotion pass through her in that instant. Love, fear, warmth, panic, hope and dread, but then she did what she had to and gave herself over to Lyana.

"Of course," Lyana held out her arm for Hope to take in his, "Tendro?"

Mirror's Hope

XXXII.

The Collegium's narrow garden was lined on either side with people of all kinds. The usually beautiful space was made even more so with large silk roses draped artfully between the real white lilies that already grew there.

It was still the beginning of spring, but the day was even more beautiful for it; the weather was balmy and the green foliage decorated with early buds.

Lyana, her arm in Hope's, stepped out of the Panarch's secret garden where the fountain stood to mark its entrance. She took a deep breath, her head held high, but no one even so much as looked her way. They were all focused ahead and trying to see what lay beyond at the far end of the gardens where the wedding ceremony was to take place.

The training yard and the building behind it had been set up as a stage, she knew, but Lyana couldn't see it from here with the trees and the people blocking her view. Still, Terrence was waiting for her and she felt her heart beat quickly in her chest with the anticipation of seeing him at the end of the garden trail, dressed in his wedding finery.

This is it, Lyana thought. *This is the moment I have been waiting for.*

She felt Hope stiffen his resolve beside her and taking that as her cue, Lyana took the first step toward her destiny.

People gasped and turned to stare at her as she passed but it was a slow process, only one a row at a time as something ahead kept their attention focused away from her. Lyana's sense of foreboding grew with each step; the faces of the people in the crowd seeming more alarmed by her presence than congratulatory.

Sure, they likely expected Caralain, but to show such disrespect to the chosen wife of their ruler...

Lyana kept on, head held high as there was nothing else for her to do. She'd committed herself now to this wedding and not even the disdain of every single person in the Collegium was going to prevent her from seeing it through.

*Terrence chose me...*Lyana reminded herself forcefully.

...or did he? Mirena questioned.

As Lyana got far enough to see past the crowd, she got her first glimpse of the stage she was headed towards. A raised dais had been constructed, large enough to hold the small wedding party and Theia Prosai, the female Panarch and Terrence Lee's counterpart, as she the only person in this realm with enough authority to marry such a public figure.

Theia, a tall and regal woman, stood in formal black Mage's robes with a podium before her, her black hair piled high upon her head. Before her stood Terrence, commanding in a stark white suit trimmed in gold that stood out brazenly against the black that was traditional. His face was an unreadable mask at this distance but one thing was certain, he had taken notice of the white of her dress through the crowd and with a single nod of his head, the music began.

Lyana stepped onto the red carpet that trailed before her at the sound, assuming she was meant to, but something about the whole circumstance still seemed wrong to her.

Jehenna stood to Terrence's right but far enough away as to leave room for the bride and D'wann stood behind Terrence and slightly to his left, as was proper for his bodyguard and friend. However, D'wann wasn't looking at Lyana or even at Terrence. He was looking off to the right, at something Lyana was still too far away to see.

Uncertainty quickening her steps, Lyana walked a little faster, a little out of beat with the music played by a team of musicians to the right of the stage. Then she saw what she hadn't known she had feared as a figure in white stepped onto the platform and made its way into full view.

With the shorter distance to travel, Caralain would make it to Terrence's side before she did and it became abruptly clear who it was that the Panarch intended to marry this day.

Lyana stopped walking and unconsciously tightened her grip on Hope's arm.

"Just remember…" Hope whispered encouragingly into her ear. "This is our day."

Lyana was caught off guard as Hope gave her a push forward, letting go of her arm as the music suddenly changed tempo and became something more familiar, something personal.

It's a version of what the musicians were playing that night at Valentino's, Lyana realized. *Our first date...*

Caralain's head snapped up at the sudden change, her confident steps shaken somewhat as she whirled around to face the musicians. Even from this distance, Lyana could read the confusion on her features. Sweeping her gaze around, Caralain did a double-take as she noticed Lyana's presence for the first time.

"No," Caralain mouthed; from here, her protest was silent.

"Go on, Lyana," Hope urged from behind her, his voice the only thing she could make out over the noise of the thumping in her chest. "You started this, now be the one to finish it."

Overwhelmed by everything that was happening and not quite sure she understood it yet, Lyana took Hope's words as an imperative and trusted that he, above anyone else, would not guide her falsely. She closed her eyes and took a step forward and then another, breathing deeply to keep herself from feeling light-headed and concentrating on putting one foot in front of the other to walk in a straight line.

The thing that finally caused her to open her eyes was the cheering of the crowd as it grew from a mild appreciation to a thundering roar with each step she took, until eventually it drowned out even the music that guided the pace of her steps.

Lyana's eyes opened and she took in Terrence's expression, as well as the hand he held out to help her onto the stage to join him. Caralain still stood halfway between the training facility door she'd exited from and center stage where she'd been headed, but the Panarch ignored her; he only had eyes for Lyana.

She looked around herself in confusion, not yet reaching for the proffered hand. *Why are they cheering…it can't be for me, can it?*

"Lyana," Terrence called to her, trying to pull her attention back to him, "Lyana."

Why is this happening? Lyana remained frozen, her mind continuing to question. *How could he do this? Not even Caralain deserves this. I know exactly how she must be feeling. I got a taste of it just now, seeing her on my wedding day, dressed in white and expecting to stand at the Panarch's side.*

Lyana couldn't help it; she turned to Caralain and met her enemy's eyes. "I'm sorry," she mouthed, knowing the simple words could never be enough.

She won't believe me, but I really had no idea that this was what he was planning.

Rage crossed Caralain's pretty face, distorting it until it was nearly unrecognizable. Her cheeks reddened, her eyes bulged and the bouquet of lilies she held in her whitened knuckles crumpled and broke apart under the force of her grip.

In one moment everything shifted as she released her grip and let the flowers fall from her hands, the crushed white petals raining to the floor. Caralain turned and fled from the sight of her ruin before her and that single instant was all it took for the crowd to forget her existence.

But Mirena didn't forget; she didn't think she'd ever be able to forget the look on Caralain's face in that instant. But Lyana was strong enough to swallow the feelings of guilt that threatened to overwhelm her and reach for the Panarch's hand, allowing him to pull her onto the stage.

"There is balance in all things," Theia Prosai stated, her pure voice carrying strongly out past Terrence and Lyana to reach the ears of the expansive audience. "Like the never-ending conflict between the Creator and the Destroyer, so too is there balance in this day and in the union of man and woman. Love is a passion and it can be a violent meeting of two forces strong enough to consume, but there is always balance in the union of two opposing forces.

"Terrence Lee, do you swear to forever join with this woman in seeking balance in your life? Do you claim her to be your chosen soul mate for as long as there is sand in the hourglass?"

"I do so swear."

"And Lyana Morelle," Theia continued, "do you also swear to join with this man in seeking balance in your life? Do you claim him as your chosen soul mate for as long as there is sand in the hourglass?"

Lyana didn't even so much as look in Hope's direction. She knew that she couldn't, both because she knew that seeing him would cause her to hesitate and also because to do so would alert Terrence to the danger that awaited him.

"I do so swear," she stated calmly, looking Terrence in the eyes and keeping his gaze locked with hers.

"By my right as Panarch, I declare this union between two consenting individuals to be lasting and valid and by the power invested in me by my training as a Mage, I will unite your souls as traditions of old bid us to do."

There was a collective gasp from the crowd at this news, or perhaps it was at the pinprick of light that appeared in the air behind Terrence, Lyana couldn't tell. The tradition Theia spoke of was one long out of use, but at one time it had been an accepted part of marriage law. Through majik, couples would have their souls bound to one another in a permanent union that lasted until death and maybe even beyond.

He was serious, then, Lyana fully realized the depth of the devotion the Panarch had for her. *He would unite his soul with mine for eternity knowing that it is an act that can never be undone, a promise that by its nature cannot be broken.*

True to the plan, the pinprick of light that had indeed appeared behind Terrence Lee grew and it was a measure of Lyana's control over Terrence, or perhaps just his love for her, that he didn't look away from her eyes even as the danger rose.

Lyana fought every muscle in her face to keep herself from betraying her knowledge of what was happening as Theia's eyes closed and the female Panarch began to gather her power for the irrevocable act that would join them together forever.

The light continued to pulse, glowing fiercely now; the eyes of the crowd were riveted upon the unusual phenomenon. Some wore fearful expressions, others enraptured by its beauty and power, and still others who didn't yet understand what was happening were confused.

It wouldn't be long now but Lyana had one last crucial job to perform. Letting herself ride the moment and the wave of emotion that crested within her, she stepped forward and raised her head to kiss Terrence, pouring as much love as she could into the gesture but praying that he wouldn't notice until too late that the act in itself was a goodbye.

As one, Lyana and Terrence shuddered as Theia's majik took hold, covering them both like a warm blanket and holding them closer together than either of them had ever believed possible.

She could feel him now, not only physically. She could feel him there beside her, connected to her like she was holding his hand, even if she wasn't.

And she always would. As Mirena or Lyana, she would never be separated from him; their souls were one.

Lyana ended the kiss and pushed back from Terrence. The light behind him was bright now, like a halo around his whole body. She felt the connection to him still, like they were touching.

It would have to be enough, because she knew she'd never see him again.

I have to do this, Mirena affirmed. *This is what is right.*

"Terrence," she told him, speaking clearly so there would be no mistaking her words. "I am with child. I'm carrying your son and his name is Grace."

"How do you know that?" Terrence asked; his eyes filled with wonder as he gazed upon the false face she wore.

"The Creator has blessed us," Mirena stated, taking off the mask she'd worn to conceal herself from him all these months, revealing her skin and the words that were imprinted upon it in dark ink.

She let the Panarch get a good look at his betrayer, but no more than that before she shoved him with all her might and he stumbled backwards, never expecting such an act from the woman to whom he had just sworn his soul.

The searing light of Hope's void-world swallowed Terrence whole and in a whoosh the words flowed from her skin, much like the manner in which they had taken up residence there. The dark ink swirled nebulously in the air, being sucked in a vague spiral into the void after the Panarch. The glowing hole in the air closed behind them, sealing shut with the power of the Prophecy that was the key to the Creator's once-prison.

Every feeling Mirena had ever felt went with those words and the absence of him was all that was left to her as she fell to her knees on the stage in front of the gathered populace of the Collegium.

She wanted tears, but none came. Only emptiness remained.

"Mirena!"

The sound of the name she hadn't used in months snapped her head up and her eyes locked onto the speaker.

Caralain held Hope by the hair. He was on his knees before her and she held a sword made of fire dangerously close to the skin of his neck as she stood behind him, making sure that Mirena had a clear view of her intentions.

"You dared to try and take everything from me," Caralain stated in a loud, clear voice, the rage Mirena had noted earlier still very much on her face. "You may have taken some things but I swear to you that I can do much worse than you can even dream of and I will pay you back in kind.

"Release them!" Caralain commanded Hope, pressing the sword a little closer to his flesh and causing him to cry out from the searing heat of it. "All of those you have taken; give them their lives back!"

A hole to the void-world didn't so much open as three familiar people appeared in a burst of light near to where Caralain held Hope hostage. The three residents of this realm that Hope and the others had taken prisoner in order to replace them looked confused at where they found themselves, but otherwise unhurt. In a moment, D'wann, Odark and Jehenna's Mirrors, the ones who belonged in this realm, each took up wary positions around Caralain to support whatever she chose to accomplish.

"You have what you want," Hope told her, speaking carefully and very much aware of the deadly weapon Caralain held at his throat. "Stop this. There's no need for more violence."

"No need?!" Caralain demanded in a dangerous hiss. "There is every need for violence and retribution. This man and his whore," she spat, addressing the crowd at large now, "have just taken your Panarch! Are you going to stand for this or are you going to make them pay for this injustice?"

A sudden roar went up from the onlookers and the audience that had gathered for a wedding suddenly began to turn into an angry mob.

"You may want revenge," Hope countered and for a wonder Caralain let him speak his piece, perhaps believing that his words would have no effect on the angry crowd or simply beyond caring if they did, "but it's the wrong answer. Don't worry yourselves about leaders. Take your freedom and do with it what you will!"

Cloaks fell from a good half of those gathered, revealing weapons of all kinds, both metal and majik, though the latter were fewer in number. Fully half of the people who had come for the wedding now bore symbols of the Creator, openly declaring religious defiance unseen in the Collegium or elsewhere for over a hundred years.

Mirena could see that Tendro and Elizabeth were among them, as was Odark from the Mirror World; the one without the scar. Her friends and her sister had led the People of the Light here from the Temple in force to rise up, now that the Panarch was no longer able to stop them.

And rise up they did.

The angry mob spurred by Caralain's words and the attack they'd just witnessed on the Panarch was no real match for the armed Soldiers of the Light, but in their anger they tried anyway and they fell in droves.

It was a massacre like none other, the followers of the Light forced to the violence they so condemned in order to free themselves and stand up for what they believed in and those that had stood for the Panarch now rallying around Theia Prosai to keep her from falling too.

At some point during the chaos of it all, Caralain disappeared and Hope with her. No doubt she had used her majik to escape to only the Creator knew where.

Mirena watched emotionlessly as people of both persuasions died in front of her eyes. Blood and death was everywhere and having been both Lyana and Mirena for some time now, she had friends on both sides and she didn't have it in her to be grateful that those she'd brought over with her from the Mirror World were some of the lucky ones.

Eventually Mirena came to herself enough to stand and even later than that she found herself able to walk. On uncertain legs, she walked in a straight line back down the red carpet Lyana had used to get to this place, stepping over the bodies of those that had fallen, her white dress soaking up the blood that had been spilled in celebration of her wedding vows.

...Everything has a price.

This was mine.

XXXIII.

*T*imelessly strong, the immovable Sentinal Stones stood like a circle of gravestones before her, marking the place where Mirena Calanais' life would soon end.

She didn't want to leave without saying goodbye but she just couldn't face her friends and allies after everything that had happened.

We won…but what did we win? She questioned, feeling empty. *I've lost everything…*

The memory of his face was strong in her mind, his pain at her betrayal the most vivid memory of all. *Terrence Lee…* Mirena was certain that even if she died right here and now, she would never be able to forget the look on his face as she turned on him and betrayed him more completely than even a tyrant such as he deserved.

She felt the tears start again, a sharp reminder of what she had lost; what she had given up. She took one step toward the waiting Sentinal Stones, then another, her back straight with determined pride.

How can I go on without them? Without Terrence? Without Hope? Even my sister, Elizabeth, wants nothing more to do with me. Jehenna and the others have gone back to their lives; I can't be a part of theirs anymore.

Was I destined to be so alone?

The tall stones welcomed her with open arms, the green grass within them a peaceful place. She was almost there; it would all be over soon. Reaching the center of the circle of standing stones, she put her hand up against the central pillar to steady herself as emotion overtook her.

It's not supposed to be this way!

There had been promises made, vows to always love one another and to never be apart. Who would have ever believed that it would end like this?

The marriage and the life they'd begun to build together simply didn't exist anymore and it was her own fault, as much as she felt that circumstances had driven her to the decisions she had made.

There had been no goodbyes, no telling her that he loved her and begging her to stay and to fix what she'd broken.

Terrence is gone...Hope is all but lost. There's nothing left for me here but to be alone while surrounded by others. If I'm going to be alone, I should at least be by myself instead of being constantly reminded of what I've lost.

Mirena lifted her head and her eyes locked onto the symbol carved into the stone that represented the realm that was a mirror of her own. She felt the majik that was her will surge within her. From this moment onwards, she would make her own way and try to walk a path that agreed with her conscience. She would no longer do what was necessary instead of what felt right.

It was an ending but she was determined that it would also be a beginning. At the end of this long and bumpy road, she finally knew where it was she was supposed to start and it wasn't in the place she was from.

Here, in this new world, Mirena – *no, it's Mira now...just Mira*, she resolved. *I won't be Mirena Calanais anymore and my husband wasn't around long enough for me to claim his name as my own.*

Mira straightened her back and set her shoulders, taking a deep breath to compose herself and lock the tears away. This was her chance for a new life and no matter what she was leaving behind she had to take this opportunity to try again. She had nothing to lose, since right from the beginning it had all been destined to fall apart.

The garden was in full bloom here, the green foliage plentiful and the flowers sweet-smelling. This place was pure and clean just as it should be and though it looked exactly the same, it truly was nothing like the world she had left behind.

White walls gleamed brightly, beckoning her, and without further hesitation Mira started forward. There was a man here she needed to see, although the pain of seeing him might just be more than she could bear at present.

"Name?"

Lee's secretary was a bright redhead and polite as always, though never personal. Mira didn't know the woman's name but she knew she could be trusted through past experiences.

"Mira," she replied, giving no last name. This was a new start, she was only Mira now. There was no Lyana Morelle anymore and the Mirena Calanais of her world was dead now. "I need to see Terrence Lee. It's important."

It didn't take long at all for Lee's door to open and the Panarch of this world greeted her with a friendly smile.

"Mira. It's good to see..." Lee hesitated, taking in Mira's appearance and her expression. She still wore her wedding dress, though it was torn and dirty around the hem. Around it she wore Terrence Lee's own gold-trimmed black Mage jacket. Her arms were not in the sleeves but the garment was draped over her shoulders. "Please, come in."

She followed Lee into his round office. Considering his great position the room was smaller than one might expect, but the book-lined walls and the cluttered desk suited Terrence perfectly and so too did it suit his Mirror in this world. He was a grand man by virtue of his status, but he had never been grandiose.

Conversely, Mira knew that she looked sad and tired. Her blond hair hung limply around her shoulders, her complexion was paler than ever before and she had dark circles beneath her once bright blue eyes. She couldn't even muster up a smile to greet this man whom she so admired and in her world, loved.

By his hesitation in taking his chair, Lee didn't know whether he should remain standing or not. In the end he settled for pulling Mira's chair out for her and helping her into it despite her bulky dress.

"The others told me that you had succeeded," Lee began after a moment of awkward silence during which he'd taken a seat on the edge of his desk. "Did something happen between Hope and yourself, or were there further complications following everyone's return?"

Mira took in a deep breath and tried to speak, she really did, but seeing his face was a torment as much as it was a blessing.

The last memory she had of her realm flashed before her eyes. The screaming, the sound of tearing cloth and the smashing of mirrors and vases; she had gone into a wordless state of rage and despair and even for this version of Terrence she couldn't bring herself to relive the final moments of the mission again. However, the Panarch would expect nothing less than a full explanation from her and she knew Lee deserved the truth, so she steeled herself to answer his questions as best she could.

"They are gone," Mira finally stated; her words simple and devoid of emotion. "Hope was taken by Caralain. And Terrence..." She hesitated, the name touching on the void in her heart. "My husband is dead."

The tears fell freely from her eyes. *This is the first time that I've admitted the truth out loud.* There had been those to see it happen but hearing herself say the words, telling her story to someone was wholly different and it brought the reality of it crashing down upon her.

Mira fell as she tried to get to her feet to flee from it all, her strength giving out at last. The tears came and she didn't stop them; when the sobbing started, this time she didn't hold back. And if she was screaming by the end of it, wordlessly demanding why it had to come to this, she didn't care anymore if the whole world heard her; this one or her own.

Mira didn't hear or feel Lee get down from his perch, but he was there a moment later, holding her as she rocked and cried on the floor of his office. He didn't speak for there was nothing to say and he knew it better than most, having lost the love of his life just as suddenly as she'd lost hers.

"I love him," she heard her own voice rasp; "I want him back."

"I know."

"It's my fault he's dead," Mira confided. "I hate myself! Is this how you lost her? Lyana? Is this what it felt like? How did you get through the pain? How are you still getting through it?"

"I'm so sorry..." Lee whispered instead of answering her. "I made you her Mirror, didn't I? By giving you that face...I made you lose me the way that I lost her.

"The pain never fully goes away," he continued, filled with sadness and regret. "It will stay with you forever; the guilt, the hurt, the loss. But in time you will be able to push through it and keep living; the days that pass get easier with each one that you manage to outlast."

Mira put her arms around Lee, pretending for just a moment that she held the one she loved and not the man who had only been her friend. She buried her face in his chest, taking in the smell of him.

"I'm pregnant," she whispered. "I'm pregnant with his child and now I'm all alone..."

Lee's hold around her tightened; for her pain and for his, he held her close.

"Whatever you need," he told her after some time spent in silent closeness. "It's not my child, I know that, but whatever you need, I'll help you in any way I can."

"I don't want to go back to my realm," Mira said, pulling back from him. "I can't face that place with Hope and Terrence gone, but once I have my son, Grace, I plan on going to save Hope. I just need a safe place to be until then."

"Like hell I'm going to 'wait out here'! That's my sister in there with your Panarch and a little wooden door is not going to keep me from going where I please!"

The door swung open and there she was. It was Elizabeth; her Elizabeth and not this realm's pale copy.

*Maybe I didn't lose her completely...*Mira felt a slight flicker of hope. *She came after me; maybe she doesn't hate me after all.*

Standing behind her and looking a little sheepish as he tried to calm Lee's secretary was Odark. He was this realm's Odark and not the scarred one whom she last had seen standing with Caralain following her marriage to Terrence.

I'll have to thank him for bringing my sister back to me, Mira resolved. *She could never have travelled through the stones on her own; it had to have been with his help.*

"There you are!" Elizabeth exclaimed, hands on her hips. "Did you think that hiding here was going to be good enough to keep me from finding you?"

"Elizabeth..." Mira began, struggling to get to her feet.

Lee gave Mira a hand up and then retreated to behind his desk to give the twin sisters a moment's reunion.

"Come here," Elizabeth commanded, holding her arms out expectantly. "I did warn you that this would happen; you're so emotional..."

Mira stumbled into her sister's waiting arms, holding her bony form gratefully.

"I'm sorry," she said at last, "I love you and I never want to lose you again."

"Of course you don't," Elizabeth told her. "What would you do without my sass to keep you going?"

"Like I was telling Elizabeth on the way up here," Odark interjected with a slight clearing of his throat, entering the room and bringing the small space to its maximum capacity as he shut the door behind himself, "I might have a temporary solution for you girls."

"Really?" Mira questioned, feeling another surge of the unfamiliar emotion; hope.

"My family owns a cottage up North in Nefall," Odark explained. "It's not large, but it would be enough for the two of you...and the baby. You know, until you decide what you want to do next."

"We wouldn't be imposing?" Mira asked.

"We never use it and no one really knows about it. It belonged to my Mother...and she's been gone a long time. I thought it might be a possible solution, since you can't stay here in the Collegium with your Mirror, Mirena, and this realm's Caralain, due to return any day now."

"You make a good point," Lee agreed. "I'll have to check with Tendro for the precise day, but they are expected back in the Collegium soon, I believe."

"You don't have to do this, Odark. Not for me," Mira told him. "You've already done so much more than I even have a right to ask of you."

"It's no more than you deserve," Odark responded, clearing his throat a little uncomfortably in the face of her gratitude. "You gave me a place to stay in your realm and I'm just returning the favour. It's been days since we've last seen you and you're still in your wedding dress. From where I stand, I haven't done enough..."

"Thank you," she said at last, there being nothing else to say.

Closing the short distance between them, Mira wrapped her arms around Odark in a grateful hug and to her surprise he held her back just as tightly.

Epilogue

Hope's world spun and shifted. It twirled with him inside of it, all of it filled with colours and noise and most of all, pain.

He couldn't stop it or block it out and he couldn't escape it. He was trapped within his own mind and left there to be driven mad, blind and deaf from the taxing strain on his senses.

"Comfortable?"

Her voice came from everywhere at once. It came from within him and all around him and even the colours and their incessant buzzing couldn't drown it out.

Caralain.

Hope tried to speak and acknowledge her, maybe even ask her to help him escape this place. But it seemed that in addition to being trapped here, this place had also made him mute.

"I know you must hate me," she said, her words bouncing around painfully in his skull, "but I don't hate you, Tendro. No, I hate her. Lyana, Mirena, Mira, whatever her name is.

"I blame her for taking Terrence from me. I almost had him, but then she took him from me like she took you away from me."

Hope tried to tell Caralain that she was mistaken but the colours and the sounds wouldn't let him. This place was all he was now; all he would be until she decided to help him. It didn't look like that was going to be the case. By the sound of her words filled with a bitter scorn, she'd been the one to put him here; wherever this was.

"You think you know what it was like to have your heart broken because you watched your little whore marry my Panarch?" Caralain demanded. "Well, welcome to the future, Tendro because *that* was only the beginning…"

To be continued…

In *Mirror's Heart*

Coming soon

M|W mirror world publishing

Mirror's Hope

Murandy Damodred

Co-founder of Mirror World Publishing and co-author of Neo Central and Mirror's Hope, Murandy (left) loves dark fantasy with strong romantic sub-plots. She's got a background in Drama and Communications and developed her fiction writing skills through roleplaying and working on screenplays.

Justine Alley Dowsett

Also co-founder of Mirror World Publishing, Justine (right) is an entrepreneur and a jack-of-all-trades. She authored Neo Central and Mirror's Hope with Murandy and the Crimson Winter trilogy on her own. Her education background is also in Drama, but she's does a bit of everything, including producing video games and sewing mascot costumes in her spare time.

To learn more about Justine Alley Dowsett and Murandy Damodred or their current projects visit: www.mirrorworldpublishing.com

Mirror's Hope